THE BROKEN SHADE

MICHELE POAGUE

THE BROKEN SHADE ©2020 by Michele Poague

For information contact:

Publisher
Bent Briar Publishing L.L.L.P.
Denver CO
roseliterary@aol.com
bentbriarbooks.com

Author
info@michelepoague.com
michelepoague.com

ISBNS
978-1-942665-17-5 SC
978-1-942665-12-0 HC
978-1-942665-13-7 EPUB

First Edition: March 2020

10 9 8 7 6 5 4 3 2 1

Praise for The Broken Shade

"…there's more to this house than meets the eye, including a story of love, heartbreak, forgiveness, and an intriguing house guest – one who winds up changing the course of Freja's life forever…Instantly, I was enthralled with this book from beginning till the end. I appreciated the plot, the dialogue, the characters, and the imagery. Each one of these components accentuated the other to create a fantastic read. The bits of historical information and the idea of the situations within this story being real, according to the author, made me appreciate this novel and the author for writing this engaging and well-written content." [MorganLee, LitPick Reviewer]

"Readers who like their romances tempered by engrossing life dilemmas with a dash of the supernatural added for good measure will find *The Broken Shade* a powerful and fine story of bittersweet endings and new beginnings." [Diane Donovan, Senior Reviewer, Midwest Book Review]

"The author gracefully balances a number of seemingly disconnected storylines and side plots in *The Broken Shade*. Between Freja's family life, personal life, professional scene, and unique hobbies, she's a well-rounded character who, despite some shallowness and tendencies to make wrong decisions when it comes to men, is admirable in her drive and thoughtfulness. Such a packed plot leaves little room for the narrative to drag, making this story a real page turner. Homeowners will appreciate the detailed process of Freja's remodeling project, which comes with its many frustrating and sometimes comical setbacks. The ghost story will appeal to mystery lovers and history buffs…. a high-energy, tightly packed story with a likable protagonist who has a unique and compelling story to tell. I hope to see this novel adapted for the big screen one day." [Laura335, LitPick Reviewer]

More books by Michele Poague

Praise for The Healing Crystal

Heir to Power
"…I was surprised at how much I liked this. Not because I didn't think it sounded good, but there weren't any of the usual aspects that make me fall in love with a book, like high action and steamy romance. Yet somehow, I can't stop thinking about it. The story completely captivated me." [Library Canary]

Fall of Eden
"…Fall of Eden is the second book in The Healing Crystal series. As I started this series, I thought I knew what would be in the story. Let me tell you, if you have preconceived notions when you start reading, they will soon be thrown out the door. This series will lead you in one direction and as soon as you get comfortable, hang on, it soon switches gear and you are off in a new direction. I liked this aspect with Michele's writing." [S. Staley]

Ransom
"With _Ransom_, the final book in _The Healing Crystal Trilogy_, Michele Poague has brought about an exciting and more-than-satisfactory conclusion to a distinctive and epic narrative of a post-apocalyptic cosmos – one which might be more real than imagined especially considering the life and times we live in today…" [Julie PK]

Praise for The Candy Store
"An orphaned 1980s teenager travels through time to the Jazz Age to discover the mystery of her identity in this sweetly confected historical fantasia… Poague's vibrant characters and piquant period details make for an entertaining voyage into the past… An engaging, bittersweet saga about finding a place to belong." [Kirkus Reviews]

"Reading The Candy Store was like savoring a bittersweet chocolate bar that has a surprise twist in flavor at the last bite. The novel was a delicious combination of sci-fi, time travel, historical fiction, and romance." [Star 360, LitPick Reviewer]

Dear Reader:

Most of the situations in this story are real although they may seem quite unlikely. The characters are a fictional blend of many people I've come to know and love while working at Shotgun Willies Gentleman's Cabaret in Glendale, Colorado. The political and world events are correct, as is the technology of the day. And yes, the two men who partied with their dead friend are verifiable. It is up to you to decide where real life and fiction part ways.

This novel is dedicated to my extended family at Shotgun Willies. It was a wild and wonderful 36 years!

Michle

Acknowledgments

This work wouldn't have come into existence if not for the following people: My dear friend Deborah Matthews-Dunafon, owner and manager of Shotgun Willies, my friends at the club who made my time there both fun and interesting; Carie Riasati, Gwen Gladman-Smiley, Matthew Dunafon, Scott Brock, Linda Anders, Cliff Crihfield, Jim White, Kevin McGee, and a cast of hundreds I don't have room to list.

I would also like to acknowledge my family, who gave me the courage to keep working on that old house through tough times. I would especially like to thank my close friend, one-time roommate in the house, and editor, Lois Deveneau.

THE BROKEN SHADE

CHAPTER 1

When I was a little girl, back in the sixties, I dreamed of being a successful interior designer, hosting fabulous cocktail parties, and having lots of boyfriends. If I could go back and have a conversation with my eight-year-old self, I'd tell her to be a whole lot more specific.

My name is Freja Hedvig O'Connell. Freja is not a good name for blending in at the local public school, where my nickname was often Frigid, an image I grappled with for years. I get my long legs, ample rack, and blond hair from my Swedish mother and my dark eyes, hot temper, and propensity to shoot whiskey from my Irish father. He also passed on to me a bit of the gambling gene, which explains why I'm usually in over my head.

Twenty years later, in the summer '86, fashion designers are putting their labels on the outside of clothes, girls in my line of work all have big Texas hair, and neon spandex is the fabric of the moment; which is cool if you have a good body, but truly painful if you don't.

∞

September heat radiated through the window glass where I was holed up at my sister's house, discussing last summer's discovery of the Titanic after seventy-five years at the bottom of the ocean. There is an eeriness to raising the dead, be it an old ship or my love life.

"You want to tell me again why you did it?" Shannon asked.

"Did what? Blow my life's savings, break up with Dirk, or leave Las Vegas with my tail between my legs?" Looking out the window as a swarm of teens rolled by on inline skates, I sighed.

"All of the above," she said, pouring hot water into my cup and handing me a teabag. "You want cream in that?"

I nodded.

My sister Shannon and her new husband had a small one-bedroom apartment near Capitol Hill in Denver overlooking 13th Avenue. Two days earlier, I'd shown up on her doorstep, broke and depressed.

"I couldn't handle the drinking anymore, mine or his," I said. "It was bad enough Dirk lost another job because he was too drunk to get to work. I could deal with that. What I couldn't take was him driving when he was too hammered to walk. I didn't want to watch him die, or worse yet, see him kill someone else."

Shannon set a plate of homemade cookies on the table in front of me. "I'm sorry it got that bad. I always liked Dirk."

"Leaving him is the hardest thing I've ever had to do." I bit on my lower lip. "After the break-up, I was feeling dead inside. I'm sure that's why I went to the Gold Strike Casino that night."

Shannon curled up in an overstuffed chair. "How much did you lose?"

"Eighteen thousand dollars."

"Wow," she said, biting into a warm chocolate chip cookie. "I don't believe I've ever held eighteen thousand dollars."

Shannon and I were not new to gambling. On more than one occasion, as children, we'd been awakened in the dead of night and hustled into the family car when our father's latest scheme had fallen through. He was more inclined to the horses or the next best pyramid scheme, while craps and poker were my ruin. I'd lived in Las Vegas for five years without falling victim to the bug, but once it bit me, I was lost. Depression and gambling go hand-in-hand.

"I couldn't stay in Vegas," I said. "I'm not strong enough to stay away from the craps tables or Dirk. I'm sure I'd talk myself into taking him back again like I have so many times before."

"So, what are you going to do now?"

"When I was flush, I loaned Dad ten thousand dollars for a start-up business. Before I came to Denver, I called him to see if he could pay me back."

Shannon's eyes bugged out. "What did he say?"

"His plan to make a fortune flipping houses crashed when the housing bubble burst. He doesn't have the cash, but he offered to give me a one-hundred-year-old house he won in a card game. He quick-deeded it to me for the ten-grand. All I have to do is make the mortgage payments."

"Oh, Fre. Have you seen the house?"

∞

My dad showed me the house at night, the shadows hiding many flaws. That's one of the reasons why bars and nightclubs are dark.

We pulled up to the curb in front of a two-story Victorian number.

"It looks cool," I said, getting out of the car. "Not much grass."

"The yard is only about a hundred square feet," he said. "Shouldn't be too difficult to plant some grass in the spring. The place has been empty—for a while."

I followed him across a small porch, and he held the door open for me. I found the light switch, but nothing happened when I flipped the switch.

"Most of the lights burned out," he said. "I haven't been here to replace them."

And so it was by flashlight that I had my first tour of the place that would change my life forever.

CHAPTER 2

On the right of the entry was a wooden staircase leading to the second floor with a landing about two-thirds of the way up. My dad shined his light down the hallway in front of us. "Straight ahead, you'll find the dining room and the kitchen beyond that. Check this out." He waved the light to the left, where a doublewide doorway led into the living room. Ten-foot-high ceilings and ten-inch-wide woodwork gave the room an elegant feel. Residual light from the streetlamp on the corner shown through the wavy glass of the round top picture window. A car drove past; it's bass thundering loud enough to rattle the ancient pane.

"What's with the hole in the wall?" I asked.

The focal point of the room should have been the fireplace. Tall and narrow windows framed the opening, but the mantle was gone leaving a cavernous hole, stuffed full of bricks.

"Someone stole the mantle," he said.

"Someone came in and walked off with the fireplace mantle? Who would do such a thing?"

"Some of these houses had exceedingly nice woodwork in their day. Look at this." He passed his light over the heavy wooden pocket doors. "She's something, isn't she?"

Running my hand over the wood, I nodded. "Yes, beautiful woodwork," I opened the doors to the parlor. There was one tall window to the left, and the doorway to the right led back to the dining room. The house was empty of furniture, meaning I wouldn't be spending the night, so I waved off the chance of seeing the rest of the house for a day when I could see more details.

"We should get going," I said. "I'm expected at Shannon's."

He carefully locked the door behind us, although I didn't think a burglar would find a reason to go inside since they'd already stolen the mantle.

"Thanks for the tour, dad. Is there any chance I could use that old truck you have in the backyard? I sold my car to buy my plane ticket." *And to pay off some debts.*

He nodded as we headed for the car. "It's not in the best shape, but it'll get you home most days."

"Fair enough."

We took 6th Avenue west to Lakewood, where my parents recently moved. Traffic was light, and there was just enough moonlight to see the outline of the mountains.

"How are Connor and Aiden?" I asked.

"They're doing well for themselves, but neither of them will be driving a Mercedes any time soon."

"Still selling used car parts?"

"Yeah. They do better selling whole cars, but the junkyard still has its customers."

My brothers, Aiden and Connor, live in the Highlands area of north Denver. Both are in their thirties and as far as I could tell, marriage isn't on either one's horizon. My oldest brother, Sheamus O'Connell Jr., is a software designer for Martin Marietta.

My dad turned onto Wadsworth Boulevard. "Sheamus and Jackie Jo just bought a house in Bonnie Brae. A lovely little house, but if you asked me, they paid too much for it."

"That's a nice neighborhood," I said. "Are they finally thinking of having kids?"

"They haven't said anything to your mother or me, but if they're going to do it, they best do more than think about it."

"That's a long drive to work for Sheamus. I would have thought they'd move to Highlands Ranch."

"Puts Jackie Jo closer to Children's Hospital."

Jackie Jo is a pediatric nurse Sheamus met while attending C.U. Boulder. They'd been married since they were twenty-two. Sheamus would be thirty-seven in the spring. "She would make a great mom," I said. "But, I don't think it's going to happen now."

"Yes, she would. Something your mother reminds him of whenever we see them. After fifteen years, you would think there would be at least one or two." He pulled into the drive of their fifties style ranch home. "Mom must be out playing bingo. She'll be sorry she missed you."

"Give her my love. I'll come by tomorrow if I can. I need to do some job hunting."

"Here's the key to the dodge. Keep a close eye on the oil. There's a leak I haven't had time to fix."

"Thanks, Daddy," I said, kissing him on the cheek. "Hopefully, I can get a car of my own soon."

Sliding into the driver's seat of the army-green, thirty-five-year-old truck, I adjusted the mirrors, waved goodbye to my dad, and turned the ignition.

Grrrumph, bang, cough, cough. It died.

"Give it a little more gas, honey," my dad said from the doorway.

Grrrumph, bang, cough, cough, rumble, rumble. It was running, but I wasn't sure how long it would be. I shifted into reverse and slowly let out the clutch. Bang, cough, cough. It died again. I had to repeat the process three more times before heading downtown.

∞

On the way to Shannon's house, I stopped to pick up some cleaning supplies and a dozen light bulbs. Thinking this was going to be fun, I added some dishtowels to my basket. Some paint and a little elbow grease and I'd have a beautiful new home. In the car, I sang along with the Eurythmics, *"sweet dreams are made of these. Who am I to disagree?"*

Of course, I still needed a job to pay the outstanding mortgage, utilities, and buy food. I'd left all my money and my dignity in Las Vegas. Coming to Denver would give me a chance to turn my life around. This time, I was going to take my time and make something of my life. Working as a cocktail waitress in Vegas was easy and good money, but now it was time for me to decide on a real career. I could go back to school. I'd dropped out of college when I met Dirk, but Denver had some fantastic art schools. Feeling good about where I was headed, I pulled up in front of my sister's apartment.

∞

I stashed my little bag of cleaning supplies next to the couch and sat down. Picking up the newspaper, I scanned the help wanted ads. There were dozens of computer tech jobs, being the hot new industry. IBM was selling the Commodore 64 for home use, and two years ago, Apple Inc. introduced the Macintosh 128k personal computer with its graphic interface and mouse. Because of its simplicity, elementary schools were using the Mac. Unfortunately, I knew nothing about computers or designing software. I also had no accounting or medical training. "I can't seem to find any decent jobs here," I said to Shannon.

She was in the kitchen, heating Sloppy Joes for dinner. "What are you looking for?"

"I don't know. Something that will pay the bills."

Shannon set a plate of carrots on the coffee table in front of me. My sister believes Sloppy Joes are healthy if you substitute carrot sticks for potato chips.

"I told you to apply at Shotgun Willies." She set some celery sticks next to the carrots. "I know the girls make a ton of money."

"I don't know. It's a strip club." I went to the pantry and grabbed a bag of chips. "I was hoping to find something else."

"It's a Gentleman's Cabaret." Shannon frowned at me but didn't take the chips.

"That's just the PC way to say titty bar."

"It's a nice place, and waitressing is all you've done."

"I know. I was hoping to make a change."

"You can always look for a new job after you have one."

She was right, but I was still hesitant. "I don't know. What do the waitresses wear?"

"The manager said the waitresses aren't topless."

"I can't imagine any cocktail job in Denver paying what I was making in Vegas."

"You don't need as much money here. Your house payment is only four hundred and eighty dollars." She set the hot dish of ground beef on the table and began ladling it over fat hamburger buns. "You could almost cover that working at McDonald's."

"I need a car. I'm sure Dad will want his truck back, and I don't want to run up a debt with him."

Shannon smiled. Our dad is good at keeping score, although more often than not, it was he who owed us money. Not unlike our older brothers who borrowed and loaned money as a side business out of a salvage yard. Gambling is in our blood. Shannon takes after my mother, levelheaded and pragmatic.

"You're too tough on Dad," she said. "He would give you the shirt off his back if you asked for it."

"I know. But he usually doesn't have a shirt to give." I piled chips beside my sandwich and settled down in front of the TV to watch the Golden Girls.

Pulling open a folding TV tray, Shannon sat beside me. "I think you should check out the club. The manager is genuinely nice. He's cute, too."

"That's just what I need. I came here to get away from men."

"What made you believe there were no men here?"

"You know what I mean. I've had my fill of bartenders and bass players." I had been head-over-heels for Dirk. After four years, I realized I was never going to save him from himself. The gambling wasn't new to me; I thought I could handle it. After all, my mother was still married to my father. It was the drinking I couldn't bear to watch — too many nights, lying awake, wondering if he had run off the road or landed in jail.

I tried to move on by dating a guitar player from a local lounge act, but Vegas is a small town. Dirk and I had many mutual friends, so I always felt his presence. When the musician started boinking a coworker, I decided it was time to leave Sin City. I showed up on my sister's doorstep with a couple of suitcases and less than five hundred dollars in the bank.

Tucking a light brown curl behind her ear to keep it away from her sandwich, she said, "This is a nightclub manager we're talking about."

"Where I come from, a bar manager isn't much higher on the list."

"You could hang out with him for fun. I definitely would if I wasn't married."

"He's that cute?"

"Yeah, he's that cute."

Swallowing a bite of sandwich, I nodded. "I'll think about it."

∞

The next morning, I went back to the house. In the daylight, I cringed. It had the saddest little front porch. Years of settling had caused the front of the cement step to sink deep into the ground, pulling the porch roof away from the house. Rain and snow fell between the house and porch roof, leaving black streaks on the rust-colored brick. Someone had carved an array of names and symbols into the wooden posts and kicked out most of the balustrades.

Most of the woodwork was gouged and painted over a dozen times. The floors, covered with hideous olive-green shag carpet, hadn't seen a vacuum in years. This project was going to take so much more than cleaning and paint.

The second floor was no better except that it was smaller, three bedrooms and a bath, and therefore, would need less work. The bedroom at the top of the stairs was so tiny it couldn't hold more than a single bed and a small chest of drawers. Calling it a bedroom was unfair. Even the walk-in closet in my Vegas apartment had been larger. The room didn't have a closet. The second bedroom was larger and had a tiny closet - only two-feet by three-feet - but a closet all the same. Built at a time when taxes were calculated on the number of rooms in a house, a closet was considered a room because it had a door. Most folks had wardrobes for their clothing, and, well, most folks didn't have a modern girl's wardrobe.

Dominated by a massive claw-foot tub deep enough to fully immerse myself - something I would often do - the bathroom wasn't a total loss. The toilet, however, was scary and straight out of the twenties, including a pull chain for flushing. A tiny sink in the corner completed the ensemble.

Loud banging on the front door told me my brothers had arrived.

"Freja, it's Connor. Aiden's with me. Dad let us know you wanted the old waterbed he had in the basement. We got it in the truck."

I raced down the stairs to greet my older brothers. "Thanks for bringing it," I said.

Aiden's laugh shook his red curls, the only redhead in the family. He glanced around the front entryway and whistled softly. "Freeman," he said, punching me lightly in the shoulder." Dad got you again, didn't he?"

I puffed out my lower lip. "Not totally. The bathtub is nice."

Connor stepped inside. "We have some other things in the truck," he said, eyeing the living room. "Mom said you needed a dresser and a kitchen table. It looks to me like you need everything."

"I guess I came to Denver packing light."

"Had to sell it all?"

"Not all of it, but it was easier to give it away than drag it with me." The truth was, I didn't want the memories haunting me.

As I followed my brothers to the truck to help them unload, I saw my neighbors sitting on their porch across the street. I waved as friendly as I could. "Hi, I'm Freja. I'm just moving in."

"Hon," the large black woman said, "I kin see that. We was jus' wonderin' why."

The boy to her left gave me a toothy grin, and I felt much better.

I helped Connor carry the headboard up the stairs. Aiden followed with the footboard. The master bedroom was roomy, with a closet nearly as big as the third bedroom. I suspected it was once a nursery. Morning sun glared off the cracked and chipped plaster through two southern windows and one east-facing window. It could have been worse; it might not have been large enough for the king-size waterbed.

Crossing the hall, I had to rethink the waterbed. The floor sloped noticeably toward the bathroom door. That much weight upstairs might bring the whole place in on me. We set the solid pieces of furniture down in the master bedroom.

"I need to find a regular mattress for it," I said. "I'll sleep better knowing I won't wake up in the living room one morning. Where's the base and side rails?"

"I think Dad used them to make sideboards for the truck you're driving," Connor said, stretching his back.

I peeked outside the east window. Sure enough, the sideboards on the Dodge were a beautifully varnished dark wood.

"Oh well," I said. "The mahogany headboard has deep bookshelves and a nice mirror. It should make a decent dresser. I can throw an air mattress on the floor, and the footboard will make a great make-up table if I can find some cinderblocks or old peach crates."

"I saw some cinderblocks in the alley," Aiden said. "I'll go get them. Just got to machete my way through the jungle." The back yard was a large patch of weeds four feet high.

"Thanks. My peach crates are storing my vinyl collection."

Connor whistled. "How did you get all those albums here?"

"UPS. It cost more than my plane ticket."

"No doubt."

Aiden came in the back door. "You might want to replace the missing bricks in the wall. I saw a couple of cats climb through the hole headed for the basement."

"Seriously?" I said.

"Yep. It looks like it's missing about ten bricks or so."

I rubbed my temples. I hated the thought of going into the basement. "Would you look at this kitchen," I said, opening the metal cabinets over the sink. "It must have been remodeled sometime in the thirties. It has to be hiding a full fifty-years' worth of dirt and grime in here."

Connor smiled. "Not to worry, since you don't cook anyway."

I stuck my tongue out at him. "I may not cook much, but how am I supposed to store cocktail ice in a box that's smaller than my make-up case?"

"You want to ride out to Lakewood with us to pick up another load?" Connor asked. "Mom said she had some more furniture in the basement."

"Sure. Can't do much here without a wrecking ball."

"I wasn't gonna mention that," Aiden said, jabbing my ribs.

Another trip to my parent's house in Lakewood and I had enough furniture to fill two rooms if I wasn't picky. I now owned a sweet Formica-topped 1950s style kitchen table with two chairs, a brown and green plaid couch with matching chair, and an oversized coffee table that didn't match anything.

My mom gave me some old curtains, but since I didn't have any hardware, I hung up what I could with thumbtacks. I didn't believe anyone would notice a few more holes in the severely damaged woodwork. Pulling up the green shag carpet would have to wait a few days. I didn't know what I would find underneath, but it had to be better than the ratty old shag. Besides, I didn't own a vacuum cleaner and, judging by the amount of crap on the floor; the last tenant hadn't either.

After Aiden and Connor left, about four o'clock in the afternoon, I took stock of the house thinking about the recent disaster in Ukraine. The Chernobyl melt-down started with a simple safety test. I sat down on the stairs and cried.

CHAPTER 3

Late September in Colorado can be finicky. I've seen it snow one day and be in the eighties the next. On this beautiful afternoon, I was hanging out at the convenience store where Shannon worked as the day manager. We were discussing the advantages of having a car with a standard straight-stick in the snow when this dark-haired, green-eyed, God's gift-to-women strolled into the store to buy a cup of coffee and a box Hostess Donettes.

"Hi, Nick," Shannon said. "This is my sister, Freja."

"Freja? Interesting name."

"It's Swedish."

"Nice to meet you, Freja." He smiled, and my heart pounded just a little.

I'm not usually tongue-tied, but I could barely nod and smile in return. After he left, I asked Shannon, "Who was that doll?"

"That's Nick. He's the guy I was telling you about. You know, the general manager at Shotgun Willies."

"The topless place?" I stepped out of the way as a customer came to the counter.

"Yeah. You should seriously consider working there. I know the girls make tons of money because they come in after work and spend about a hundred dollars a night on junk." Shannon rang up a pack of Lucky Strikes and a two-liter bottle of Coke. "That will be a dollar-eighty-two," she said to the man at the counter.

The lanky guy of twenty-something dug through his pockets for change.

"I can't work there," I said as the guy left.

"Why not? You've always been a cocktail waitress, and they make bank there."

"I don't know."

"I told you, the waitresses aren't topless."

"For sure?"

"Yes, for sure. I asked again last week. And I know Nick is single. He asked me out."

"You're married."

"Yeah, but you aren't."

"True," I said, "but while I have vowed to be a good girl and find a nice man, Nick is gorgeous, and a nightclub manager would be a step up from a blackjack dealer, bartender, and bass player." *Could he even make me forget Dirk?*

∞

At home that night, I wandered through the empty rooms of the old house. It was going to be a lot more work and money that I'd first thought. It was so like me to jump into something without thinking it through. This neighborhood was in an especially bad part of town. I had no idea where I would find the money for tools and materials. If that wasn't enough, I knew virtually nothing about remodeling a house, and this place was going to take a lot of restoration. Staring at a four-inch gap between the baseboard and the floor at the bottom of the stairs next to the front door, I surmised there was a broken floor-joist below. Feeling deeply depressed, I wandered into the kitchen.

A massive monstrosity of a gas stove with deep metal drawers had replaced the original wood-burning unit. Across a narrow aisle from the gas-behemoth was a combination white metal cabinet and sink. A tall window five-feet high and a foot-and-a-half wide let the evening sun throw beams of light across the yellowed linoleum floor; the only section not covered by the hideous green shag carpet. While the entire kitchen was eleven-by-eighteen feet, the stove and sink was crammed into a tiny five-by-six-foot nook next to the basement stairs. That left the remaining twelve-by-eleven feet of the kitchen space for the teensy weensy, 1940s refrigerator, complete with a wooden door for the freezer.

Taking out the stove that once produced heat in the room meant there was no heat duct. The remaining chimney had an attractive tin pie pan blocking the hole where the stovepipe once vented. Since the large room was mostly unnecessary, I hung a quilt over the doorway so I could use the entire room for a refrigerator during the winter.

The second floor wasn't in any better shape. The wood floors were gouged and split. Being pine and not hardwood, cleaning them up would be a delicate job. Carpeting would go a long way to making it look better, but I've never been a fan of carpet. I have a childhood fear of tiny bugs hiding between the threads, waiting to attack me while I sleep. I saw something like that on a TV commercial, and the image has never left me. It didn't help that my dad used to tease me about being snug as a bug in a rug.

The basement was just dark and scary. Rickety wooden steps led down to the main room of dark grey cement walls. Through a narrow doorway was another room with a furnace and filled with old wooden doors leaning upright against a wall. A fast estimate was about thirty to forty doors. The rest of the basement contained a dark crawlspace full of scary things.

Since the weather would be turning colder, patching the holes in the brick outer walls took priority. I would worry about things like electrical and plumbing once I was able to keep the stray cats from living in the crawl space. Walking past the heavy abandoned doors, I felt a sense of foreboding, like the way I felt right after losing eighteen-grand.

I headed back upstairs and sat down on my air-mattress bed and made a list of repairs. I couldn't fix my dad, and I couldn't fix Dirk, but the house, broken and in need, represented something I could control. I added stripping the floors and tearing out the lathe and plaster to the list. I would need to replace the shingles on the roof someday but making the inside livable was critical. With its intricate Victorian gingerbread trim, the outside of the house would be fun to paint in an *I-like-working-stupid-hard,* sort of way. As I dropped off to sleep, the list of projects was already overwhelming.

I needed a job! So the next day, I slipped into my sexiest three-piece suit, the one with the three-inch slit up the back of the skirt and my favorite black stilettos. I felt like I needed a little pampering. Maybe I wouldn't get a job, but I might get a date, and that would take my mind off the house and Dirk for a while. I parked my dad's truck at the Target store behind Shotgun Willies so no one would see what I was driving. I know I should be thankful, and I was, but there was no sense bragging by parking it by the front door.

The double doors to the club were heavy oak. I pulled one open and peered into the darkness. Stepping inside, I was assailed by the smell of old cigarette smoke and stale perfume.

My eyes adjusted to the dark, revealing a man in a cheap suit standing behind a counter. "ID please," he said with no preamble.

"I'd like to see Nick, the general manager," I said, handing him my driver's license.

"Sure, but any manager can do your audition."

"Oh, I'm not here to audition," I shouted over the strains of Billy Ocean's *Caribbean Queen.*

He inspected me, head to toe, and pointed to a table about three feet away. "Take a seat."

I felt my way to the table. The club was exceedingly dark, which was a good thing. Had I been able to see what was going on, I would have run away, but before my eyes could fully adjust to the dark, handsome Nick was sitting in front of me, flashing an incredible smile.

He took my resume and examined it. "Good experience. I see you worked at the Stardust in Las Vegas."

"Yes, only for about a year. I liked working at the marina on Lake Mead better; fewer tourists, more locals."

"Can you be here Thursday at seven?"

"Sure."

"Great, see you then." Tossing me one more smile, he got up and disappeared into the darkness.

Feeling bummed when he walked away, I'd hoped to have a little more time to flirt. He appeared to be impressed with my Las Vegas experience, although I think he would have hired me even if I couldn't read. Judging by what I saw as my eyes adjusted, the main requirements for working in this establishment were my being five-foot-seven and weighing one-hundred-twenty pounds. I'm sure it didn't hurt that I have waist-length curly blond hair.

∞

It was early evening when I drove the Dodge truck to the Highlands to visit my brothers. Their shop was on a hill overlooking the Valley Highway and the Platte River. Lower downtown had flooded several times before they built the Cherry Creek Reservoir in 1950 and Chatfield in 1975. The west side of the city was mostly rundown warehouses and railroad tracks. Denver saw its first skyscrapers as high-rise office buildings sprang up on the southeastern side of downtown during the oil boom of the seventies, then the real-estate bubble burst in the early eighties, leaving lots of office space vacant. The city was in slow recovery, and I was counting on the northeast properties rising in value again.

I found Aiden in the garage. "I could use a car," I said. "It's nice of Dad to loan the Dodge to me, but it's not exactly my style."

Aiden laid down the wrench he was using to tighten the battery post on an old Ford Galaxy. "I don't know if I have much here. How much do you have to spend?"

"Thing is, I don't have any money right now, but I did get a job."

"If you weren't my little sister…"

I nudged him in the ribs. "You know I'm good for it."

"Yeah, you've always been the responsible one. Hard to believe you need a loan from me."

"I should be able to pay you at least two hundred a month. What do you have for that price?"

Aiden led me over to the small lot where he and Connor had used cars for sale. Most of the vehicles were at least ten years old. I wandered passed the '73 Dodge Colt and '74 Ford Falcon. There was a black '71 Buick LeSabre and a '79 Red Pontiac Grand AM that looked pretty rad. "I was hoping for something a little newer and a little flashier," I said.

"I have an '83 Toyota Celica Coupe. Not a good family car."

"Do I look like I'm starting a family?"

"No, but it might be more than you want to spend. I need to get four thousand for it plus interest."

It was baby blue and perfect. "I love it. How much is the interest?"

"Seven hundred."

"No way! I'm your sister."

"I had a guy offer me forty-two cash. He's coming over in the morning."

I opened the trunk. "Good size."

"The back seats fold forward so you can carry snow skis if you want."

"Really? When did you pick up snow skiing?"

He laughed and showed me how the seats lay down. A lot of the people who grew up in Colorado didn't ski. We were no exception.

"I can haul two by fours in here," I said. "Sold!"

∞

Aiden followed me to Lakewood to drop off the truck. Mom was in the yard watering the junipers.

"Hi, Mom," I said. "I'm dropping off the truck. Aiden sold me a new car."

She turned the faucet off. "Are you two staying for dinner? I made a roast."

"Sure," Aiden said. "Connor's at a car auction in Colorado Springs."

I didn't have a thing in my house to eat, and roast beef sounded a lot better than a burger. "I'll stay if you have enough."

"I always have enough."

True. My mother always made enough for a family of five, even when it was just her and dad at home. She froze the leftovers to serve on the nights she went to bingo or a church social.

Once we were seated at the table, Dad came in and took his place at the head of the table. He'd been in the basement working on a table he was refinishing. "How's the house coming along?" he asked.

I held my tongue, feeling he'd taken advantage of me. "Fine. It's going to be a lot more work than I thought."

"If anyone can do it, you can. You're incredibly talented. More than that, your tenacious."

Mom scooped potatoes onto her plate. "Shannon said you got a job waiting tables."

"Yeah. It's going to be okay for a while, but then I'd like to go back to school."

Dad sliced the roast and pushed the plate toward me. "I know my little girl. You'll learn plenty working on that house. You've always been handy with a hammer. Speaking of—there's a toolbox on the back porch. Just some odds and ends."

Aiden swallowed a mouthful of roast beef. "Are those Connor's old tools?"

"Yeah. They've been sitting here for a couple of years now. I figure he bought new ones when you two remodeled the auto repair shop."

My brother smiled at me. "You should find enough to get started wrecking the place."

"It's already pretty wrecked," I said.

∞

Mom packed a box of cookies for me and sent meat, potatoes, and gravy with Aiden. I would have taken some roast beef, but I didn't trust the refrigerator. By the time I got back home, it was after ten. Even though I'd replaced most of the light bulbs, it was still creepy coming home at night. Deep shadows from the unlit rooms greeted me as I opened the front door. I quickly turned on every light in the house. I'd lived alone in a small apartment the last year I was in Vegas, but this house was so big it unnerving.

In Vegas, I'd always slept in the buff, but I wasn't comfortable here, so I slipped an old T-shirt over my head and snuggled into bed. The sound of cars driving up and down the street kept me awake most of the night. Sometime around two, I thought I heard someone knocking on the door, but I might have been dreaming. The house made the usual house noises, like the furnace kicking on, but they were all new sounds to me.

Living in a space where, for more than one hundred years, different families with many different experiences had lived, I felt an emptiness universal to old homes, especially large ones. Like shadows of the past; there but not there.

CHAPTER 4

The morning sun woke me around eight. Groggy from lack of sleep, it took a moment to orient myself and unwind my T-shirt. I had mom's cookies for breakfast while planning my day. The first step was to make the place a little more livable by cleaning the bathroom. I scoured and scrubbed for over an hour. The room was still scary. I made a mental note to paint before the week was over.

From the bathroom, I moved to the bedroom. I was going to be spending most of my time in these two rooms while I tore out and remodeled the rest of the house. The last owner had slapped that green shag carpet down in every room, including the stairs. It was totally gross. By three in the afternoon, I had every stitch of carpet in the dumpster. The metal kitchen sink was hopeless, but it would be a decent place to clean up paintbrushes

The cookies had worn off, so I scrounged through the bottom of my bag and counted my change. I had enough for a burger and a couple of domestic items. After a stop at Wendy's, I headed to K-Mart for a set of fluffy bath towels. I have my priorities.

The bathtub was fabulous. Covered in bubbles, I could almost forget about the challenge before me. Although I lived alone, I got out of the tub and closed the bathroom door. The house was so large and old; it was creepy. I felt like someone was watching me.

I reported to work the following night, and the manager on duty gave me my uniform. "Holy crap." I'm not all that shy, but this thing was little more than rhinestone cuffs and a collar with a bowtie which could best be described as a white lace dickie, t-back thong underwear, and fishnet stockings.

Once dressed, the manager pointed me in the direction of a girl with black hair and blacker eye make-up. Pepper, aka Debbie on her paycheck, came across like a Goth biker with a severe Princess Di haircut. She was cute in a forbidden sort of way, but the scar on her cheek and sleeve of tattoos suggested she didn't take crap from anyone.

"Hi, I'm Freja. The manager told me you would train me."

Looking at me as if I had just slept with her husband, she said, "Really? Freja?"

"Yes. It's Swedish." I smiled the best I could, considering she was freaking me out a little. "I have a lot of experience with serving drinks. I worked in Vegas for a few years."

She rolled her eyes and pointed toward the bar. "Grab a tray from the bartender. It's pay as you go, no cash tabs."

That was the norm for most bars, although I'd recently worked in a casino where the drinks were complimentary. "How much are the drinks?"

She rolled her eyes again and blew out a sigh. "Ask the bartender when you order," she said as she strutted away.

"Wait, where is my section?"

"Your section? There aren't any sections. Go. Sell drinks. Oh, and don't serve a dancer without getting a drink ticket from her. Some of the girls are under twenty-one."

That was the end of my training. Nervously, I walked to the bar and waited for the bartender to notice me. Rail thin and sporting a stylish mullet, he appeared too young to be serving drinks. He was flirting with the nearly naked girl sitting at the end of the bar. By her state of undress, I figured she must be one of the dancers.

Pepper came in behind me and nearly pushed me aside. "Hey, Bobby! Put your pecker away. I need a bourbon-water, two Jack-coke, a Bud, and a Coors-light."

Bobby jumped to fill her order. "Twenty-six, fifty," he said, opening the three bottles of beer. Setting the beers on the bar, he held out his left hand to her while ringing in the drinks with the right. She passed him a hundred-dollar bill, and he returned the change in ones and fives. I was shocked by the price. A dollar was the average price for a bottle of beer in most places.

Once Pepper cleared the service well, Bobby regarded me with a smile. "First night?" he asked.

"Yeah. Three seventy-five for a beer? Are you kidding me?"

He nodded toward a table-height, hexagon stage where a girl in a barely visible G-string had her legs wrapped around a guy's head. "The same price as the airport and the only thing taken off there are planes."

I cringed, thinking the money had better be better than good. "Do you think I could get a tray and set-up?"

"Sure."

He was back in a few seconds with a serving tray and a big black plastic ashtray. "You want a rocks glass for your quarters?"

"That would be great. Could I get a bar towel, too?"

He cocked his head and narrowed his eyes. "What for?"

"To wipe the tables when guests leave and to clean up spills."

He laughed. "You plan on spilling a lot?" It wasn't a mean laugh, but I still felt dumb.

"I just like to be prepared."

"Sure," he said, reaching for a towel. "I don't think anyone ever asked me for a towel before they spilled their drinks. You want it dry?"

"No, just damp enough to clean the tables. Can I get some matches, too? I have a lighter and pens," I said as I grabbed a stack of napkins.

He stared at me as if he didn't quite know what to make of me. Another waitress came into the well and glanced my way. She was tall, sporting a Farrah Fawcett hairstyle on steroids. I looked down and saw she was wearing low heels. Even with my five-inch platforms, she was a good two inches taller. In her three-inch heels, she was taller than any of the men standing near the bar. "Two eighteen hundred, no training wheels, coke back, and three buds," she called to Bobby.

He poured her drinks and headed to the cooler for the beers.

Setting the shots of tequila on her tray, she said, "Hi, I'm Ginger."

"Freja."

"For reals?"

"Yes. It's Swedish. It's my first night."

Shaking her head, she handed Bobby two twenties for her order; he gave her back a stack of ones and three quarters.

I eyeballed her tray, noting she had a glass for quarters and a dirty plastic ashtray, nothing else.

Dumping the cigarette butts in the trash, she said, "Bobby's cute, but it ain't like he's gonna buy any drinks from you." She tilted her head toward the room. "Money's out there." With a Pepsodent smile, she reprimanded the bartender, "Bobby, stop flirting and, like, let the girl make some money."

He grinned. "Baby, I hate to see you get jealous when I flirt with other girls."

"And then you woke up," Ginger, aka Carolyn on her library card, said, placing her tray on her left hand. As she turned, she clipped the edge of the bar and nearly spilled her drinks. As her hand shot up to steady the beer bottles, she gave me a wink.

Bobby watched her saunter away. "Ginger's cool. She used to be a dancer, but she's a little clumsy."

"She's gorgeous."

"She's got nothing on you."

"Thanks. I've never been to a place like this."

"As Ginger said, if you want to make money here, the trick is not to spend too much time with one guy. Get in and get out quick. These guys will try to talk your ear off if you let them and you can't sell drinks that way. Of course, if a guy is paying for your time, that's another story."

"Thanks. I'll remember that." I turned to look at the room. It was dark and very crowded. The sound system was blaring *"...I may be crazy, but it just may be a lunatic you're looking for..."*

I went to the stage closest to the bar and walked the room yelling 'cocktails' the same way I used to when I worked the blackjack pits in Vegas. I had twelve orders before I made my way around the entire stage. I tried lapping a few of the other dance stages, but my tray was filled with drink orders before I could get thirty feet from the bar.

"How many waitresses are working tonight?" I asked Bobby as he filled my order.

"Ten, I think."

"Where are they? I'm swamped."

He pointed to a table where two waitresses were sitting with an older man in a nice suit.

"Why are they sitting there? Are they on break?"

"No, he's probably tipping a lot of money. You'll see."

Sure enough, one of the girls came to the bar and ordered a cognac. Not a tray of drinks like I was holding, just the one. She didn't stop to solicit another order on the way back to the table, either. I realized I had at least half of the club to cover. Pepper, on the other hand, worked the way I worked. She didn't sit and shoot the bull with the guys, just in and out. I figured that was why the manager wanted her to train me.

By the end of the night, my feet were on fire, and I wasn't sure I wanted to come back. I hadn't counted my money while I was working because I'd been too busy to give it a thought. When I went to the dressing room to change, I counted my tips for the first time and decided I would stick it out for a while. At a time when the minimum wage was less than three-fifty an hour, I had made close to forty dollars an hour. At this rate, I would be able to pay off my car in half the time.

∞

Since I had decent cash coming in, this was an excellent time to get started on some major house projects. My original supply list had paint and wallpaper. It only took a couple of days to realize the old plaster walls need much more than a coat of paint. Bricks and mortar were now first on the list. The hole was located on the wall behind the basement stairs, and the stairs were a cobbled-up mess, more a ladder than a staircase. Eventually, I would replace them but today, I would settle for shoring up the stairs with a couple of studs.

By Friday of my second week of work, I'd made enough money for a trip to H B Woods, a hardware store that was not in my immediate area. The fact was, there weren't too many places in my neighborhood that I was willing to go inside. I like shopping at H B Woods because the guys who work there are so helpful. They know how things work, unlike the new supercenters that hired high school kids who don't know the difference between a jigsaw and a circular saw.

I pulled into the parking lot and felt a familiar rush. I love shopping. Not like most girls who can spend hours at the mall. No, given the choice of a thousand-dollar shopping spree at Macy's or a home improvement store, you'll find me breathing in the scent of fresh-cut wood every time. I took woodshop in high school, not because I thought I would be good at woodworking but because I love the smell of cedar, oak, and pine. If I'm not gazing at lumber, you might find me dreaming in the paint and stain aisles or going gaga over some new fancy molding or bathroom fixtures.

∞

Standing by the fresh-cut lumber trying to decide how much I could get in the back of my Toyota, I looked up to see a gorgeous blond beach bum with the bluest eyes I've ever seen. He asked me if I needed help as he stared back into my eyes, waiting for an answer.

"Uh... I need a few studs and some bricks," I stuttered like an idiot.

He was dressed much like me in a green-and-black plaid flannel shirt and denim jeans. Only his shirt looked a lot nicer on his broad shoulders. He was buff, not steroid buff, but rad genetics buff.

"How many do you need?" he asked.

"I'll take eight two-by-fours. The cement can wait, but I'll need a box of decking screws."

He tilted his head as if he wanted to ask me something. Instead, the corners of his mouth tipped up. He had adorable dimples in his tanned cheeks that could use a shave. He was scruffy in a sexy kind of way.

He loaded the studs onto my cart next to the grinder, two five-gallon utility buckets, a bag of mortar, and sixteen red bricks. When he turned around, I could see his jeans fit perfectly in all the right places. Did I mention that I like the guys who work here?

"I can ring you up over here if you're ready to check out."

I thought for a moment. "That should do for now." I followed him to the checkout lane.

He was fast on the register. He must have known all the SKU numbers by heart. "That comes to twenty-one, eighty-seven."

"That can't be right." I scanned everything I bought and calculated the damage. "It has to be closer to forty dollars."

"It's okay; I gave you my employee discount."

"Seriously? You didn't need to do that. Thank you."

"You're welcome. I wanted to." His smile widened, and his dimples deepened. He brushed a lock of blond hair out of his eyes and asked, "Do you need help loading these things?"

I felt so thankful for the discount. I didn't want to put him out further. "No, that's fine."

"Here," he said, "I got this. Where are you parked?"

As we stepped past the sliding doors, I pointed to my little blue Celica.

"You're kidding," he said.

"No. The backseats fold forward. I can lay the studs between the front seats. Just need to leave room to shift."

After we finished cramming everything in my car, I said, "Thank you. You're sweet."

"Don't let it get around, okay?"

"Sure. By the way, I'm Freja."

"Sawyer. It's my pleasure."

I opened the driver's side door. "Thanks again, Sawyer. See you next time."

"Hope so," he said, and he jogged back to the store.

∞

Since I didn't need to be at work until seven on Saturday night, I spent the rest of the day bracing the stairs and patching the hole in the wall. I hadn't spent much time in the basement as it seriously creeped me out. Technically it was only a half basement. A three-foot crawl space existed under the parlor, living room, and entry hall. I wasn't looking forward to crawling around in the creepy darkness, but I needed to know why the entryway floor had dropped, pulling away from the baseboard. But not today. I had a hole to fix first.

The original brick walls were covered with a white powdery efflorescence and were as soft as butter. That required me to wrest out several full courses of old brick to find a stable place to start rebuilding the wall and closing the impromptu cat door. With the grinder, I cut away the loose bricks and filled the hole. I had about eight times more mortar than I was going to need, but I realized I was going to be short on bricks.

Since I was planning on tearing out and replacing the entire fireplace one day, I grabbed a chisel and ripped out enough of the old brick from the original firebox to finish the basement wall. They didn't match the original wall, but I was going to paint over them anyway.

Upon sealing the hole in the wall, I felt a sense of accomplishment I hadn't felt in years. Spirits renewed; I set off on the next project. I'd need instructions on framing, plumbing, and electrical systems. I didn't know the first thing about rebuilding the front porch, so the second item on my list was "How To" books. I'd hoped the store would be open Sunday because that was my next day off.

∞

I was becoming more at ease going to work, knowing I would be making great money. The club was dark, smelled of cigarette smoke, and most of my coworkers wouldn't speak to me. Ginger, aka Carolyn to her dentist, and Bobby were the exceptions.

The club, crowded with young men of all types, was a new experience for me. Every other place I'd worked was about fifty-fifty men and women. Here was a room full of testosterone, and I can't say that it was all dreadful. There were some fine-looking men here.

The music was so loud; I nearly had to sit in a guy's lap to hear his drink order. I'm not sure that wasn't intentional. When the song ended, the music lowered, and the DJ announced the next line up of dancers. Like a morning radio show announcing the winner of an all-expenses-paid trip to Mexico, he sounded exultant. "On stage five, we have the lovely Lexus, and on stage four, please welcome pretty Porsche. On stage three for the first time tonight, we have beautiful Bentley." There was a Mercedes and a Jaguar as well. No, this wasn't a fancy car commercial.

I quickly learned how important it was to choose the right name when working in a strip club. I can see where it would be awkward to have seven Cindys working in a place that doesn't use last names. Even the cocktail waitresses had aliases. I usually worked shifts with a Sugar, Pepper, Spice, Cinnamon, and Ginger. Luckily, there wasn't another girl using my name so I stuck with Freja because it was easier to remember.

The entertainers came in all sizes and attitudes. The large-busted blond was the mainstay but there were some rounder girls and some small-breasted girls to attract the men who didn't like the Loni

Anderson type. There were even a few girls who looked pre-teen. I found that disturbing.

The only time I had much to do with the entertainers was when they ordered a drink. Management didn't like the girls getting hammered, so they had to give me a permission slip every time they wanted a drink. Most of the girls were cool about it, but others, you would have thought I asked for their first-born child.

While ordering my drinks, I mentioned to Ginger how surprised I'd been about the tips I was making. "Part of the reason I made rad money in Vegas," I said, "was because waitresses made union scale and the drinks in the casinos were all free."

Ginger cleared dirty glassware from her tray. "So, like, topless clubs are totally different because the customers are like ninety-nine percent male." She garnished a fresh drink and dumped her ashtray. "And look at all the cute guys who come in here. Gotta watch out for the married ones, for sure. Some of these dipsticks will try to fool you by taking off their wedding rings. And if you go out with, like, a good-tipping regular, he'll think he doesn't have to tip as much cause now you're friends."

"Nick told me we're not supposed to go out with the customers."

"Yeah, I know. Just don't be a bonehead."

"I've had enough of men for a while. I only need to work two days a week and can survive on one if I need to."

"For sure, but you'll get used to the money pretty quick. Soon it will be a better car, better clothes, more parties."

"I got a lot going on. I told Nick I only wanted to work Thursdays and Fridays."

"Everybody works Saturdays. It's like the World's Largest Bachelor Party in here; you've seen the flyers."

"Maybe he'll let me work the four to midnight shift. I like leaving before the dancers. I'm not a prude, but some of these girls make me uncomfortable. There's no filter, and no subject is taboo with them."

Ginger laughed. "Fuckin' A. You might think you're not like, a total prude, but I see the way you avoid looking at the stages."

"I feel funny looking at naked girls."

"For sure. You'll get used to that, too."

Of course, she was right. Dealing with drunken men wasn't new to me, but the added testosterone of a man surrounded by naked women was more of a challenge. The occasional shot of whiskey helped, but I noticed my tips went down when I imbibed. Not because I made less money; more that I tended to drop it on the floor. I only know this because Ginger retrieved it for me on several occasions.

Before Ginger left at midnight on Saturday, she brought me a hefty 3oz snifter of B & B. "So, like, one of my best customers insists you have a drink with him," she said, leading me to the table. "This guy is good for fifty to a hundred dollars a night, but you have to drink with him."

I sat down, feeling a little guilty for not waiting on the guy at the next table who had an empty glass.

"So," he said with a touch of a slur. "Ginger tells me you're from Las Vegas."

"I lived there for a few years. I recently bought a house in Five Points."

"That's a rough neighborhood. Is it an original house?"

"Yes. It's over a hundred years old."

"They say most of those houses are haunted."

I laughed. "I don't believe in ghosts."

Ten minutes later, my drink was gone, and I had a crisp fifty tucked in my garter. The B & B had me feeling good enough to have another when the guy offered.

"I should get back to work," I said. "I'll be back after I've made a round."

∞

Later that night, I cornered Nick by the ice machine. "I only want to work Thursday and Friday," I said. "I don't need more shifts than that."

"Are you in school?"

"No, but I hate working Saturday."

"Can't you give me at least three days?"

"Do you think I could work the four to midnight shift?"

We compromised.

"Tell you what," he said, smiling in that way that tickled me deep inside where it had no business. "You give me a nine to midnight shift on Saturday, and I'll give you four to midnight Wednesday, Thursday, and Friday."

I made twice the money on Wednesday as I did on Saturday, and I genuinely hated getting home so late, but I said, "Okay." I'm such a sucker for a cute man, and whenever Nick asked me to do anything, I said yes.

CHAPTER 5

Ginger and I went to the Landmark Hotel restaurant to have breakfast after work the following night. She pulled out a flask and poured something in her coffee.

"I'd like to be an artist, for sure," she told me over her bacon and eggs. "I like painting and sculpture. I once sold a painting at the People's Fair for like fifty dollars."

"That's impressive," I said, munching on cantaloupe and cottage cheese. "I once sold a couple of children's dolls at a fair. Not a big market for princess dolls, but it was fun."

"So, how is the house project coming along?"

"Overwhelming most days, but I met a super cute guy at the hardware store."

"Did you like, ask him out?"

"No, I'm trying to stay out of trouble."

"Men are no trouble. I like men. I like sex too, and not, like, always in that order."

I told her about my bitter break up with Dirk. "I'm feeling a little gun-shy right now."

"You need to forget about that guy."

"That's not as easy as it sounds. A chunk of my heart is gone."

"You should come to Vegas with me next month. A new guy is just what you need; nothing like, serious. Just for fun."

"I'll think about it." And I did. There was something in Sawyer's eyes that made me twitter.

Ginger and I talked for three more hours, drinking coffee spiked with Yukon Jack, meaning I didn't get home until well after four in the morning. I rolled to a stop at the curb. I'd left the porch light on because I didn't like going to the door in the dark. I had my hand on the door handle when I noticed two women standing on my little porch. Dressed in dark clothes with dark skin, they were mostly shadows.

"I don't think anybody's home," the shorter of the girls said. "I tried earlier but didn't get an answer."

Stepping off the porch, the two of them headed toward me. My heart was pounding.

"You lookin' for the dudes that live here?" the taller one asked.

"No," I said. "My husband is the only guy who lives here." I didn't want to tell them I lived there alone. I was sure they were harmless, but I didn't know why they were knocking on my door in the middle of the night.

"You live here?" Her eyes popped wide.

I nodded.

"You got any liquor?"

"No. I just got home from work."

"You sure you ain't got any booze?"

"I'm sure."

The shorter girl tugged on her friend's arm. "Let find Sparky. He should know someone."

I waited until they turned the corner before I got out of the car.

∞

On Sunday, I was back at H B Woods, stocking up on reading material. Soon my arms were full of books, and I strolled to the checkout counter. On the way, I saw Sawyer standing in the doorway of the office talking to a man in a suit, probably his boss. I smiled as I passed and took my place in line. A moment later, he waved me over to a different checkout lane.

"I can take you here," he said as he inserted his key into the register.

"What? In front of all these people?"

He cocked his head slightly to one side as he replayed the conversation. I'm not positive, but I believe his cheeks pinked just a little. His eyes flashed as he grinned.

"Thanks," I said. "You didn't have to open a register for me."

"I like waiting on you. You buy interesting stuff."

"Just books today."

He picked the first book up and scanned it, Banner Press, *Handyman.* "This is an excellent choice. I have this one at home."

"I couldn't decide between that one and the *Reader's Digest Home Improvement Guide,* so I'm getting both."

"The Guide is better for big projects, but both of them cover basics pretty well."

"I picked up Bob Vila's *This Old House* because it said there might be some surprises in a house as old as mine, and the *Old House Catalog* is so I know what to call things when I need to replace them." There were eight other books in the stack, including one on electricity, plumbing, doors, and windows, and framing and drywall.

"I just have to ask you," he said as he stuffed a copy of *How a House Works* in the sack. "What kind of project are you working on?"

"I have an old house that needs a lot of work. A new kitchen and bath, new windows, and I need to rip out the plaster and lathe and replace it with drywall."

"I gather you want to know what the building crew is doing? That's smart to have a good understanding of construction so you won't get ripped off."

"I don't have a crew. I'm going to do it myself."

His lips curled into a broad smile showing white teeth and sexy dimples. "Really? And do you have a lot of experience remodeling a house?"

"No, but how hard can it be? It's all in these books."

"Well, if you ever need a hand, I know a little bit about the remodeling business."

He was sweet and cute in that beach bum kind of way, but I'd sworn off men. No more bad boys for me, and he was obviously a chick magnet. He was friendly, but his coworkers appeared to work twice as hard as Sawyer, so I figured he was either incredibly laid back or just unambitious. What a shame; he was super cute. *Down girl. Wait until Mr. Right comes along.*

My past track record, where men were concerned, was pretty sketchy. I couldn't be trusted to keep a level head around a charming man. My biggest weakness is being unable to say no, even when it's something I don't want to do, like working four days a week instead of two. Big, sad eyes melt my heart, and tears will completely undo me. Accepting the house from my dad had given me the chance to immerse myself in a massive renovation project, leaving me no time to get in trouble. Or so I thought.

∞

Friday night started a little slow, but, even then, the tips were excellent. There is a lot to be said for a virtually all-male clientele. I'm sure the uniform helped as well. The job became more manageable once I'd learned my way around.

Ginger, aka Carolyn on her apartment lease, was bubbly and cute even though she wasn't particularly graceful. She was good at flirting with men, probably because she liked them. I was a decent enough waitress but a little gun-shy when it came to flirting with someone I didn't want to see socially.

I stayed clear of Pepper, aka Debbie, to her parole officer. She didn't smile at me and was very curt whenever she spoke. Tattoos and the dark, goth look were things I rarely saw in Vegas. I wondered how she made money.

I was standing by the front door waiting to greet the next guest when the DJ cued up Rick James. *"She's a very kinky girl, the kind you don't take home to mother…"*

As if on cue, a tall businessman came in and asked if Pepper was working. I pointed to the back bar. "She's working the back half of the room tonight."

Handing me a ten spot, he smiled and said, "Thanks."

It was still a mystery to me, but obviously, Pepper had her regulars who helped pay the bills. You just never knew what turned a guy on. It was a mystery fashion and make-up companies exploited.

After work, I stopped at the Landmark hotel restaurant to have something to eat with Ginger. She made me feel welcome, where most of the other girls were about as friendly as Pepper.

"I'm going to Vegas for Halloween," she told me over her Denver Omelet. "I have a friend who works at the Aladdin." She pulled out her flask and poured Yukon Jack in her coffee and a little in mine.

"That's cool." I had cantaloupe and cottage cheese for breakfast. It helped counteract the double cheeseburger I had for lunch. "I like the strip for its architecture, but I always played at the local casinos. The odds were supposed to be better."

"So, like, did you win a lot?"

"No. The odds might have been better, but that didn't mean they were in my favor."

"You should come with me."

"I'm trying to stay out of trouble."

"This would be so, like good for you. A chance to get away."

"Perhaps," I said, sipping my spiked coffee. "I'll think about it."

She beamed. "We'd have a riot!"

Ginger and I talked until well after three in the morning. She was so full of life, and my house was so dead. I almost hated going home.

∞

Later that night/early morning, I lay on my bed, skimming through the home improvement books I'd bought, taking stock, and making notes. Basic construction was straightforward: two-by-fours and sheetrock. I studied the book on wiring, and other than hooking the final wires to the breaker box, it didn't look too hard. Basic flooring and subfloor construction were simple enough. Beams sat on sills, and the subfloor went over the beams. As much as I didn't want to do it, I would have to crawl under the floor to figure out what was wrong with the entryway. I'm not a big baby, but it was dark, so checking out the crawl space would wait until daylight.

∞

Saturday morning, I woke up at seven to the sun shining through my east bedroom window. Without the leaves on the big Sumac tree across the street, the morning sun was killer. I'm not a morning person. If I'm up at seven in the morning, it's because I haven't been to bed yet.

Rubbing the sleep out of my eyes, I stumbled down the stairs to the kitchen, careful not to step on anything more dangerous than a dust bunny. Opening the metal draw of the stove, I pulled out a roll of aluminum foil, wishing it was a cup of coffee. Dragging my tired body back up to my room, I taped the foil over the windows. Much better. The bed was still warm, so I curled up and tried to sleep.

Damn, not going to happen. Half an hour later, I got up and wandered into the bathroom. I didn't need to be at work until nine that night, and I had several projects on my immediate list. There was probably a rotted or broken floor joist under the front stairway. That required pouring new cement footings in the crawl space so I could jack up the floor. While I was exploring under the floor, I could see what would be needed to alter the fireplace. I was planning to replace the missing mantle with solid brick. *Try walking off with that!*

Like the stairway, to add that much weight on the floor, I needed to reinforce the fireplace from underneath. The problem was…there are spiders in the crawl space, big spiders. I'm not fond of anything sporting more than four legs, and anything with more than six puts me in a cold sweat. It would not be out of the ordinary for me to move out and give my apartment to a hefty arachnid. Bug bombs were the answer. I slipped into jeans and a sweatshirt, not bothering to remove last night's makeup.

I made a shortlist and then hit Wendy's on the way to H B Woods. There's nothing like a classic double cheeseburger and a frosty for breakfast when you have a hangover.

∞

At the store, I stacked six fifty-pound bags of cement on my cart. I found a jack that would rise four feet; six, two by six studs; two rolls of painter's plastic, and a case of bug bombs. I was tossing ten-inch bolts into a plastic bag when Sawyer came up behind me. His longish blond hair was held in place by a blue bandana, and his blue eyes were shining.

"New project?" he asked.

"Yeah," I said, stretching my back. "I shined a flashlight into the crawlspace by the front door. It looks like the floor joists have slipped off the sill. The landing at the bottom of the stairway has dropped about four inches."

He casually leaned against the shelving end cap. "What are the two by sixes for?"

"A floor joist or two might be broken or rotted." I held up a ten-inch bolt. "Once I pour a cement footing, I'll set the jack and raise the joist and floor. If the joist is broken or rotted, I'll bolt the new studs to the old one and splint it into place."

Sawyer tilted his head a fraction and studied me. His dimples deepened as a smile crossed his lips. "Thought this through, didn't you?"

"Pretty much. The hard part will be carrying full buckets of cement through a three-foot-high crawlspace, and that's after I dig a three-by-three-foot hole. It's not like I can get a full-size shovel in there."

"You're amazing. Are you ready to check out?"

"Sure, but you don't have to give me your discount."

"I know. But I like checking you out."

"Are you flirting with me?"

"Would that be a problem?"

"No." I was about to tell him I liked checking him out, too, when one of the cashiers called him over to her register.

"I'll only be a minute," he said. "You can go to register one."

I watched him interact with the cashier. She was pretty and in her mid-twenties. She smiled, saying something to Sawyer I couldn't hear, but I knew the look. He said something back; she laughed. As I thought, total chick magnet.

Back at his register, he gave me the discount again. I frowned at him. He added another five dollars to the total, and I felt better.

"Let me help you lug these to your car." He grabbed the cart and wheeled it straight for my little blue Celica.

"Aren't you supposed to be on the register?"

"I would have stayed if there had been someone in line behind you."

"Okay. I don't want to keep you from your job."

He graced me with his dimples again. "You should let me worry about my job."

"You can put the cement in the trunk," I said.

"Best to distribute the weight a little more evenly. If I set these bags in the backseat, will you be able to lift them out?"

"Sure." I picked up a bag and set it on the floor in the front. "Would you fold down the seats in the back, so I don't have to bend over as far?"

"I like it when you bend over."

I shook my head. "Men," I said, feeling a familiar tingle in my belly. He was cute in an unkempt, Rob Lowe kind of way. Guys like Sawyer had a dozen girls on a string, and I didn't have the energy to compete for his attention, but I enjoyed it all the same.

The weight of the cement lowered the car a good five inches.

"You might want to wait on these last two bags," he said.

Holding the driver's door open, he flashed a playful smile, but his eyes were intense. I slid into the seat and lowered the window.

"Thank you," I said. "I truly appreciate your help."

"Drive slow. One good bounce, and you'll lose a tire." He shut my door bent over to look through the window. "I can deliver the studs and the remaining cement tomorrow. I remember you said you were off Sunday through Tuesday."

"Oh, no. I can come back for the rest."

"That would be at least two trips in your car. I won't charge you."

"What would your boss say?"

"Don't worry about my boss. What's your address?"

I don't typically offer my address to strangers, but he was so sweet, and I knew where he worked if he got all weird on me. I gave him the information. "Not much I can do before tomorrow anyway. I don't know how to thank you."

"You can show me a couple of your projects or maybe have a drink with me."

"Maybe." I smiled as I shifted the car into first gear. He was definitely flirting with me now. I shook my head. Why can't I ever be attracted to a doctor or a lawyer?

∞

Before leaving for work Saturday night, I set off ten bug bombs hoping the gas would sufficiently dissipate before I got home. Being Saturday, I would have to work until two. If I stopped at the Landmark for breakfast after work, I could kill a couple more hours.

I hated working Saturdays. The club was packed with young guys who acted like they'd never seen breasts before. It was a big night for bachelor parties, attracting men who had spent most of their nights at the local dance club or playing ball with other guys. It would have been almost comical if they didn't tend to stand in the aisles, keeping me from waiting on my tables.

Rounding stage two, I took orders from three new guys; two Coors, two shots of Jack Daniels, and a seven and seven. They were cute, pleasant, and sober. As Ginger pointed out, Shotgun Willies is a great place to work if you like to look at hot guys. With three to four hundred guests a night, there were bound to be some nines and tens. A great looking guy might come in often enough to get to know him, but honestly, who wants to date a guy who hangs out in strip clubs?

At the bar, two cowboys were shooting tequila, no training wheels.

"Can I buy you a shot, Honey?" said the one with the scraggly beard.

"No, thanks. I need to handle money, and I turn into a hot mess on tequila."

"My kind of girl," he said with a grin.

I smiled back and placed my order with the bartender.

"Can I see your tits?" This from the second guy, a thin man who looked like his nose had been broken at least once. It wasn't hard to guess why.

I shook my head. It was a question asked of me a dozen times a night.

"Don't mind my friend. He ain't got no class. But seriously, why don't you dance?"

And there was the other question I'd been asked as many times as the first. "I don't want to dance," I said.

"You got something to hide?" said the nose.

"No. I just like to wait on tables."

"You'd make more money." The bearded guy slid a shot my way.

"I make enough." I slid it back. Truth be known, I would have loved that shot, but it was early in the night, and I couldn't afford to drop another twenty.

Nose stood up. "I need to shake hands with the general. Can you point the way?"

I tilted my head toward the DJ booth. "See that big sign there that says, restrooms? You can look there, but I wouldn't be surprised if you only find a private."

That's the way it went every night at the club. Propositioned for many things that made me blush, I made a lot of promises to guys whom I was positive I'd never see again or at least hoped I wouldn't.

∞

I decided against going to Vegas with Ginger. I needed to work on the house, and I'd only been in Denver a month, not long enough to miss it. As it was, Ginger had an after-work date that night, so I ate breakfast alone and sketched ideas for the kitchen remodel on a paper napkin. The bearded guy from the bar walked in. That was my cue to leave.

"Hey, aren't you the waitress from across the street?" he asked, drifting over to my table.

"Yes. Sorry, I was just leaving."

"I just stopped to get a sandwich to take up to my room. My buddy is passed out."

"He was shooting them pretty fast."

"We both were. We had a fun time. That's a real classy place."

"Well," I said, grabbing my jacket. "I got to run. Nice to meet you."

"You, too. Hope we'll see you when we're back in Denver."

When I got home at four, the house smelled terrible, but my eyes didn't sting, so I thought it was safe enough to steal a quick nap.

CHAPTER 6

The following morning, I slipped into boot-cut jeans and a red and black, plaid flannel shirt. There wasn't any food in the house, so I grabbed my wallet and headed for the grocery store two blocks away. The air was crisp, as it often is in October, and the walk helped clear the fog from my brain. In my mind, I sorted through the projects on my list.

The grocery store had an excellent deli, which meant I could go for months without ever having to cook. It was close to home, and even though I was usually the only one of my particular shade in the store, the clerks were friendly. I paid for my sandwich and headed back to the house. About a block from home, I saw an elderly woman struggling with several heavy bags of groceries.

"Can I help you?" I asked.

She backed away from me and frowned. I recognized her as the woman that lived in the house to the south of me.

"I'm Freja."

"Freja?"

"Yes. It's Swedish. I live next door to you."

"I know who you are. Not many white gals in this neighborhood." She appeared a little less wary but wasn't ready to hand over her bags.

"I could carry a couple of those for you since we're going the same way."

She scrutinized me for a moment and came to a decision. Handing me a sack full of canned goods, she said, "Don't know why they always put all the heavy stuff in one bag. It'd be much easier if the weight spread out a bit more." She adjusted the remaining bags between her dark and wrinkled hands. "It's nice of you to help an old woman. I'm Haddie."

"Nice to finally meet you."

"That house you got needs a lot of work. Thought they would tear it down when it was empty for so long. Sad how things fall apart, and there's nothing you can do."

"Have you lived here a long time? My house was built in 1889."

She glanced sideways at me, and a smile played across her red lips. "Been around this here area nearly ninety years."

"For real?" She didn't look that old to me.

"I grew up in this neighborhood. The house you just moved into was built the year my parents married. There was a young doctor with three little girls who lived there when I was in school. A nice white man named Henderson. Lost his wife to Diphtheria, I believe."

"You've always lived next door?"

She shook her head. "My parents bought the house next to yours in 1909. My father was a doctor, too." She stared longingly at another large brick house in need of major repair as we strolled past. "It was a nice place to live in those days. People didn't hate each other the way they do now. Henderson moved out a few years later. I must have been attending Manual High school by then." She shrugged. "A man named Tyler or Taylor moved in then. I didn't pay a lot of attention."

"You must've seen a lot of people come and go."

She cautiously stepped off the curb into the street. I had to resist the urge to reach out and steady her. She spoke like a proud woman and might be offended by my assistance. A car with its stereo blasting nearly ran us over as it took the corner at high speed. The young black man driving yelled for us to get out of the street. To my surprise, Haddie flipped him off and continued as if nothing happened. "I moved back here after my mother died in 'sixty-one. The twenties were tough, but the sixties were appalling."

She stopped at the wrought-iron gate of her front yard, and I handed her the bag of canned goods. "Thanks for telling me about the neighborhood. It's fascinating."

"We'll have tea sometime. You seem like a nice gal."

∞

I cut across the patch of dirt to my front door and let myself in the house. Sitting down to eat at the Formica table, I thought about all the families who might have lived in the house, wondering who they were and what had become of them.

After brunch, I laid the plastic over the dirt in the crawl space because I refuse to touch even dead spiders. It was cramped in there, and I kept banging my head on the floor joists knocking down more dirt. I prayed there were no dead spiders mixed in with the debris but too scared to look. I crawled around in search of the right place to reinforce the floor. As I got close to the fireplace, I could see light coming through the floor above me. Sure enough, one of the floorboards was loose. With my flashlight, I popped it up. Interesting. Nailed to the sides of the joist were two strips of wood just wide enough to hold the six-inch-wide piece of flooring in place. The floorboard could be removed from the living room area to give access to the crawl space, but why would someone want to have a hole in the crawl space? I like to keep the spiders and centipedes in their rightful place.

Creeping closer, I laid my hand on something hard and rectangular. I carefully pulled the plastic back and shined my light down. No way I'm picking this up if it has a spider on it.

It was a small wooden box. Imagine my surprise when I opened it and discovered it was full of money. I studied a thick stack of twenty-dollar bills. I didn't recognize the man on the front of the old bill, Cleveland. I knew he was a president, but all my twenties had Jackson on them. I looked closely, shining my flashlight over the paper. The date was 1914, and the flower-shaped seal and serial numbers were in blue. Fanning them, I saw a couple that appeared more real. There were a few Jacksons mixed in. The dates on those were from the late twenties. Holy investments, Batman, I just found someone's sixty-year-old stash of cash. The few hundred-dollar bills in the mix had the same seal but in red. Although it was Franklin on the face of it, I'd never seen him pictured in profile like this. Printed on the front was the *United States of America,* but the bills didn't look real.

Under the money, I found a dainty crystal beaded bracelet and a diamond ring. The stone was tiny, but it picked up the glow from my flashlight and scattered radiant drops of color around the crawl space. I stashed the money back in the box and stuck the ring and bracelet in my jeans pocket and finished mapping out the new supports.

∞

Several hours later, I was up to my neck in hot water in the deep claw foot bathtub. Looking up at the tiny window above the sink, I could see light snow piling up on the ledge. That's something you get used to in Colorado. It can snow any time between the last weeks of September to the first weeks of June, and there are exceptions to that. The water felt divine as I lay back to enjoy the soapy bubbles, wondering about how much the antique money was worth. The ring and bracelet were no second prizes. It was like an early Christmas present.

My favorite album, *A Little Touch of Schmilsson in the Night,* played on the turntable in my bedroom. Soft music drifted in, easing my mind as the hot water eased my aching muscles. I closed my eyes and hummed along with Harry Nilsson as he sang, *"I wonder who's kissing her now?"*

Unexpectedly, I could hear someone singing along with us. I opened my eyes. "OH CRAP!"

A young black woman was sitting on the back of the toilet, staring right at me. She was wearing a costume of some sort, trimmed in black tassels and sequins.

"Who the hell are you?" I shrieked, grabbing my towel from the floor.

She didn't say anything as she rose and walked through the door. Not through the doorWAY, through a two-and-a-half-inch, solid core, wooden door. I can cuss with the best of them, but there are times when even my best truck driver swear words aren't enough.

In my hurry to follow, I slipped in the tub, dunking my head and my towel in the water. "Crap, crap, crap." I scrabbled out of the bathtub and grabbed something to cover me. The closest thing I had was an over-sized hand towel. Cautiously, I opened the door. I didn't see anyone as I made my way out of the bathroom and into my bedroom. I scanned the closet; no one in there either. *Well, that was just too weird.*

Standing there in half a towel, I shook my head. I must have fallen asleep in the bathtub and had a crazy dream. I was so thoroughly rattled that when I heard a banging on my front door, I screamed bloody murder. I had barely stopped blaring when Sawyer burst into my room.

"Freja! What's wrong? Are you hurt? I heard you scream."

I had forgotten he would be delivering my wood today. I blinked back tears. "I uh, I'm okay now. You just startled me when you knocked on the door."

"I didn't mean to frighten you. You don't have a doorbell." He looked a bit apprehensive. "Are you sure you're okay?"

"It's fine. Really. I don't usually freak out when someone knocks on the door." I felt the heat rise to my cheeks as I realized the towel I was holding up was only covering the absolute essentials. Sawyer must have seen my blush because he turned away but not before looking me over from head to toe.

"I'm so sorry to barge in," he said. "I thought you were hurt."

I stepped into my closet to find something to wear. "Thank you for coming to my rescue. I didn't mean to scare you. I just had a weird…" To say I had a bad dream sounded pathetic. "I forgot you were coming over. I'll only be a minute."

"I'll unload the wood and the rest of your cement."

"Thank you. You're a doll."

While he went to unload the truck, I slipped into a clean pair of jeans, my favorite flannel shirt, and my only pair of sneakers. Passing by the mirror, I cringed. My hair was a tangled wet mess, and the dirt from the crawl space had left streaks of mud on my face. I rubbed the water out of my hair as best I could with my little towel, wiped my face off, and went to help Sawyer.

His Ford pick-up truck was about a hundred years old. Grey primer was the dominant color with streaks of red and white. The back bumper was missing, and the left headlight hung at a precarious angle.

"Nice ride," I joked.

"It's a favorite. Besides, I wouldn't want to put these supplies in a car as sweet as yours."

"Thanks again. Are you sure I don't owe you something for delivering this stuff?"

He smiled slyly, and his dimples deepened. "No, I already got more than I was expecting. We're all good."

We placed the studs in the hallway, and I gave him the fifty-cent tour of the rest of the house. He stared thoughtfully at the crawl space as I explained my plan, nodding when I outlined my idea for the new fireplace mantel. As I was showing him the cool pocket doors that led to the parlor, we heard glass crashing behind us. Someone had thrown an empty wine bottle through my front, picture window.

"Damn it," I said as I went to find a broom. "That was an original window. It's going to cost a fortune to replace a glass pane that large with a round top."

Sawyer picked up glass shards, depositing them in a five-gallon bucket I'd been using for a wastebasket. "Most of the houses here have cut the window in two, a square and the half-circle. It's rare to see one like yours."

"That would save me some money when the next guy throws a rock through it. I've been finding crap in my yard since I moved in.

Yesterday there was a syringe in the front yard. They didn't exactly put out a big welcoming committee for me."

"Maybe they think the house is empty. You don't have any homey touches like grass or drapes, and the foil over the windows upstairs reminds me of a crack house."

"I have curtain rods, but I want to finish the walls and the woodwork first."

He smiled. "So, in about four or five years, then?"

"Poo," I said as I blew out a sigh. He was right. It would require years to tear out the lathe and plaster, rewire the electricity, hang sheetrock, and then there's tape, texture, and paint.

"Don't get discouraged," he said. "Seems to me you have a brilliant plan so far. You might need some help, though."

"No, I don't." *Yes, I do.* I didn't want him to know that. "It can't be that hard to nail Drywall to the studs, and the wiring is pretty straight forward." I did a mental eye roll. I sounded like my mother. When my dad went to prison for selling land that he didn't own, my mother raised us alone. She never accepted help from anyone and got her back up when someone implied she couldn't do whatever she had set her mind to do. "Well," I said. "If you don't mind, I could use some help covering this window."

His lips curved into a slight smile, and I wondered if it was because he genuinely wanted to help me or if he could sense my inner dialog. "What do you want to cover it with?"

"I have some old doors in the basement. I should leave it broken until I finish the walls. No sense in challenging some dipstick to throw another bottle through it."

We scrambled down the basement stairs to my storeroom of solid core doors.

"Odd collection," Sawyer said as he chose a ratty-looking door.

"My dad was getting into the house-flipping business. He won these in a card game."

I couldn't see his face, but I heard him chuckle.

Helping me carry the door to the living room window, he asked, "So, do you have any big plans for the holidays? Do you have any family in Denver?"

"Yeah, three brothers and a sister." I held the door over the window while he pounded in the 16 penny nails. "I'm working Halloween, and I'll be at my sister's for Thanksgiving. I work weekends. This house is going to cost me much more than I thought it would." I handed him another nail. "What about you? Anything special?"

"No, I don't have any family here. There, that should hold up to the next bottle."

I thought briefly about asking him to my sister's place but decided I wasn't ready to bring a stranger home to meet the folks. "Well, thanks for the help with this and for bringing the framing studs over. What do I owe for the delivery?"

"It was in the bill when you ordered it."

"No way!"

"Way."

I tried to remember everything he rang up that day. "Are you sure?"

"Absolutely."

"Well, okay." I walked him to the door. "Thanks again."

"Anytime."

As I watched him drive away, I wondered if he volunteered to bring my order because he was genuinely interested in me or just a natural flirt. I can be naive at times, and there is nothing more embarrassing than trying to seduce someone who isn't attracted to you. He was sweet and sincerely hot. Not in a Richard Gear sort of way, more like Jon Bon Jovi.

CHAPTER 7

Hot rollers and blow dryers are a couple of the greatest inventions of the twentieth century. As a child, we had to sleep on uncomfortable plastic rollers and wet hair. Today, I could wash out the plaster dirt, dry, and set my hair in less than an hour. I had my rollers in and was attempting to apply false eyelashes when I caught the reflection of movement in my mirror. Spinning around, I scanned the room, but nothing moved. Glancing back in my mirror, I suspected it was a shadow of clouds passing the bathroom window, but I couldn't shake the feeling that I wasn't alone. Was this feeling a carry-over from looking at Halloween costumes earlier?

It was Friday and, dressed as a fairy complete with three-foot, wings made of wire and lace, driving to work was a challenge. I had to straighten the wires once I got out of the car, but it was one of my favorite costumes.

The night started okay, but the crowd was drunker and rowdier than usual.

I cruised up to a shiny glass-topped stage to wait on a young man. He was sloppy drunk, sliding out of the black metal chair. As I leaned over to change the ashtray, he leered at me and wrapped a sweaty arm around my thigh. With crossed eyes, he said, "I'll ha' 'nother Bud, Tinker Bell."

"Seriously?" I said. "You might be treading a fine line here. The line between obnoxious and incapacitated." I backed up, disengaging his grip.

"Yer cute. I should take you home." And then he swallowed what I suspected might be the vomit laced burp that's supposed to tell you you've had enough alcohol. Making a god-awful face, he mumbled, "I wanna do you all nigh' long."

"Dude!' I said, "You can't even keep your head up. How're you gonna keep your dick up?" But he didn't answer. His eyes rolled back in his head, and he slid the rest of the way to the floor. A moment later, the doorman was carting him out to a taxi.

While I cleaned up the place where my suitor had so gracefully evacuated, Mötley Crüe belted out, *"Girls, Girls, Girls,"* as seven girls on seven stages shimmied and shook for several inebriated men, all of whom made rude comments to me about granting their explicit wishes.

Grumbling to Ginger, aka Carolyn on her phone bill, at the bar about distasteful, uncensored men, I didn't realize Bobby had been listening. He smiled sweetly at me and told me to ignore the ones who had been harassing me.

"If they want a drink badly enough, they'll come to the bar."

"They keep making rude remarks," I said.

"Which ones are they?"

"Those two, over in the booth by the shoeshine stand."

"You want I should kick them out?"

"No. I can deal with it."

I scooted by the table, and the guys waved at me. Against my better judgment, I strolled over and asked what they needed. I had to ask twice because the guy on the right either lowered his voice, or Madonna belted *"Like a virgin"* exceedingly loud just then.

"We'll have a Jim Beam and Coke and a Scotch on the rocks. Bring a couple of Kamikazes, too. Make it three. I think you could use one."

"I don't like to drink while I work." They had pushed their empty glasses to the very back of the booth, meaning I had to lean over the table to reach them. As I did, I felt something clammy on my butt cheek. I whipped my arm back and caught the guy on the side of the face. Dumbfounded and embarrassed, I started to cry and ran away from the table.

"What happened?" Bobby asked, coming out from behind the bar as I staggered up.

"They – they – he bit me," I said, choking back a sob.

"Where? Where did he bite you?"

"On the upper-most back side of my thigh," I stammered.

"Where?"

I blinked back tears. "On my butt."

"Let me see."

I shook my head. "I hit him before he got a hold of – of – of any meat."

Bobby stifled a giggle, and I realized how silly I sounded.

"Tell Nick. He'll kick them out."

I was embarrassed all over again. "No. It's okay."

"No, it isn't," Bobby said and took off to find Nick.

By the time Nick took care of the offenders, I had composed myself.

"You going to be okay?" Nick asked when he came back inside.

"Yeah. I'm good. I've never had anyone bite me before."

Bobby puffed out his chest. "Well, they won't be back."

"They were rude earlier." I pressed my lips together and then let out a sigh. "Saying stuff like I want to eat your panties."

"I can understand that," Nick said.

The look in his dark eyes brought a lovely heat to my cheeks.

"Sorry," he said. "Sometimes we get some real jerks in here. After a few drinks, these guys will say out loud what a lot of us men are thinking." His smile was genuine. I felt a flutter in my belly and glanced down, afraid to meet his eyes. I was picturing how I might have reacted if Nick had been the one to bite my ass.

Nick reached over and lifted my chin. His eyes were dark and serious. "Are you going to be okay?"

"Yes. I'm okay. I was just a little shook up." Reflecting on the situation and how I handled it, especially the way I told Bobby what happened, made me start to chuckle. "I'm fine now. I just learned a valuable lesson."

For the rest of the night, Bobby was super sweet to me. We started joking about several customers, and he told me some of the horrors he'd seen over the four years he'd worked at the club.

∞

I worked with Bobby again on Saturday night.

"Sometimes, I just have to laugh at the insanity," Bobby said as he placed bottles of beer on the bar in front of me. "You don't believe me? Check out the stages right now."

I peered around through the dark, smoky haze but didn't know what he was talking about.

He waved a hand toward the DJ booth. "The music is so loud; sometimes the dancers can't hear their names. The DJ makes sure the girls know they're being called by positioning certain girls up at the same time."

"What do you mean?"

"He has Randi, Brandy, Bambi, Candy, and Mandi all up at the same time because the names rhyme. That way, Candy can't say she thought he was calling Randi, and so on."

"That's brilliant, but how do they know which stage to go to?"

"They usually follow the same girl all night. On the occasions they get moved on the list, they can see which stage is open." He came out from behind the bar again. "I need to see a man about a horse."

"Did I need to know that?"

He smiled. "No, but I wanted to get close enough to ask you if you would have breakfast with me after work."

"Sure. Will the Landmark be okay?" Ginger was in Vegas, and it would be enjoyable not to eat alone.

He nodded and skipped off to the restroom.

Breaking my vow to steer clear of men, I had breakfast with Bobby the following night as well.

∞

Sunday-morning sunlight drifted around the foil that covered my bedroom windows. I yawned and stretched. The cement under the front sill and fireplace should be hardened enough to set the jacks today.

I rolled out of bed and slipped into my ratty jeans and a long-sleeved T-shirt, threw a bandanna over my hair, and went to the refrigerator. I needed fortification to go back in that crawl space. Not much to choose from. There was a half jar of strawberry jam and a couple of mystery boxes from the last time I ordered Chinese. I also had two pieces of pizza leftover from last Tuesday. Since the Chinese food was at least a week old, I tossed it and had pizza for breakfast.

Munching on a cold slice of pepperoni, I rounded the kitchen corner, and my heart stopped. I thought I saw someone cross from the front door to the living room where I'd left the jacks.

"Hello? Who's there?" I backtracked to the kitchen and picked up a three-foot board. I'd have opted for a knife, but I only had three, a butter knife, a paring knife, and a pocketknife. The two by three seemed like a better alternative.

I made my way into the dining room and nervously glanced into the parlor — no one in there. Slipping through the parlor, I checked the living room. No one there either. I must be seeing things. I checked the front door; no one was outside. The door was locked, which was good because I had a bad habit of not remembering to do that.

∞

By the time the jacks were in place and the floor joist under the stairway was splinted, I'd calmed down. The bracing for the fireplace mantle would wait until tomorrow. I was ready for a break. I wiped off most of the black dirt that sifted from the floorboards on to my face and threw a sweatshirt over my blackened T-shirt. I needed another stud for the fireplace brace and a new drill bit. After a stop at Wendy's, I drove to H B Woods.

From the lumberyard, I saw Sawyer chatting it up with a pretty girl in a business suit. She had his full attention, so I slipped passed them and went to the tool aisle and picked up a package of drill bits. When I turned around, I nearly knocked him over.

"Uh, hi," I said. "I didn't see you walk up."

"I saw you come in."

"You looked busy."

"That's Lynette. She's a sales rep."

"She looks professional," I said, realizing I was dressed rather poorly.

"I suppose."

"How is it going?"

"You know, same wood, different day." He grinned. "What's the project?"

"Bracing the floor. I finished the floor joists under the front stairs, but I broke my last bit."

He smiled and nodded at the package in my hand. Lynette called him over to the desk, where she had a perfectly manicured hand on top of a stack of catalogs. "I'll take you on register one. I won't be long."

"You're such a tease."

"What makes you think I'm teasing?"

Oh boy. "I'll be at the register," I said.

It took him a while to get away from Lynette, so one of the other cashiers helped me. I was loading the wood into the car when he caught up to me.

"Sorry about that," he said.

"Don't worry about it. You're a popular guy."

"Let me get this," he said, taking the board from me and sliding it past the gearshift.

"You're spoiling me," I said as I slid into the front seat.

"You look like someone who should be spoiled."

"Such a sweet talker. If I don't see you before, have a nice Thanksgiving," I turned over the ignition.

He held the door open for a moment. "I hope to see you, but if not, you have a wonderful Thanksgiving, too."

I tried to tell myself not to care how many chicks hung on Sawyer. I had more important things to do than getting mixed up with a hardware clerk. I was usually an all or nothing kind of girl. If I was ever to have a decent place to live, the house had to come first. As I pulled on to Holly Street, it started to snow.

When I got home, I unloaded the wood and took a long warm bath. Lewis & Floorwax on the radio kept me company. Bruce Springsteen singing, *"I got a bad desire, oh, oh, oh, I'm on fire,"* wafted through the room like a lullaby, making me miss the touch of a man. Music had a way of jacking with my emotions.

CHAPTER 8

Bobby was thirty-one and charming in a disarming way. He was also one of the few people at the club to befriend me. Like Dirk, Bobby regarded me as if he thought I walked on water, which was flattering. He was also not terribly bright, which brought out all the mothering instincts I tried so hard to ignore.

The day-time DJ was getting married on Sunday, and Bobby asked me to go with him to the wedding. It was basically an employee outing, so I said yes. We were pretty good friends now having had breakfast after work several times. On Sunday, I met Bobby at the club because I wasn't ready to show off my residence to anyone.

The wedding, held at the Wellshire Country Club on South Colorado Boulevard, was beautiful. Someone had a lot of money: the reception boasted an open bar plus several bottles of champagne on every table. I was pretty loose after a few glasses of free champagne

Bobby looked stunning in his black tuxedo. Something I learned about my coworkers, they all made more money than they knew what to do with, so limousines and tuxedos were common. I was feeling fabulous in a spectacular red dress I bought for the wedding. Yes, I'm a sucker for long gowns and romantic talk.

Cocaine was the drug of choice at this point in the 80s, so I wasn't surprised to see several guests partaking in the party favors. It was never my thing, so I drank champagne instead.

The band was fantastic, playing mostly seventies love songs and a few from the sixties. The dance floor stayed busy all night long.

"Are you having a good time?" Bobby asked.

"Oh, yes. The band is awesome."

"Would you like to dance?"

"Sure." I nearly bounced out of my chair. I love to dance, and most men hate it. Of course, dancing makes me thirsty. I don't usually like champagne, but it was a wedding.

Several dances later, I was feeling super good. Bobby was holding me close as the band sang, *"And I'm gonna keep on lovin' you, cause it's the only thing I want to do."*

"You are so beautiful tonight," Bobby whispered in my ear. "You're a wonderful dancer, too."

"Thank you. I'm about three sheets to the wind right now."

"You seem very much in control."

"Well, I've had some practice."

He laughed. "You're super sexy. That dress fits you in all the right places."

I was eating it up: the dancing, the champagne, the flattery. That was why, when he asked to take me to a hotel room, I agreed.

He was a gentle lover and didn't seem to care that I might have been overly enthusiastic. I hadn't been with a man since my breakup with the bass player last year.

The next day, I was hungover but still feeling the afterglow of an enjoyable romp in the hay. When Bobby asked me to meet him at the same hotel the next night, I did.

What a fool I can be. I was trying not to get involved with anyone, and least of all, Bobby. He was a friend, and I ruined it. When I wouldn't go to the hotel with him the next night, he cried. I tried to tell him I just wanted to be friends. I felt like an ass.

∞

The week before Thanksgiving, I finished bracing the floor for a new brick mantle and started tearing out the molding on the main floor. Most of it was a total loss. The pieces of wood piled up in the dining room as I worked. I would begin tearing out the lathe and plaster soon and then the place would be seriously unlivable.

The club would be closed until seven on Thanksgiving, so Nick gave me the day off. Had I realized the club was going to have girls wrestling in mashed potatoes the night before, I would have asked for Wednesday off as well. As it was, Ginger, Pepper, and Sugar took the night off. It would have been nice if one of them had warned me.

When I got to work on Wednesday, stage one was featuring a wrestling ring complete with corner pads. The floor of the ring was about the depth of a kiddie pool and filled nearly to the brim with warm instant mashed potatoes. I helped pass out plastic trash bags to guests who were sitting in the first three rows from the stage. There was a hole cut out of the bottom to put their heads through. It wasn't enough.

Two girls got in the ring wearing bikini tops and G-Strings. They circled each other, waiting to make the best move. Walking through mashed potatoes on a plastic mat is like trying to walk on ice with wet shoes. Wrestling in the glop is like trying to catch a greased pig. Before either girl could execute the first attack, they slipped. SPLAT!!! Slimy mashed potatoes went flying everywhere. On the chandeliers, on the ceiling, on the other stages, and of course, covering nearly every person in the ballroom because the place was packed with people, like a Saturday night.

As I delivered a beer to stage five, a gob of potatoes landed in my hair and ran down my back. Gross. The floor, covered in potato mash and other assorted crap, soiled my shoes so badly I'd have to spring for a new pair of stilettos before my next shift.

The ramp leading to the restrooms, installed to meet ADA code, was used like a Breathalyzer by the staff. If you stumbled up the ramp trying to get to the john, you'd be cut-off. It was so slippery from gooey mashed potatoes everyone had to pull themselves up to the restrooms by the handrail. Most of the entertainers and about half of the guests were drenched in potatoes by the end of the night.

∞

Thanksgiving Day was a perfect Colorado sixty-two degrees and dry. Dressed in sandals, jeans, and a light pink sweater, I knew enough about Colorado to throw a coat and a pair of boots in the back seat of the car. In 1983, Denver got twenty-two inches of snow on Thanksgiving, but today was a more typical Indian-Summer day.

I stopped at Safeway and picked up a couple of pumpkin pies and some whipped topping. Shannon would be making a turkey with all the trimmings. She got an A in Home Economics while I typically slept through the class.

My parents, my brother Sheamus, and his wife, Jackie Jo, were in Breckenridge for the week. Sheamus won a free vacation, and none of us blamed them for wanting to spend Thanksgiving week in the mountains.

When I got to the steps of Shannon's apartment building, Aiden and Connor were pulling up in a 1978 Monte Carlo.

"Hey, Guys!" I shouted as they rolled to a stop. "I got pumpkin pies for dinner."

Aiden opened the door. "Great. I got two cherry pies, and Connor picked up a peach." You can never have too much pie.

"Awesome," I said. "We never fail to have dessert. I'm guessing since Mom and Dad won't be here; we won't have sauerkraut."

Aiden laughed. "I didn't bring any."

"Me neither," said Connor.

My mother frequently served sauerkraut for Thanksgiving because it was good for digestion, and just as often, it went untouched. Shannon, on the other hand, was a traditionalist. There would be turkey, stuffing, potatoes, gravy, green beans, corn on the cob, acorn squash, cranberries, and of course, Watergate salad. The smell of culinary delights wafted over us as we hastened in the door. My stomach growled loud enough to cause Aiden to turn around.

"Hungry?" he asked.

"Starving more like it. I haven't eaten since yesterday morning. I've been saving myself for today."

"Silly girl, you're supposed to eat big meals every day before Thanksgiving to stretch your stomach."

I had the beginnings of a solid muffin top and didn't think it was a good idea to practice. I tried to balance the double cheeseburgers with cottage cheese and cantaloupe, but the burgers were winning.

Once settled at the table, Shannon asked me about my job.

"It's okay. I make rad money, but men can be real jerks sometimes." I told them about being bit as I passed the potatoes to my right.

Connor frowned. "I should break the guy's leg."

"He was drunk. He thought he was cute."

"No one treats my sister like that. You can find another job."

"Not one where I can make a thousand dollars a week." I buttered my roll.

Aiden stopped mid-bite. "A thousand dollars a week?"

Connor ladled gray over everything on his plate, including the cranberries. "I don't want you working there."

"Conn, it's not your decision," I said.

"It's degrading, Fre." Aiden and Connor usually called me Freeman unless they were mad at me. Fre meant Connor was just a little upset with me.

"Not really. If some idiot wants to give me fifty dollars for bringing him a couple of cocktails, I would be dumb not to accept it. It's not like I'm doing anything wrong."

Aiden swallowed his bite of turkey. "Why would a guy give you that kind of money for a drink?"

"Some men have more money than brains," Shannon said. "If I had a body like Fre, I'd be working there, too. She makes more in one night than I make in a week at the store, and I'm a manager."

Shannon's husband, Eric, nearly choked on his potatoes. "I don't think so."

Before Shannon could argue, Aiden asked again. "Why would a guy give you that kind of money?"

I played with my Watergate salad. "Lots of reasons. Some guys have a LOT of money. If you make three or four million a year playing football, it's no big deal to throw a few hundred dollars around. If you have a company and you're trying to impress new clients, you don't want to look cheap. You could just be lonely and want a pretty girl to pay attention to you."

Connor pursed his lips. "You can buy more than a little attention for fifty dollars."

"Really?" Eric asked. "And how would you know this?"

Aiden laughed as the blood rose to Connor's cheeks.

"If you haven't been in the place," I said, "don't judge it." I immediately regretted my words. The last thing I wanted was to have my big brothers see me in that tiny excuse for a uniform. "So, how's the wrecking business going?" I asked Aiden to change the subject before my brothers could plan a field trip.

"Not bad. We got a line on a few nice cars out of California. Conn and I are planning on heading west next week."

Shannon cleared away the turkey to make room for the pies. "You two will be home for Christmas, won't you?"

"Of course," Aiden said, jamming me in the side. "We haven't had Christmas with Freeman for several years."

She set the pie on the table and passed out plates. "No way, Shannon," Aiden said. "I can't eat another bite. Save the pie for after the game."

The television had been tuned to football all day. "The Game?" I asked.

Connor pushed back from the table. "A little touch football to work off the first round of turkey." He ruffled my hair. "You still remember how to play, don't you?"

"You boys go play," Shannon said. "Fre and I will clear the table and do the dishes."

I wanted to go out and play with the boys, but I couldn't leave Shannon with all the clean-up. "Go on, guys. I'll save you a piece of pie," I said.

While the boys played touch football in the parking lot, Shannon and I enjoyed some girl time. I missed having my sister close by during the years I lived in Vegas. Dirk had been my world, and I wondered if it would have crashed and burned if I had had her sage advice and pragmatic shoulder to cry on.

CHAPTER 9

The other waitresses seemed to accept me after the incident with the butt-biter as if being humiliated by a customer was a rite of passage. I think the fact I didn't run out the door showed them I was made of tougher stuff than they first thought. If only I felt brave. I'm a colossal pretender, afraid of so many things.

In truth, I was getting used to seeing half-naked women everywhere, and the men were no more obnoxious than men in any other bar. Because the entertainers held most of their attention, they rarely noticed me except when their beer was empty.

Like the entertainers, the waitresses came in assorted denominations. Cinnamon, aka Barbara to her hairstylist, was short, but her six-inch pumps brought her to five-eight. A lion's mane of red curls draped over her pale, freckled shoulders.

"What was it like to work in Vegas?" Cinnamon asked. "Did you get to schmooze with a lot of famous people?"

"The money was rad, but finding real friends was challenging. It seems to me everyone in Vegas is on the take, using others to advance their position." I cleared the empty glasses and bottles from my tray. "They call it juice, being connected to the right people who can get you into the right places or get you the right jobs."

Cinnamon rearranged her drinks and garnished them with limes. "I've never held a job before coming to Shotgun Willies. I got married right out of high school. And then I had my three boys."

"How old are your boys?"

"Middle school. My ex walked out on us two years ago."

"Where did you learn to waitress? You're terrific."

"Waitressing is just like being a wife," she said, squeezing a lime into a gin and tonic. "He asks you for something, and you smile and go get it." She adjusted her napkins for the third time. "It isn't rocket science."

"It's a little harder than that," I said. "You have to carry a heavy tray, add and subtract, and know who ordered which drink. There's a huge room full of husbands out there."

"The corners of her mouth turned up. "I'm only looking for one."

A stunning waitress who could have passed for Diana Ross's younger sister said, "That's all you need if he's the right one." Sugar, aka Corrine to her manicurist, gracefully emptied her tray with a perfectly manicured hand. "Cinnamon thinks she'll find the perfect man here. It can be done, but you'd have to kiss many frogs to find a prince. And seriously, who wants a husband who hangs out in a place like this?"

I didn't tell her I'd already kissed more frogs than I cared to remember. "Did you find your husband here?" I asked, noticing the exquisite marquise-cut diamond on her left hand. It had to be more than five carats.

"Oh no," she said, her brows knitting together. "I met Jim at Harvard."

I tried to hide my surprise. Why would someone with a Harvard education wait on tables in a topless club? Before I could ask, she said, "Jim used to practice law, but lately, the stock market has been a better source of income. He's a broker now." When that didn't seem to answer the look in my eyes, she added, "I only work the occasional Friday to have a bit of play money, and that's the day Jim likes to play golf. There aren't a lot of places a girl can make seventy dollars an hour without being tied down."

Seventy dollars an hour? I thought I was doing good making forty.

Cinnamon nodded. "Raising kids is very expensive."

I knew better than to ask Cinnamon how much she made, but I would have to take some lessons from these girls. Clearly, they knew how to work this room better than me. Bopping to the strains of Madonna's *Material Girl*, I went out to the ballroom, determined to make money.

∞

There seems to be some unwritten rule that being someone's date for a wedding is practically an engagement. It would have made more sense if it had been a family wedding. After all, it's not like he introduced me to his mother. Unfortunately, Bobby now thought I was going to marry him, and I felt like a total scumbag.

"Come on," he insisted. "I told my folks about you. My baby sister is dyin' to meet you."

"What were you thinking? You should have at least asked me if I was free for Christmas."

"I just figured, since we hit it off so good…"

"We spent two nights in a motel."

"That's cuz you wouldn't let me come to your house."

"My house is a construction site. I sleep on a mattress on the floor right now. I went to the motel because they have nice beds."

"Oh, that hurts."

"That isn't the only reason, but come on, I'm not your fiancé."

I didn't mean to lead him on. Frankly, I don't know how he could have jumped to the conclusion I was any more than a fling. Apparently, there wasn't as much wild and crazy sex among the employees as gossip would have you believe.

I had to smile when he paraded a new girl in front of me the next day. I should have pretended to be at least a little hurt to make him feel better, but I'm not much of an actress, and I was annoyed by his presumption. Bobby made sure to tell everyone that he and London were going to Aspen for Christmas.

"I thought you were staying in town with your parents," I said, setting drinks on my tray.

"I was going to surprise you with the trip, but then you blew me off."

"Bobby, I have to work all weekend. I couldn't have gone with you anyway."

"But it's a condo in Aspen. You could have called off sick."

"I don't ski either." I handed him the money for my drinks

He frowned and rang up the order. "You don't know what you're missing."

The trouble was, I knew very well what I was missing. I would have loved to spend the weekend learning to ski in a fancy resort, but I knew I'd be taking advantage. Bobby wasn't long-term relationship material.

Once more, I vowed to save myself for Mr. Right. No sex unless I'm seriously considering marrying the guy. I quickly realized that would never work, so I modified it to only if he's truly special and has at least some husband potential. I reeled in my inner slut and went back to work. It was a hectic night, and I didn't have time to sort out my sex life.

CHAPTER 10

The next afternoon while getting dressed for work, I had the same unnerving feeling that someone was watching me. I checked the sheets hanging over the windows, but they were secure. To mitigate the uneasy feeling, I dropped an album on the turntable. Most of the time while getting ready for work, I chose something a little harder, like Van Halen or AC/DC, to get me in the mood. Today, I wanted the smooth sexy sounds of Dean Martin.

"You're nobody 'til somebody loves you," filled the air, and I sang along as I applied blush to my cheeks. I stopped mid-stroke when I heard a female harmonizing. I'd never noticed that before. A chill ran up my arm as the song ended. I continued applying make-up when a shadow in the mirror crossed behind me. Once again, I turned around, but no one was there. The window on the south side was open a fraction, and a breeze moved the curtain. I admonished myself for being so jumpy. I've always liked living alone, but the past three months had me feeling small in a very big house.

∞

I started my weekend by tearing out the rest of the brick from the firebox of the original fireplace. The previous owners decided they didn't need the air draft and filled in the firebox. The brick and mortar had been tossed in sloppily so there were plenty of places to get my pry bar in and rip out whole chunks. There was something very satisfying about tearing into a wall at the end of a workweek. I cleaned out dirt and bits of broken bricks until late in the night, Bruce Springsteen blaring from my portable Sony cassette player. Every once in a while, I would find myself looking around the room.

Sighing, I attributed the uneasy feeling to the size of the house and the amount of dust I was kicking up. I decided it was time to go to bed so I turned off the Sony tape player and headed up the stairs. There was a knock at the door but not recognizing the man on the front step; I chose to ignore it. Wondering if he had been the source of the feeling of being watched, I took a three-foot-long stud up to bed with me. I had trouble sleeping that night. It was frustrating because I needed to be up early. The first of the month, I had ordered two pallets of ivory brick from Robinson's Brick Company. The delivery was scheduled for some time between eight in the morning and noon.

I got up at seven-forty-five, then immediately laid back down on the bed and fell asleep. It was eleven o'clock before the flatbed pulled up outside. I had them come through the alley and place the brick near the back door. It wasn't the kind of neighborhood to leave anything valuable on the front porch. My brick had been delivered on three, six by eight feet wooden pallets.

The weather held out so I buried myself in the house. Once I'd hauled a full pallet of brick into the living room ten bricks at a time. I set up the brick saw on the empty pallet making a small deck of sorts to cut the half bricks that would be needed for every other course. The brick saw required water, so over the following week, mud and bits of brick became the main landscape features in my backyard. As I used up the brick on the second pallet, I found it more comfortable to stand on the pallet rather than in the mud puddle I'd created. Inspiration struck. I headed back to H B Woods.

A couple of guys were unloading lumber in the back of the store.

"Hey guys," I said. "Do you think I could have some of those old pallets you have stacked in the corner?"

The older of the two men shut off the forklift. "Those?" he said, pointing to several dozen pallets of assorted sizes. "What do you want with those?"

"I want to use them in my backyard to keep my feet clean."

"Most people plant grass," said the younger one, leaning against a stack of two by fours. "But if you want them, it will save us from having to haul them off."

"Great. I'll need about thirty to make a deck across the back of the house."

I grabbed two and hauled them to my car. Crap. I could only fit four at a time in my car. Back to the dockhands I went. "I'll take these four today. It isn't like I need all thirty pallets now." I thanked the guys and went home with my prize.

∞

At home, placing a couple one by twos, between the slates in the pallets, I lashed six pallets together, creating a deck nearly eight feet by twelve feet. This was a perfect place to set up the brick saw since it needed a constant flow of water and standing in a pool of water while working with power tools was a good way to curl my hair permanently.

Cutting the bricks was much more difficult than I'd imagined and messy, too. The saw spewed mud up one side of me and down the other. The dry mortar settled in my hair while mixing small batches, and, even wearing my Isotoner Gloves, my nails took an incredible beating.

There is a reason brick masons apprentice for years. I spent hours upon hours plumbing and leveling every single ivory brick. As I mixed up a new batch of mortar, the bricks I'd just set began to tilt to the left. I rarely got a brick set right from the start, and by the end of the project, I discovered I never wanted to build something out of brick again. The last batch of mortar had been too thin. The fact that I was going to have to scrape off the mortar and start again had me so upset I grabbed my SOB tool and threw it across the room, screaming Son-of-a-Bitch. Today, my SOB was my trowel, and, of course, it was the next tool I needed.

Before I could get up to retrieve it, I heard a knock at the door.

"Everything okay?" Sawyer called from the doorway.

"Yes," I said, getting up. I pushed the hair out of my face and went to the door.

Sawyer beamed when he saw me, and I felt better about my outburst. I pulled the trowel out of the plaster wall under the stairway. "I wasn't expecting company."

"The guys on the dock said you needed some pallets. We just throw these away, so I thought I'd bring some over and see how it went with the joist project."

"I set the jack and mounted a splint next to the joist. It was rotted through. I finished framing under the fireplace but climbing up and down those rickety stairs to the basement makes me think that's a more important project. It's super nice of you to bring over the pallets." I stepped out to see the back of his truck loaded with pallets. "I didn't need that many."

"I'm transporting the rest to a friend who cuts them up for firewood."

"Oh. Well, thanks," I said, wiping the wet mortar from my gloves onto my cutoff denim shorts and grabbing a nice-looking pallet. *I know what the term "friend" means — usually a girl but not quite a girlfriend.*

"What are you going to do with these?" he asked.

"For the cost of a few one by twos, I can build sort of a deck across the back of the house. Keeps me out of the mud."

"You don't say?" His dimples deepened. He was grinning at some joke I didn't catch.

I helped him carry a couple of pallets through a gate on the side of the house. Once there, he inspected my makeshift deck. "I'd have never thought of this. You're brilliant."

"Resourcefulness is what I call it. Work with what you have."

We carried the rest of the pallets to the backyard, and by then, it was almost dark.

"I'll put these together in the morning. Thanks again for bringing these by."

"My pleasure."

I followed him down the narrow sidewalk to the front of the house. "I was going to order a pizza. Would you like to stay? It's the least I can do."

"I would love to stay, but I have to get up to Evergreen tonight."

"That's cool. Maybe some other night?" *Definitely a girl - probably spending the night in front of a roaring fire. Just wait until I have my fireplace done. I'll show him a fire.* Then I mentally kicked myself for thinking that way.

He had that look on his face again, the look that made me wonder if he could read my thoughts. "Are you ready for Christmas?" he asked. "Shopping all done?"

"Almost," I said. "I haven't been home for Christmas for several years so this is going to be special. Tips have been nearly doubled this month. I'm feeling rich."

"What did you ask Santa for this year?"

Looking at him, I was thinking a night with Sawyer would be nice. "I don't actually need anything."

He tucked a curl behind my ear, and I thought I was going to wet myself. His eyes twinkled, and I was sure he could read my mind.

"Think about it," he said. "You still have another week."

I walked Sawyer to his truck and thanked him again for bringing the pallets over. As he drove off, I found myself wishing he was the kind of guy with a real job, not a part-time salesclerk at a hardware store. As cute and flirtatious as he was, he must have a dozen women on a string, a real heartbreaker. Not what I needed at this stage of my life.

I was too tired to eat so I went up to take a well-deserved bath. In the bathroom mirror I saw my hair pushed up on my forehead and streaked with mortar. So much for staying out of the mud. It was little wonder Sawyer was so quick to leave. I certainly wasn't the classiest act in town.

∞

The next day I stopped at K-Mart. They had Poinsettias on sale, so I bought one for my neighbor, Haddie, along with a box of assorted Celestial Seasons tea and some nuts. I picked up some perfume and bath oils for the waitresses, gloves and scarves for the bartenders and valet, and a tie and tie tack for each of the managers. I didn't spend a lot of money, but I wanted my co-workers to know I appreciated them.

Haddie was just coming home when I pulled up in front of the house. Her arms were full of groceries, light snow covering the shoulders of her woolen coat.

I jumped out of the car and ran to her side. "Hi," I said. "Can I help you?"

She nodded. "Getting mighty cold out here."

I took the heaviest bags from her while she unlocked the door. "I would be happy to take you to the store when you need to go."

"Walking is good for me. Don't want to shrivel like an old lady."

"Well, if ever I can be of help, please ask."

"Would you like to come in? I could use a hot."

"Sure. I picked up a little something for you today." I went back to the car and got the things I'd purchased.

She met me at the door, her eyes glistening as I handed her the gift.

"It's beautiful," she said. "Oh, and tea. Aren't you thoughtful?"

"I'm terrible with plants," I said. "I can kill a plastic plant."

"All they need is a little love."

Her home was cozy and warm. Antique furniture adorned the living room. She probably didn't think of it as antique since it was likely she'd had it all her life, but it was extraordinary to me.

"I have hot water on the stove," she said. "Do you like cream or sugar in your tea?"

"No. Just black."

"These are wonderful flavors. Is there one you would like?"

"Blackberry, please. Are you doing anything for the holidays?"

"I'll attend church with my daughter and her family. We'll have dinner at her house afterward. I have two grand-daughters and five great-grandchildren, who will all be home for the holiday."

"That sounds wonderful; I said, sipping my tea. "I have family in the area, too. I'm really looking forward to this Christmas. Can you tell me any more about the people who lived in my house before I moved in?"

"Well, let's see. I was away raising my own family for most of that time. I live here until shortly after high school. I was lucky. Few people had the money to attend high school. I worked in a greenhouse then. It was there I met my late husband, Will. He'd been working there since he was thirteen. We married in 'seventeen, and we bought a small house on Welton Street."

She went to the kitchen and brought back a box of Girl Scout cookies. "I have to buy these. Grandchildren know a soft touch. So, it was a few years after the Great War when we were forced to sell the house and moved in with friends. Must have been the summer of twenty-six. The twenties were hard on the neighborhood with the rise of the Klan, most notably Mayor Stapleton and Governor Morley."

I stopped mid-sip. "Stapleton? As in Stapleton airport?"

"Yes. He was a powerful Klansman in the twenties."

"No way! How could a KKK member become mayor or governor? That's... That's..." I didn't know what to say. It was unthinkable. Having been born in 1960, I had no real experience with pre-Civil Rights Movement America.

She shrugged. "The Klan focused on Catholics and Jews saying they posed a threat to the "nation's Protestant ideals. For all their hate, they were in favor of fair elections and reducing crime. They peddled many ideas the average white voter could support. The Klan sponsored big family picnics, auto races, and other public events. They were well-liked in those days."

She paused as if gathering her memories. "All their good deeds and promises did little to cover their hatred of Negros, Mexicans, and Italians but they were rich and powerful men." She stirred sugar into her tea. "The American West and, in particular, this neighborhood had been fairly integrated before the turn of the century but during those years, most white folks moved to the new neighborhoods to the south and east where we weren't welcome."

My understanding of history was tainted by what I saw on television and what I was taught in public school. I was beginning to wonder how much I didn't know.

"So, the mayor made all the white people move out?"

"Not exactly. It was a sense of community, and we still have a lot of that today. By the mid-twenties, about ninety percent of this area was black but it wasn't a poor neighborhood. We had doctors and lawyers and successful businesses. It was a swinging place in those days." Haddie sipped on her tea and smiled.

"We had the biggest jazz scene between California and St. Louis. I remember dancing to the tunes of Louis Armstrong, Ella Fitzgerald, Nat King Cole, and Duke Ellington. The Rossonian was the best-known lounge but we also had the Casino Cabaret, Lotus Club, and Benny Hooper's ex-servicemen club."

"I like jazz music," I said. "Not as much as I like rock and roll, but I like to switch it up now and then."

Haddie nodded with a grin. "It's not just you. Jazz brought white people into Five Points who'd never been there before," she said, taking a second cookie. "They mixed with us. Found out we didn't rub off. No such thing as segregation in the jazz scene."

"Music has a way of doing that." I placed my hand over my cup when she tried to add more water. "I've got to go. I love talking with you, but I have presents to wrap."

"By the way, have you ever heard about any of these houses being haunted?" I asked, shuffling toward the door.

Haddie laughed. "Silly superstitions. I don't believe in ghosts." She sipped her tea. "But a lot of people do. I've heard of a few places in town that are said to be haunted. My friend swears the Peabody-Whitehead mansion on Eleventh and Grant is haunted."

"No way!" She had my full attention.

"Apparently, the Queen Anne mansion was first inhabited by William Riddick Whitehead, a surgeon who had a vast majority of his patients die on the operating table, or soon thereafter. There is also a story about a jilted woman who hung herself on her wedding day. I've heard her name is Eloise."

"Has your friend seen Eloise?"

"No, but she swears a disconnected phone rang, not once but several times, while she was living there. As they do with most big mansions, they chopped it up into apartments in the fifties."

"Did she move out?"

"Haddie nodded. "Yes. It was sold again and became a bar and restaurant. It might be office space now."

"Do you believe her?"

"Child, it's hard to say. Strange things do happen. The gossip around town is that the Croke-Patterson-Campbell Mansion is haunted. The man who built it never lived there claiming there was an evil spirit in the house."

"I've never heard of a new house being haunted before."

"Some people are very superstitious. The Patterson family moved in and lived there for several years. The place changed hands several times and about ten years ago, the new owners did a major remodel. The construction crew claimed they would leave after a hard day's work, and the next day, their work was sabotaged, and tools were missing. From what I've heard, the crew got two large guard dogs to watch for intruders. A couple of days later, the dogs were found dead on the sidewalk, having jumped to their deaths from a third-story window."

"Wow." My skin began to crawl. Dogs have senses we humans don't have.

Haddie smiled. "Dear child, you look like you saw a ghost." She patted my arm. "Now don't get in a tizzy over this. It's all poppycock.

No one ever heard about the Stanley Hotel being haunted until they made that movie a couple of years ago. Those are all silly stories to scare children and the weak-minded."

I could feel myself calming down. She was probably right. "Thanks for the stories."

"Any time. I like having visitors." She held the door for me. "Come back soon."

"I will."

I slept uneasily that night. I couldn't get the vision of those dogs jumping out a third-story window out of my mind. Was it just old houses in general that gave you the feeling of not quite being alone? I've lived alone many times, even in some old houses that had been converted to apartments. You often heard noises in the night, but it was usually just the neighbors or the old boiler in the basement.

∞

On the way to work the next day, I tried to get the ghost stories out of my head, tried to think of them as stories to scare kids. What was I thinking, asking her to tell me ghost stories when I was already more than a little freaked out by my house? Just for reference, I drove by the Croke-Patterson-Campbell house. It was a huge Chateauesque style mansion boasting an arched double door entrance and turrets on each corner. It gave the appearance of a haunted centuries-old French castle. Thing is, I really didn't believe in ghosts, so why was I so jumpy?

CHAPTER 11

The holidays in a strip club can be genuinely fun or seriously depressing depending on your point of view. Most of the waitresses had children, so I told Nick I would work Christmas Eve if he needed me as my family planned to gather on Christmas Day. Working the holidays would earn brownie points for the times I wanted extra days off.

Charisma and Exotica were sitting with a group of cowboys from Wyoming who were in Denver celebrating a friend's divorce. The DJ had them singing, *"All my exes live in Texas,"* and those boys couldn't have been in better spirits.

On the other side of the room was a man here on business, missing the time he would have spent with his kids while they were on school break, and the table I was serving was the saddest of all.

"So, I've never seen you here," the older man said, removing his dark wool coat.

I set a napkin on the glass top table. "I've only been here a few months. I'm Freja"

"Freja? That's different."

"It's Swedish."

He laid his coat over the chair next to him. "Is Desire working?"

"No, she's in Vail for Christmas."

"Yes," he sighed. "So many of these girls have real lives."

"How about you? Do you have plans for the holidays?"

"Not this year. I'm not married, and I don't have any children. You can bring me a Meyers and Coke."

"What about brothers and sisters?"

"No family here."

"Yeah, it was a pretty lonely time of year for me when I was living in Nevada. I'm really looking forward to spending Christmas day at my parents' house."

It was a slow day with most of our regular customers out of town or home with their families so I stood at his table longer than I normally would have stayed. "So, what do you do for a living? You can see what I do."

He smiled. "I'm a high school history teacher."

"Really?" I glanced over at the stage where nineteen-year-old Serenity was baring her everything, and then I turned back to the man at the table. There was something creepy about a schoolteacher looking at young, naked girls.

Faith pulled up the chair next to him. She was over twenty-one but came across more like fifteen. "Hi, Gene," she said, all bubbly and cute.

"Would you like something to drink?" he asked.

She shook her head. "Not today. I have to meet my folks later."

He slid a twenty into her cleavage. "How are your boys? Did they get everything they wanted for Christmas?"

"Almost. You know boys, there's always something more they want." She fluttered her fake eyelashes at him. Reaching over, she grasped his hand. "The only difference between men and boys is the price of their toys."

Her act was a bit too much for me; I had to slip away. I felt bad for anyone who didn't have family to spend the Holidays with and a teacher would be especially lonely during the school break. I did a stint of student teaching in high school and I know how many evenings and weekends are taken up with grading papers and outlining lessons. Having nothing to occupy his time during the long vacations was just sad.

I eyeballed the table where he was laughing at some unknown story Faith was telling. She always had funny incidents to share, and I could understand why he chose to spend Christmas week with someone like her.

Back at the other table, my cowboys were drinking and tipping as if this would be the last time they'd ever see a girl. I've heard there aren't many girls in Wyoming. The divorcé was spending the most money. He'd maxed out his American Express card and was working on the Visa.

"Bring us another round," he said as he got up from the table.

Charisma stood and latched on to his arm. He unhooked himself. "'Scuse me darlin', but I need to paint the snow."

She frowned, and he said, "Now don't you be an addle pot. I'll be back as quick as a mouse in a hen house." He turned to leave the table as a big woman in a classy three-piece suit stomped across the floor towards him.

"What in Tarnation is she doin' here?"

All the men at the table turned to see what he was talking about. One of the younger men stood and backed away "Damn, she looks mad as a March hare."

The woman was waving some papers. "The jig is up, Rusty. I canceled the credit cards."

"Bully for you!" he said.

"You think you can spend my share of the ranch before the divorce is final? Well, this here letter says you can't spend a dime."

"I can't hold a candle to you, Faye. What, with the Mercedes you had to have. The calico curtains from New York. You're just the most persnickety woman I ever met."

Placing her hands on her hips, she sneered. "If you think I'm gonna get the muddy end of the stick, you're cracked. My father gave me that land."

"Quit yer yammerin'. I made that ranch. It was up the spout when I took it over. You and your folks didn't have enough credit to buy cow chips."

By this time the manager and the doorman had stepped between them.

"You'll have to leave ma'am', Nick said as kindly as he could. "We don't allow unescorted women in here."

As Nick led her towards the door, she was still waving the paper. "Not another dime, Rusty."

Now that the threat had been removed, the younger man sat back down and took a swig of his beer. "Cowboy up man, she can't do that to you."

At first glance, Rusty appeared rattled, but he recovered quickly. "She ain't as smart as she thinks she is. I sold the whole shebang to my sister when she bought that damn Mercedes three years ago. She's burned through all the money I got from the sale. I ain't worth a lick now. The cards I'm using are hers and you can bet the farm she ain't cancelled them cards."

∞

Being Christmas Eve, it was positively dead after nine o'clock. So we closed a little early. I was starving and since virtually everything was closed by the time I left work, I stopped at a Seven-Eleven and picked up a box of donuts. When I came out of the store, an old man asked me if I had some change for the bus.

"It's not my business," I said, "but the busses don't run this late."He started to turn away. "Wait. Do you have someplace to go? I can give you money for a cab."

His eyes crinkled and I suspected he was smiling under that ragged mop of facial hair. "I could use that. I have an army buddy in Englewood who would probably put me up for a few days."

I hadn't noticed the military jacket covered in grime. Judging by his age, he was probably a Viet Nam Vet. My heart hurt to see a man, who had risked his life for me, begging for spare change. One hundred and ninety-two dollars was all I had left of my tips after buying toothpaste, hairspray, milk, and donuts. I gave it to him and wished him a merry Christmas.

∞

The next morning, I drove out 6th Avenue feeling good. I'd only been in the house for four months; however, I'd accomplished a lot. I fixed the floor under the front stairs, patched all the holes in the brick walls, and removed about half of the molding. I'd also nearly completed my new fireplace mantel and the floor beneath it.

I still had a ton of work to make the house livable and it was going to get a lot worse before it got better. Luckily, my job afforded me three-day weekends. That would go a long way to speeding up the process if I didn't get side-tracked by anything stupid.

Denver rarely sees a white Christmas because December is one of the driest months of the year although four years ago Denver had twenty-four inches of snow on Christmas. I was living in Vegas that year so missed the blizzard of the century. Anyone from the area will tell you, any season in Colorado is blizzard season. When I was a kid, we had four inches of snow in June. Today, like Thanksgiving, was a sunny and crisp forty degrees. Traffic was light, the streets were dry, and the snowcapped mountains in front of me were stunning.

My parents' house was warm and inviting. Traditionally decorated, circa 1962, including a revolving aluminum tree, lit from the floor by a rotating color wheel to show every ornament. Seeing that old tree made me feel as if I were five years old again, excited to open presents and play with my new Easy Bake oven. The last real baking I've done. Customarily, we don't exchange many gifts, preferring to give things like coffee and tea or disposable items. I'd gone overboard because I hadn't been home for a long time and the rest of the family seemed to have caught the same bus. Presents were piled high around the tree. I couldn't have been happier when my dad gave me a power drill with every size bit imaginable.

During the years that dad was away making license plates for the state, mom couldn't afford a lot of expensive toys, but I never felt cheated. I could entertain myself with a cardboard box and a roll of fabric. One Christmas, when I was in high school, mom made a dress for me because we couldn't afford "store bought" clothes at the time. It was one of my favorite dresses. Every time I wore it, I felt her love.

Mom remained loyal to my dad through those hard years. We all knew how much she missed him and how hard she'd had to work to care for us. A single woman with five kids was somewhat of a rarity in the sixties.

She was no pushover. When she picked dad up at the gates, she laid down the law. She wasn't going to uproot her family in the middle of the night ever again. He would run alone if he ever needed to run again.

My parents are doing better financially these days. Dad still likes to play cards and bet on the dogs once in a while but the drinking and running with mobsters has given way to eating too much pasta and watching Miami Vice or Hill Street Blues.

∞

While my dad and brothers played football in the front yard, Shannon, my mom, and I sat at the dining room table assembling a jigsaw puzzle and drinking eggnog. After a few months of living in a rundown house with unfriendly neighbors I missed the simple comforts of security and family.

"How's the job?" my mom asked.

I didn't want a repeat of Thanksgiving, so I just told her it was paying the bills.

"Have you found a new man yet?"

"Mom, I'm not looking for a man."

Shannon smiled. "I tried to tell her that."

I munched on a homemade popcorn ball. "I just want to get the house done. A man will only get in my way."

"You can't be alone all of your life," she said, giving me that *trust me, I know* look. For all his faults, my mother loved my father.

"Aiden and Connor aren't married," I said a little sterner than I meant to. "I'm only twenty-eight. I've got time." Not to mention, my last few relationships had crashed and burned.

"Men can have babies when they're ninety, not so with girls. Shannon at least has a husband."

Shannon rolled her eyes as she refilled my mug. "Eric and I are looking for a house in Englewood. The schools are better there, and it's closer to his work."

My mother's mouth dropped open. "Are you going to have a baby?"

She shook her head. "Not today, but we're trying."

With those words, my mom forgot about me finding a man and started giving Shannon advice on getting pregnant. Having had five children in eight years, I didn't think Shannon needed much assistance in that area.

∞

An unexpected Christmas gift came from Shannon and Eric who had recently bought a new dining set. "We don't have any place to store the old set," Shannon said. "Could you use it?"

"Sure. It's a major step up from using my table saw. Don't know how I'll get it home. It won't fit in my Celica. Maybe I can borrow Dad's truck."

"I guess you didn't notice, the truck is up on blocks. Eric can bring it to your house tomorrow."

"That would be totally awesome."

When the sun dropped behind the mountains, the men came in for more pie and ice-cream. Dad popped a VHS tape in the recorder and we all settled in to watch, *It's a Wonderful Life*, followed by, *Miracle on 34th Street*.

CHAPTER 12

The next day, Eric and Connor came over with a beautiful oak dining room table and china hutch. I had to move the piles of molding to the kitchen. I didn't see myself using that room for much more than storage for the next year or so. The dining room pieces were perfect for an old Victorian house. Too perfect. All the dust and crap from remodeling the house would have the furniture ruined in weeks. I made a trip to the hardware store to pick up several sheets of painter's plastic to cover them. There were about a dozen choices for plastic tarps.

"Painting already?" Sawyer asked, leaning, arms crossed, against a Sherwin Williams display. I hadn't seen him walk up.

"I'm covering some furniture my sister gave me. I don't want it to get all scratched up."

"Did you have a nice Christmas?"

"Very nice. And you?"

"It could have been better." He looked me over, taking in my dirty jeans, sweatband, and sweatshirt, my hair in a knot on top of my head, held in place by wooden sticks. The *Flashdance* workout-look was so popular, lots of people wore sweatbands. I was wearing one to keep the sweat out of my eyes.

"I've been working on the fireplace and moving furniture."

He nodded. "You're a hard worker." He brushed some dust and cobwebs off my shoulder. "I bet it's looking great."

I wanted him to ask me out for New Year's Eve, but one of the pretty cashiers called him away.

"Sorry, I can't stay and chat right now," he said. "The 50ML is best for covering your furniture."

He followed the cashier into the office. I strolled around the store looking at decorator items I wouldn't be needing for a long time. I was killing time to see if he would come back, but after twenty minutes, I started feeling foolish. I grabbed a box of plastic sheeting and left.

∞

New Year's Eve is a big date night and a strip club isn't exactly the kind of place a girl wants to be taken. I was still new in town and since I spent all my free time working on the house, I hadn't found a date, so I offered to work. It was slow for a Thursday but made a bit livelier with the complimentary champagne the managers were handing out. Although I was off at midnight that didn't mean I had to go home. Nick was working, and after a couple of glasses I was shamelessly flirting with him. Four shots of whiskey and I'm fine but give me two glasses of champagne and I'm a giggling bimbette. I still blame the champagne for making me stupid enough to sleep with Bobby.

I'm not sure if Nick was too much of a gentleman to take advantage of my drunken state of if he truly wasn't interested in me. Either way, I related to the loud rock voice of ACDC screaming, *"I'm on the highway to hell."* He suggested I get something to eat before driving home, so I stopped across the street at the Landmark for breakfast. I ate there regularly because it was handy. I never had much food in the house. It was easier to eat before I went home or on the way to work each day. My days off were covered by pizza and Chinese delivery.

The Landmark restaurant was quiet with the occasional couple strolling in from a party being held in one of the hotel's convention rooms. It was well after midnight and most of the guests had gone to their rooms. The waitress brought my cantaloupe and cottage cheese and asked if I needed anything else.

"No, this is good," I said.

She refilled my tea. "You eat pretty healthy. Must be how you keep your figure."

"I don't like to eat a lot before going to bed."

"A pretty girl like you should have had a date tonight."

"Thank you. I had to work." I cut my cantaloupe into bite size pieces.

"Do you work across the street?"

"Uh huh."

She studied me for a moment before scurrying back to the kitchen. She probably wanted to tell me to "get a real job" but was too nice to say it.

∞

The hall light was on when I pulled up to my house. Suddenly stone-cold sober, a knot formed in my stomach. *I never used the hall light.* Gingerly opening the front door, I stepped in and surveyed the front room and hallway. The house was always a wreck of boards and boxes, so I didn't spot anything out of place until I got to my bedroom.

All my dresser drawers were open, bits of clothing strewn from one side of the room to another. My cheap costume jewelry was gone except a single lonely earring. My stereo was missing and with it, the Beastie Boys album I'd been listening to while I dressed for work earlier that night. Even my freaking bedspread was gone.

I checked the rest of my house. They had stolen the beer and vodka but left me with a box of crackers. I went to the living room and pulled up the floorboard, looking for my little box of treasures. Thank heaven for small favors. I pulled it up by the fishing line I'd attached to it and opened it. Everything was still there, my tips for the last two weeks, the antique money I'd found, the ring, and the bracelet. I was so glad I'd stashed the antiques back in the crawl space instead of in my jewelry box. It had only made sense to store my tips there as well. It saved me a trip to the bank every day.

Feeling a rattled, I slipped the bracelet over my wrist and watched the tiny crystal beads glisten in the light. It was so pretty I immediately felt better. I stashed the cash back in the box and went to the dining room to call the police. I was sure the burglar was gone but I reported the break-in, and they told me they would send a car.

The back door had been kicked in, so I found a couple two by fours and nailed it shut while I waited for the police. I never used that door much anyway, now that all my bricks were cut.

As I turned to go up the stairs, I saw her again, the young woman in the red dress with the black fringe. I was shaking, not sure if it was from the violation of the robbery or because a strange woman was perched on the landing of my stairs.

"Hello?" I called to her. No answer. "Hey. Can you hear me?" I still had the hammer in my hand. Originally an implement of war, my hammer would suffice nicely tonight if this girl went crazy on me. I often thought of this tool as a type of divining rod used to locate the most expensive part of anything I was trying to fix and then destroying it, but tonight it would double as a weapon.

I called to her. "Who are you?"

She turned toward me, looking confused as if she had only just noticed me. "I don't know," she said softly and faded away.

"Holy apparitions, Batman, I have a freaking ghost in my house."

CHAPTER 13

Tiptoeing up the stairs, I called to her again. "Hey, who are you? It's okay. You can come out. I just want to talk to you." She wasn't in the bathroom or the first bedroom. I went into my room; empty. I hesitated to look in the closet. I've seen my share of movies and I know there are certain places you're never supposed to look. I set my hammer on the dresser. "Come on out. Please. I just want to talk." In truth, I was unnerved, but it was also kind of cool. She didn't look scary or mean. She was pretty and exquisitely dressed. I loved the feather and sequin headband and the fringe on her dress was to die for. OK wrong word, but she did look amazing.

After checking the entire upper floor and not finding the girl, I sat on the bed and mourned my missing chenille bedspread. It wasn't particularly nice, but I'd had it for years. It had once belonged to my grandmother. I imagined the burglar wrapped his booty in the spread and drug it out the backdoor without giving it a second thought. "I hate this," I said to out loud to myself, and the invisible girl. "I've never had a stranger rifle through my things, and it feels horrible." I didn't know if she could hear me but talking to her made me feel less alone. "I don't know what I was thinking when I took over the payments here. The place is falling around me faster than I can slap it back together. Just look at those cracks in the plaster." I stared up a particularly long crack in the ceiling. "What I need is a big dog. I need a killer Rottweiler or German Sheppard. Should I try to sell the place?" I got off the bed and ambled over to the doorway. There was an old gaslight fixture on the wall. I ran my hand over the intricate door trim. "I imagine this place was elegant eighty years ago. Maybe if I stripped the paint off this door frame..." The original gas light fixture was covered with layers of paint and surely hadn't been used since sometime in the 1930s. Gazing across the hall toward the smallest bedroom, more of an oversized closet, an idea popped into my head. "This room is definitely too small to be a bedroom but if I remove the wall next to the stairs and add a railing it would make a fabulous loft office or art studio. I could look over and see the front door from my drafting board or desk." I strolled around the room, imagining what it would look like without the east wall. "The lighting would be so much better. This window does nothing. It might have if it were on the south side of the house but here on the north it's practically worthless." I went back to the hall leading to the stairs and glanced up. There was an access panel to the attic next to the light fixture. "Of course, I would have to see if the rafters ran parallel or contrary to the wall. It could be super cool." I designed the room in my head while I waited.

∞

It was nearly forty-five minutes before the cops arrived. Police aren't there to prevent crime, only to clean up the broken pieces after the deed has been done. It was obvious I was going to have to learn to protect myself. I could buy a new door, better locks, and a dog; a big dog.

Three uniformed officers wondered through the house. One older guy asked, "How long have you lived here?"

"Since the end of August."

"You live here alone?"

"Yes."

"Why? This is a pretty rough neighborhood," he said. "A girl like you isn't safe in this area."

He wasn't telling me anything Haddie hadn't said over the past month. He made more notes on his clipboard.

"My dad gave me the house. I want to fix it up. It's kind of cute."

He shook his head and followed another uniform to the kitchen. Looking at the studs nailed to the door, he asked, "Did you just do this?"

"Yes. I was a little freaked out."

His smile appeared understanding. "We'll take a look outside. I believe they're gone now. Might want to consider getting a security system. Or a mean dog."

The officer filled out a form and had me sign it. There was nothing they could do. "You have a few days to come up with a list of goods stolen but I don't think you'll ever see your stuff again. You were lucky you weren't home. Burglars can turn nasty when confronted by a homeowner."

Yikes. I hadn't thought of that. I escorted the officers to the front door and locked the deadbolt after them. As the police car drove away, I could see the pinking of the eastern sky not yet bright enough to light the dirty snow in the front yard.

Dejected, I went back upstairs to list everything that was stolen in the robbery.

∞

I must have drifted off because the next thing I knew, someone was pummeling on my front door. I rubbed my eyes and tried to clear my head. When I saw the state of my bedroom, everything came flooding back, the anger, the fear, and absolute violation. "Coming!" I shouted down the stairs. The front was locked tight. I'd thought about nailing it shut but I was going to need it.

My clothes were wrinkled from sleeping in them, so I brushed out the worst of it and opened the door to a bright-eyed Sawyer.

"What time is it?" I asked.

"Eight o'clock."

"What were you thinking, coming over at eight in the morning on New Year's Day."

He looked abashed. "I'm sorry. I should have realized you would be out late. I can come back."

"No. It's all right. Come in." I opened the front door and motioned him in.

He eyed my wrinkled clothes and messy hair. "Rough night?"

"You might say that. Someone kicked in my back door and robbed me,"

His pale blue eyes turned dark and he frowned. "Are you okay? Were you home?"

"I was at work when they came in. It was probably kids. They took the stereo and some jewelry but left most of my non-power tools. I real thief knows the value of a good pry bar. It's the only tool perfect for completely destroying one hundred-year-old molding you're trying to remove to reuse."

I led him to the kitchen. I would have offered him some coffee or a beer, but I didn't have a coffee maker and the thieves took my beer. "Would you like a glass of water? Sorry, it's all I have." I grabbed a glass from the drain board and filled it.

"That's okay. I was in the neighborhood and I thought I'd see how it went with the decking project."

I sipped my water and shuffled to the kitchen table. A box of hand tools had been turned over on the floor by the back door. "Crap! Now I'm going to need another circular saw. I guess someone couldn't resist that." I sniffed, shaking my head. "And a new drill. Damn it. My dad just gave me that for Christmas. It was still in the box."

He leaned against the fifty-year-old metal stove. "Do you have homeowner's insurance?"

"Yeah. Thankfully. I can replace most of what I had but I feel so violated."

"Come on, let's get you a cup of coffee and a hot meal."

Over a McDonald's coffee and fries, Sawyer told me about Christmas with his sister. He'd taken her to the Colorado Ballet to see the Nutcracker.

"So how was it?" I asked. It was hard to imagine him in a suit watching a ballet.

"Not my cup of tea but she loved it."

"I've never been to the ballet before. Someday it might be fun to go." I sipped on my coffee and watched him stuff ketchup laden fries into his mouth. "So." I said as blithely as I could. "Have you ever seen a ghost?"

He blinked at me as if he wasn't sure what I said. "A what?"

"Never mind. Tell me more about your Christmas."

CHAPTER 14

Early January was dry with temperatures in the forties; perfect weather for shopping for new tools. I get turned on in a hardware store like most girls will swoon over new shoes. A lot of the power tools I'd lost in the robbery had been hand-me-downs from my brothers. There is nothing quite like a shiny new electric screwdriver to make a girl feel pretty.

I strolled through the tool aisle and saw the object of my desire, a pneumatic nail gun. One of these babies full of brads is like shooting a BB gun. Give me some 16 penny nails and we'll talk self-defense.

From experience, I knew a circular saw would be great for cutting my studs too short and a jigsaw would help me hopelessly mutilate any other woodworking project. I needed practice with the scroll saw but I figured I'd learn enough using the others before I got to the finish work.

Meandering down the aisle, looking at all the tools, gave me more ideas for the house. I needed a reciprocating saw to cut through all the plaster and lathe, not to mention the hundred-year old nails and screws. A belt sander would probably leave ripples in any piece of furniture I tried to refinish but I wasn't planning on doing much of that. I bought it anyway. I added up the prices in my head as I moved to the next aisle. I still had enough money to get a few more tools. I hadn't received the insurance check but my tips for the week had been excellent. I studied the large box on the shelf. A table saw is great for launching wood across the room but could also double as a workbench, and what the heck, I threw in the band saw, too. Now my cart was full.

At the counter, a young girl began ringing up my new toys.

"Is Sawyer here?" I asked.

She shyly blinked a couple of times. "No," she said. "He's in Vegas this week. Is there something Paul can help you with?"

I didn't know who Paul was. "No. I just wanted to say, hey."

"He'll be back on Saturday."

"No biggie."

She smiled. "He's a hottie, isn't he?"

"Yeah, he is."

∞

On the way home I picked up a classic double cheeseburger and a frosty. I'd have to pay for my poor eating habits someday, but all that shopping had made me hungry. Eating my lunch in the car, I watched homeless people roaming up and down Colfax Avenue. I was feeling lucky to have only lost some fake jewelry and a few old tools. In a moment of munificence, I rolled down the window and waved to a woman pushing a shopping cart. "Here," I said, handing her a twenty, "have a nice day."

Her eyes glistened. "Thank you and God bless you."

"Someday I may need a friend."

"You can always find me here if you do."

I nodded and rolled up the window as she parked her cart and went inside Wendy's.

A few minutes later I pulled up in front of my house, excited to open my new tools. While dragging the first big box from the car to the living room I heard a noise in the kitchen. A shiver ran up my back. Once your home has been invaded, you're never quite the same again. I picked up my war hammer and crept into the dining room to find the window had been broken. I must have interrupted the party because they appeared to have scrambled out the parlor window when I came in.

They were truly starting to piss me off now. Good thing I just bought that power-nailer. It took most of the afternoon to finish but I covered every main floor window with a solid-core wood door from my dad's collection. The only window I didn't cover was the one in the kitchen by the stove because it was only a foot and a half wide and I didn't think anyone could fit through it. It left the place dark, but I felt safer.

The rest of the day I used a sledgehammer to tear out lathe and plaster. Hitting things made me feel better. I needed to get the place down to the studs before I could run the wiring. I had most of the walls torn out of the living room and half of the parlor before I gave up, exhausting most of my anger.

After a well-deserved soak in the claw-foot tub, I tried to work on my house plans. I uncovered the dining table and a couple chairs to have a flat surface to draw house plans. Most of the remodel would require replacing the electrical system, the plumbing, and cracked plaster walls. I thought a double doorway from the kitchen to the dining room with French doors would open the room nicely. I drew it in. On the south side of the parlor I would build a window seat with built-in oak shelves creating a nice library. The living room was pretty much as is. It would need new sheet rock of course and I'd have to replace the big picture window. I was concentrating on my drawing when the girl appeared in the seat on the other side of the table from me.

"Shit!" I said, and a scribble of pencil streaked across my plans. "Don't scare me like that. I thought I was alone." And just as quick, she was gone again. "I'm sorry," I called to her. "I didn't mean to yell at you." But she didn't come back. I suspected she was more afraid of me than I was of her.

∞

The next day while working at the back bar with Cinnamon, aka Barbara to her kids' sitter, I told her the reason for the blisters on my right hand.

"You should have a gun," she said. Shaking her head made her soft red curls shimmer. "You were lucky they didn't come in while you were home. I have a loaded thirty-eight under my pillow." She slapped her round and ample butt cheek. "No one is getting a piece of this unless I agree."

"I've never had a real gun. They scare me. I have a nail gun."

She grimaced like my mother did when she thought I was being silly. "I'm serious, Freja."

"I wouldn't know what to do with a gun."

"Don't worry. I have a friend who owns a gun store. He'll give you lessons if you want." Cinnamon didn't look like the kind of girl who hung out with gun store types but over the past few months of working there I'd learned that no one was who you thought they were. The girls here were more real and honest with each other than anyplace I'd worked before. The façade they put on to do their job was only playacting. The brightest girls often pretended to be airheads and the most innocent looking were usually the wildest. There were always exceptions to every rule, but I learned not to prejudge.

I stepped aside to let Pepper, aka Debbie to her motorcycle mechanic, pass as she came into the well to empty her tray. Tough looking with a dark Gothic flair, Pepper kept to herself and intimidated the crap out of me. I expected she had an arsenal of weapons, probably carrying right then, although I had no idea where she would hide a gun under her infinitesimal uniform.

As usual, she ignored me, but I noticed while Cinnamon had her back to us, Pepper moved the napkins on Cinnamon's tray slightly to the right. Her eyes met mine for a fraction of a second before she sauntered away, her face a blank.

"Maybe it wouldn't hurt to be prepared," I said to Cinnamon as I watched her replace the napkins in their original position. "But, I think the doors will be good enough."

"You're going to want windows again one day. Come, meet Dave."

I followed her over to a table where a muscular man in a tight T-shirt and full sleeve tattoos sipped on a drink. A black leather bomber jacket laid across the back of his chair. Diamond, Jade, Emerald, and Sapphire were currently entertaining him. These girls were sweet and innocent-looking, while I imagined this guy should be sitting with the likes of Pepper.

Cinnamon set drinks on the table for the girls. "This is Freja," she shouted over the strains of *Eye of the Tiger*. "She's been having trouble with people breaking into her house. Freja, this is Dave Langley."

He looked like a cross between a member of the Hell's Angels and the Fonz. He stood up and held out his hand. "Freja? How unusual. Is it your given name?"

"Yes. It's Swedish," I said as a way of explanation. "It's not like I had to change it because there was already a Freja working here." I shook his hand politely. He held mine a fraction longer than he needed to, not in a creepy way, but in a sincerely *'nice to meet you'* kind of way. He was charming and bad-boy sexy.

"Are you looking for a security company," he asked in a low firm voice, "or is this something you want to handle? I can provide either."

"I don't know," I said. "Cinnamon thought I should buy a gun, but I don't know the first thing about them. I'm afraid I'll shoot myself."

"Don't believe the media hype. People rarely shoot themselves by accident." He reached into his wallet. "Here's my card. Come to the shop, and we'll talk about what you need."

"Thanks. I'll do that."

"Now, if you'll excuse me, the lease is up on my beer. I'll be right back, ladies."

Dave looked like a tough biker, but he had the voice and manners of a real gentleman. All the stereotypes I'd learned as a kid flew out the window in this place. Maybe it was because the place was so dark that people let their guard down, and you could talk to them. Certainly, not all of them were cool, some were every bit the jerks and sleaze bags you'd expect to find in a titty bar, like the guy who bit my ass.

CHAPTER 15

The next day I stopped by Dave's shop. All the guns in the cases were pretty, shiny, and scary. If I hadn't been so angry about the burglary, I wouldn't have dreamed of buying a gun. I couldn't help envisioning what might have happened if I'd been at home when the thieves broke in. I called the cops, but they took forty-five minutes to arrive. If it had been someone set on hurting me, I would have been dead by the time they showed up.

Dave showed me several handguns, but I was drawn to the shotguns and rifles. He had several used rifles on a table in the corner.

"What are these?" I asked.

"Those are Soviet rifles." He picked one up to show me. "This is the SKS model. It was replaced by the AK-47 on the front lines. They used it for second line service and still use it for ceremonies. These particular rifles were actually made in China, known as the Type 56 Carbine." He turned it over so I could see how it was loaded. "It has a conventional layout, with a wooden stock and grip. The barrel is four inches longer than the AK, so it has a slightly higher muzzle velocity."

He handed it to me, and it wasn't as heavy as I had expected. "It's pretty cool," I said placing it up against my shoulder and aiming at a blank wall, probably blank for that very reason.

All military SKSs have a bayonet attached to the underside of the barrel. This spring-loaded hinge retracts and extends the blade.

There's a cleaning kit in the buttstock and a cleaning rod under the barrel. A good thing about this model is you can field strip it without any tools. Overall, it's a good gun but shotguns are better for home defense."

He pointed out a few models and then led me back to the case of handguns. "Now for personal protection a handgun can be carried in the car or your purse. You'll want something with some stopping power. A twenty-two can drop a man if you hit him in a vital area but a forty-five will usually stop him just by the look of it." He laid a couple of guns on the counter. "Let's see how these feel."

I couldn't stop thinking about the rifle. It wasn't as scary as the handguns. I'm sure my bias was from watching too many crime dramas as a kid. Six-shooters were for outlaws; I wanted to be the Rifleman. By the end of the day I had an SKS rifle, five boxes of ammunition, and my first gun class. The class was all about handling the gun safely when loading, unloading, and cleaning it. I was still nervous but feeling better about it. I set up some time with Dave for range practice.

On the way home I stopped at Listen Up to see about getting a new stereo. I'm not a connoisseur of music, I just like to listen to tunes. The overwhelming choices of quality and gadgets sent me back to K-Mart. Simple rack and turntable in hand, I returned home to find my doors had held.

∞

I was off the next few days, so I stayed up all night playing with my new drill press. After several attempts, I discovered the press was excellent for ripping wood out of my hand and launching it through the closest window. Fortunately, the solid core doors I'd nailed over them protected the glass. Can't say it did much for my cup of tea.

I was just getting the hang of preventing the subject of my project from smacking me in the chest when someone knocked on the door. Shutting off the drill, I glanced at my five-dollar K-Mart watch. It was four in the morning.

The front door had a large window covered with a curtain, not very secure but at least I could see who was out there. At the door, I peeked through curtain of the only window I hadn't covered with wood. Two dark-skinned men were pacing back and forth on my porch. Both appeared to be in their teens and the taller one was wearing a gold chain worth more than my house. It was no one I knew and not the kind of guys I normally hang out with, so I pretended not to be home.

One of them knocked again and then tried the door. Thankfully, I'd remembered to lock it when I got home. I ran up to my bedroom where my gun was stashed under the bed. My hands were shaking, and my breath was coming in short spasms. After loading it, I sat at on the stair landing with my SKS pointed toward the door.

I was startled awake by a banging on the door. "I definitely need to get a doorbell." Daylight was streaming through the window and I could see the silhouette of Sawyer through the glass. "I set the rifle aside and rubbed the sleep out of my eyes. "Be right there," I called to him.

Opening the door, I squinted into early morning sunlight; early for me, late morning by most people's standards. "Yeah?" I said.

"Did I catch you at a bad time?"

I shook my head, mostly to clear out the cobwebs. "No, I was just getting up."

He sized up my clothes. I was fully dressed although a bit wrinkled. Glancing up the stairs he couldn't help but notice the rifle standing in the corner of the landing. "Are you okay?" His eyes softened with concern.

"Yes. I was working on the drill press last night when two guys started banging on my door. I perched at the top of the landing where I'd have a good shot at them if they tried to come in."

His gaze slid past me and into the living room where he could see my latest handiwork. "I couldn't help noticing your new window coverings. Did you board up every window?"

"Yeah, the little brats broke in again. They didn't get anything the second time, partially because I didn't have anything left to steal and partially because I interrupted their fun."

"And the note on the door?"

"I'm sure that helps, too." The note said, *"come on in if you think you're faster than a speeding bullet."*

He nodded, knowingly. "I stopped by to tell you the store has some stuff that's slated for the dump as a write-off."

"What kind of stuff? I'm going to need some sheetrock soon."

"Lights, vanities, sinks, and counter tops. Things that are discontinued are marked down to a fraction of the original price. If they don't sell today, they get destroyed."

"What exactly do you mean by a fraction? Is it better than last weekend's sale?"

"The vanities are normally two to three hundred dollars. They're going for twenty bucks."

"That's my kind of sale but I can't fit a vanity cabinet in my car."

"I can give you a ride."

"Excellent. Give me a minute to grab a clean sweatshirt."

I grabbed my gun and stashed it in my room. Running a brush through my hair in front of the mirror, my face resembled an east coast road map; wrinkles from where I'd fallen asleep against the stair balustrades. Lovely.

Sawyer was waiting in the truck where the Bellamy Brothers sang about a redneck girl. As I got in, I saw the ghost in the bedroom window. A chill ran up my spine. I peeked over to see if Sawyer had noticed, but his eyes were fixed on the road in front of us.

I stole another peak at the window. She appeared upset, almost angry.

∞

When we got to the store, Lynette took him away for a while, then another man in a suit, maybe his boss, pulled him aside. "I'll be back in a few minutes," he said. "Pick out anything you like, and I'll check you out on Register One."

I thought he was in trouble and I started feeling guilty. I would hate to see him lose his job trying to sell me a ten-dollar light fixture. I found a vanity I thought would work well once I got around to remodeling the bathroom.

It was nearly forty-five minutes before he came back to see what I had loaded on the flatbed cart. I probably added a few extra things because I felt bad for him.

"I see you picked out a quality vanity," he said. "We stopped carrying that brand."

"Why? If it's good quality I would think you would want to keep it in stock."

"The company was bought out by a large conglomerate and now everything is being made in China."

"Seems to be the way of things these days."

He loaded my treasures into the back of his truck, but his mind was on something else.

"Is everything okay?" I asked.

"Yeah." he said opening the door for me. I climbed into the truck and buckled myself in.

He was quiet as we pulled out of the parking lot. A cold front was moving in and the temperature dropped twenty degrees before we got back to Five-Points.

"Wow. Where did this come from?" I asked to make conversation. "It was fifty-five degrees not even an hour ago."

"Do you need a jacket? I have one behind the seat."

"No. I'm fine. It won't take long to unload the truck. Would you like to stay for dinner? I don't have anything in the house, but we could order out."

He turned toward me; his eyes scanning my body, landing on my eyes. "I would love to stay but I can't. Something's come up and I have to go back to work."

"Maybe another time," I said not actually believing it and knowing it was probably for the best. As much as I was in the mood for some male attention, I didn't want a repeat of the Bobby fiasco.

He may have had to leave because of his boss, or maybe he had a date with Lynette. She held his attention whenever she was in the store. At any rate, I had work to do.

∞

February weather was crappy, and I spent hours reading how to books, making notes, tearing out plaster, and feeling more overwhelmed each day. How was I going to shingle a roof with a twelve-twelve pitch or fix a chimney that leaned precariously to one side? I still needed to run new wiring, new plumbing, and hang sheetrock. It was sad that I should be feeling so depressed when spring was right around the corner. If you ask me, February is a bad month for Valentine's Day. It only serves to remind single people how miserable their lives are during the most depressing month of the year. Seriously, couldn't they have stuck this holiday in July or August so I could go to the beach or a park?

It wasn't just the house that had me wanting to run away. There were days I truly hated my job and the idiots who pestered me for dates each day. How many times do you have to tell a guy you can't see him outside of the club? Strangers knocked on my doors at all hours of the night, and I had a ghost that liked to startle me at the most inopportune times. She would appear on the edge of my bed while I was reading or drawing, my scream sending her to wherever ghosts hang out when they're not scaring the crap out of you.

∞

On the fourteenth, flowers congested the front door. Most every entertainer and the cocktail staff had boyfriends or regulars who sent roses or the occasional bouquet of mixed flowers to the club. The scent was overpowering. At the seven o'clock shift change, several girls couldn't take home the flowers from their regulars, so they left them behind or gave them away. I love flowers so I took home four bouquets. It didn't do much to cheer up my house, but I noticed the girl seemed to like looking at them. I tried not to frighten her away by watching from the corner of my eye. She appeared more often now but was still frightfully skittish.

A big surprise came late one Tuesday night near the end of February. I was in the living room putting my tools in a box when I happened to glance up the stairway. The girl stood on the landing watching me for several minutes. She pulled a gold cigarette case out from an elaborately beaded bag. Extracting a cigarette from the case, she appeared to have forgotten what to do with it.

I nearly dropped my pry bar when she said, "I am vexed. I half thought you were a snake charmer. I was brought to understand you were not such, as time confirmed you offered them none of your hooch." She glanced out the window behind her as if expecting to see someone out there. "Scoundrels come seeking though you cast them out. I find that is perfectly divine as bootlegging is a wicked business."

It was hard to follow her conversation because there was an obscure timbre to her voice, like a jazz song with too much going on to find the melody. I swallowed back a rush of fear.

"I don't know why people come here." I said softly, not wanting to upset her. "Maybe the guy who lived here before me was a bootlegger. I rarely have more than the occasional beer or bottle of whiskey in the house."

"I fear it would be a hard row to hoe should the bulls catch on. You don't need that hokum." She returned the cigarette to its case.

"No, I don't," I answered, not understanding but not wanting to disagree. I wasn't sure what she meant by snake charmer or who these bulls were. Her language fascinated me.

"The world has grown very corrupt. Though truth be uttered, you appear practical. That's to say, I approve of cutting one's coat to the cloth."

As she crept down the stairs and around the newel post, my heart began to pound. I forced myself to stay still. After all, a ghost is a ghost and not quite natural. She stared into the living room, where I stood stock-still, but she didn't enter.

"My name is Freja. What should I call you?" I asked. "I hate to keep calling you Girl."

She stopped at the doorway of the living room, wringing her hands. "I must beg your pardon," she said, a puzzled frown wrinkled her brows. "I'm all balled up inside. I should know my own name, but it skitters from my mind, like chasing a rainbow." She looked as if she might cry at any moment.

"I'll try to help," I said. "What can you tell me about yourself? Obviously, people who knock on the door disturb you."

She gave me a reprimanding frown. "I don't like rascals coming to the door looking for hooch. You should make them stop."

"I don't like it either but there isn't much I can do until they figure out I don't have any booze."

Distracted by something, she turned and drifted down the hall toward the dining room. I waited to follow at a safe distance but when I came around the corner she was gone. I replayed the conversation in my head wondering if her strange accent was British or French.

CHAPTER 16

The following Monday, I got in a little practice on the shooting range. Dave said I was a good shot because I could hit the target nine out of ten times. I didn't always hit the silhouette man in the chest or head, but I got close enough to scare the crap out of him. I prayed if it ever came down to it that that would be good enough.

"Keep practicing," Dave said, handing me another box of shells. "You have to get comfortable with it. Let it become second nature to take aim and fire." He drew his forty-five and fired off six rounds. His little silhouette man was very dead.

He stood behind me and adjusted my stance. "Feet apart just a bit." He slid his leg between mine and tapped my foot. His warm breath on my neck sent heat to my nether regions. I sighed.

"You're doing fine," he whispered, his lips close to my ear. "Any new sport can be intimidating."

It wasn't the sport that was intimidating; it was him. His dark hair was tied back in a ponytail and his torn jeans were sexy in a relaxed way. Built like a Greek god, his sleeveless muscle shirt showed his tattoos didn't end at the shoulders. I tried to imagine what my mother would say if I brought him home for dinner. I suspected she would faint upon meeting him, although maybe not. She was a bit bohemian and stronger than she appeared. My dad, on the other hand, had more in common with James Dean than Dean Martin so he might like Dave. I shook my head to get rid of the thoughts.

We went through another box of ammo and I began to relax. My aim was slightly better because I'd stopped closing my eyes every time I pulled the trigger.

Dave began putting his forty-five away. "Would you like to have a drink later?"

"Uh, no. Not today. I need to stop by the hardware store before it closes." I locked the bolt open on my rifle to let the barrel cool and began cleaning up my empty casings. It's not like I was firing an automatic, but it never hurts to let it cool. It also makes sure the rifle is unloaded. "The house keeps me super busy. Another time?" I was torn, part of me wanted to have a couple shots and get to know him, the other part of me was afraid of having a couple of shots and getting to know him.

"I'd like to see your house."

"Someday. It's a mess right now." I packed my rifle in a carrying satchel. "We should practice again next week."

He smiled and held the door open. "I'm free on Tuesday. You're off work that day, aren't you?"

"Yes. I'll let you know if I can make next Tuesday."

"You should learn how to handle a handgun."

"I don't know," I replied.

Dave made the forty-five-look cool, but that was because Dave always looked cool.

"The SKS is a great gun if we're ever invaded by another country but self-defense is quite different."

"I'll think about it. This is all I can handle right now."

After leaving the shooting range, I went by H B Woods to pick up blades for my Saws-All and to see if there was anything I needed. As luck would have it, there was another sale on lighting fixtures. Lights and vanities are much more fun to buy that sheetrock. I studied each light; not sure any would fit in my final design because I didn't have a final design.

"Looking for new lighting?" Sawyer asked from behind me.

"Yes, no, maybe."

"I like a decisive woman."

I puffed out my lower lip a fraction and furrowed my brows. "I can't decide what I want. This chandelier might look nice in the dining room or the living room. I could mount it in the parlor, but you only have one. I'm not sure it would look right if all three were different."

He led me to another shelf. "These all have the same style and color but this one is a flush mount while these two are traditional. Would you like something in crystal?"

"No. That's going to be too ritzy for my house."

"Traditional it is, then."

I hesitated. "I like that one over there, but nothing matches it."

"Most Victorian homes have eclectic decorating."

"Sold!" I said. "I'll take that and maybe I'll find something similar later."

"What about the second-floor rooms?"

"Since I have to rob all the fancy woodwork from upstairs to complete the main floor, I'll make the upstairs more modern."

He led me to another aisle of lights. After about thirty minutes I had everything I needed to install my new light.

"You're quite the salesman," I said plunking three metal electrical boxes on the flatbed.

He winked. "I try."

"Did you get in trouble the other day when you helped me with the vanity and sinks?"

He looked confused. "In trouble?"

"Yeah, you gave me a ride home but had to go right away. I thought you got in trouble for leaving work."

"Oh, no." An odd smile curved his lips. "Just had to handle something."

"A hot date with Lynette?"

His smile widened and he slid a finger across my shoulder. "Is that jealousy I detect?"

I felt heat flush my cheeks from his touch. "Uh, no." *Maybe.* "I just noticed you were talking to her before we left. I was more concerned your boss might be mad at you for spending so much time with me."

He leaned closer. "I think I'll be okay, but I like that you care."

I wasn't sure I believed he wasn't in trouble, but it was hard to think with him breathing on my cheek.

I stepped back to clear my head. I swear he was holding back a laugh. He probably toyed with women like this all the time. My heart sank. I didn't need this.

"So," I said, breathing out a sigh. "I've started tearing out the plaster and lathe. Do you think half-inch drywall will work? Three-quarter is so heavy."

"Half-inch works for most projects. When you do the kitchen and bath, I recommend cement board anywhere water might splash on it."

"I'll need about twelve sheets for the living room."

He was walking me to the register when one of the cashiers called him over.

"Sorry," he said. "I need to go."

"Sure, I understand. We all need to make a living."

"This will take a while, so Sam will check you out."

I grinned. "I'll be checking him out, too."

Sawyer stopped for a moment. "He's married."

"I didn't say I was going to take him home."

All the while, Sam was looking back and forth between Sawyer and me as if he didn't quite know what to do.

∞

On Saturday night, Ginger, aka Carolyn on her driver's license, set her cocktail tray beside mine. "You have a new customer up in the elevated section."

I turned to see a sexy looking man of about thirty stretching his long legs under the table. Three girls immediately sat down at his table. I didn't know him, but if Houston, Dallas, and Austin were at his table, he was a big tipper.

"Thanks," I said to Ginger. "It's been a little slow for tips tonight."

"His name is Jason Vaughn. He owns a tie company or something." She smiled, knowingly.

I quickly headed to the table take his order. He was dressed in an Armani suit that probably cost more than my last car.

"Hi, I'm Freja. What can I bring you?"

"Freja. Really?"

"Yes. It's Swedish." He smiled, and I thought I would wet my pants; he was totally hot. "What would you like?"

He peered into my eyes. "I'd like to buy you a drink. Oh, and one for each of my girls here."

"I don't drink when I work," I said with my best smile. "I tend to lose all my hard-earned money but thank you."

"Well, here's a twenty so you can buy a drink later."

SWEET. It's going to be a good night.

∞

Sunday morning, I moved my bathroom vanity, and a four-foot bathroom counter with dual sinks—complements of the super sale Sawyer turned me on to—into the parlor. Clearing space to start hanging sheet rock in the living room, I realized I should have done that before building the new mantel but live and learn.

The ceiling rock had to go up before the wall. According to the books, the wall helped hold the ceiling in place. I ran Romex twelve gage wire from the center of the ceiling to the wall leading to the front hall for the switch and dropped more down the wall between the living room and the parlor. Eventually it would go through the ceiling, connect to the light in the parlor and make its way to the breaker box in the kitchen.

After shutting off the gas in the basement, I tore out the old lighting fixtures; no way I was good enough to restore those. I capped the ends of the pipe and started on the ceiling. I couldn't get to the window molding without tearing off the doors covering them but there were other walls I could rock.

It was late. I decide to take a break and have something to eat. A half a Domino's Pizza sat in a cardboard box on a stack of lumber as I perched on a step stool, eating cold pizza and admiring my accomplishment. The girl appeared. She was standing in the doorway to the parlor.

"Hello," I said nearly choking on a pepperoni. I had been wondering when she would come back again. I hadn't seen her since shortly after Valentine's Day. I turned down the Sony, silencing Chris de Burgh crooning, *"...lady in red is dancing with me..."*

The ghost glided toward me and my heart began to beat faster. She *was* the shade of a dead woman after all. Curiosity held my feet firmly planted in the dust and bits of plaster that covered the floor.

"I don't know if you remember, my name is Freja." She studied me and seemed to be taking a lot in. I took a chance and asked again, "What's your name?"

She blinked at me. Her eyes glistened with unspent tears and she shook her head.

"Do you know where you are?" I asked gently.

Again, she shook her head, no. "I don't know where I am. My head is going round and round."

"You're very pretty and that's a lovely dress you're wearing. I don't think I've ever seen anything quite like it."

She glanced down at her dress and seemed surprised, as if she hadn't ever seen it before. I felt sorry for her. She appeared lost, as her dark eyes darted around the room. "Have a seat," I said pointing to a box. "Sorry I don't have any furniture in here."

"You are only too kind." She settled gracefully on the box of drywall mud crossing her legs at the ankles and pulling them to the side. "Where is this place?" she asked.

"You don't recognize it?"

"No." She appeared confused. "I am often conscious of an undercurrent of foreboding. The room is familiar to me, but I know it not."

I told her the address and gave her an approximate location relative to downtown Denver. She silently considered my words.

"I've been living here for a few months now," I explained.

"Yes," she said. "You spoke long into the night. There were men who visited quite late though I know not the uniform they wore."

For a moment, I was confused and then I remembered the night I had been robbed. "I didn't know you were listening. That was a bad night for me." I set my half-eaten pizza down.

She glanced at the box. "I will open my heart to you. It proved a considerable strain. I was quite frightened."

"So was I. It's safe now. I boarded up all the windows so the bad men can't get in. Is my work on the house disturbing you?"

"I was wont to remark I rather enjoy having you here. The house is mournfully quiet when you leave. A sudden madness comes over me and I feel anxious in the silence."

She felt anxious? I couldn't tell her how much she was freaking me out right then. The logical part of my brain was screaming, "There's no such thing as ghosts," while my heart was breaking at the sight of her distress. "I'm glad you feel better when I'm here."

"I should not be in this place, but I cannot leave. For some considerable time, I have tried to find passage out, but I keep waking in this room." Getting up once more, she stepped through the parlor doorway and stood not two feet away. Her skin was a flawless chocolate and her eyes heavily lined with a dark smoky shadow, not the shadow of death, but the elegant shadowing of carefully applied make-up. Her lips were deep red and perfectly shaped. I was reminded of Halle Berry, the 1985 first runner-up for Miss U.S.A. Beautiful and graceful but with an air of misery.

Looking a little less frightened, she moved around the edge of the room, skirting the sawhorses holding my impromptu workbench.

I wondered if she knew she was dead. The first time I saw her, she had walked through a solid door but now she seemed acutely aware of the objects in the room.

"I have to work to afford this stuff," I said, tapping the bag of mortar at my feet.

"May I know what it is?"

"It's what's left over from our new fireplace."

"You remade the fireplace?"

"Only the mantle." I picked at a piece of pepperoni. "Can you tell me anything like your name, or where you came from?"

She looked pained. "No, don't urge me please. I cannot remember. I do not share this with you with the abject of softening your heart and arousing your pity."

"This house must mean something to you since you're here. What about friends or relatives?"

Looking agitated, she began pacing. "I believe I may have lived in Denver some months ago. I was set to travel. It was most needful and urgent, but I cannot remember if I was coming or going."

That was a start. "Did you live here?"

She shook her head, studying the pocket doors to the parlor. "I do not know. I do not believe so. The word Baxter is fixed in my mind."

"Could that be your name?"

"It does not feel like my name. It is a place, I'm mostly certain."

"Could it be the name of a street?"

Someone banged on the front door. I nearly jumped through the roof, knocking my pizza box onto the floor. The girl vanished. I glanced at my watch. It was ten minutes to four in the morning. This was freaking me out.

I peeked through the curtain cover window to see who was out there. It was two women about my age. I couldn't see anyone else. I called through the door. "What is it?"

"Sparky sent us to get some whiskey. He says if the lights on, you got whiskey for sale."

My porch light was on. It had been on all day again. "I don't have any whiskey."

"Why you got your light on then?"

"I didn't know it was on."

From the other woman, "Sparky says you do."

"Who is Sparky?"

"Everybody in this here neighborhood knows Sparky."

"I'm sorry," I said, "I don't know anyone named Sparky and I don't have whiskey."

"You sound like a white girl. You got beer?"

Leaving the chain on, I opened the door, so I didn't have to yell. "No, I don't have anything."

"We got money."

"I'm sorry, you must have the wrong house."

"He says it's the one with the boarded-up windows. Used to buy from you all the time."

"I've been here for six months and I've never sold anyone beer or whiskey. Were the people who lived here before me bootleggers or something?"

"Sheesh." The taller one said as she turned away. "How we gonna keep a party going without beer."

The shorter girl shook her head. "Wish we'd have known that a couple hours ago. Stores weren't closed then."

I closed the door and through the open curtain I watched them shuffle down the flagstone sidewalk. It dawned on me then why people might have been knocking on my door in the middle of the night. Most of the times I heard knocking, I was in bed, so I hadn't been sure it was the door or the house. After discovering the house was haunted, I still didn't know for sure.

It was late, so I tossed out the rest of the pizza and cleaned up. I didn't sleep well as my mind kept drifting to thoughts of the dead woman haunting my house. By eight in the morning I decided to get up and take a bath. Maybe I could get a nap in there.

Hot bubbly water engulfed me, and I closed my eyes. It couldn't have been more than five minutes before I heard someone banging on my door. Crap. What is it now?

Wrapping myself in a towel, I went to the landing and looked at the door. Though the still open curtain, I could see Sawyer smiling up at me. So much for being able to pretend I'm not home.

I waved to him and went back to my room to throw some clothes on. I twisted my wet hair into a knot and stuck a plastic stick through it.

He was waiting patiently for me on the front step. I could see sheetrock in the back of his truck.

"Hi," I said opening the door. "I didn't order sheet rock."

"I know. I had some left over from another order. I thought you could use it."

I was unnerved by his forwardness and couldn't help thinking he'd stolen it. "What do I owe you?"

"It's only a couple sheets."

"How much?"

He was staring at me in a funny way.

"What?"

"Nothing. Let's unload the truck."

We unloaded eight sheets of drywall and I asked how much it would be for the sheetrock and delivery. Again, with the funny smile. "Nothing," he said. "It was covered in the last bill."

I thought about it but wasn't going to argue. "Your timing sucks," I said. "I need to finish my bath and be to work by ten-thirty. Sage is on vacation and I'm working her day shifts this week."

He sighed. "My timing sucks, except…"

"Except what?"

He grinned and lightly thumbed my nose. "Go finish your bath."

After he left, I went back to my bath. The water was cold, so I refilled the tub. As I took my t-shirt off, I realized I'd put it on backwards. "Geez." I hit my head with my hand. Why was it I was always a mess when I saw that guy?

CHAPTER 17

I spent the next few days at the library looking for the name Baxter. It was the closest thing my airy roommate could think of that might be a name. The phone book had dozens of Baxters but I had no way to make a connection. I didn't find a street name either. For all I knew it might be a first name. There was a small community in Pueblo county that was called Baxter. I took down the limited information. It might help her remember something. I needed more information before I could help this girl cross over, supposing that's why she was here. She seemed less shy around me, showing up and scaring the crap out of me almost daily.

Later that day, I was moving scrap wood to the storage room that I hoped would one day be a kitchen. The girl stood in the hallway, watching me with great interest.

"How are you today?" I said.

She nodded slowly and I thought she was going to say something when the phone rang. I crossed the dining room to answer the phone. Still watching me, she cocked her head to one side.

"Hello?" I said into the receiver.

She crossed the room and studied the phone. "May I know the nature of this instrument?"

I looked down at my hand holding the receiver of my black Trimline phone. I could hear the voice on the other end saying, "Freja? Freja, are you there?"

Bringing the receiver to my ear, I said, "I'm kind of busy right now, Mom. Can I call you back?"

"Sure, hon. It's not important. Bye."

"Bye, Mom."

The girl walked to the other side of me, looking at the phone as if it were a snake.

"It's a telephone," I said reassuringly.

"I see no crank. How do you ring one up?"

I didn't have one of the newer phones with the push buttons; mine still sported a rotary dial. "Everyone has a seven-digit number. You pick the number and turn the dial." I showed her how the dial worked. "Then it rings on the other end of the line."

"Nertz."

"What?"

"I have never known of a contraption such as this."

Being from a foreign country, I guessed there were a few things she might not have seen before. But not knowing what a phone was, is just crazy.

Once I had assured myself her questions had been answered, I called my mom back.

"I just wanted to know how you were doing," my mother said.

"I'm fine. Working on the house."

"Well Easter is coming up, and I was wondering if you would be bringing a friend."

"I don't think so."

"Freja, you need to get out there and meet someone."

"I'm really okay. A man would just get in the way."

"A man could help you with the remodeling."

"He would just insist on doing it his way. I have my own ideas."

"Well, think about bringing a friend. Your father and I like to meet your friends."

"I'll think about it. Bye, Mom." And I did think about it. I wondered what they would say upon meeting my friendly ghost.

∞

On the way to work, I went by the hardware store. I didn't really need anything, but I wanted Sawyer to know I could put my clothes on right.

I looked around the store but didn't see him. It must have been his day off. Another nice man asked to help me, so I ordered a dozen sheets of drywall.

"Is Sawyer around?"

"He's working at the Englewood store today."

"Really? I didn't know there was another H B Woods."

"Used to be seventeen stores. Now, there are only five."

"All in Denver?"

"No. I think there are a couple in Kansas and Nevada."

I nodded and paid for the sheetrock. Forty-five dollars with delivery. Now I knew for sure, Sawyer hadn't charged me for the rock or delivery. He would probably lose his job if his boss ever found out. Why couldn't I like guys who were honest, hardworking, and successful?

∞

Work was as stressful as my search for clues about my ghost. I was tired of slogging through dust in the house, but slinging cocktails while flirting with men I'd never give the time of day in the real world was just as annoying. It seemed like most of the customers lately were rude and disgusting and Bobby was still pestering me to resume our relationship. Had the money not been so good, I would have fled Shotgun's.

"Why are you so sad these days?" Sugar, aka Corrine on her Discover card, asked me as she refilled the napkins on her tray. "You're usually so cheerful."

I shrugged and blew out a sigh. "I'm tired of men."

Sugar nodded. "Boyfriend troubles?" She glanced over at Bobby as she said it.

"Oh, hell no. That was just a rebound of sorts. I'm not dating anyone."

"Hunuh, we should do lunch. Jim and I have a good friend you could meet."

I unloaded empty glasses from my tray. "I don't know. Men complicate my life."

Sugar was a striking woman with large cow eyes. Dressed in designer clothing, she was as thin and graceful as Josephine Baker. Her husband was a stockbroker for Charles Schwab and they lived in a high-rise apartment overlooking Cheeseman Park. He had a Jaguar and she drove a cherry red Mercedes 380SL convertible. I would guess Sugar brought in forty thousand a year in pocket money. She and her husband were commonly known as DINKS, double income – no kids. The fact that the girl made all her money working one day a week didn't matter.

"I think you'd like Rick, and he'll be visiting us next week.

"I'm not looking for a man right now," I replied.

"He owns a paint store in Arizona and his portfolio is sweet. You're a pretty girl and you're smart. You shouldn't ever waste your time on men who can't make your life better."

I couldn't help but think she was talking about Bobby. I handed the bartender money for the drinks I'd ordered. "I don't care how much money a man has. I care whether he treats me right."

"Any rich man can be as nice or as piggy as any poor man."

"Good point."

"So, I can pencil you in?"

"I don't know. I don't want to get mixed up with anyone."

"What if it goes well? Isn't that worth the risk?"

"Love stinks."

She sighed. "Hunuh, love and marriage are two different things." She shook her head sadly. "And I'm not asking you to marry him."

I was taken back by her comment. "Don't you love your husband?"

"Of course, I love Jim, but marriage is much easier when you aren't fighting over money."

I thought back on the fights my parents had. The times my dad gambled away our possessions and we fled in the middle of the night. I believe there were times my mother regretted loving a man like my father. "I guess it can't hurt."

"Then you'll meet Rick?" She flashed bright white teeth when she smiled. "Next Thursday, for lunch?"

I nodded. This wasn't the first time she'd tried to set me up. "Sure," I said, "but I work at four on Thursdays." This was a good way out, if the date went horribly wrong. I could fain having to go home and get ready for work at one. Lots of girls needed three hours to dress, right?

∞

The next Sunday, I was musing about what the name Baxter meant to my friendly ghost while cleaning baseboard woodwork with a drill. The paint had filled the decorative channels and all the paint stripper in the world wouldn't clean them as quickly as running a drill bit down the grooves. It was close work. Too much and you would end up cutting into the wood. I just wanted to strip off the first thirty or so layers of paint.

As I leaned in, the drill spun up my hair like a fusion powered curling iron and attached itself to my head. "#@*#@!" I said in my best truck driver language and immediately jerked on the cord, unplugging the bastard.

There was a pounding on the door. "#@*#@!" I repeated, as I made my way down the hall to the door. It was him, Mr. Timely. Sometimes I believe he waited outside my door until he heard me swear. I opened the door and motioned for him to come in. "I'll only be a minute," I said trying to untangle my long hair.

It took him about thirty seconds to figure out why I was holding the drill up to the side of my head. He pinched his lips together tightly, not trusting himself to speak. He held up a finger, turned, and darted out the front door. I know he was trying to be nice, but everyone within two miles heard him laughing. I waited, patiently. The drill was heavy, not one of those cheap generic drills, it was a full-size Makita. My arm was getting tired, so I laid my head on the newel post and waited some more.

The door opened, and Sawyer came in wiping tears from those beautiful blue eyes. He took one look at me resting my head on the newel post and went back outside.

"Aw, come on," I wailed. "I could really use some help here."

He came back in and, between fits of laughter, he managed to get the chuck in place and loosen the bit. My hair would never be the same.

"I brought your sheetrock order." He was biting on his lip, and I felt like kicking him.

"You know I have a phone. You could call and let me know when you're coming over."

"You've never given me your number."

He was right. I never thought to give it to him, and he never asked for it. I don't know if I was hurt or annoyed, but I wanted to kick him again. I found a menu from Domino's Pizza and scribbled my number on the back.

He gazed around the living room, inspecting my drywall effort. I'd gotten better as I moved into the parlor but some of the seams were going to require a lot of mud. "How did you do the ceiling in here?" he asked. "Did you hire some help?"

"No. I made a big 'T' from a couple studs and wedged the drywall against the joists before screwing it in place. Then I wedged the next piece in place."

"Brilliant."

I smiled. He always made me feel good about myself. "I still have a lot of plaster to remove."

After unloading the materials, I asked if he wanted to stay for pizza.

"Sounds good," he said looking around the room. I'm sure he was wondering where we were going to eat dinner.

"I'll need that menu back."

He appeared hurt.

"To call for Pizza," I said. "Unless you want Chinese."

"No, pizza is fine."

After calling for dinner I gave the menu back to Sawyer. "We can eat upstairs. I have a couch in the second bedroom. I don't think it's too dirty." He was wearing clean jeans and a nice sweater. "I can throw a blanket over it."

A smile played across his lips and his eyes twinkled. "I'm sure it's fine the way it is."

I felt a thrill run through my belly.

He followed me to the kitchen where I grabbed a couple bottles of beer from the refrigerator. "You look nice today," I said handing him a bottle. "Not your usual delivery uniform."

An errant blonde curl fell over his eye and he brushed it back. "Sometimes I like to wear clean clothes." He motioned to the stairs. "Shall we?"

"Sure. Let me grab some paper towels."

We had barely sat down when there was a knock at the door. Sawyer jumped up. "I got this."

"I should be paying for your dinner. It's the least I can do since you keep delivering my supplies."

"Consider it my way of taking you to dinner."

"You mean. Like a date?"

"Yeah. You never have time for any other kind of date."

He was back with the pizza a moment later. We were both silent throughout the first attack.

"Wow. I'm famished," I said grabbing another slice. Two is all I can usually eat unless I haven't eaten all day, which I hadn't.

"So," he said. "Have you lived here long?"

"No, only since last August. I moved here from Vegas."

"Didn't you like living in Vegas? I've heard it's a pretty good time."

"It's a small town. When you split with a guy you want never to run into him at the local grocery store."

He nodded solemnly. "Bad break up?"

"He drank a lot. I couldn't handle worrying about how or when he was getting home. He would call me and say he was on the way and three or four hours would pass. Then he'd call again and say he was really on the way this time. He did that one too many times. The thing is, I never cared how long he was out or where he was partying. I just hated believing he was on the way home and not showing up. I spent hours agonizing over whether or not he was in a ditch somewhere. I just couldn't endure the constant worry."

"You still love him." It was a statement, not a question.

"Yeah, probably always will. Leaving him was the hardest thing I've ever had to do."

"Not interested in dating." Again, it was a statement, not a question.

"I kind of went out with this guy from work and it was a disaster."

Sawyer raised an eyebrow. "How bad could it be?"

"Bad. I feel like a jerk. I kind of used him because I was feeling lonely."

"Moving to a new town can be a challenge."

A beeping sound came from a little black box on his hip. He glanced down and scowled. "I have to go. This has been fun. We should do it again."

"Sure," I said walking him to the door. "Stay longer next time?"

"Hope so." He leaned over and kissed me lightly on the cheek.

What the hell? He can be so charming and sexy one minute then he treats me like his sister. I went upstairs to clean up the pizza. Only two types of people wear pagers: doctors and drug dealers. I knew he wasn't a doctor. Drug dealer would explain a lot. In the back of my mind, I could hear the words of Glenn Frey, *'I'm sorry it went down like this, someone had to lose, it's the nature of the business, it's the smuggler's blues.'*

With my dad, it was pyramid schemes and gambling. With Dirk, it was drinking and women. Why was I always fascinated by trouble?

∞

So much had happened over my weekend I forgotten about my lunch date with Rick. On Thursday morning Sugar, aka Corrine to her accountant, called to get my address.

"I'll meet you there," I said. Having once been stranded without a car on a high school date left me cautious when it came to blind dates and some dates that weren't blind. I never went anywhere without a way to get back home on my own terms.

"We can pick you up," she said. "Rick rented a limo so we can have cocktails during lunch and won't have to drive. He made reservations at the Chateau Pyrenees in the Denver Tech Center."

Wow, I thought. This guy does have money. The Pyrenees is pricey and how many people rent a limo for the afternoon when a taxi would have done the job.

"No, I need to run some errands down south, so I'll be in the area. I'll meet you at the restaurant."

"Be there at noon, K?"

"I'll be there." I hung up and went to my closet to find something to wear. I wanted something nice in case I liked him and not too slutty if I didn't. I settled for black spandex pants, a thigh length, fluffy white sweater, and a wide red belt with matching pumps. I pulled my hair up into a banana clip and backcombed the curls out over my shoulders. It was cold enough for a coat, but I didn't want to ruin the look. I added pearl earrings and dabbed on a little *Skin* by Bonne Bell, my go to perfume since the tenth grade.

As I shut the front door, I saw the girl standing at the top of the stairs. I wanted to go back inside and talk to her, but I was running a tad late as it was. I opted for a wave instead. To my surprise, she waved back.

CHAPTER 18

When I got to the restaurant, Corrine, aka Sugar to her bartender, was waiting for me in the entry. She was dressed to kill in a spandex gold Lame' Versace dress, her perfect figure was outlined in elegance. I suddenly felt under-dressed.

"You look great, Hon," she said, kissing me on the cheek. "Rick is going to love you." Seizing my hand, she led me to a table near the back where Jim was standing.

"Hi, Jim," I said, sliding into the booth. "I'm sorry I'm late. Traffic was a bear."

"No biggie. We only just arrived ourselves. Here comes Rick."

The man who joined us was nice looking, tall, not too heavy. He appeared to be in his early forties, a little older than my usual dates. Dark curly hair trimmed short. Tailored suit, obviously expensive. Cufflinks by Dior.

Jim motioned for his wife to slide to the back of the booth next to me. "Excuse me," he said. "I need to drain the snake. Please order a Tanqueray Ten and tonic for me. I'll be right back."

Corrine blew him a kiss and motioned to Rick to slide in beside me. "This is the adorable girl I've been telling you about," she gushed, making me feel a little pimped. "Isn't she the cutest thing? We work together at the Gun."

He smiled shyly and I felt better. He didn't look lecherous. "Rick Winston," he said, holding out his hand.

"I'm Freja O'Connell."

I held out my hand and he lightly kissed it, not creepy but sweet. "Lovely name."

"It's Swedish. Nice to meet you."

He smiled charmingly. "Thanks for coming. Corrine said you weren't much for dating, and meeting someone new is stressful, I know. I lost my wife a year ago and dating seems so..."

"Foreign?" I offered.

"Yes. I guess I'm out of practice."

The waiter stood by the table. "I'll have a Johnny Walker Blue neat," he said and turned toward me "What would you like, darlin?"

"I'll have Yukon Jack straight up." His brow raised a fraction, but he didn't say anything. If he can drink straight scotch before lunch, I can have whiskey. Corrine ordered a Cape Cod and a drink for Jim.

I sipped my water. I wasn't good at small talk. "So, Corrine tell me you own a paint store."

Rick brightened. "Actually, I own a chain of stores. Thirteen to be exact."

"Wow. All in Arizona?"

"No, I have two in Phoenix and one in Tucson, the rest are in southern California, Nevada, and New Mexico."

"What brings you to Colorado?"

"Well, Darlin, you do." He smiled. "And golf. I like to play golf with Jim. I'm semi-pro and so is Jim."

Jim arrived just ahead of the drinks. "What did I miss?" he asked.

"Nothing," Corrine said. "Rick was telling Freja about his stores." I couldn't help wondering if they had a bet on how this lunch date was going to turn out.

Lunch was a blast. I know nothing about French food, so I allowed Rick to order for me. We started with Steak Tartare, followed by a salmon tarragon salad, Quenelles of Pike in Lobster Sauce, and Pan-seared Foie Gras complimented by a bottle of Taittinger Champagne.

Rick topped of my glass and signaled the waiter to bring another bottle of champagne. "So, you used to live in Las Vegas?"

"I lived in Boulder City most of the time. I was only in Vegas proper for about two years." I sipped more champagne knowing I was feeling the effects but a little too buzzed to care. "I worked at the Stardust when I first moved there."

"Most people think "Bugsy" Siegel was the man behind Las Vegas but that isn't true. There were a dozen motels and casinos open before "Bugsy" Siegel opened the Flamingo, including Club 91, The El Rancho, and The Golden Nugget. Bugsy was famous because he was a known mobster and was murdered six months after he opened the Flamingo. There was a lot of speculating going on."

"Yeah," Jim said. "I always thought he started Vegas."

"Actually, Vegas began as a trade route stop on the Old Spanish Trail between Mexico and California. Its laws to allowed for "quickie" divorce after six weeks of residency leading to the nick name 'Sin City.' It wasn't until 1931 that the Nevada Legislature repealed its gambling ban; the same year the Boulder Dam project began."

"You know a lot about Vegas," I said.

"It's one of my favorite places."

"It was mine too until I broke up with my ex."

"Oh, Darlin, I'm so sorry. You need to create new memories."

"Corrine swirled her champagne in her flute and sighed. "I love Vegas. The shows are splendid, and the food is to die for, not that this isn't a fabulous restaurant but the buffets there are ridiculously cheap."

"They aren't cheap," I said. "Most people leave five times the cost of the meal in the slots or at the tables."

"True," Jim said, refilling Corrine's flute. "We haven't been there in months."

Rick raised his glass. "We should go today. We can catch a flight this afternoon."

"I can't go. I have to work. I have a shift in…Oh my god, in an hour."

Corrine waved her hand, "Just call in. They won't care."

"Yes, they will. I'm the only four o'clock waitress."

"Trust me," she said, "that you never call in or miss work makes you abnormal. All the girls call off if they have something better to do."

I didn't know if it was the champagne or the company, but I definitely wanted to go to Vegas with these people.

Rick signaled the waiter. "Yes, sir."

"Could you bring us a phone?"

"Yes, sir."

A few moments later, I was giving the day manager some hogwash story about having to leave town to care for my sister. Once I was off the hook for work, I handed the phone to Rick who dialed Continental Airlines and booked four first class tickets to Las Vegas.

"We leave at five-thirty," he said. "I went ahead and booked four tickets for the ten o'clock showing of Beyond Belief. It's a great show."

To celebrate our decision, Rick ordered a round of Grand Marnier Cuvee Speciale Cent Cinquantenaire 150 liqueur at eighty-five dollars an ounce. I couldn't tell the difference between the eighty-five dollars stuff and plain old Grand Marnier. I watched Rick sip his after-dinner drink and tried to make up my mind if he was stupid rich or just stupid.

The limo whisked us to the airport for our flight. With no checked bags we went straight to the gate and boarded the plane before anyone else. I'd never flown first class and the seats were spectacular.

Jim buckled his seatbelt and turned to Rick. "I heard a couple Vegas mobsters, Michael and Tony Spilotro, were found buried in an Indiana cornfield," he said. "The paper said they were beaten to death."

Rick buckled his own belt and offered to do mine.

"I got this," I said. "But thanks."

Rick peered across the aisle at Jim. "Vegas has a colorful history. I've been following the Spilotro story since seventy-five. It started when a guy named Allen Glick managed to get a Teamsters loan and assume control of the Stardust. He wasn't what you would call Vegas royalty, young for someone with that much "juice' as Freja called it. He was in his thirties when he became president of ARGENT. ARGENT is an abbreviation of Allan R. Glick Enterprises."

The airline stewardess passed us each a warm towel and asked what we would like to drink. Rick ordered more champagne. "No sense in changing now."

We settled back while the rest of the passengers boarded. Once the plane was in the air, Rick continued with his story. "Glick hired Frank "Lefty" Rosenthal to be his assistant. Lefty had connections to Chicago. Lefty hired Tony Spilotro as the new casino boss. According to gossip, Spilotro was a hit man who also worked for the Chicago outfit."

"I thought the gaming commission didn't allow mob connections," Jim said.

"Well they didn't allow anyone with mob connections to own a casino and Glick was squeaky clean.

"I heard the Stardust was shut down for skimming," Corrine said.

"They didn't actually shut down," I said. "I was working there when the Feds came in and roped off the slot machines. I didn't know what was going on. It makes sense now."

The stewardess brought us a filet and green beans for dinner, refilled our champagne glasses, and asked if there would be anything else.

Rick nodded. "Please bring us an Irish Coffee when you pick up our dinner plates."

I was still feeling quite buzzed and wasn't sure I needed another drink, but I love Irish Coffee. I slowed down on the champagne to save room and my head.

Rick took a bite of his filet. "Skimming isn't stealing in the usual sense. It isn't exactly taking money that belongs to someone else. Skimming is hiding income from the IRS to avoid paying taxes. Casinos make and pay taxes on millions and millions of dollars. So what if a casino owner took a handful of cash and went to dinner. He owned the place, so it was his money. Who is he stealing from — himself?"

"I hate the IRS," I said. "They have too much power for their own good."

"Don't you know it, Sister," Corrine said.

Rick smiled. "Despite all the Fed's money spent on all the investigations, the only thing they could get the owners on was good old tax evasion."

Jim wiped his mouth and set down his napkin. "You're saying the IRS closed down the Stardust for walking around money?"

"It was a bit more than that," Rick said. "There were so many nickels, dimes, and quarters coming into the count room every night, it was nearly impossible to count them, so they used scales to weigh coins. The scales were calibrated so when four thousand quarters was placed in the hopper, it only registered as nine hundred dollars. The "extra" one hundred dollars in quarters were deposited in special banks for the change girls to sell."

"No Way! Those banks hold thousands of dollars." I handed handing my plate to the stewardess.

Jim said, "The paper last January said Chicago mobsters were convicted for controlling the Stardust and Fremont casinos."

Rick passed a coffee to me. "Glick wasn't indicted. He probably testified and is now hiding in South America under a new name."

"Who killed the brothers?" Jim asked.

"My guess is the mob." Rick said. "Several people may have participated. Mickey and Tony weren't well liked."

The flight was a mere twenty minutes with the time change. Waiting for us as we stepped into the warm Nevada evening, was another white stretch limo loaded with more cocktails.

From the airport, we took Paradise Road to Tropicana and headed for the Strip. The Hacienda was a couple blocks south of the Tropicana, the debut hotel for Siegfried & Roy. While I lived there, the team of magicians worked at the Lido in the Stardust Hotel. I guess with all the nasty skimming business it made sense to them to move to the Frontier.

As we passed a sign touting Sammy Davis Jr. and Jerry Lewis at Bally's, Rick said, "Did you know, the Moulin Rouge was the first racially integrated hotel in Vegas?"

Turning to get a better look out the window I said, "I always meant to see the Rat Pack when I lived here. I never quite found the time." As we made our way south, I added, "Bally's used to be the MGM before the fire in 1980. Things change so fast here. Look, there's the Barbary Coast. Good cheap drinks with great lounge acts."

David Copperfield was playing across the street at Caesar's Palace. I didn't correct Rick when he said the television show Vegas was filmed at Caesars Palace instead of the Desert Inn. Having lived here for a while, I knew a bit about the place. I didn't want to make him feel bad, or worse yet, get into a pissing contest over stupid Vegas trivia.

A bit further down the strip, the Flamingo advertised fifty-cent shrimp cocktails. "When I lived here," I said, "the buffets were usually ninety-nine cents. The Treasury had free food after midnight. That helps a lot when you don't have a job right away."

Corinne laughed. "I'll bet."

Rick added, "Unfortunately, after the Stardust incident the IRS requires every department to make a profit." He smiled at me. "Did you know Las Vegas show girls made their first appearance at the Desert Inn in 1957?"

Jim grinned. "You two are just fountains of information, aren't you?"

Rick laughed. "I love this town. I spend a lot of free time researching it's history." He reached over and caressed my knee. "One of my many hobbies. There," he said pointing out the window. "That's the Silver Slipper and Frontier; where we're going to see the show tonight. We'll go down to Sahara and circle around. It's hard to make a U-turn here."

We drove on, and the blinding lights of Las Vegas' largest porte-cochere flashed with enough vigor to incite a seizure. The Stardust. From the outside, you would never know they'd been through so much drama. The two-story motel stretched out behind the casino towards Industrial Avenue. We passed several empty lots along Las Vegas Boulevard that were surely worth millions and I wondered what the owners were waiting for.

Pointing to the Las Vegas Hilton, Rick said, "The MGM wasn't the only fire. In 1981, eight people were killed in a fire at the Hilton."

"Good thing we aren't renting rooms," Jim commented under his breath.

Passing one of my favorite places, I said, "I've had dinner in the top on the Landmark. I also had my second biggest craps table win there."

"Where was you're biggest win?" Corrine asked.

"The Las Vegas Club downtown. It wasn't more money, but the percent of winning was larger."

"How much did you win?"

"I started with three dollars and walked away with thirty-five. I was playing fifty-cent craps. Think of how much I would have won if I'd been playing fifty dollars a pop instead of fifty cents."

Rick laughed.

"It's easier to be daring when you don't have a lot at stake."

∞

The casino floor was packed. I was glad I'd dressed for lunch. Many of the women wore evening gowns and most of the men were in suits. There was the occasional low-life looking tourist in shorts and a flowered shirt, but most people respected the casinos and dressed well.

The casino bosses all dressed in the same uniform. It didn't matter if they worked at Caesars or the Hacienda, casino bosses always wore black silk suits, white shirts with either solid white or solid black silk ties, high polished black shoes and big gold cufflinks.

The cocktail uniforms were themed to match the name of the hotel and all the dealers wore black pants and an apron over their pockets so they couldn't pocket chips.

∞

After the show we had a several hours to kill before our flight home. We made our way to the valet where we had left the limousine parked. The doors of the hotel opened, and a cool night breeze blew through my hair. I turned into the breeze to keep my hair out of my face and saw him across the drive. Dirk was getting out of his Galaxy 500. He stared straight at me, and I felt the weight of our five-year relationship settle on my shoulders. I gave him a little finger wave and stepped into the limo.

"Are you alright?" Rick asked.

"Yeah. I just saw a ghost."

Corrine appeared concerned but didn't ask. I felt sick and, at the same time happy that he saw me doing well. I couldn't tell if he was drunk, he was dressed in a white shirt and black pants, so I guessed he was working as a dealer again. Since he was valeting his car, I guessed it wasn't at the Frontier. He would probably lose all his tips for the day and be trashed by morning. Henderson was a long drive home from the Frontier. I tried to shut out the anxiety I felt. I turned and stared out the window. He wasn't my problem any longer but seeing him again made my stomach hurt. Over the limousine sound system, Joan Jett sang, *"I hate myself, for loving you…"*

We stopped at Caesars to kill some time. Jim and Rick were betting heavy on craps while I was trying to hold onto the same twenty-dollar bill I started with. I love craps but the money can disappear in a blink of an eye.

Corrine and I were at a dollar blackjack table. She lost another hand and leaned toward me. "I'm going to get more money," she said, as casually as if she was offering to get me a drink. "Would you like some?"

"No. I'm good."

"You'll never make any money betting two dollars." She had been playing with hundred-dollar chips and I felt sick every time the dealer snapped up her chips and dropped them into the rack.

"I'm going to play Quarter Poker," I said, getting up from the table. I threw the dealer a dollar and made my way to the slots. About an hour later Corrine found me and showed me a stack of chips.

"I made most of it back. I'm down twelve hundred but Jim is up four."

"So, you're down eight hundred for the night. I've lost forty dollars, and I'm contemplating suicide." As tempting as it was, I knew better than to chase money. It was a lesson I'd learned the hard way.

"Rick will give you money to play with and you can win it back."

"I can't take his money to gamble. It's enough that he bought that fabulous lunch and flew us out here for the night."

She shook her head. "Hon, aren't you ever going to learn? He wouldn't do it if he didn't want to. It makes him feel good."

Although she assured me it was untrue, somewhere in my mind, I was convinced I would have to pay it back and the payback would be on Rick's terms. I could be wrong. He could just be a guy having fun, but long ago, I learned not to go into debt if I could help it.

Around six in the morning, Rick and Jim found us sipping black Russians in the lounge. The band was a performing traditional lounge act, some good jokes mixed with decent twenty-year old music.

Rick sat beside me. "Are you having fun?"

"Yes. The band is great."

"I did okay tonight; I didn't kill it but I made back the plane fare."

That was good because the plane fare was almost three thousand dollars. "I'm glad," I said, and I meant it. "The crap tables can be harsh. I've only come out ahead a few times."

"Would you like to play? We still have a half hour before we need to go to the airport." He slid a stack of chips toward me.

"No, I'm too tired to play." I slid the chips back across the table. "Too much to drink. I have to be on my game to play craps." He looked hurt. He brightened when I said, "But you can buy me another drink."

CHAPTER 19

Saturday, I was better rested, and in the zone, slinging drinks and cracking jokes. Even the cloying smell of stale cigarettes and cheap perfume didn't bother me. Jason came in and asked for me; meaning I made excellent money that night.

"You're the best waitress here," he said. "I never have to ask you to empty my ashtray; and pouring beer into a cold glass for the ladies is a nice touch of class."

"Thank you. I try to give you the service you deserve. When you're spending the kind of money you spend, you shouldn't have to ask for anything."

He handed me another twenty. "I just wanted you to know, I noticed."

Jason was awesome. It's great to have a customer comment on your skills as opposed to only mentioning your legs or ass.

Nick stopped me to say he missed me on Thursday. I didn't know whether to be flattered or paranoid. He most likely saw through my story, but he was cool about it.

Later, while standing at the bar, Nick came up behind me close enough to be flirting but probably only to be heard over the music. From the gigantic sound system *"That you won't forget about me"* wafted across the room at about ten thousand decibels.

"Someone left you a gift at the door," he said, skewering an olive from the garnish tray.

I glanced over at the door. "Dang. That's big." Next to the door admission counter was a Schefflera houseplant about the size of a living room recliner. "How I'm I going to get that home?"

Grinning, Nick said, "Bobby has a truck."

"No way am I going to ask Bobby for anything. He's like quicksand."

Nick laughed and went off to do some managerial duty.

I checked out the card on the plant. *'I had a great time. Hope we can get together again soon. Love R.'*

Rick was nice but I wasn't sure how much I liked him. I know I didn't not like him. I was flooded with guilt because he'd spent so much money on me, and I wasn't sure I wanted to go out with him again.

Back at the bar, Bobby was giving me the stink eye. "What is it?" I asked.

"Nick said you wanted me to give you a ride home. If you want to kiss and make up, don't go through Nick."

"I don't need a ride, Bobby. Nick was teasing you." I gave him a placating smile.

"Oh fine. You think this is funny? Girl, you broke my heart and now you want to get back together."

"I didn't tell Nick I needed a ride or that I thought we should get back together. Bobby, we only went out a couple times and you've been seeing London for months now."

He straightened up and put on his best macho face. "Yeah, she's the real deal."

I rolled my eyes. London was a flake. Unfortunately, Bobby wasn't much brighter.

Not more than an hour later, Bobby asked again if he could give me a ride home. "Bobby, we aren't getting back together."

"I don't understand why not. London doesn't mean anything to me. She's just fun to hang out with."

I set my dirty glasses on the bar. "I didn't mean to lead you on, but I don't want to be tied down. I have too much going on right now with the house and all."

"Could I still take that plant to your house?"

"No. That's sweet of you to offer but I'll figure something out." I was feeling bad about the way we had broken up but seriously, can't a guy tell when sex is just sex?

Bobby chilled out, and the rest of the night went smoothly. Jason was a respectful guy and an excellent tipper. I ended up making just under three hundred dollars after tipping the bartender and the valet. On the way out the door, I told Nick I would come back for the plant in the morning. I could always borrow the old Dodge from my dad.

∞

Sunday morning - ok it was afternoon before I got up - I moved my new vanity and sink once more, this time, into the kitchen. I'd already stacked several studs against the west wall and piled tools on the sink and stove. Since I had no idea what I was going to do in there, it was becoming a storage room. I had a narrow path to the refrigerator just in case I wanted to use it for beer.

I started tearing out the lathe and plaster between the living room and parlor. Revealing the structure of the walls would allow me to run new electrical wires and plumbing. Swinging a sledgehammer to the strains of Cheap Trick singing, *"I want you to want me,"* was relaxing. Black dust drifted down covering me and everything else in the house. When I reached the corner, I realized the outer walls would have to be framed over because the plaster was applied directly to the brick. To not lose too much space in the rooms I added two by twos to my shopping list to frame the outer walls and tossed in some insulation for good measure.

April isn't usually the warmest month but even seventy degrees can be uncomfortable when you're covered in dirt. The black dust turned to mud when it hit the sweat on my skin. I know, women don't sweat; they glow. Well, I was glowing in black streams that day.

Before the plaster could come down, the woodwork had to come off, which wasn't a bad idea since most of it was a total wreck.

As I worked, my ghostly friend was telling me about the home of someone who I gathered was her employer.

"…as if I would not show proper respect according to their rank and station." She paced nervously. "But the misses couldn't do with only three courses; soup, meat, and dessert. No. They had meals in five styles; so many sauces and dressings." She set her hands on her slender hips. "And the pastries, it was a regular olla podrida."

I looked up from the chunk of plaster in my hand. "A what?"

"The cake shops will get you up a dinner for a dozen. She would have none of it. Nearly threw me out on my ear."

It was fascinating to hear her talk about something she remembered. I had learned not to pressure her for details, but to gently coax information. "I love fashion. What was she wearing?"

"A silk-lined hood and a green brocade gown. Patent-leather slippers with a fragile heel. A lady is judged by her foot gear." She looked down at the black leather ankle boots she wore and frowned. "You can always tell a fine lady by her shoes.

"It was a dinner party?" As I swung for the outfield a loud banging on the door startled me into missing the inside wall and hitting the brick. Soft as it was, it crumbled leaving a serious dent. I rolled my eyes as I headed to the front entry.

I opened the door to Sawyer. "I wasn't expecting you."

"This a bad time?"

"Only if you're allergic to dust."

He shook his head. "You should wear a mask. You don't know what's in those walls."

"I'm hoping the house is pre-asbestos."

He smiled.

"So, what brings you to my side of town?" I asked.

"Sheetrock. Something you definitely can't carry in your car."

I peered past him to his truck. He had several sheets of plywood and a dozen sheets of drywall. "I won't need more drywall for at least a couple weeks maybe a month or so. It's going to take me awhile to tear out the rest of the plaster."

"Doesn't go bad." He casually leaned against the door frame.

"I don't know how to thank you."

His eyes drifted down to my feet and back up. "I'll think of something."

My belly tingled. "Are you off today? I don't want to keep you."

He grinned. "I'm all yours for the next two hours."

"Oh. I have you all to myself for two whole hours."

"If I'd known you wanted me longer, I'd have made plans."

"If I'd known you were coming over, I might have had you deliver a plant. It's at work and it won't fit in my car."

"Must be a big plant."

"And I have no idea where to put it." I waved my arm, indicating the mess that was my dining room.

"You have the space if it can handle the dust and the dark."

"Maybe you should keep it. I'm not sure I have the time to nurture anything right now."

"Why did you buy it?"

"It was a gift from a guy I went to Vegas with last week."

Some of the intensity went out of his eyes. "Well, if you don't want it..."

I brushed the hair out of my eyes and noticed my hands were covered in black dust. "I must look frightening."

The playfulness returned to his eyes. "You can be scary."

I stuck my tongue out. "Let me help you unload the truck. By the way, what do I owe you?"

"Have dinner with me and it's on the house."

I studied him for a moment. "I'm not that kind of girl. I'll pay my bills and go to dinner with you because I want to, not because you buy building supplies for me."

"Understood. Forty-nine, eighty-seven."

I ran up the stairs and grabbed fifty dollars from last night's tips. In the mirror I could see I was covered in black dust from head to toe. My blue eyes popped out in my black face. I called down to Sawyer. "I'll only be a few minutes. I need to clean up."

I heard him laugh "Take your time."

I scrubbed my face and covered my hair with a scarf. Changing into a clean pair of jeans and a stretchy t-shirt, I almost looked presentable.

On the way down the stairs, I saw the girl standing in the living room. Sawyer must have noticed me looking past him and he turned around. The girl had slipped into the parlor and out of his sight. I shivered.

"What do you think of the fireplace?" I asked.

"Your mantel looks nice," he said. "You must be proud."

"I am proud, but I see a couple of mistakes where the brick is uneven." I pointed them out to him.

He shook his head. "Amazing. I would never have seen that."

"I wanted it to be perfect."

"People will find enough flaws in what we do. No need to point them out."

I rolled my eyes. Of course, he was right. "To complete the look, I want a picture or mirror to hang above the mantle. I want something that will transcend time. Something new that looks old or something old that looks new."

"Try estate sales. We don't carry the kind of piece you're looking for."

"Not that I've seen," I said. "Let's unload the truck so you aren't late for your next appointment."

∞

After unloading the sheetrock and plywood, I followed Sawyer to the club to pick up the Schefflera. I could have called the doorman and told him Sawyer would be picking it up, but they didn't know Sawyer, and I wanted to make sure no one gave him a tough time. The music pounded as we walked in the front door. The doorman set down a Rubik's Cube and asked for Sawyer's ID.

"This is my friend, Sawyer. He's here to pick up my plant. As our eyes adjusted to the dark, we could see a chair holding a plant; taller than the doorman. Sawyer shook his head. "That's a big plant."

I held the door open as he carried the plant out. "It was a nice thought," I said. "But Rick has never seen my house. I tried to explain what I was doing but I'm not sure he was listening."

Sawyer set the plant in the back of his truck and secured it with a thin rope. "If I hadn't seen it for myself, I'm not sure I would believe it either."

"Thanks for taking care of this. It truly is a very nice gift, and I'd hate to see it die."

"Won't he wonder what happened to it the next time he comes over?"

"If I can help it, he'll never see my house."

"I feel special."

"You are special." I leaned over and kissed him on the cheek.

He wrapped his arms around me and pulled me close. "I wouldn't mind seeing more than your house."

My breath caught in my throat and panic thrummed through me. I lowered my eyes. Sawyer was ridiculously hot. *Down girl*, I told myself. *He's not for you.* It was all I could do to pull back. I couldn't afford to get distracted by another playboy, or possibly a drug dealer. Not only was I afraid of getting my heart stomped on again, I was pretty certain Sawyer, or anyone else for that matter, would think I was bat shit crazy if they heard me talking to my ghost. "You'd better go before one of us gets in trouble."

He glanced down at his watch with a sigh and kissed me on top of the head. "Oh, I can see you *are* trouble."

CHAPTER 20

After Sawyer left, I saw Ginger, aka Carolyn to her bookie, in high waisted Calvin Klein skinny jeans complete with white fuzzy leg-warmers, crossing the parking lot.

"What's up girlfriend?" she said.

"I just gave away that huge plant."

"I tried to get over here as fast as I could. I was hoping you'd introduce me to your friend."

"That's Sawyer, the guy from the hardware store."

"I wouldn't mind seeing his hardware," she said with a grin.

"He is hot, but he must have a dozen girlfriends. I see him talking to all the girls at the store."

"That's the kind of man I like. I find that most men totally see women as either a baby factory or a one-night stand. I can handle the one-night stand, it's just if you, like, want to see him again, he starts thinking about babies. Oh, they don't say that until about a month or two into the relationship."

"You don't want to have children?"

Ginger laughed. "I don't have the hips to make babies. And I might be allergic to children. It stems from the time I lost my baby doll when I was five. I knew then I could never be trusted with a child."

"You were five. You could hardly be responsible for losing a doll."

"Doesn't erase the guilt. I loved that doll. I was heading downtown to like totally check out a new brewpub. Do you want to come?"

"I should get back to work."

"You're working today?"

"On the house, not here."

"Come on. Take a day off. You might meet a construction worker willing to finish your house for you."

"I don't have any make-up on, and my hair is in a rag."

"Whatever. So, we go to a dive bar."

That wasn't a bad idea.

Over a beer, Ginger asked me why I didn't go out with Sawyer. "The man is super fine."

"I'm not sure I want to get involved with a man who sells sheetrock at a hardware store. I've had my fill of lazy men. When I settle down, I want someone I can depend on, someone who won't spend my paycheck faster than me, and someone who won't sleep with my girlfriends while I'm at work."

"And you totally know this Sawyer is like that?"

"Let's just say I don't want to risk it. Besides, he might be a drug dealer."

Surprising me, she laughed. "Girl, half the guys who come in the club are drug dealers. Where do you think all that cash comes from?"

"That might be true, but I don't go out with customers. I have my house to think about.

After a couple drinks, Ginger wondered off with a tall, dark, and handsome stranger so I waved good-bye and headed back to my car.

Driving past the parks I could see daffodils and crocus swaying in the breeze. The weather had been warm and dry the last few weeks but with Colorado, it can snow any time of the year. I needed to winter water my weeds. I could wait until summer to tackle the roof and front porch when I could count on blistering heat giving me an awesome tan.

On the way home, I stumbled across the estate sale from an old candy store across from the Oxford Hotel. There had been a fire in the store and most of the property had been destroyed. I was rummaging through the items for sale, mostly baking goods that I had no use for, when I saw this gorgeous round mirror with beveled edges.

I picked it up. It was heavy and undoubtedly antique.

"Oh, that isn't for sale," the old woman said. "I don't know how that got out here with all this other stuff."

"It's so beautiful. It would be the perfect complement to my new mantle." I was proud of the work I'd done, and I showed her a picture of the fireplace. "I'm restoring an old house on Clarkson Street."

An old man, who I assumed was her husband, ambled up to us. "Maybe it's time to let it go, Jay. She seems like a nice girl."

The old woman took the picture and studied it. I've been in a few houses in that neighborhood but never seen a brick mantel quite like that one."

"I had to build a new one, someone stole the original. That mirror would be just perfect for the house."

"Did you do this yourself?" she asked.

"Yes."

"She reminds me of someone I met a long time ago," the old man said. The woman glanced at her husband, and he nodded his head. "Things change," he said. "No one knows the future."

The woman giggled softly. Caressing the mirror, she said, "Maybe it is time for a new home. I hope it brings you as much happiness as it has given me."

"I promise to take care of it."

She smiled at me and nodded. "It isn't the first time it's been sold at a garage sale." Turning to her husband, she sighed. "Should we tell her its history?"

The old man's eyes glistened. "It's been in the family for nearly six decades, but it's only been in our home for a year."

I was surprised by his statement, and even more surprised that they would let go of an obvious family heirloom. "Should you sell it?"

"We're moving in with our daughter and she doesn't have a lot of room for memorabilia. It feels right," he said. "It should be in your house." With that, he took my twenty dollars and carried the mirror to my car.

"Thank you, again," I said. "I truly love it."

He beamed. "I can tell. Good luck with the house."

When I got home, Shannon was parked outside my door.

"Hi, Shannon. What are you doing here?" I pulled out my new mirror.

"Eric's out of town and I thought I'd come over to see what you've done to the house." She scrutinized the yard and dilapidated porch. "And to share some good news."

I unlocked the door and let her in. She wasn't any more impressed with the inside than the outside. I set the mirror down in the hallway.

"Pretty mirror." She slipped past me and wondered into the dining room. "Seriously, Fre. You should get some help. This is a huge project."

"I can do it. It's just going to require some time."

"But to live like this…" She strolled to the kitchen and took a seat at the Formica table.

I slid a stack of papers and books to the side, so she had a place to set her leather Coach bag. It was a beautiful bag, but I'm not one to carry a purse. It's impossible to leave the contents of your pockets under the table at a restaurant, unless of course you are doing something under the table other than eating; but that's a story for another time.

Shannon looked longingly at the dining table cover in plastic.

"I would just ruin it if I tried to use it now." I walked over to the answering machine and clicked play. Rick's voice greeted me. "I just wanted to tell you what a wonderful time I had. I hope we can do it again soon. Call me." He left his number for his home, his car, and his office.

"He sounds nice," Shannon said. "New boyfriend?"

"I went out with him once. He flew me to Vegas for a show."

"Wow."

"He's nice but I don't have any real feelings for him." I told her all about the lunch and the trip. Corrine must have given him my number.

"Well, money isn't everything," she said when I finished.

"Are these your plans?" she asked looking over the graph paper.

"Yes. They aren't finished yet. I can't figure out what to do with the kitchen. It has a door in the middle of every wall."

"Well, I suppose if anyone can do it, you can."

I poured us each a glass of orange juice; dropping a splash of vodka in each. "So what's the news?"

"I'll have plain juice, please."

"Whatever." I poured her a new glass of juice and kept the two originals for myself. "So?" I asked.

"So..., Eric and I are going to have a baby!"

"Oh, that's so awesome!" It was awesome for her. I, on the other hand, didn't know if I wanted kids. It isn't that I don't like kids, I love them, but it seems like there weren't enough hours in the day for everything I wanted to do as it was, and finding a good man wasn't exactly easy. "I'll bet mom is over the moon."

"Yes. She's already shopping for diapers."

"What about the house? I never heard any more about it."

Shannon sipped on her juice. "We're still looking. The one we had an offer on had roof damage and the basement leaked."

"That's too bad. I'll sell you this one cheap."

She laughed. "No thanks. It's too much work for me."

Shannon and I shared a delivery pizza and talked about raising children until late in the night. I promised to throw a baby shower and babysit whenever she needed me.

When Shannon left, I placed the mirror above my new mantle. It was the first 'finished' spot in the house. Had I actually thought it through; I would have framed and sheet-rocked the living room walls first, but finishing the fireplace gave me a sense of accomplishment I genuinely needed. I'd been in the house nearly six months and this was the only thing I had to show for my time. Everything else I'd done over the winter was behind the scenes, under the floorboards, or just a torn-up mess.

The phone rang. "Hi Mom," I said. "What's up?"

"Did you hear about Shannon and Eric?"

"Yes. I'm happy for them."

Your father and I are having a little party to celebrate this weekend. Can you come?"

"As long as it's Sunday."

"Done. Please bring your boyfriend."

"What boyfriend?"

"Freja, you've been here six months, surely you have a friend you can bring."

"We'll see, Mom. I got to go."

My mother was the salt of the earth, but I suspected in her younger years she was a bit of a firecracker; after all, she was attracted to my father, a bit of a con-man and gambler. Life had dealt her a hand that required her to work two jobs to raise five children alone. She was our caretaker even when we lived a hundred miles away. She never flinched and never complained. She was a tough role model so it wasn't hard to understand why I felt I could never live up to her standards. I was glad my sister had the courage.

I fell asleep that night imagining what it would be like to have a baby. My dreams, on the other hand, reminded me of late-night calls from the drunk tank. The worst of it was when Dirk would call from a bar to say he was on the way home and hours would pass. The whole time I worried he'd been in an accident. It was always a roller coast of fear and the last thing I wanted was to raise a child alone.

I awoke to find sunlight pouring in the slits between window frame and the foil. When I went downstairs, I found my roommate in the living room. "Has this only arrived?" she said passing a slender hand over the beveled edge. "It draws me."

"I bought it at a garage sale yesterday."

She scrutinized the mirror. "I know this piece but understand it not."

The girl had me stymied. The mirror was old certainly. Figuring out how my friend might be connected would be a serious challenge. "Can you recall where you might have seen it before? Does it have anything to do with the name Baxter?"

Her head tilled to one side and she closed her eyes. A soft smile spread over her lips. "It was a good place. I knew the love of friends."

"Could it have been in a candy store?"

Her dark eyes opened; the pain visible. "The feeling retreats, and I am lost in darkness once more."

As she faded into mist, I shuddered. I really wanted to help her.

On my way to work, I drove by the little store where I bought the mirror. The shop was closed. I hoped the lovely couple hadn't left Denver. The radio played, *"You spin me right round, baby. Right round, round…"*

CHAPTER 21

The following day the store was open. The new owners were moving furniture in. "Do you have contact information for the couple who used to live here?"

"No," said a middle-aged woman holding a bolt of fabric. "I think it was someplace in the mountains, but I don't have an address."

"Could I leave my number in case you hear from them?"

"Sure, but it isn't likely. The realtor made all the arrangements." She gave me a card.

"Thank you."

"I hope it helps."

When I got up the next morning, I called the number on the card, but the realtor wouldn't give me any information. When I couldn't tell her why I want to get in touch with them, she mumbled something about privacy and hung up. A dead end; very disheartening.

Staring at the mirror again, my practically translucent roommate declared, "I bear a connection. I recall a young woman with hair of light red. She, no, it was her brother who played music. He was my friend. We would play music and go to picnics with his family. Oh, how grateful we should be. I was not an outcast in their eyes."

"Do you remember anything else about him?"

"He also had red hair. He assisted me when I needed counsel." She turned and looked at me. "I am losing my spirits and almost my wits. Why will it not come to me?"

"I don't know, but don't give up."

∞

As I got dressed for work later that day, the phone rang. I let the answering machine pick it up.

"Hi, this is Rick. You must be busy with your house and all. I just thought I'd let you know; I might have a buyer for it. Call me."

My spectral friend perched on the bedside. She looked disconcerted. "There is a strange recording. Like a radio. Is this man offering you proof of his gratitude?"

I thought about her question but honestly didn't know how to answer. "That was my answering machine. When I don't pick up the telephone, it records the message."

"How grand!"

"Yes, it saves me having to talk to people when I'm busy."

"We didn't have a telephone. I would have been delighted to speak to someone over the wires."

I mentally reminded myself that so many things I took for granted would be very strange to her. I could only imagine finding myself in a future with self-driving cars, replicators, and Star Trek communicators. My Sony Walkman was great, but what if I could have ten-thousand songs on it?

"Do you remember anything more about the name Baxter?"

"I do not. I believe this knowledge is in my mind but out of reach. What is the malady, amnesia?"

"We'll keep trying. Something will trigger your memory."

∞

I took a week off in April to work on the house. It was windy and cold adding to my depression. What I really needed was a week on the beach with a margarita in each hand. I was tired of tearing out plaster and tired of being covered in dust every day. Removing the plaster had taken much longer than I thought it would. As much as I felt like bagging the whole project, it was too far gone to try and sell.

Rick was a constant reminder of that. He left another message asking me to call. I felt bad for not getting back to him, so I called.

"Hey Rick."

"Freja. It's so nice to hear from you. I was just thinking about coming to Denver over spring break. Arizona is crazy with tourists then. I could get a room at the Brown Palace. Would you like to stay there for a week?"

Yes, I would love to stay there instead of my house, but you know, strings. "I have to work all week; but thank you for the offer."

"Really Freja. You don't have to work that much. Let me take you on vacation. Would you like to go to Cancun?"

The offers kept getting better, making me feel even worse. "Thank you, no. I just wanted to say hi."

"Have you ever been to Hawaii?"

"I just finished my vacation. I got a lot done on the house. I have to go now."

"Wait, I have someone who will buy your house. Then you would have more free time."

"I really have to hang up now. Thank you for a wonderful trip to Vegas. It was fun. Bye."

I hung up and felt worse for calling. How do you tell a nice man that you aren't interested in pursuing the relationship?

∞

Tearing out plaster and hanging sheetrock, I spent days on end thinking about Sawyer and all the reasons why I shouldn't be thinking about him. He flirted with me, but I was never sure if he was serious. I toyed with the idea of bringing him home to meet the family for Easter Dinner. We had never been on a real date so meeting the family seemed a bit premature. I pushed the thoughts from my mind and concentrated on the house. As if remodeling a house wasn't a big enough project, how do you exorcise a ghost? Truth be told, I wasn't even sure I wanted her to leave. She was perfectly harmless apart from showing up unexpectedly and scaring the crap out of me.

∞

On Saturday night, there was a beautiful Rabbit fur coat with my name on it at the front door. The note was from Rick saying, "Happy Easter. Please call me. I have a buyer for your house." Lately, I'd been letting the answering machine pick up to avoid his calls. Sugar, aka Corrine on her passport, must have told him about my break-in because the last two times he called, all he could talk about was getting me out of that house and into something nicer. As often as I told him I liked my house, he didn't seem to believe me. He went so far as to offer to buy it from me for double the market value. It was tempting but I couldn't help believing the gift would come with strings.

Over the blaring sound of Wham singing, *"Everything she wants,"* I told Sugar I wanted to return the coat. "I don't feel comfortable keeping it if I'm not going to see him again. It feels wrong." I moved my tray over to the side to let her set hers on the bar. "Keep the coat," she insisted. "How would you feel if you gave someone a Christmas gift and they gave it back? That would hurt his feeling much more than just telling him you don't want to see him again."

"I feel guilty."

"You have nothing to feel guilty about. You went on a date and you're just not interested in him." She dumped cigarette butts from an ashtray and wiped it out with a bar towel.

"He spent so much money on me."

"Hon, he didn't spend a dime more than he wanted to. Besides, the man is worth millions. He probably didn't spend more than a month of interest on just one of his smallest investments."

I was still feeling uncomfortable as I approached Dave's table where Kitten was telling Bubbles how one of her regulars had recently paid off her car. Kitten was a smart girl, married with two kids. All her regulars knew that. It still floored me how men would spend ridiculous amounts of money on these girls who never went out with them. Not to be out done, Toy had to show off a diamond necklace she was given the night before.

"Ladies," Dave said getting up. "Mother nature is calling. I shall be back soon. Freja would you bring us a round?"

"Sure."

"How is your aim lately. Are you getting any practice?"

"Oh, it's fine." The truth was, I never went to the range without him. I was still nervous about handling my gun and prayed I'd never have to actually use it. As if he could read my thoughts, he said, "The only way to get comfortable with a weapon is to get used to handling it. Remember a tool can't do anything without your help."

That's what I was afraid of. I still had a bruise on my chest where a piece of wood on the drill press whacked me. "I'll come by on Monday for some practice if you're going to be around."

"Sure. You have the spirit and natural talent; all you need is the confidence."

∞

When I got home from work, the answering machine was going crazy. Six missed calls. I click the play back.

Rick: "I hope you got the coat. I couldn't resist. I have a friend who is an appraiser. I gave him your number. Call me."

Mom: "Freja, are you home?" Click.

Mom: "Freja?" Click.

Rick: "Freja, the appraiser's name is Michael Duran? Call me." Click.

Mom: "Freja, I have some wonderful news." Click.

Exasperated Mom: "Freja, Connor and Bridgett are engaged. Isn't that wonderful? The wedding is set for September ninth. I'm so looking forward to meeting Rick. Shannon told me all about him. He sounds like a good catch. Call me." Click.

That was my mother; always wondering why I couldn't seem to catch a man. The truth was, at the moment, I had more men in my life than I could handle.

I rewound the tape and went to bed.

∞

The next morning, I dressed in jeans and a thick grey sweater. It was cold and snowy as I headed to Lakewood for Easter Dinner. I turned over all the clues in my head but couldn't link my roommate to the name Baxter or to the candy store where I'd bought the mirror. I needed more to go on. There might be a clue in her accent, but I still couldn't place it.

Mom was waiting by the door when I pulled up. I could see in her face she was disappointed that I was alone. "Hi, Mom," I said, kissing her on the cheek.

"No Rick?"

"It was just one date."

"Good to know you're dating. Come in. The ham is getting cold."

Dad got up from the living room recliner. "How's the house project going?"

"I should shoot you for that one, Dad."

He laughed heartily. "You're the only one of my kids who could tackle it. You'll thank me in the end." He ruffled my hair as we walked into the dining room where Shannon was setting the table.

"I meant to ask you the other day," she said, "did you ever go out with Nick?"

I grabbed a stack of plates and helped her set the table. "No."

"Any hope?"

"Not likely."

Connor and Bridgett came in wishing everyone a happy Easter. I looked around but didn't see Sheamus and Jackie Jo. "Where's Sheamus?"

Mom set a large ham in the middle of the table. "Eric, Aiden and Sheamus are in the garage. Your dad bought a new car."

"I'm here," Jackie Jo said coming out of the bathroom. I had to tinkle. What did I miss?"

Shannon handed her a bowl of fruit salad. "Fre didn't bring a date."

Jackie reached in her pocket and pulled out a ten.

"I can't take your money," Shannon said. "I knew she wouldn't bring him."

"But I can take it," said Aiden coming through the garage door.

"Really guys. You all took bets on whether or not I'd have a date?"

Aiden punched me in the shoulder. "I'm four for four."

That was my family in a nutshell. If there was a question about anything, my family would take bets on it.

During dinner Bridgett asked Shannon to be a bridesmaid at their wedding.

"I'm going to be big as a house by then, Bridgett."

"Oh, I know." Bridgett said. "It will be so beautiful. It's good luck for all the bridesmaids to be pregnant. My maid of honor is due in September."

I nearly spit out my milk. "Isn't that cutting in a little close."

Bridgett smiled. "She's due at the end of the month. We'll be married by then."

The rest of dinner was spent discussing wedding plans and baby names. Feeling a little left out, Aiden and I went out to look at dad's new Ford Taurus. Sitting in the front seat we shared a Pepsi being careful not to spill in the seats.

"It's just you and me now," Aiden said. "The bachelors."

"You really should tell mom and dad. You know they love you. They'll understand."

Aiden blew out a sigh. "I don't know how to tell them. Should I just announce it over desert. Hey mom and dad, I'm gay."

I took a sip of the Pepsi. "I don't know. That's kind of how you told me. When my girlfriend in high school had a crush on you, you just told me girls didn't do much for you."

"I begged you not to tell anyone."

"I didn't. You told Shannon when we were camping. I don't know how or when Connor found out."

Aiden rolled his eyes. "I told him before we got out of high school."

"Does Sheamus know?"

"I don't think so, but I could be wrong. He's never tried to set me up with a girl."

"I think you should tell them. Take them to lunch or something. Do you have a boyfriend?"

"Yeah."

"You should let us meet him."

"I'll think about it."

∞

Early on Monday morning I slipped on my jeans and a light sweatshirt and headed to the range for a couple hours of shooting. Dave was right, and after a few hours of practice, I was less intimidated by the gun. I was a long way from becoming a big-game hunter, but at least I could clean my gun without my hands getting sweaty.

The downside of going to the shooting range with Dave was the fact he was sexy. It had been months since I'd been with a man and between Dave and Sawyer, my libido was flipping out.

We had just finished packing away our guns when Dave leaned into me, pressing me against the wall. "Do you have any idea how hot you are?"

I pressed my hands on his chest, not pushing him away, just feeling his powerful muscles under his t-shirt. "Um. I…"

His dark eyes twinkled and there was the roughness of passion in his voice. "You're speechless?" His lips were almost touching mine.

"I truly like you Dave…"

"But," he said pulling back. "There's always a but."

"I'm not ready for a relationship."

"I don't know if you've noticed but I'm not a relationship kind of man."

"I'm not ready to have a non-relationship that involves sex."

"Too bad. I've been told I'm gifted."

I didn't doubt that for a minute. That was a whole different problem. I might get addicted to his gifts and I wasn't good at sharing."

CHAPTER 22

May is spring in some places, but Colorado doesn't have regular seasons. We get seventy degrees one day and twenty the next. This was one of those seventy-degree weeks and I wanted to plant some grass in the front yard. My neighbor, Haddie, whose yard was right out of a *Better Homes and Gardens* magazine, had offered to help me restore the patch of lawn and plant some roses under the front picture window; the window that was still covered by an old door. The porch was sinking into the ground, pulling the weathered roof away from the house. No way climbing roses would fix that. I needed to re-pour the cement floor and add new posts. I really wanted to buy a whole new front porch and have someone else install it. Today I would settle for stacking garden pavers and planting some potted roses.

Another trip to the hardware store and I was another two hundred dollars poorer. After loading my cart with grass seed, flowers, and the makings of a raised rose bed, I picked up a ceiling fan with a light to eventually go in my bedroom, and a closet organizer I wouldn't need for months. I also ordered another dozen drywall sheets.

Sawyer was in deep conversation with a man in a dark suit, so I didn't interrupt them. The suit took him into the offices in the back. I wasted another twenty minutes, hoping for a chance to say hi, but I started to feel like a stalker.

When I got home, the answering machine was blinking. Four hang-ups and a message from Rick. "I have a great deal on a condo by Cheeseman Park. Nothing down and only eight hundred a month. I'll be in town next week. I hope I can see you. Call me."

I considered changing my out-going message to tell everyone they had the wrong number. The message currently said:

"Hello. If you are selling something, I have everything I need. If you are wanting to buy something, I am sold out. If you are soliciting money for charity, I am broke, but if you are a friend, you have three seconds to compose an outstanding message which will inspire me to call you back."

None of the messages were ever inspiring.

∞

The next day while getting ready for work, the girl abruptly appeared on my bed. "I must know, what is the meaning of this you do?" she asked.

Startled, I dropped my hot roller and it rolled into the closet. "I'm curling my hair," I said chasing down the errant roller. I sat back down at my dressing table. Removing the rest of the rollers from my hair, I carefully placed them on the metal rods. The girl quietly watched as I combed and teased my hair into immense deluge of blond curls.

She cocked her head to the side. "You have lovely curls and surely are the envy of many socialite friends who must tie rags into their wet hair each night to effect curls of such grace."

"Thank you," I said. My hand shook a little as I applied my eyeliner. As many times as I'd seen her, the fact she was a ghost could rattle my nerves at moments. She was making casual conversation now, but at any moment, she could blink out and then reappear when I least expected her.

"I cannot wear my tresses long," she continued, "as it has great tendency to tangle. Despite the barber's recurrent shearing and the fervent use of a stiff brush my curls insist on springing into crisps waves, refusing to lie flat."

Her black hair was cut into a short bob held tightly to her scalp with a headband of sequins and peacock feathers. A puzzled frown wrinkled her brow.

"You're getting dolled up once again. Are you going out on the town or to a swanky party?"

"No. I have to dress like this for work. I wait on tables."

"You're a working girl then?"

She was silent for several heartbeats, and then, "What kind of industry is it that would have you dress in that manner to serve food?"

"I serve cocktails."

Her eyes got impossibly larger. "Jeepers Creepers! You can't mean to say you work in a gin joint?"

"You might call it that."

She frowned and her nose crinkled ever so slightly. "I've no earthly right to grumble, having done my share of gigs in a friend's speakeasy. Is it a nice one?"

I didn't know how to answer her. What's a nice bar? Certainly not one with half naked women, but as topless clubs went, yes, it was nice one. "It's okay, I guess."

I sprayed my hair in place. "Tell me about your fabulous dress. You look like you're going someplace special. Dinner or a night out on the town perhaps?"

She ran her hand over the beaded bodice. "I adore this dress. It makes me feel positively ritzy. Here in the middle-west, did you ever see such a thing?" She took a slight bow and began to sing. "Pack up all my cares and woe. Here I go, singing low. Bye-bye, blackbird."

"You have a beautiful voice."

"I very much love to sing. One of my favorite songs is *I Wonder Who's Kissing Her Now*." She looked tickled remembering it.

I was excited. "I heard you singing that song the first day I saw you." She knew songs by Joe Cocker and Harry Nilsson, that was a start. Both songs were older, from the sixties and seventies although she appeared younger than me.

She nodded. "I know not how it comes to me." Staring off into space, a tiny crease formed between her brows. "I love to sing *Stepping Out*."

"Oh. I know that one, too. Joe Jackson, Right?"

She sat down on the bed once more and the smile slipped away. "It's as if my mind is filled with shadows, and of a sudden, a memory comes to me much like a flash of light. I can see that small illumination but nothing else." Her eyes filled with tears. "Why can't I see more?"

Now I was convinced she didn't know she was dead. How do you tell a person something like that? "Let me play some songs for you. Music could help you remember. Maybe Baxter is the name of a singer."

I slipped past her to the shelf where I kept my albums. I couldn't avoid all the construction dust, but it helped to keep the stereo under plastic in my bedroom. I started with Joe Jackson. Setting the album on the turntable, I cranked the volume and started bopping to the rhythmic sounds. Looking at her I could see she didn't like the song. "What is it? Do you remember something bad?"

"No. I've never heard this song before."

"Could you have heard it done by someone else?" I couldn't think of anyone who might have covered the song.

"No, I don't believe I have." She shook her head. The sequins on her headband sparkled and the small peacock feather danced gracefully. I'd seen a headband like that somewhere, but I couldn't place it. It was totally vintage. Then it crossed my mind that she must have died in that dress and it wouldn't have been vintage at the time. Goosebumps raced up and down my arms. "I'm going to play Bye, Bye Black Bird. You said you know that one."

She watched as I searched through my albums. I was sure it was on one of my collections. Not having luck there, I went to the album I knew she would remember, *A Little Touch of Schmilsson in the Night*. She studied my every move as I started the album, fascinated by the turntable.

"I've never seen one of these contraptions before. It makes no sense in my mind."

"It's very new. I just bought it a couple weeks ago."

The music filled the room and Harry's angelic voice sang, *'Lazy moon, come out soon.'*

"Yes, I know this one." She began to sing along, gliding around the room. During the break between songs she said, "Thank you ever so much. The sound of music fills my heart with warmth."

"I'm going to see if I can find more songs you know. There's a great record store on 13th Avenue that has just about every song recorded."

∞

On my way to work I stopped at Wax Trax. My ghost liked older songs, so I purchased an album by Glenn Miller, two by Bing Crosby, and one by Benny Goodman. I wasn't crazy about Benny Goodman, but I enjoyed Glenn Miller.

Work was a real drag that night. It was hard to keep my mind on work. It became my mission to know who my misty roommate was, and why she was trapped in my house. Don't get me wrong—I liked the company, when she wasn't startling me. It was like having a roommate who never ate your food or left the bathroom a mess.

When I got home from work, I played a Bing Crosby album. My wispy friend appeared; sitting on my dressing table, which was actually an old, peddle-operated Singer sewing machine. I'd learned to sew on it as a child and when my mother was going to toss it out, I snatched it up. I don't collect antiques; I just needed a table. The little drawers on the sides were perfect for stashing things like clippers and tweezers the other side held what little jewelry I still owned.

I played *Swinging on a Star* by Bing Crosby, but she didn't know the song. *The Way You Look Tonight* by Fred Astaire didn't ring any bells either.

"These are lovely tunes," she said, "but I know not the lyrics."

Next, I played *String of Pearls, Moonlight Serenade,* and *In the Mood.*

She smiled. "Glenn Miller is a local boy." She was looking at the album cover lying face up on the bed. "He was a talented trombonist from the University. If my recollection is true, he went to New York. I remember him playing with a local band here; Boyd Senter's band."

I was excited, yes, shocked that she knew Glenn Miller and that he was from Colorado. This was a real clue to whom she was. If I could find out more about him, it might lead me back to her. Odd that she knew of him but didn't know his most famous works. She most likely didn't have access to his music. I scanned the jacket to see when he had recorded the album. On the cover was a car with Indiana plates from 1940 but the copyright date was 1975. I'd bought it new. The music must have been remastered. Unfortunately, there were no liner notes to speak of. My best guess was late thirties to the early forties.

I was off the next three days and hoped to get the last of the plaster down before returning to work on Wednesday, so while working on the sheetrock and stripping the trim I played music for my friendly ghost. When I went to work, I left the radio on to keep her company. Most of the newer music didn't impress her but she loved Van Morrison, Carlos Santana, and B. B. King. It was surprising how many songs had been covered by current artists. She would sing along with the songs she knew, occasionally learning some different tunes. I played her favorites over and over, hoping she would remember something new.

"I love to listen to the wireless. I so enjoy the stories and the sounds of George Gershwin. His musical hour was preceded by the Farm Report which we never missed."

My ears perked up. She was remembering something. "Who was with you?"

She glanced over at me and looked surprised to see me there. "I cannot see the faces, though it must be my family. I feel at home there by the wireless."

"What were you listing to at the time." I set my reciprocating saw down. "You looked like you were enjoying yourself."

"I believe it was the Grand Ole Opry. They changed the name you know."

"What was it before?"

"National Barn Dance. Is that not a ridiculous name?"

"Do you like Country Western music?"

She drifted past me and settled on a five-gallon bucket of drywall mud. "I think western music is in my repertoire but not my preferred."

While yanking the remaining slabs of plaster from the parlor walls, I asked her if she might be a professional singer. The dress she was wearing surely should have been on a stage and I couldn't picture her wearing the sequin headband with the fluffy peacock feather to the park.

She thought about it for a while. "It is certainly possible. While you play many songs of which I am familiar, I'm unacquainted with these arrangements."

"I'll keep trying to find recordings you'll recognize." I wasn't sure when they stopped producing 78s but my turntable still had a 78 speed. It was worth a try.

Hefting my Saws-All up to the door jam, I cut through the nails holding the woodwork to the wall. It was less damaging that trying to pry it off. The heads of the nails were small, but they did a real number when I tried pulling them out. "It would be nice to have some friends to help tear this down and haul it out."

She began singing, "*Nobody knows when you're down and out.*"

"Wait, I know that song." I brushed the plaster dust off my hands. Come with me," I said. "I have that song by Janis Joplin. You sound just like her."

Up in my bedroom, I took the plastic sheets off my album collection. "Here, listen to this."

The arrangement was different, but the voice was spot on.

I played a couple more albums for her. She knew all the words to *T for Texas* and *Who's Sorry Now*.

"These songs were staples for my band. Nertz, Freja! I had a band. My memory is returning!" She grinned showing perfect white teeth against her red cupid lips. She looked so happy.

"Who was in your band?"

That quick; the smile faded, and she shook her head. "It's all cluttered up. I sing. On occasion, play the piano. I remember playing the organ in church when I was very young."

"Don't stress out. For now, let's just play some more music."

I tuned the Sony to a country station where Randy Travis was *'diggin' up bones.'* It was a nice break from my usual rock. I went back to work tearing out plaster. After about an hour, she asked me to change the station. Evidently, eighties country music wasn't to her liking. I tuned into National Public Radio and she glowed. This was her element. For me, tearing out plaster to Beethoven wasn't as satisfying as hitting the wall with a sledgehammer to White Snake.

CHAPTER 23

Leaving for work the next day, I saw Haddie pruning her roses. Slipping her sheers into her apron pocket, she struggled to her feet.

"Hi," I called to her. "Those are beautiful. I wish I had a green thumb."

"It's just a hobby. At my age I have a lot of time to devote to flowers."

"Well, it definitely shows. By the way, do you know anything about Glenn Miller?"

"He's a Colorado boy. I'm pretty sure his plane went missing over the English Channel during World War Two. I never cared for his musical style."

"He must have died young. When did he have time to write all that music?"

"I don't remember when he was born. Some artists are very prolific."

"I suppose. Too bad, though."

"War always consumes the best and the brightest."

I waved good-bye and headed for work.

That night I asked the DJ what he knew about any artists from the thirties and forties or if he knew where I could find early jazz recordings. "I'm familiar with the music," he said as he wrote down the line up of entertainers to be on stage next. "It's not what I usually listen to but it's classic stuff."

"I have a friend who said Glenn Miller went to CU Boulder. Didn't you go to school there?"

"I was there for a year, but I don't know about Miller. Hold on, I need to get my girls up." He pulled the microphone close to his mouth and read off the grease board, "Now on the red stage, stage four we have the irresistible Isis. Joining you on the orange stage, stage number three will be the alluring Athena. Passionate Persephone will be stepping up on blue number two, and right here in front of me on the purple stage is the electrifying Electra." He scanned the room to see if the girls made it to stage and erased the top line of the grease board. "I've heard he was originally from Nebraska and later moved to Fort Collins or Fort Morgan. Or Fort Lupton, one of those fort places. It would make sense that he went to CU. You should ask Ted Goldstein."

"Who's Ted?"

He pointed across the room to the guy sitting in the shoeshine booth. "He usually comes in on the weekends and sometimes on Wednesdays. He works in Lakewood at the Government Archives on Sixth and Union."

"Thanks." I headed over to introduce myself to Ted. He was older, receding hairline, and hawk-like eyes. His button-down shirt had small, embroidered polo player on the pocket. He wore dress slacks and carried a leather briefcase. Aurora was just collecting her money for a foot massage when I arrived.

"Can I buy you a drink?" he asked Aurora with the gravelly voice of a two-pack a day smoker.

"Sure," she said, batting her fake eyelashes. "I'll have a Jack and Coke. Leave it here, I have to pee."

Ted smiled at the departing girl. "And I'll have a Bacardi and Coke," he said, handing me a hundred-dollar bill. "Bring me about twenty ones if you don't mind."

"By the way," I said, "I'm Freja.

"Freja?"

"Yes, it's Swedish. I understand you work at the Government Archives in Lakewood."

"It's the National Archives at the Federal Center, and yes I do."

"Cool. Let me get your drinks. I have some questions, if you don't mind."

"I always have time for a pretty girl."

When I returned, he paid for the drinks and tipped me ten dollars.

"Thank you," I said. *Information and money. Bitchin'.*

He motioned for me to sit down. It was pretty slow, but I didn't like us sitting with guests. I thought it was kind of rude to my other guests if they were watching, especially if they wanted a new drink or change. I set my knee on the chair.

"I'm looking for information about Glenn Miller."

"The Glenn Miller?"

"Yes. I have a friend that said he used to play in bands around Denver."

He sipped his drink and nodded. "The library should have several the old newspapers on microfiche, that would be a good place to start looking. I'd check out the entertainment pages, too. What year are you talking about?"

I had no idea, but it had to be before World War Two. If he was twenty-something during the war he must have gone to CU in the late thirties. "Sometime in the thirties or early forties, I think. He died in World War Two."

"The National Archives has military records. How old is your friend?"

I couldn't answer that. She appeared to be about twenty, but I had no clue how long she'd looked like that. Aurora returned and handed me her drink ticket.

When I didn't answer Ted, he said, "Are you looking for his family or other friends of his?"

"Other friends."

"Why don't you come out to the Federal Center on your day off and I can help you look. We have war records dating back to the revolution. If Glenn Miller died during World War Two, we might have a last known Colorado address. From there you might find people who knew him.

"That would be awesome. Thank you, and thanks for the great tip."

He smiled as his eyes swept over me from head to toe. "You're welcome. I love to help."

Before I left the booth, Aurora said, "You should ask Gene. He's a history teacher."

I thought about it for a moment. Gene seemed like a nice enough guy. I'd met him over the Christmas break. Quirky as he was, he loved to match his shirt and tie to Desire's costume, going so far as to change his shirt and tie when she changed costumes. When Desire wasn't working, he would spend money on Faith, but didn't change his shirt or tie for her. It creeped me out that he was a high-school teacher and seemed overly infatuated with the young-looking girls. Still, it wouldn't hurt to find out what he knew about Denver during the thirties and forties. Unfortunately, it was the end of May and, due to finals and graduation, Gene hadn't come in for a while.

∞

The Federal Center was closed on Sunday, so I put it off until Monday. On the way there, I stopped at Wendy's for my usual breakfast. The drive out 6th Avenue was pleasant in the middle of the day but sucked big time during rush hour.

Ted met me at the door. He was dressed in a dark suit, carrying his leather briefcase; in which I imagined held precious state secrets.

"Hi PTY."

"Huh?"

"PTY. Pretty Young Thing."

"Really? You're quoting Michael Jackson?" That was too geeky.

After checking us in at the reception desk, he led me to an elevator. The second floor held America's military history. There were few people sorting through the microfiche, so it was easy to find a couple readers next to each other. After showing me how to search the files, Ted ogled me like a rare steak.

"Can I do anything else?" he asked.

"No. I got this." I had the urge to move a couple of machines down.

"Remember to return them exactly how you found them." He showed me once more.

He helped me search for a few minutes and then asked, "What's the connection again with your friend?"

"She said she knew Miller when he lived in Denver. I think she's looking for his family or something. She has trouble with her memory. I'm trying to help her sort out her past."

"That's sweet of you." He stared at me for a moment. "You sure do a lot for this friend of yours. The obits might be a good place to start."

"The obits?" I didn't have her name yet.

"There are dozens of obituaries posted every week. They usually list surviving family."

"Well, duh. I guess I should have thought of that."

"Narrowing it down to the day he died would help a lot."

We found Glenn Miller in the war records, but nothing that would tie him to my house. He did indeed come from Colorado, but I couldn't make a connection to my ghost.

I wrote down his information. I wasn't sure how long before him she had died but I was narrowing it down. It must have been before December of 1944.

In the chair next to me, Ted planted his hand on my leg, not on my knee, but high enough to make me uncomfortable.

"Excuse me," I said jumping up. "I need to use the little girl's room."

He pointed down the hall. "On the left."

In the Ladies room I splashed my face with water. Ted was probably in his late forties or even early fifties and that wasn't a high school ring on his left hand. Now I had to figure a graceful way out of this. Running out the back door wouldn't work, as I might need the archives again. I went back to the reader and pretended nothing had happened.

Ted seemed to guess his move had rattled me and he was less creepy the rest of the day, often going off and doing whatever it was he did there.

Searching the census reports for the Denver area. I found the name Baxter, but it was a dead end. Maybe it was the name of a friend. Without knowing which County to look through, it was impossible to narrow the search to something manageable. My airy friend spoke as if she was still concerned with alcohol prohibition, but the war came later. She must have known Miller before he joined the service.

Next stop was the library to find out when Glenn Miller wrote his most famous works. After hours of searching I discovered *A String of Pearls* was written by Eddie de Lange and Jerry Gray, and then released by Glenn Miller in 1941. *In the Mood* was written by Joe Garland in 1939 and recorded on Bluebird by Glenn Miller and his band in August of that year. I was down to sometime between December 5, 1920 when prohibition began and the release of *In the Mood* in 1939; a nineteen-year window.

∞

When I got home, I tossed my notebook on my desk and threw myself across the bed. Ted's pass had discouraged me. I was hoping for a platonic relationship. He wasn't a bad looking guy. He dressed in sharp designer clothes and had the body of a man who cared about his health even though he smoked. He always carried a leather briefcase that made him look important. The real issue was that the man was married and at least fifteen years older than me. Why was it, that guys you liked, didn't like you, and ones you didn't like, sprang up like the dandelions in my yard?

The girl sat next to me on the bed. "You are all balled up about something. Did you have a sour day?"

I didn't tell her I was searching the archives because that would have led to telling her what year this was. I didn't think she knew was dead and I didn't know how to tell her. "Men."

She smiled softly. "They can be wearisome. There is a very wide gulf between what a man says and what he means."

"There is usually a much wider one between what he wants and what he gets."

Her eyes twinkled. "I find you must ask them a question in just the right manner to get the answer you wish to hear."

I sat up. "You're right. I guess I've been asking the question wrong." I told her I'd gone to the record store to find music and the clerk made a pass at me.

"Why, the impudent creature!" She sighed. "I cannot be totally surprised when you dress as you do."

"What?" I was wearing faded jeans and a t-shirt.

"You have all the charms though your attire leaves little to the imagination."

I couldn't imagine what she would think if she saw me in my work uniform.

CHAPTER 24

Some bartenders flip bottles, some bartenders tell jokes, some bartenders are charming, while others set their hats on fire. I arrived at the bar as Dan's black cowboy hat petered out. As usual, the crowd at the bar enjoyed the show. If he wasn't setting fire to dried coffee creamer, he was flirting outrageously with the girls. Dan tried to sleep with every girl he met, at least that's the way it seemed to me. He once received an award for his *'silver tongue'*. Come to think of it, he got that for asking a girl when she was due. Unfortunately, the girl wasn't pregnant and left the club in tears. It was rumored that the maintenance man made repairs from an old waterbed frame he got from Dan. They say they were notches carved into the headboard for every girl he nailed. The summer of love was over, and the winter of AIDS was turning everyone cold. Guys like Dan made me nervous.

When I approached the bar, Dan blew flame from his mouth and sauntered over to get my drinks. "That uniform looks great on you, but I rather see it on my bedroom floor," he said, smiling like the Cheshire cat.

"Are you offering to do my laundry?" I said. "I can bring it over tomorrow. I have a couple more things that need washing while you're at it."

He wasn't a bit phased by my retort. He was used to being turned down several times a night. It was surprising how many times he succeeded. I gave him my order and paid the bill.

Shotgun Willies attracts a lot of major sports stars and professional musicians. Most of these stars were friendly if not generous. In fact, one of the pro running backs had a crush on Spice, aka Linda to her bank. He spent a lot of money on her during the off-season.

This particular night, I was working stage six and the surrounding tables when one of Denver's more famous sports stars came in. Jupiter and Venus were doing double trouble on stage. The girls wear five and six-inch stiletto heels, and the stage floors are black glass. Needless to say, they can be slick. This moron sat down at the stage. and bumped the college kid next to him. "Hey, you know who I am?"

Of course the kid knew who this guy was, everyone in Denver knew him.

"Buy me a beer," the super-jock said loud enough for me to hear from the other side of the stage, and that's saying something because the music in the club was about as loud as a fighter jet taking off.

I came around to see if I could calm him down. He was totally trashed at this point and I wasn't comfortable bringing him any more alcohol.

"Bring me a beer. He's buying." He bumped the kid again. The poor college kid, thoroughly enamored, would probably be telling his kids and grandkids about this night for years to come.

"You don't have to buy the beer," I said to the kid.

"Oh, no. I'd love to buy it."

"Come on, he's had enough. He can hardly sit upright in his chair."

At this point, our celebrity began pitching dimes onto the stage. A guy who was worth multi-millions was bumming beers and throwing dimes at the entertainers. I was appalled.

Nick was standing by the bar signing drink tickets for Saturn and Mercury. When I told him what happened, he came over and explained how dangerous it was to have coins on the stages.

Moron didn't care. "You know who I am?"

"Yes, I do," Nick said. "You're 86'd."

Now the kid at the stage was mad at me. Not that I would be missing out on a big tip; college kids were notoriously cheap, except the guys from D.U., those were mostly trust-fund babies, but his lack of understanding upset me.

∞

Gene was sitting at a table near the center of the room. He had his sweater tied around his neck like a man from a fashion ad. I slunk over to him, feeling bad. He and Jupiter were talking about the latest scandal with Jessica Hahn and Jim Bakker. Apparently, the Assembly of God church had him defrocked.

"People get so upset about extramarital affairs," Jupiter said. "I don't understand all the hubbub about Gary Hart. Just because you have a girl sitting on your lap doesn't mean you wouldn't make a good president."

Gene shook his head. "It's that he lied about it."

"Everyone lies."

She was right. It was rare to find anyone who was truthful all the time. Setting Gene's drink down asked, "I hate to interrupt, but how much to you know about Denver's History?"

"It's not my area. I teach American History. You look upset."

I told him about my run-in with the super-jock. By the time I vented the worst of it, Neptune sat down and asked for a Sex-on-the-Beach. I collected her drink ticket and went back to the bar. Apparently, Faith and Desire were off that day.

Back at the table, I set the drink down. "Seven dollars," I said. "Is there anything you can tell me about Glenn Miller?

Gene gave me a ten and waved me off when I tried to hand him back the change.

"Well I do know a bit," he said. "Glenn Miller attended Fort Morgan high school. He graduated in 1921 or 1922. From there he went to college in Boulder."

"1921? Are you sure?" That placed him in Denver in the early twenties, older than I'd thought. The dress my roommate wore made more sense now, not what I would call a flapper, but it had a dropped waist and handkerchief hemline. For months, I'd been searching the thirties and forties, narrowing it down by the song releases. I realized then her dress could be from the early twenties.

Gene wrapped an arm around Jupiter "He played music around Denver for a few years. He joined the service and his plane went down in 1944. What a shame. He was a talented man. I guess it's true what they say; the good die young." He slid his hand to the back of my knee. "Let me take you to dinner. There is a lot more information I could share, but it's noisy here."

I backed away, disengaging his hand. I leaned over the table so he could hear me over Soft Cell's *Tainted Love*. "You know the rules. I can't meet you outside the club."

He smiled. "I know quite a bit about Denver and more than that, I can find out anything you want to know."

"I'll find it in the library but thanks for what you told me. I didn't know Glenn Miller played music in the twenties. He was more popular in the thirties and forties."

∞

Later, when Ted came in, he sat at his usual table. He set his briefcase on the floor beside his chair in the usual spot. I imagined he was meeting some underworld spy, selling government secrets. The briefcase was probably filled with his mail. Mary Jane, Sativa, and Indica sat down. So much for meeting a foreign emissary.

I asked him what he knew about old jazz music as I delivered his usual Bacardi and Coke. "I'd like to find some old recording of movies or music from the 1920s. I was hoping the archives might have some old recordings."

"The Federal Archives would have information on military service, but I don't believe they would let you borrow any recordings they might have. If it isn't governmental property, they wouldn't be storing the information there."

"You mean they might have recordings from Area 51?" My imagination flitted to the briefcase.

Ted laughed. "If they do, I haven't seen those, and I doubt they would let you see them either."

I changed his ashtray and set his drink on a fresh napkin. "Video One or Blockbuster Video have a nice selection of popular movies but not really what I'm looking for."

"Did you try silent films? The soundtrack was often musical."

"That's a great idea."

"Why don't I meet you at the library tomorrow," he said. "They have a collection of film and sound recordings. I could help you with your research."

There was no way I was going to meet Ted anywhere after the fiasco at the Federal Center.

"I wanted to the share old recording with my friend. She's like super into old jazz."

"I don't think they allow these items to be removed from the Library. You should have your friend come with you."

"That won't work."

"Why not?"

"She doesn't leave the house." No way, I was going to tell him she was a ghost and couldn't leave the house.

"Is she too old?"

"Yeah, that's it. She's incredibly old. She was born somewhere around the turn of the century."

"I can't picture you hanging out with an eighty-year-old friend."

How could I have been so blind? Of course, Haddie would be about the same age as my roommate. That's whom I should be talking to, not this guy.

"She's my neighbor," I lied. "She loves to sing. I was hoping some old recordings would help her memory."

Ted offered to buy drinks for the girls sitting at his table. I collected their tickets and before I left, Ted scribbled a phone number on his napkin. "Call me if you change your mind and want my help." His smile seemed sincere, hardly lecherous at all.

CHAPTER 25

I got up on Sunday morning, bright and early for me, (about ten), and with sledgehammer and catspaw, I went to work to the sounds of Tina Turner belting, *"What's love got to do with it?"* I used pliers to pull out the nails. Pliers are a very useful tool for rounding off bolt heads and giving you blood blisters; only out done for damage by the vice-grips. The lathe was nailed on with square-sided nails. Interesting. They had to be made by pouring hot metal in molds. You would have thought they would be rounded on at least one side. I thought about keeping them because they were kind of cool. By the time I'd pulled out about five or six hundred nails I was over it and into the trash they went.

My vapor roommate was making regular appearances now and talked more often. "Is everything going smoothly with you this day?" she said, appearing on her usual five-gallon bucket of drywall mud.

Yanking on a piece of plaster, I said, "Most men are totally lame. They either sponge off a girl, cheat on a girl, or they can't put an intelligent sentence together."

Little lines formed between her brows and she blinked at me. "Most men can't walk?"

I stopped mid yank. "Huh?"

"Most of the gentlemen you are acquainted with are lame. Is it polio?"

I laughed. "No. That's what I call a guy who is un-cool or uh, unacceptable, stupid, or a jerk"

"Un cool? You slay me. I'm to guess you mean a Reuben."

It was my turn to blink. "Rueben?"

"Yes. An unsophisticated man, a bumpkin."

"Yeah. That's it," I said pulling out more square nails holding dust-covered lathe. "So, what would you call a guy who mooches off his girl and can't keep a job? I've known a few of those."

"Well a four flusher is a person who pretends to be wealthy. He runs with a social class above his own and lets others pick up the check."

"I've met a few of those guys, too. They always have to go to the john when the check hits the table."

She tilted her head. "The John?"

I explained and then leaving her in the house, I drug a fifty-gallon plastic trashcan to the alley and emptied it into the city dumpster. I probably should have rented a roll-off dumpster, but I did so little each week I didn't think anyone would notice a few extra pounds of plaster, not to mention, a dumpster would require building permits.

My friend couldn't come with me and it's just as well. The alley was a dilapidated place with trash strewn about and broken liquor and beer bottles everywhere. It was probably a nice place in her day but in 1987, I refused to go out to the alley at night.

Back inside, my misty roommate explained that she and her friends called a man who didn't work a dew dropper. Sadly, she couldn't remember any of the names of her friends.

I pulled down more plaster. "A couple of the guys at work seem nice but I can't bring myself to get serious about a dude whose aspiration is to tend bar. I genuinely can't decide if I even want a man of my own."

"It would be a tragedy to be left to wither on your maiden stalks."

My head popped up. "Maiden stalks?" I stared at her a moment, thinking about her choice of words. The term wasn't something I was familiar with.

"You are not so young," she said, as she followed me into the next room."

"You sound like my mother."

"That is not so bad a thing for me to care. You would do well to have someone looking toward your future interests."

I shook my head. "I'm pretty good at taking care of myself."

She sighed. "What is it to me? I shan't say another word."

I felt bad that I'd turned down her offer of advice, but women didn't often marry at eighteen in these days. "While we're on the subject of men, what would you call a man who was perfect, or close to it?"

She paced back and forth through the parlor, trying not to step on piles of plaster. "If he's strong you might call him a big six. If he's attractive he would be airtight."

I pulled down another chunk of wall revealing a broken stud and two cracked ones on either side. "Well, crap. This needs to be fixed." I got down on my hands and knees to clean away the broken lathe and check the sill for cracks.

She bent over to watch me. "You didn't tell me what you would call a rich and good-looking man."

"Mine." I teased. "Though most girls would call him a stud."

"Like a horse?"

I thought about it for a second. "I guess. It usually means the guy is sexually attractive."

"Nertz! Isn't that the ant's ear? The man who brings building wares to you, would you call him a stud?"

"Sawyer? Well, he's nice, and he's good looking. But his job isn't much better than a bartender." I didn't want to tell her I was fairly certain he was a drug dealer, too.

Sitting on the floor, I pulled up my goggles to see what was written on the funeral memorial I'd just found in the wall. It had slid under the wainscot where the wall met the floor. The service was for a man of sixty-three and dated 1908, meaning this little piece of paper had been in the wall for eighty years.

She stood in the doorway watching me.

"Did you know anyone named Samuel Baker?" I asked.

She shook her head. "I don't believe I do."

"Well that was a long time ago. The service was held at the Baptist church right around the corner. Did you go to church there?"

She cocked her head and blinked her eyes but didn't answer. This was the way most of our conversations went. Little by little she remembered trivial things about her past. Sometimes it was a word or a random name. She was about to say something, but an unexpected knock on the door frightened her, and she vanished.

Getting up from the floor and pulling off my googles, I went to the front entry. It was Sawyer. His smile lit up his face and his dimples were ever so charming. "Hi. I have some sheetrock in my truck," he said.

"I wasn't expecting you today."

His grin grew impossibly wider. "Want to give me a hand?"

"Sure," I said wiping my dusty hands on my cutoffs. "Let me clear a space in the hallway for it." Somewhere in the mess that was the dining room was a broom. Locating it, I started sweeping fine black dust and bits of plaster from the hall.

"You really should wear a dust mask when you tear this out," he said, holding the dustpan for me. "A lot of this is coal dust. Bad for your lungs."

He was right, but I hated masks. They were so hot and hard to breathe through. The goggles, on the other hand, kept the dust out of my eyes. "I have some masks around here somewhere."

We carried several sheets of drywall into the hall and leaned them up against the stairway. I barely had room to get past them to the dining room when we were done.

I invited him to dinner, imagining this was like our fifth sort of date. "I'll order Chinese," I said.

"Chinese delivery?"

"Yeah," I said. What was he expecting; my kitchen is a construction site. Not that it would have made any difference if the kitchen had been finished. The only thing I kept on hand was the occasional beer and ketchup. The ketchup came in those cute little plastic packages and had been there so long I couldn't remember where they came from. Oh, and there was a box of macaroni & cheese on the shelf. It was still there because it requires milk and butter; two things my refrigerator rarely sees.

"That's fine, unless you would consider going out with me."

"Going out would mean taking a bath, and once I do that, I won't want to tear out more plaster. Would you rather have pizza?"

"No, Chinese is good."

I went to the refrigerator. No beer. "We could go out. I don't have anything to drink."

"Tell you what, order dinner, and I'll grab a six pack."

"Awesome."

"Mind if I use the boy's room first?"

"Of course not. What do you like to eat?"

"Beef and Broccoli, Peanut Curry, just about anything," he said, disappearing up the stairs.

Scampering to the phone, I mentally replayed the morning to see if I'd left any incriminating items in the bathroom. After he left to pick up the beer, I checked the bathroom. Whew. Clean. Then I glanced in the mirror. Horror of horrors, my face and neck were completely black. White circles around my eyes made me look like a something out of a horror movie. The blue handkerchief on my head was totally black. My formerly red, Led Zeppelin t-shirt was black. The only thing I could see in the mirror was a ring of white around my eyes and my teeth. I needed a bath. Washing my face wasn't going to be enough.

I ran bath water and waited for the sound of the door. He was back in less than ten minutes. "My wallet is on the table saw," I called to him when he opened the door. "I'll just be a minute. I needed to wash up."

"Sure thing. Want a beer with your bath?"

I thought about it for a moment. It was tempting. "No, I can wait."

The bath took longer than I'd planned. I had to change the water twice. I threw on a clean pair of jeans and a flannel shirt. So much for finishing the dining room tonight.

Towel drying my hair, I returned to the kitchen to find Sawyer dishing up a plate of hot food for me. I was famished. Pulling up a step stool I offered him a seat at the table saw, while I sat on a five-gallon bucket of drywall mud. I would have used the dining room table, but I'd stacked molding and drywall in front of it. I'm such a great hostess.

I sipped my beer. Time to find out who this guy is. "Do you go to college?" Fingers crossed.

"No, I had to drop out after a year." Some of the light went out of his eyes and I figured this was a sore subject. He probably ran out of money. College isn't cheap. Topic change.

"I never got your last name, Sawyer. We've been friends now for nearly a year now."

He chuckled. "You've never asked. It's Bradford. Sawyer Christian Bradford." His beeper went off, but he ignored it.

"That's a very nice name; so American. My real name is Freja Hedvig O'Connell. I'm glad my mother married my father because O'Connell is a lot easier to spell than Svenhufuud, and it doesn't require a pronunciation guide. My mother's name is Annika, but everyone calls her Jo. Go figure."

I scooped more fried rice onto my plate. "I've been told that my Dad was named Sheamus Seabiscuit because Grandpa Liam won five thousand dollars in 1937 when Seabiscuit won the Brooklyn Handicap at Belmont Park. Grandma still thinks Grampa shouldn't have bet their life savings on that race. My dad and I take after Grandpa Liam."

We were laughing over silly names when halfway through my peanut curry I saw my delicate roommate in the corner of the room. Her head tilted slightly to one side; looking at Sawyer's back. I wasn't ready to make introductions, if he could see her at all, so I packed up my Styrofoam dish and said, "Well, just look at the time. Best I get to work now."

Sawyer stood. "It's nine o'clock."

"I want to get this done tonight. I'll see you later."

I was walking him towards the front door when he stopped and turned around. His brows furrowed. "That was odd," he said. "I thought I heard someone say my name."

"You must be tired." In truth, the girl had said she liked Sawyer. Although she whispered it to me, he'd heard it. That meant he could probably see her as well.

At the door, I handed him a sack of leftover Chinese food. "Thanks for the delivery."

He was shaking his head as he hurried to his truck.

∞

I was going to go to bed, but it was early. I was wearing my last pair of clean jeans so a trip to Smiley's Laundromat was on the list. If I wanted to work more tonight, I would have to put my dirty clothes back on. The laundry was open twenty-four hours a day, so I opted for that job instead.

Sitting on the folding tables watching cars drive by on Colfax, I thought about the implications of Sawyer being a drug dealer. The War on Drugs was gaining momentum daily. Nixon had declared Drug Abuse "public enemy number one," and created the DEA. Reagan expanded the War by establishing mandatory minimum prison sentences for drug possession. As little as an ounce of pot could put you in jail for ten years. I mentally kicked myself for even thinking about taking those kinds of chances. In high school I dabbled a little with pot but once I was old enough to drink, I switched to alcohol. Nancy Reagan did a decent job with her "Just Say No" program, and advertisements for D.A.R.E. were plastered on billboards across the nation. I was scared witless to try anything harder. I never thought of myself as a prude but could there be something about my naiveté that attracted troubled men like Dirk and Sawyer?

∞

Back home with clean clothes, I felt rejuvenated and started to work on the house at one in the morning. You don't need that much sleep when you're in your twenties and motivated. I worked through the night and by four o'clock on Tuesday, I was dog-tired, but I pushed on until five. I could now see from room to room through the bare studs. Fine, grey dust covered everything, and I was feeling depressed by the amount of work that still lay before me. I roamed through the first floor, trying to imagine what it would look like when it was done.

Even though I don't cook much, I know kitchens can make or break a house. This kitchen was giving me fits. There was a door in the middle of the south wall to the back porch, a door on the north wall to the basement, and a door in the middle of the east wall that led to the dining room. No matter how I arranged the room, I had a hallway running through the middle of the workspace.

There was a knock on the door, and I turned to see a strange man in a suit scanning the porch. I opened the door. "Can I help you?"

He started to put out his hand but seeing me covered in black dust, he snatched it back. "Michael Duncan. Rick Winston paid for an appraisal. Can I come in?"

I was furious. The nerve of that guy. I'll call him for sure now. "Come on in." I said. "I'm in the process of remodeling."

He stepped gingerly through the door, trying not to dirty his suit. "Thank you. How many bedrooms do you have?"

"That depends. I really only have one decent closet at the moment."

"Bathrooms?"

"One. Look, I don't want to waste your time. I'm not looking to sell, and no one is going to want to buy a house that's nearly stripped down to studs. I don't know what Rick told you."

"I did a drive by appraisal and it came in at forty-two-five. Rick thought that was low and wanted me to see the inside. I have to say; I think the original appraisal was a little high."

"My mortgage on this is forty-seven."

"The market took a hit, and this is more than a fixer-upper."

"Tell me about it."

"I'll leave the first appraisal as it is."

"Do what you need to." I opened the door to let him back out.

∞

I went up and soaked in the tub. A thin film of and plaster dust floated on top of the black water. I changed the water and dreamed of the day I would have a shower. After rinsing again, I toweled off and slipped into an oversized t-shirt. Construction books littered the bed and most every flat surface of the room. I push the books aside and sat down on the bed. My latest kitchen drawing spread out before me. I picked it up and made some changes. The washer and dryer would work well where the stove and sink currently sat and I wanted the sink under the window but everything else was a mystery. Before I could do anything to the second floor, I had to finish removing the dining room ceiling plaster and lathe. That would only require a couple more days and with luck there wouldn't be any big surprises under the mess. Unfortunately, my luck had run out.

CHAPTER 26

When I got up, I called Rick. "What were you thinking? I didn't need an appraiser. I'm not looking to sell my house. I LIKE my house."

"Why don't you let me put you up in a nice apartment. You can keep working on the house, but that's a really bad neighborhood."

"It's not that bad."

"I have a small condo downtown you could use."

No way. I would be living in his place. Would I even have my own room? "I don't need it. Really."

"Think about it."

"No. Bye Rick."

∞

Once the ceiling was down in the dining room, I could see three of the second story floor joists had split and were sagging precariously, which explained why the floor in the bathroom and hall sloped at about a thirty-degree angle. CRAP! Good thing I had the next two days off. Not that I actually believed the plaster had been keeping the bathroom from crashing into the dining room, but I would feel safer with something under it now that I knew how badly it was damaged.

I needed to rent some floor jacks. All Season Rental had what I needed and with the backseat down I was able to squeeze six of them into the car. It would require a couple weeks to raise the second floor to anything near its original position. If I raised it too fast, I might break something else, like the rafters. It took a hundred years to come down; couldn't expect it to go up in a day.

Since the bathroom wall was centered over the dining room, I assumed it wasn't a load-bearing wall but just to make sure, I climbed up in the attic to check.

I studied the layout of the rafters and the ceiling joists. They ran counter to the lower levels. On the main floor, the wall running from the kitchen to the front door divided the living room from the hall and stairwell and parlor from the dining room; right down the center of the house. That was definitely a load-bearing wall and was directly under the wall dividing the second bedroom from the bathroom.

In the basement, another wall was directly under that. After close inspection of the other joists, I found no more cracks or rotted wood. That meant, for all the sloping floors and cracked plaster, the house was structurally sound, not very pretty, but sound.

This would take six jacks capable of covering a ten-foot span. I placed three jacks in the dining room to raise the second floor and three more in the basement to keep the pressure from breaking the first-floor joists. Once the broken joists were pressed into place, I could splint them as I did for the joists under the front door.

This left only the upstairs and the kitchen walls to be torn out. Since there was nothing above the kitchen, and the attic was undamaged, I really hoped I wouldn't find any more major problems.

I placed a sheet of drywall against the studs in the parlor and screwed it in place. The next one needed to be cut. I laid the T-square over the marks and began cutting when my roommate said, "The news is distressing."

"What?" I missed my mark and had to recut the sheet.

"On the wireless. The news of the riot. Eight guards were killed."

"Where? What radio?" My radio had been off all day.

"The penitentiary."

I placed my newly cut sheet next to the other one. "The penitentiary in Canon City?"

"The inmates set fire to the mess hall and the chapel. The horror of it all." Agitated, she paced the room.

"You said you heard it on the radio. Do you remember where you were."

Coming back to herself, she tried to recall more from the bit of memory. "I was preparing for a recital. We had seized a brief respite from the labor of practice when the news came over the wireless." Her distress made me wonder if she knew someone in the penitentiary. I didn't get the chance to ask because the phone rang.

"Hello?" I expected it to be Rick and I was ready to tell him off again. It was my mother.

"Were planning a baby shower for Shannon. Can you come over on Sunday?"

"Sure. What time?"

"Two in the afternoon. I can't wait to show you her bridesmaid dress."

"It's a little soon for that isn't it? She just going to get bigger every day."

"Bridgett picked out the best style possible, so easy to alter."

"Okay. I'll see you Sunday. By the way. Did Aiden take you and Dad to lunch?"

"No. Why do you ask?"

"No reason. Bye, Mom."

"Bye, Hon."

I really felt for Aiden and wished I could help him, but this was his cross to bear.

After I hung up, I looked for my friend but as often happened when she was upset, she didn't return for some time.

Over the next couple weeks, I cranked the jacks another fraction. The large cracks in the plaster on the bathroom walls narrowed with each turn. That wasn't going to save them from being torn out later, but it made the room look healthier than it had looked in a long time. With my Sony radio and cassette player to keep us company, my airy friend and I sang along with Dire Straits, *"Money for nothing,"* and a few hundred other songs.

While letting the house groan with each turn of the jacks, I worked on wiring the living room and parlor and hung drywall where I could. The dining room couldn't be finished until the upper floor was near its original level. I was stuck in the parlor as well because the plumbing needed to go through the north wall to reach the bathroom.

The big four by eight sheets could be hung either up and down or on their side. The ceilings were ten feet, so that meant I had to add another two feet of sheetrock no matter which way I placed the full sheets. I discovered, after some mistakes, it made taping easier if the extra seam was closer to the floor. I used a utility knife to score the sheetrock and then snap the seam to break it. While it worked great on the sheetrock, I also discovered the utility knife is especially useful for slicing work clothes, but only while being worn.

Having the seams closer to the floor, meant furniture would cover my less than perfect taping. I couldn't finish the south wall of the dining room because it was also the north parlor wall and would have new plumbing to the bathroom. I couldn't really finish the living room with the doors over the windows, same for the parlor. For now, I had to dance around the floor jacks in the dining room and step over large pieces of half-stripped molding. Although I ran the electrical through the lower rooms, I couldn't hook it up to the breaker box. I had extension cords running throughout the house from kitchen to the upstairs to light my way.

The thought of having to tear out the upper floor before finishing the first floor had me in a sour mood. I was tired of the dust and mess. I wanted this to be over. Like tearing out plaster, hanging dry wall in the summertime is just stupid. On the ninth of June, a big bolt of lightning took out about two million tires at a place called Tire Mountain. Three tornadoes also touched down in the Denver area. I found myself wondering if my insurance would get me out of this mess, halfway hoping my place would be next to be hit.

When I got to work on Wednesday night, Rick was waiting at the bar. He carried a huge vase with three dozen red roses. I cringed. He was making this hard.

He gave me the beautiful flowers. "I wanted to say I'm sorry. I shouldn't have been so presumptuous. I was only thinking of making your life better."

"My life is fine. I don't need a place to live and, quite frankly, all this money you throw at me, makes me uncomfortable."

"I want to do things for you. You're smart and funny, and you have a great body. I don't think you know how rare you are."

I shook my head. "You're a very sweet man. I just don't think I'm the girl for you."

He left looking dejected, and I felt terrible. It didn't seem fair that those we like rarely like us back.

I looked over at the bar where Bobby was hitting on a new waitress. *Men*, I thought with a growl. Bobby still insisted we would eventually get back together whenever he thought I was being friendly to him. It made working together awkward. Lately another waitress was showing an interest in him. I was torn between warning Saffron, aka Susan on her car title, and letting her take his mind off me.

Dave never let me forget he was interested in more that teaching me to shoot. On more than one occasion I gave serious consideration to his offer, but I knew he would just toy with me. Sawyer was, well, he was Sawyer.

Even the customers seemed more handsy than usual and I felt like screaming every time one of them asked me why I wouldn't go home with him. I was frustrated that I still knew so little about the girl haunting my house. The heat of the early summer added to my stress making me want to get away from all that testosterone. Not that I had many female friends to hang out with other than my sister and my "not quite there" roommate. Ginger spent most of her free time in Vegas.

I wanted another vacation to work on the house and have time to get to know my roommate. Unfortunately, lots of other girls take the summer months off. Oh well, I always looked forward to hitting things when I got home from work.

Over my regular days off, I managed to get a lot of sheetrock up, making the rooms look all white and clean. It was hot work but well worth it.

∞

When Jason came in on Wednesday night, he came up to the bar and kissed me on the cheek. "I'll have a Crown Royal on the rocks. I'll be next to the DJ booth," he said, as Foreigner pined, *'I want to know what love is.'*

"I'll be right there." A lot of the guys like to sit by the DJ booth because all the girls went up there several times a night to check the dance list or hit the john. It was the best spot in the club to check out the entertainers.

By the time I got there, Jason was surrounded by Satin, Velvet, Chiffon, Cashmere, and Chenille. I made my way to the table and set his drink down.

"Would you ladies like something to drink?" he asked and of course they all ordered drinks. Most of the girls were good at maintaining control but a few of the girls didn't handle alcohol very well. Chenille was one of those.

"I'll need drink tickets, please," I said.

Velvet gave me a little attitude, but they all got up to get permission slips from the manager on duty.

"Would it be possible," Jason smiled almost shyly, "to invite you to have dinner with me?"

I was surprised and flattered. He'd never asked me out before. I was used to being hounded every night by lame guys, but Jason seemed different. He often over tipped without asking for anything in return. Some guys gave you a five-dollar bill and expected you to go home with them at the end of the night. "I'm not supposed to go out with the customers."

He smiled. He knew the club's policy as well as me. "It can be our little secret."

I liked the idea of dating someone like Jason, but it was against the rules. It's not that I never break the rules but this one was in place for my protection. I could still see the images of the dead girls the manager showed us when telling the staff that serial killers look like everyone else. "Maybe," was the best answer I could give him before the girls returned. That put me in a much better mood. Jason was such a nice guy, I was tempted.

At the bar Ginger, aka Carolyn on her birth certificate, told me, "Jason started coming in when his marriage fell apart. That was like about four years ago. He dated Cinnamon, for a while."

"What happened? Why did they break up?"

Ginger set her drinks on her tray and refilled her napkins nearly knocking over a bottle of beer. "You'd have to ask Cinnamon. Jason's never said a bad word about her, but she was pretty upset. She most likely expected more than he was willing to give. It was like only weeks after his divorce."

"Rebound." I glanced at Bobby behind the bar and cringed.

"For sure. You'll never know if you don't say yes."

"It's against the rules."

"Whatever you say, Miss goody two-shoes." She turned and left the station nearly smacking into Cinnamon.

Righting her tray and straightening her ashtray, Cinnamon, aka Barbara to her pastor sighed. "Ginger's a sweet girl but the poor thing can't walk and chew gum at the same time. She broke her foot last year when she fell off a curb."

"Fell off a curb?" I grabbed the beers Dan set on the bar.

"She said she stepped off the wrong way."

"I didn't know there was more than one way to step off a curb." Shaking my head, I delivered the beers to stage one.

∞

The next morning before work, I sat on my bed, pouring over books on kitchen remodeling. I examined the drawings I'd done, and measurements I'd written down. I still didn't have an acceptable plan. It was driving me nuts. No matter what I did, it was a big hallway from the dining room to the back door or the basement. I wanted the sink under the window, but that meant walking between the refrigerator and the sink to get out the back door. The only thing I knew for sure was the stairway to the basement wasn't going anywhere.

I was on the twentieth drawing when the girl appeared at the end of my bed.

"You appear to be flummoxed."

"I can't seem to figure this out. The kitchen," I answered her confused look.

"Houses have their own life. In time it will come."

I set the papers aside. "I need to crank the jacks again and get ready for work."

She followed me into the dining room watching intently as I cranked the jacks and searched the upper floor for new stress fractures.

A short while later, I sat down at my makeshift dressing table and began the task of painting my face with all the tools from my magic box, otherwise known as my make-up bag. The girl sat on the end of the bed watching me as she often did when I got ready for work. Most days she seemed fascinated by my hot rollers but today she was studying my simple jewelry.

"That's an interesting bracelet," she said watching me slip the crystal bracelet on my arm.

"I found it here in the house. There was a ring in the box, too. Here, do you want to see it?"

"I would like that very much."

Reaching into the wooden box, I pulled out the ring. "I lost most of my jewelry in the robbery. Not that I had anything particularly nice. Now I keep these in a safe place when I'm not wearing them."

I slipped the ring on and held out my hand for her to see. "I love costume jewelry for work. Expensive looking jewelry makes the guys think I'm worth more."

She studied the ring on my finger. "Jewel?" she said and shook her head, blinking several times. "No, jewels. Jul, juli. Julianne. My name. My name is Julianne!" She floated up off the bed in her excitement. "My name. I remember my name. Julianne."

She wrapped her arms around her waist and did a little pirouette. "Julianne Florence Rosa Parker. My name is Julianne Florence Rosa Parker."

I jumped up, nearly knocking my eye-shadow box to the floor. "That's Awesome! Julianne. What a beautiful name."

She danced across the room, repeating her name, "Julianne, Julianne Parker."

I joined her in her excitement. My first solid clue. With a name, I could finally figure out when and how she died, and why she was here. I was fairly sure I had the era down to about a ten-year span. She was acutely aware of prohibition, so she had to have died before repeal or shortly after. Miller was popular in Denver. My research found Miller had written *Moonlight Serenade* in 1926 and *Room 1411* with Benny Goodman in 1928. She knew Miller before he went to New York to play with Benny Goodman.

"Can you remember anymore?" I asked her as I changed my shirt.

She looked a little crestfallen, but her joy wasn't completely diminished. "It is a great joy to know one's name. Alas, I must hold this moment in my mind for fear it escapes me once more."

I hated to leave her, but work was more important at the moment. I played a couple of her favorite albums as I finished dressing. "Are you going to be okay here?"

To my surprise, she laughed. "I have no place to be, but here. I bid you good day."

I didn't want to think about the day she would leave me forever.

Work was a blur that night because I was excited by the possibilities opened to me by knowing her name. Julianne. My roommate's name was Julianne Florence Rosa Parker.

I wanted to share my good news with everyone but that was off the table. Instead, I just had a good night and made great tips.

∞

When the sun crept in my bedroom window, I found Julianne patiently waiting for me to wake up. "You have my history to date," she said. "Now tell me of yourself. The most I have been able to learn is you tear up the house at odd hours of the day and you work in a gin joint that has you dress your face as if you were to be on the silver screen."

I gave that some thought. Was make-up less common for the average girl in her day? Hollywood portrays the Twenties as flappers drinking, smoking, and dancing the Charleston in fancy clubs. Not knowing anything about gin joints, I couldn't tell her the difference. "Well, I also like to play pool," I said. "When I was in high school, I used to hang out at the local pool hall. I didn't gamble for money, but I rarely had to pay for more than one game. I'm fairly good at it."

Her eyes widened as they often did when I said something, she thought shocking. "Small credit to you if you are," she said. "A billiard hall is no place for a lady. The game is known to lead the innocent down a path of wickedness."

Her vehemence surprised me. Pool halls weren't church social gatherings, but I didn't for-a-minute believe my love of 8-Ball led me toward anything more than a little mischief. The social etiquettes of her life were far more stringent than mine. "It's not unusual for a girl to hang out in a bar to dance or play pool. That's where I met Dirk." That gave me pause to re-think her comment about the path of wickedness.

She was appalled that I met Dirk that way. "There is more real solid worth in Sawyer's little finger than there is in a pool hustler's whole self. Why the happiness you should have with him."

"Sawyer's a nice guy, I guess. I met him in a hardware store."

"So, what has your tail under the rocker?"

I smiled at her phrase. Sometimes I did feel like a long tail cat in a room full of rockers. "I don't know. He doesn't seem to have a lot of ambition. He's had that truck for a year and it's still missing a back bumper." On the Sony, Kenny Loggins sang, *'footloose, footloose.'*

"It is considered a dreadful thing for a woman to marry a man for his money." Julianne said. "It should be fully as mean a thing for a man to monopolize a woman's time so that she cannot make money for herself. Sawyer has said nothing against you working in a gin joint."

"True enough. Either Sawyer doesn't think badly of my job, or doesn't like me in that way, or he's too polite to mention it." Julianne had me thinking about the future, knowing I couldn't wear that silly thing they call a uniform forever. "I could go back to school," I said. "Or I could take up bartending or work at a Denny's."

"For you there is something vivid and more adventuring."

"If the market bounces back, I can flip houses. Next time I won't try to live in the house while I fix it up. That's a lesson learned the hard way."

I was beginning to think I wasn't ready to find a man. Over the past year I'd come to realize I could care for myself. I wasn't living in a mansion, but I wasn't anyone's pet, either. Since I wasn't dating anyone, no one cheated on me. So long as I had Julianne to talk to at night, I wasn't terribly lonely.

I left for work feeling as if a major weight had been lifted.

∞

I was feeling so good about learning Julianne's name; I'd decided to go out with Jason. It doesn't make sense to me now, but it was the only excuse I could come up with at the time.

I met him on the following Tuesday night at the Target store behind the club. He seemed like a nice man, but I wasn't ready for him to see where I was living. I wasn't sure if I would ever be ready for someone to see my house.

I love emerald green, and Jason drove an emerald green, '86 Jaguar. I also love Jaguars.

He pulled up next to my car and smiled. "Would you like to drive, or shall I?"

I got out and locked my car. "I would much rather ride in your car."

He smiled and opened the car door from inside. I slid into the soft leather seat. Classical music drifted from the radio and he smelled of Quorum aftershave.

"Have you ever been to Strings for dinner?" he asked.

"No. I've heard it's a nice restaurant."

"You'll like it."

I was petting the seat. The soft tan leather was fabulous. "I like your car."

"Would you like to drive it?"

"Oh my gosh, no. I'm sure I'd wreck it."

He laughed. "Do you usually wreck cars?'

"No. I've never had an accident, but I might be due. Not worth taking the chance with your car."

At the restaurant I was feeling a little under dressed. I only owned one skirt and it was hot pink snakeskin. The black angora sweater helped tone it down a little, but I was still a little punk for the place. Jason ordered wine and I pretended to like it. It was so dry I had trouble opening my mouth after swallowing a drink. I've always been more of a whiskey girl.

We talked about nothing and everything for the next two hours. We flirted and drank and flirted some more. I was feeling that warm buzz that comes with good food and a few cocktails.

He ran his fingers down my arm. "My mother accuses me of never dating nice girls. I must admit, I've had a bit of a crush on you for a long time."

I felt my face warm. Couple more drinks and I would probably prove his mother right.

He held my hand and ran his thumb over my knuckles. "You shouldn't be working in a place like that. You should be working in a five-star restaurant. You're a classy girl."

I was flattered. He didn't know me, and I tried to picture how he would feel walking into my wreck of a house. Not that I was going to let that happen tonight. That has to be at least date four or five, if ever.

He refilled my glass of wine. By now it tasted fine because I couldn't taste it anymore. "I have a friend who works at the Black Angus," he said. "You would make good money there and wouldn't have men pawing at you."

"You mean, men like you?" I teased.

"I try to respect the girls there."

"I'm sorry. You really are sweet."

He leaned over and kissed me lightly on the cheek. "You aren't like the other girls there. I can tell you're smart. I don't see you being the kind of girl who thinks she needs a man."

He was saying all the right things to make me feel like I needed him. Not forever, but he was looking good for the night. I turned towards him and his lips met mine in a soft kiss. My heart began to race and my hooha flushed with hot blood.

"I haven't been with a man for a while."

"My guess is, you don't actually miss the old one."

Was I missing Dirk? I didn't think so. What I was missing was sex. I wanted Jason's hands all over me but didn't want him to think I was easy.

"I don't feel like talking about it," I said, sliding a little closer to Jason.

"Let's get out of here."

"Sounds great."

He waved to the waiter and paid the check. "How would you like to see a movie? It's still pretty early"

"Sure." I was thinking I wanted to keep this awesome buzz going but a movie would be fine.

In the car, Jason leaned over and kissed me again, this time with a little tongue. I felt like crawling into his lap, but I held myself in check. It would be dark in the theatre. Surely, I could contain myself until then.

The Mayan was playing *Prelude to a Kiss,* with Meg Ryan. A sexy and romantic comedy that may have been a bit much for a first date. I guess it wasn't exactly our first date. Not if you consider the fact that he'd been stalking me at the club for the past few months. He held my hand during the film and surprised me with another gentle kiss right before the lights came up.

"Would you like to stop for a nightcap?" he asked. "I know a place just down the street."

I wasn't ready to go home. I wanted some more of those kisses. "That sounds good."

The neighborhood on south Broadway isn't particularly nice but the pub was upscale. As he passed the bar, he asked for a bottle of cabernet. Leading me to a booth in the back of the room, he slid in beside me. I could feel the warmth of his body touching mine.

"Did you like the movie?" he asked as the bartender poured two glasses of wine.

"Yes, sometimes Meg Ryan can be really hot." I took a healthy drink of the rich red wine. I'm not the kind of girl to sip. I drink for the effect, not for the taste.

He wrapped his arm around me. "You're a special kind of girl. You're smart and independent. I like that in a woman." He sipped his wine and refilled my glass. "Some of the girls I meet are just little girls looking for someone to be their daddy. I get the impression you are the master of your home."

"I'm the master of my wreck. I have this old place that's falling apart faster than I can tape it back together."

He refilled my glass once more. "Would you like to see my house? It's not far from here."

Then I had that one more cocktail I was referring to earlier.

As we drove toward his place, I found myself repeating an old joke. The only difference between a 57 Chevy and a cocktail waitress is, not everyone has had a 57 Chevy.

Jason's house wasn't that close. He lived in a huge house in Roxborough Park, a beautiful and exclusive area near the foothills southwest of Denver. I wasn't sure if he owned it or the bank owned it, and at the moment I didn't care. Could be the IRS was just hanging out, waiting to make a claim. I've learned that most people who have especially nice stuff are just renting, making payments that are never going to end. Real money is cash in hand and no credit card balances, not that I have that, but I know what it looks like.

We fell into his over-sized bed and played lover's games until morning light seeped through the windows. Although I felt guilty for having been so easy, he was a gentle lover and made me forget my pride with a smothering of kisses.

Later that morning, I woke to find myself naked and alone in a luxurious bed covered by a chocolate satin bedspread. I stretched and glanced around the room. It was immaculate. As I slipped out of the bed, I noticed the closet door was slightly ajar. I couldn't resist. Opening the door further, I found myself in a walk-in closet bigger than my bedroom at home. His clothes were all arranged by color; seventeen long sleeved dress shirts in varying shades of light blue and more shoes than Payless. All his slacks were lined up, all black—not a pair of jeans to be seen. I totally freaked. These were all the signs of a serial-killer nice guy; an over-the-top anal dude.

He called to me from the other room asking if I wanted breakfast. I needed to be nice. He was my ride home. "Sure," I yelled, "anything is fine."

"It will be ready in about ten minutes if you want to shower."

I did want a shower, but Alfred Hitchcock's Psycho was playing through my mind. I felt better finding a lock on the door.

Feeling calmer now that I was clean, I walked into the kitchen. Whoa! There were two little kids sitting at the breakfast bar.

"Hope you slept well," he gave me a conspiratorial wink—we, in fact, didn't sleep much at all. "This is David and Mindy. They were with their mother last night," he said, answering the question plain on my face.

"And this is Etta," he nodded toward an obvious housekeeper carrying a bag of groceries.

Before we finished our pancakes, Etta had the kitchen shining like a Parade of Homes model. I watched her as she moved a flower vase a sixteenth of an inch and straightened one of the leaves. Okay, so he didn't do his own laundry. He might not be a serial killer, but I wasn't sure I wanted to date a guy who came with two kids and an ex-wife.

I was feeling guilty, not only for sleeping with him on the first date but for realizing I didn't want to raise someone else's kids. Did that make me a bad person?

CHAPTER 27

When I got home, the answering machine was blinking. My mother wanted to know who my plus-one was going to be for Connor's wedding. Shannon called to tell me she was supposed to be part of the weeding party, but she was as big as a house. Rick called to tell me he still had a buyer lined up who would give my fifty-grand, if I changed my mind. I stuck my tongue out at the phone and rewound the tape.

Julianne wanted to know all about my date. "You little goose. You didn't come home last night," she scolded. "Nothing good ever comes from staying out after midnight."

"I wouldn't say that. He was actually very good in bed." I wandered toward the kitchen looking for a cup of coffee I knew wasn't there.

"Jeepers Creepers! You gave him nookie?" She backed away as if she'd been stung by a bee.

"It's not like I sleep with every guy I know." I never should have told her about my past. And yes, I shouldn't have gone home with him on the first night. "I've had my eye on him for several months. Dating men is like shopping for a new car. How are you going to know if you're getting a good deal if you don't take it for a test drive?"

She blinked in confusion. "A car?"

"Yeah, a car. You know, an automobile."

"I've never driven an automobile."

"No way!"

"No, I don't think I have. But what do automobiles have to do with being a tramp."

"I'm not a tramp!"

"You lived with Dirk for five years without the sanctity of a marriage license and then you lived with Sean the guitar player for a year. When you moved here, you met that bartender, and need I say where that went?"

I cleared tools off the stove. Definitely shouldn't have told her about Bobby. "That doesn't make me a tramp," does it? I felt ashamed of my past. "I'm sorry," I said.

She looked as if she would cry. "I will admit," she blinked back tears. "I'm not a virgin and I'm not married, but I loved him."

"Loved who?" I asked, setting down the teakettle.

"I can't remember," she wailed.

She appeared so stricken I wanted to hold her, but she was just beautiful mocha colored fog.

"You were in love," I said, lighting the stove. "You know you had sex, right."

She nodded, and I thought I could detect a slight blush; which was odd for a bloodless, shade of a woman. It was the way she folded into herself.

"See if you can remember anything about that night. The night you made love to him."

"It wasn't night."

"Good, you remember."

"We were in the City Park, feeding the ducks. His hair was black as night and his eyes like coal. He was beautiful. So warm to the touch was his smooth and shiny skin. His hands soft and gentle because he was a musician."

"What was his name?"

She shook her head, "I, it's. Oh! I do not know. His name is like a vapor on the tip of my tongue." Her lips pressed tight together in frustration.

"But you can see his face, right? Keep that image in your mind. We'll find him and when we do, maybe you can go home."

∞

The following Wednesday night, I saw Jason come in, but before I could get to his table, he ordered from Spice, aka Linda to her gynecologist.

"Hi," I said with a big smile when I got to his table.

He didn't look up. "Spice has my drink."

"Yeah, I know. I just wanted to say hi."

"Good to see you," he said, and began talking to Summer.

He scarcely acknowledged me, and I felt cheap and hurt. Had he been all talk? Did he ever really think of me as a nice girl? I shouldn't have slept with him. I tried to brush it off, no biggie. It was the eighties, and everybody slept around. I did have an enjoyable time. Even meeting his kids wasn't terrible, a little unexpected, but not terrible. I'd been more a fool for a lesser man.

Right away Cinnamon, aka Barbara to her yoga instructor, knew I'd gone out with Jason. I didn't know how, unless he told her. She ignored me all night and I was too embarrassed to say anything. I didn't know she still had feelings for him. She might have felt better knowing I was just a one-night stand, but that's not the kind of thing I like brag about. Leave it to Ginger, aka Carolyn at the corner liquor store, to break the ice.

"I don't know why you got to get all up in Freja's shit about this?" Ginger said as Cinnamon set her tray on the bar and rearranged her napkins for the hundredth time. "The guy asked her out, and she said yes. You went out with him and nobody like got all pissed off at you."

Cinnamon whirled around and stared at her. "Just because you're the kind of girl who sleeps with every swinging dick doesn't mean I am."

"Two dates does not constitute a relationship," Ginger countered.

So, he went out with Cinnamon twice. She must not have slept with him on the first date. I peeked over at the table where he was flirting with Summer, Winter, and Autumn. I had to hand it to the entertainers. They could usually see right through guys like Jason. It was girls like Cinnamon and me who got hurt.

While Cinnamon emptied and cleaned her ashtrays, Ginger bumped the napkins on her tray, something she liked to do regularly.

After Cinnamon arranged her napkins once more and walked away, Ginger said, "Don't beat yourself up. You had a good time and so did Jason."

"But I'm not that kind of girl. I thought he actually liked me."

"Of course, you did. And ninety percent of the guys who come in here think these dancers actually like them."

That really hurt. Ginger was one of the few entertainers who later became a waitress and she was a pretty good one, a little on the clumsy side, but good with the guys. She kept up the 'devil may care' attitude but I suspected there was a lonely girl she kept locked away. "Would you have gone out with him?"

"For sure. But I'm not his type. When a guy like that comes on to you it's hard to say no. You took a chance. It might have turned out different."

"He has two kids."

Ginger laughed. "He's probably like shopping for a mother. You know, someone to look after of the kids while he flirts with strippers."

"I don't know what he's looking for, but he has Etta to watch his kids." I wasn't that infatuated by him, but it hurt my pride to be dumped so quickly.

That train of thought brought me back to Bobby. Could it be that he really didn't want to get back together as much as he wanted to be the one to call it off? I was such a schmuck.

∞

I slept in all morning feeling depressed about Jason. When I finally rolled over and opened my eyes, Julianne was sitting on the bed. Barely awake, I had a chill run up my spine.

"I've got some common sense, and I can see that if a small wheel of the machine refuses to turn, the big wheels are bound to stick."

"What are you talking about?" I sat up and rubbed the sleep out of my eyes.

"We are more or less intimately known to each other. I can see the man has brutalized you."

"Who? Jason?"

"Is it then, that man?"

I blew out a sigh and got out of bed. "Yes, it's that man."

"Surely you've refused him?"

"Not exactly." I started the bath water and thought about the morning after. I had nearly bragged about sleeping with Jason only to have it thrown in my face the next week. "I don't think he wants to see me again."

"You're always kicking against the prick, whatever is it, that you in truth desire?"

"I don't know."

"That is the root of the problem, as I have come to understand it. You are very surely filled with some wild notion of defying fate. I'll tell you what's the matter. During your life with Dirk, you lived on excitement."

"Yeah, and I paid dearly for that."

"The whole five years with him was just a pulsing, throbbing rush, and now that it's over, any normal existence is feebly struggling to the surface. You're all to pieces."

"What about this existence," I waved my arm across the room indicating the mess that was my construction project, "do you find normal?"

A sad smile graced her beautiful face. "I should like to speak with my sister. She it was, who had some understanding of the heart."

"Sister? You have a sister?"

"Brilliant creature, with about her that mysterious touch of genius."

"What's her name? What do you remember?"

"When I was a kiddie, we played together. She is younger." Tears welled up in her dark eyes. "I remember not," she wailed.

She was about to disappear as she often did when frustrated.

"Wait. What I'm I going to do about Jason?"

She paused thoughtfully. "And just now—nothing seems quite worthwhile."

"You're right. Let's talk about music. That does wonders for the soul."

I placed a Journey album on the turntable and stepped into the tub feeling sorry for both of us. I was always in water over my head and, here's the scary part that I wouldn't say out loud: I was kind of addicted to it.

∞

After my bath, I made a quick trip to the hardware store to order two by twos for furring out the outer walls, and a couple of two by eights for steps and to splint my broken floor joists. I was feeling better because my hair was styled, and I was wearing make-up; a look I was sure Sawyer hadn't seen before.

Sawyer wasn't there and I mentally kicked myself for caring. My luck with men was abominable. Nick wasn't interested at all, and Bobby was too interested. Jason turned out to be a jerk. Rick was still pestering me to sell my house. Dave was scary, and Sawyer was, well, Sawyer.

At the register, Mike took my order and said someone would deliver it the next day for a small charge. I added a few sheets of drywall to the list as long as I was paying for delivery. Once the jacks were out of the way I could finish the ceiling. At least the house was something I had control over.

Thursday night, I begged Nick for Friday and Saturday off. "I've got a major house project to finish and I want to get the jacks back since they charge by the day. I've already had them for months."

Nick smiled that heart-stopping smile. "I always enjoy your tales of home remodeling, extraordinary as often they are."

"I have the wiring and sheetrock done in the dining room but can't hang the ceiling until the jacks are gone. With two extra days I should be able to bring the hall and the bathroom floors up to their original level."

He cocked his head. "To level?"

"Yeah, that's what the jacks are doing. I'll bolt new two by eights to the old joists to make a splint. I've been working on it for a couple months. I'm planning on tearing out the stairs to the basement this week."

"I wish you would have asked for the time off before the schedule came out."

"I know. I'm sorry. I just really need new stairs." The truth was more that I didn't want to see Jason, Dave, or Bobby.

∞

I cocktailed until two in the morning, so I was dog-tired and in a foul mood when I got home. Fortunately, beating on my walls usually helped me blow off steam. The stairway needed to be completely rebuilt, so I worked on tearing out the basement stairs. Once I had the stairs out, I used a ladder to get up and down.

I had a lot of odds and ends of lumber lying around from other projects. Framing the stairs with two by fours would be more substantial, and I was out of two by twos. The stairway would be a bit narrow but there was room for a decent landing three steps down. It probably wouldn't be to code, but I never planned to have an inspector look at it.

As I worked, I sang along with Phil Collins *'I don't care any mo-re, I don't care any mo-re, I don't care what you say...'* The truth, if I was being honest with myself, I did care. I was feeling angry and hurt.

I had my Sony cranked so loud I didn't hear the front door open. I came around the corner of the kitchen and two young men stood in the dining room staring at me. In my hand was a framing stud full of nails but I was wishing it were my SKS.

"I was told we could get beer from you," said a skinny kid in a red ball cap.

I shook my head. "I don't know who told you that, but I don't have any."

A taller, grease-stained guy leered at me, and I felt my hands tighten on the stud.

"What are you doing playing music at five in the morning?"

I realized that they must have thought I was having a party. Note to self. ALWAYS lock the front door. "I'm working on the stairs to the basement. I didn't mean to wake anyone."

"Oh. We was just driving by," said the red cap. "We heard this was a good place to get afterhours stuff."

"Sorry to disappoint you."

The tall one shrugged. "No harm, no foul. Let's hit it, Skip. Bingo's got stash, for sure."

I locked the door behind them. At eight AM sharp, I was on the phone to ADT Security Company. I chided myself, "What good is an alarm if you can't remember to lock the damn door?"

CHAPTER 28

A pot-bellied man from the alarm company was wiring the front door when Sawyer pulled up in his ford truck. I was exhausted and hadn't bothered to change clothes. I was covered in dirt from the stairwell. The knot of hair on the top of my head was falling to the side. I pulled out the pencils holding it in place, twisted my hair a bit tighter, and re-inserted the pencils. "Hi Sawyer," I called to him as he strolled up the flagstone walk.

His eyes swept over me, and he grinned. "I see you've been working hard all morning. I have some sheetrock, furring strips, and two by eight studs."

"Thanks," I said helping him unload the truck. "I wasn't expecting you to bring my stuff." In truth, I'd forgotten the supplies were going to be delivered today but I was happy to see them. I was almost finished with the framing and ready to add treads to my new stairs.

"I never pass up a chance to see what new mischief you've gotten into."

I was a little insulted by that. He thought I was a joke.

"So," he said, sliding passed the electrician. "Installing a security system? Does that mean the doors are coming off the windows soon?"

"Yes, I can't finish the sheetrock with doors over the windows."

"If it's any consolation, I'm sure you'll like having light in your house again. All that darkness seems to have taken some of the sunshine out of your smile."

I stuck my tongue out at him. "It's not the windows." I said sullenly. "I just got dumped by a guy I kind of liked."

His usual smile drifted. "Sorry to hear. Break-ups can be hard."

He set the wood down on the living room floor. "I had a crush on a girl once, but she never noticed me."

"I find that hard to believe. You're too cute."

His smile returned, and his dimple deepened. "I didn't think you'd noticed."

"Well of course I noticed. It's just…" I couldn't think of what I wanted to say.

He stared at me for a minute; then nodded as if he knew what I meant. Walking through the parlor, he whistled. "I'm impressed. And in here?" he asked, stepping into the dining room. "Are these the broken joists you told Mike about?"

"Mike?"

"He was the guy who took you're order yesterday."

"Oh, yeah. I told him that I needed to splint some joists."

Sawyer examined the jacks and broken joists. "Do you want some help bolting these together?"

"I can do it myself but if you don't have anything better to do, I'd love some help."

We went out to his truck and hauled the two by eights into the dining room. They were heavy and much longer than the ones I'd used to splint the joists under the front landing. Watching his muscles ripple under his shirt, I was glad to have his help splinting the floor joists. I'm not actually sure I could have done it by myself.

While Sawyer held the heavy beams in place, I matched the predrilled holes and slid the bolts though. The phone rang. I wasn't at liberty to answer right then so the machine picked up. "Hi Freja. Rick here. I'm going to be back in town next week. I was hoping you would be free for dinner. Call me."

I blew out a sigh, and Sawyer looked over at me. "I take it he wasn't the heart breaker."

"No. He's a nice guy."

"Do you like him?"

"I like him, but I don't *like* him, like him."

Sawyer grinned. "Can you get that last bolt in?"

"It's off by a fraction." I jumped down off the ladder and grabbed the drill. Crap. It wouldn't fit between the joists.

Sawyer dropped his arms and shook the blood back into his hands. "I got something in my toolbox that might work. This beam isn't going anywhere."

He brought back a right-angle drill and completed the hole.

"I want one of those," I said tightening the bolt in place.

"I know where you can buy one."

"Let me guess."

"I could sell you this one."

"How much."

He grinned. "With tax and labor, twenty bucks."

"I'll get the money in a minute. Now for the test," I said. "Let's lower the jacks."

We cranked them down a little at a time, alternating between the three on the main floor. We could hear the house groaning as we lowered them but after the first few turns all was quiet.

"Yea!" I shouted. "That's the ticket!"

Sawyer grinned. "Brilliant."

"Should I have moved that old claw-foot tub out before leveling the floor? It must weigh five-hundred pounds."

"How *are* you going to get that out of there?"

"I don't know. I'll think of something. Are you hungry?

He glanced at his watch. "I wish I could stay, but I need to go. I have an early flight and I haven't finished at the store."

"I'm sorry. I've kept you all day. I hope you don't get in trouble. I should have ordered something to eat hours ago. When I get involved with a project I tend to forget to eat."

He tucked an errant curl behind my ear, and my heart raced. I swallowed loudly.

He laughed, his blue eyes twinkling dangerously. "Do I scare you?"

"No," I lied.

"I'm going to be out of town for the next three weeks. If you need anything from the store, any one of the guys will deliver."

"Business or pleasure?"

"A little of both." He grinned and ran a finger down my cheek. "I'll bring you with me one day."

I didn't know what to say. He was flirting again, and I really liked it. Having Sawyer's company today made me feel better about the Jason screw-up.

As he walked back to his truck he turned. "Try to stay out of trouble."

"I'll try."

∞

The next morning, I checked the refrigerator hoping elves had deposited some left-over Chinese food in there while I slept. They hadn't so I made a quick stop at Wendy's on my way to the library. After a few hours I found several collections of twenties memorabilia, but the recordings were expensive when possible, and mostly not possible.

Giving up on music, I started with the obituaries from 1921 and worked my way forwards. Julianne was black. It was always possible they never printed her obituary. I scanned over two thousand news clippings before my eyes burned and my mood had soured to the point of giving me a headache.

Changing direction, I started looking for singers in the entertainment pages of the Denver Post and the Rocky Mountain News. Unfortunately, Julianne was probably from the wrong side of the tracks to get billing in the major papers as well. Putting away yet another dead end, I saw Ted walk around the corner of the reference materials cabinet.

"Crap. What is he doing at the library?" I dashed behind the closest bookshelf and waited for several minutes. Unfortunately, it wasn't long enough. He stood only ten feet from me when I stepped out.

"Well, hello there, pretty lady," he said walking toward me. "You should have called me. I'm very good at research."

"I didn't want to trouble you. And you work at the Archives not the library." I was feeling stalked.

"It's no trouble at all. I enjoy spending time with you. It's been months since we worked together. What are you looking for today?"

"I'm looking for someone named Julianne Florence Rosa Parker. I believe she was in her early to mid-twenties when she died. I was looking at obituaries.

"For your friend with the bad memory?"

"Yes, I was looking for her friend." I hiked my bag onto my shoulder.

"Wait. Is she connected to Glen Miller?"

I scrambled to think of something that would make sense. "I was hoping to find out how Julianne Parker died. My friend said she knew Glen Miller before she died but she couldn't remember how long before." I stepped toward the door. "Well, I'm on my way out now. I'll see you the next time."

He took my hand and squeezed it. "I'm looking forward to it."

Ted certainly wouldn't be waiting around the library every day on the chance I'd be doing research. I wasn't that predictable, was I? I slipped out the door wondering if any normal men ever came into the club. My batting average was already poor, and it seemed to be getting worse.

CHAPTER 29

Dust had me coughing and sneezing, not to mention, sticking to the sweat on my back and arms. With the exception of the walls with windows, the drywall was almost complete on the main floor of the house, meaning not close to done at all. I was hot and tired of being startled by people banging on my door in the middle of the night. After carefully installing a doorbell, I needed some fresh air. It was a beautiful late August day, and the temperature was in the upper seventies.

I'd planted roses and grass in the front, but today I decided to tackle the wild rose bush in the backyard, the yard overgrown with weeds. The thorny rose bush was nearly eight feet tall and about fifteen feet wide. It was decorated with small yellow roses in June, but most of the branches appeared dead all year long. It straddled a wire fence between my yard and Haddie's yard. In order to install a redwood privacy fence, I would have to remove the bush.

Haddie was in her backyard hanging clothes out to dry. She waved to me. "What are you planning to do with all those tools?" she asked.

I had a couple saws, loppers, and pruning shears. "This bush is almost dead. I thought I'd get rid of it."

She hiked her laundry basket on her hip and came to the fence. The bush was so overgrown I could only see the top of her tightly curled grey hair. "Far be it for me to tell you what to do, but there's still life in that bush."

"It looks more dead than alive."

"All it needs is love and care." She stepped to the far end of the bush where I could see her better. "I remember this bush when the Henderson family lived here. I must have been about six years old. It was the most beautiful rose bush in the neighborhood. My father said it was here before they built any homes, a rare wild rose bush."

I was stunned. "You mean to tell me this bush is more than a hundred years old? I didn't know roses could live so long."

"Love and care. That's all us old things need."

"I don't know the first thing about caring for this."

"I do most of my pruning when the roses are dormant, but if you're careful, you can trim roses in the summer. Pruning increases its late-season bloom. Do you have any bleach?"

"Uh, no. Why do I need bleach?"

"To keep your tools clean. Give me a minute and I'll come show you some tricks. Don't touch anything until I get back."

Not a problem since I wasn't sure where to start anyway.

In less than ten minutes she was back with a small bucket of bleach water, dipping my tools and laying them out on newspaper. She began by cutting the dead and spent blooms with hand pruners about a quarter of an inch above where the stem of the flower met a side branch. "Make sure there are at least five leaves before you cut." She pulled a branch forward with a gloved hand. "Using a forty-five-degree angle cut allows water to run off the cut surface instead of collecting. This keeps them healthier." She showed me where to cut away dead branches and suckers from the base of the plant.

"You know a lot about flowers." I piled up the clippings. "Your yard is beautiful."

"I used to work in a greenhouse."

As we worked, she told me about her life. "Colorado carnations are very popular. Not as popular as they once were, but there are still a lot of greenhouses around Denver." She clipped dead branches and bundled the clipping in newspaper. "You want to keep these away from your healthy plants. I learned gardening basics years ago.

"I do love working with flowers, but when the war came, I chose to go back to school and become a nurse. When I was twenty-two, I went to work for the Rossonian Hotel because it paid better than gardening." She cleaned the shears with bleach water and attacked another scraggly branch. "The first-floor lounge was a popular jazz club. Black musicians who passed through Denver often played there on their nights off and between concerts at the larger venues downtown. Sometimes they would come in late at night, after they had finished performing at other clubs. It was fine for a black musician to perform downtown but they all stayed at the Rossonian."

"The lounge was famous for having the best jazz talent in the country. In later years, the hotel mostly catered to white folk. While I was there, I took care of Mr. Duke Ellington's rooms. He was a lovely man. Of course, back in '25 it was called the Baxter Hotel."

"What?" I glanced up from the clippings I was wrapping.

"It was the Baxter Hotel from 1912 until 1929 when they renamed it. I believe Baxter still owned the hotel, but a Mr. Ross managed it when I worked there. That's where the name Rossonian came from. After a few years Baxter sold the hotel to Ross. It's changed hands a dozen times since then. It's a real shame."

"Where is this hotel?"

She glanced over at me as if she hadn't quite heard the question.

"The Baxter," I said. "Where is it?"

"Good lord, child. Why, it's just down the street. It's one of the neighborhood's icons."

I felt foolish that I hadn't been aware there was a hotel a couple blocks away. It was a rough neighborhood and I rarely had reason to go north.

"I suppose it's not that surprising you didn't know about it. It's been boarded up for a while now. I did see something in the paper about Mayor Peña loaning almost four-hundred-thousand dollars to a real estate company for economic development. The name was Star

One or something. They bought the hotel from Goens and Johnson. We'll see if anything happens. At the rate the gangs are moving in, it wouldn't surprise me to see all that government money flushed down the toilet."

"You said the hotel had jazz music. Do you recall a girl by the name of Julianne Parker?" Parker could have been a married name, but it was worth a shot.

Haddie flexed her fingers. There was a flash of pain in her eyes. "My hands aren't what they used to be. I always wanted to live to a hundred but now I'm not so sure.

"I can't say if I knew a Julianne Parker though I clearly remember meeting Billie Holiday." When Haddie stood, her back cracked. "That was a very long time ago. I worked at the hotel until '46 when I graduated from the University of Colorado Nursing School." The rose pruning wasn't finished but I could tell Haddie was done for the day. She stripped off her garden gloves revealing heavy swelling around her knuckles. "I'm sure you could find out more about the hotel at the library. It was the hottest spot this side of the Mississippi."

"I'll check it out. Thanks for telling me about the hotel. I love this neighborhood."

She tilted her head to one side trying to figure out if I was serious. Deciding that I must be, she said, "There's a lot of history in this town. Five Points was a hoppin' place. Good people of all incomes, and the Rossonian was Denver's premier jazz scene until the early sixties." She started shuffling toward the gate. "Things changed when wealthy black folk were allowed to move into white neighborhoods again. Those with money moved out of Five Points leaving only the poorest to carry on the memory." She eyeballed my dilapidated porch as we walked past. "Child, I hope you know what you're doing."

So do I, I thought as I waved good-bye. I couldn't wait to hit the library. I quickly stashed my tools away and jumped in the car. The library was only about a mile away. On the radio there was talk of

Reagan and Gorbachev. Our president was telling the Russians to tear down the wall separating East and West Germany. It gave me an odd feeling. My entire life was influenced by the cold war. I remembered hiding under my desk at school, waiting for the atom bomb to take us out. The Russians were the enemy. What would we do if they became our friend?

I headed up to the floor holding old newspaper clippings and magazines. I swear the librarian cringed when I started looking through the stacks of papers with dirt under my nails. I made a quick trip to the Ladies Room and washed my hands. My nails were a wreck. One day I would be done with all this house stuff and have a professional manicure.

Back at the table where I'd stacked the old clippings, I sorted through them, looking for any sign of the Baxter Hotel. It took several hours, and the library was closing as I stopped at the copier. I held an old clipping advertising a jazz pianist. Baxter was name of the hotel and the address was just down the street on 26th and Welton.

I was so excited, I ran through the house calling, "Julianne, I know what it means now. The Baxter is a hotel. They feature jazz singers in the lounge. Come out. Let me tell you about it." I looked down at the photocopy in my hand and made a decision. I didn't want to show her the article because of the date. I folded up the article and stuffed it in my jeans pocket. "The hotel down the street from here used to be called the Baxter. Does the name Rossonian mean anything to you? You might have been singing at the hotel. That's why you know the name Baxter."

At the top of the stairs, she sat, perched on the railing, swinging a tiny foot back and forth. "The Rossonian? I do remember hearing talk of this change. I hadn't realized they'd done it. Though it may just have been habit to think of the hotel as the Baxter."

I wanted to tell her it was changed in 1929 but that might lead her to ask what the current year was, and that might lead her to totally freak out. For me, it meant I had a year for her death. If the hotel changed names in '29 and she barely remembered the change meant she must have died about the same time.

"I'm going to see if I can find some flyers or billboards from the hotel that might help you remember." I headed up the stairway. "Now I need to get to work. What would you like to listen to tonight?"

"I like the songs you played last night."

"The Elvis Christmas album?"

"Yes, his voice is just the ant's ear. I adore the song about mama and the roses. My mama loved roses, too."

"That's one of my favorite songs. I play it all year."

I was walking on air. I knew Julianne was a jazz singer from sometime in the late twenties. She must have worked at the Baxter, now Rossonian Hotel, and died before the hotel changed names or shortly thereafter. I blew out a sigh. *Unless her swiss cheese mind was only focused on the years before the change.*

CHAPTER 30

While I dressed for work, I played Elvis for Julianne, and played Prince for me. She liked *When Doves Cry* and *Purple Rain*. I didn't think she would be singing either song any time soon, but I was glad she didn't hate all my music. To keep her company, I turned the radio on and left for work.

I had a good night because I'd made a major advancement in the case of my ghostly jazz singer. When Jason came in, I hardly felt anything at all.

"I'm going to Vegas again next week," Ginger, aka Carol on her car registration, said. "You should come with me."

I cleaned my ashtray over the trash. "It does sound like fun."

"We'd have a riot." She loaded her tray with drinks.

"I'm right in the middle of something."

Turning to leave the well, she said, "You're going to be like, in the middle of that for a long time. Take a break."

"I don't know. Let me see how this week goes."

∞

Gene didn't know anything about the hotel name change. "I know a lot about American history but a hotel changing ownership isn't exactly the kind of history I teach high-school students."

"Thanks anyway. I'll check the library. They must have something about it."

"Why the interest?"

"It's research for a friend."

I was standing in the well when Ted strolled through the door sporting a new Abercrombie & Fitch look. He set his leather briefcase full of state secrets down in its usual place and took a seat at his regular table.

"Hi," I said. "How are you tonight?" I set his Bacardi and Coke on a fresh napkin.

"Thank you." He handed me a ten and waved off the change. "I'm good today. What have you been up to?"

"I'm researching the Rossonian Hotel. The name changed from Baxter in 1929."

"Would that be the same Baxter you were looking for a few months ago? It was a hotel?"

"Yes. I didn't know it at the time."

"What does this have to do with your friend or the Parker woman who died?"

"I think my friend used to work there and any information, especially pictures might help her memory. I think her friend, Julianne, died about the time the hotel changed names."

Taking a sip of his drink, he looked at me with interest. "The library should have what you need. I take it that you didn't find the obituary for Julianne Parker."

I blew out a sigh. "No." I set napkins in front of Paris and London.

Ted gave me half a smile. "Bring the ladies what they want, I'm going to hit the head."

∞

When I got home that night the temperature was still in the mid-seventies and forecast to be near one hundred the following day. Without air conditioning, it was too hot to work during the day, so I spent the next two nights finishing the dining room sheetrock leaving part of the wall with the bathroom plumbing open and, of course, the two walls with the door covered windows. I didn't know what the kitchen was going to look like, and the bathroom was a whole other issue.

I woke up to Julianne standing at the foot of my bed. I was growing used to having her watch me. Sleepily, I stretched and slowly crawled out of bed.

"Something has you balled up," she said following me to the bathroom. "You didn't well sleep last night. After your discovery, I thought you would be in better spirits."

Julianne sat on the side of the bathtub while I washed my face, twisted my hair up in a bun on top of my head, and stuck a wooden pencil through it to hold it in place. "I can't seem to find an answer to the kitchen. I hate every plan I come up with and I need to start on it so I can finish the first floor." I was hesitant to take the doors off the windows. I still felt a little vulnerable, but I couldn't do anymore on the main floor.

"Why don't you work on the second floor?"

"I guess I could do that next. I could live in the parlor while I tear out the other bedrooms and the bathroom. Would be nice if I could finish the drywall downstairs, but I still need to run plumbing and wiring through the parlor and dining room and into the kitchen. I just don't know where I'm going to put it when I get there."

"That does complicate matters."

The hardest part of doing the upper floor would be the bathroom. I had a plan for the bathroom but moving the heavy bathtub was going to be a serious challenge.

I hadn't figured out what to do for the however-many-days-it-would-take to tear it out and replace the toilet. I could shower in the kitchen sink, but even as awful as that old metal monster was, there were certain things it couldn't be used for.

Back in my room, I shrugged into a t-shirt and pulled up my cut-off jean shorts. I set aside the kitchen drawings and started on the upstairs plans. I knew the hall closet would have to change and I wanted to remove a wall from the north room to make a loft overlooking the stairs. The master bedroom would just need the standard; remove the plaster and lathe, put in new electrical, put up new sheetrock, tape, texture, and then paint. It sounded simple but it was a truck load of work. *Awesome. Another wall to tear out.*

I moved my bedroom to the unfinished parlor. By closing the pocket doors, I could almost feel like I had some privacy although I could see through the wall into the dining room. I was going to have to give up my window coverings one day. I'd had the alarm system for over a month, but I still felt a little uneasy about removing the doors.

I tore out the remaining upper floor walls over the course of my three-day weekend. I was feeling motivated. I'd already stolen most of the molding to use on the main floor, so it went pretty fast.

I didn't have a lot of changes in the master bedroom. Where a wall once separated the little room from the stairway there was now wooden railing. I added a shallow closet and some shelves on the west wall of my new loft where the ceiling sloped to a knee wall.

Hauling the sheetrock up the stairs was a pain. I cut as many pieces as I could down in the living room before bringing it up.

During the next week, I tore out the linen closet and made an extra-large closet in the second bedroom; the room I'd been using for a living room. The ugly plaid couch was now in the actual living room. It was unlikely it would be there long. It was truly hideous. Once I'd learned how to frame, the sheetrock and tape went pretty fast. I was able to complete the drywall, taping and texture in the second bedroom before going to work on Wednesday.

I begged Nick for the next week off and finished drywalling the master bedroom and the walk-in closet. I hooked the new wiring to the old wires so I would have lights upstairs. I got as far as the second bedroom before I was forced to tackle the bathroom. UGH!

∞

Customarily, I would go to H B Woods when I needed something for the house, but a flyer I received in the mail advertised a sale on bathtubs and showers at the local big box hardware store. I was wandering through the lighting department when I ran into Ted.

He was with a skinny, mean-looking woman who might have been his wife. She wore a baggy and stained sweatshirt with dirty looking scrubs and flip-flops. In contrast, Ted was dressed in a polo shirt and dress pants. We pretended not to know each other. It was an unwritten rule that you didn't recognize strip-club customers in public. I thought about all the time and money Ted spent at the club, wondering if that was the reason his wife looked so cross. My house may cost a lot and might give me fits, but it never cheated on me.

With delivery, the shower, toilet, and tile were more expensive than I'd originally planned. Although I had almost everything I needed to start on the bathroom, I drove by the H B Woods anyway. I didn't see Sawyer's half-restored truck in the lot, but I went inside to see if there was something I had to buy.

"Can I help you," a young man asked as I meandered up and down the plumbing aisle.

"I'm trying to decide on a shower head. Is Sawyer around?"

"He's left for the day. Can I give him a message?"

"No. It's cool. Just haven't been in for a while."

Depressed, I went home and shut the water off in preparation of moving the bathroom appliances out to make room for the new ones. I took out the bathroom sink, which was easy, and disconnected the bathtub. I would save the toilet for the last possible moment.

Before going to bed, I struggled to carry my new toilet and bathtub upstairs. The toilet was much heavier than the fiberglass tub, but easier to carry with a rope strapped around it. The molded sink and countertop were heavy but still easier than the previous items. The vanity was awkward because of the shape. I turned it on its back and used a rope to pull it up the stairs, sliding it on the edges of the treads. That gave me an idea.

∞

The next morning, I struggled to flip the cast iron bathtub over so I could slide it across the hall floor. After tying a rope around the four claw feet, I double wrapped the other end of the rope around the corner post of the loft. Dragging the tub to the top of the stairs, I loosened the rope and slowly let the tub drop down the first step. That worked, only eleven more steps to go. The next two steps went smoothly, and the bathtub was on the landing. The line of the remaining steps was more direct and longer, so I tied the loose end of the rope around my waist. I didn't want to take the chance the tub was too heavy and might pull the rope through my hands. I could imagine it sliding down the stairs, gaining speed and crashing through the front door. The rope wrapped twice around the post and several times around me. I loosened the rope at my waist a fraction for every inch the bathtub moved down to the next step. I was feeling good about things when halfway down the stairs, I ran out of rope. With one end of the rope tied to me, and the other to the bathtub, I held it in place with my hands, I was afraid to release either end of the rope. I considered my dilemma for several minutes.

Julianne stood in the loft, watching me. It would have been extremely convenient for her to have been more than fog at that moment.

"You appear to be in trouble."

"You don't say."

"Is there some direction you can give me?"

I thought about it long and hard but couldn't come up with a damn thing. I tested the balance and weight of the bathtub. Nope. If I let go, it would slide the rest of the way down the stairs. Its weight was too much for me to hold back without the rope pulley. As it was, the rope was pinching my waist pretty good.

The doorbell rang. I glanced up to see Sawyer peeking through the window.

"I can't get to the door. I'm a little tied up."

He tried the handle. Of course, I'd remembered to lock the door this time. "You look like you need help," he shouted through the door.

I didn't want to admit it. "I guess you could break the window." I blew out a sigh when the glass shattered. He reached through the window and unlocked the door. Climbing the steps, he held the tub in place as I untied the rope. Slowly we inched it down to the lower landing.

Once settled, Sawyer untied the cord from the tub. "That was interesting."

I could feel my face turn tens shades of red. "I guess I should have measured the distance better." I sat down on the steps feeling like an idiot. "I'm glad you came by when you did. I don't know how long I would have been stuck there."

"I'm always glad to help. I've told you that before." He lifted my chin and gazed into my eyes. "Anytime you need a hand, I'm happy to come over. There's no shame in needing help. Even guys like me need help sometimes."

"I didn't want to bother you."

"You came by the store yesterday looking for me."

"I was in the area. I just stopped to say hi."

His face lit up. "I'm sorry I missed you."

I stood up and cracked my back. "One of the guys said you were gone for the day."

"I was shopping."

I never thought about him doing something so mundane. "What were you shopping for?"

He smiled. "It's never too early to shop for Christmas."

"It's a hundred degrees outside. That doesn't exactly put me in the mood for Christmas shopping."

"It's my sister's birthday next week."

Oh, he has a sister. This was news. The dolly was standing in the living room. Sawyer retrieved it and tried to wedge the dolly under the lip of the bathtub. "This won't work. We need to turn it around."

"What did you get for her?"

"A gift certificate for Macy's."

"That's a little spendy for my blood." Tipping the bathtub on end, it was much easier to turn with the two of us.

"Anytime you want to go shopping at Macy's, just let me know."

"Ok, next time I'm in New York, I'll call you."

Sawyer muscled the tub out the back door and down the back steps. Again, I was thankful for his strength. I went to the kitchen and grabbed a soda for him. When he came back in the house, he smiled. "Thanks. That's hard work. How were you planning to get that out the back door?"

"I hadn't thought about it. My main concern was getting it out of the bathroom so I can install the new sink and toilet. I can't go very long without a bathroom."

He finished off the cold drink in three long swallows. "I had planned to ask you if you'd like to go to a movie this afternoon, but I can see you're preoccupied."

I grimaced. "I can't leave. The grocery store will get tired of seeing me. I need a place to water the flowers."

"I know you don't need the help, but I'm free this afternoon if you want to move the toilet."

"Great! I'll buy lunch."

He shook his head. "I got it."

The bathroom had flooded often enough the original floor was trashed. We spent the next three hours tearing out the flooring and laying a new subfloor. The sixteen-inch by sixteen-inch tiles had to be set and dry before we could replace the toilet, tub, and vanity. We set a huge fan in the room to help set the tiles. The sun was setting when we finished the grout.

I sat back on my heels. "Wow. I'm famished."

Sawyer wiped his hands on a rag. "Me, too. Let's eat."

"Should I order pizza?"

He stood and headed down the stairs. "I told you, I got this one."

He went out to his truck and came back with a cooler and a picnic basket. Smiling, he wrapped an arm around my shoulder and led me to the kitchen. Setting the containers on the table he began pulling out the contents; fried chicken, baking powder biscuits, coleslaw, and a bottle of wine.

"Wow," I said. "You had this in your truck?"

"I was hoping you would join me for a movie and lunch today."

"Oh. OH!" I bit on my lower lip. "And I kept you working all day. I'm so sorry."

He motioned for me to sit down. "One day you will be finished with this project and we can catch that movie."

The kitchen table was covered in dust and bits of drawings. Every other room in the house was half finished, and the couch was covered with tools. It was a warm August evening, so we opted to carry two kitchen chairs out to the pallet patio. I grabbed the cardboard box my sink came in and used it for a table.

"So, you have a sister, and she likes to shop at Macy's." I bit into a biscuit drenched in honey.

Sawyer leaned back and crossed his ankles. "Christine. She's in college. She likes clothing, but I can never pick out something that she wants or when I do, it doesn't fit."

"I don't like people picking out my clothes either."

"You would be easy to shop for. I would just buy you a nice tool chest."

I laughed. He was right, my tools were all over the house. "I could use some more of those old pallets to make my deck a little larger. I'm planning on stacking them two high so there is a little more of a step down to the grass."

"Have you planted grass back here?" He glanced over the weeds that were nearly three feet tall.

"No. But I will someday."

I was feeling good having shared a bottle of wine. I'm a bit more of a straight shots person but drinking wine makes me feel like an adult. I suspected Sawyer filled my glass more often than his own. My thoughts strayed to more illicit contemplations but whenever I pictured Sawyer in my bed, all I could see was unfinished walls and wires running everywhere. I was covered in dirt and dog tired. As sexy as he was looking at that moment, I couldn't bear to let him run his strong hands over me before I had a bath. I was about to talk myself into not caring how tired and dirty I was when his beeper when off.

"Do you have to go."

"Not right away. What about your family? Sisters or brothers?"

"Yes, three brothers and a sister. My brother, Connor, is getting married next week, and Shannon is going to have a baby in October."

"Are you excited?"

"Yes. It will be my first niece or nephew."

"Family is important." His beeper went off again.

"How about you? Any plans for children?" It was the wine talking.

He grinned. "Not in the next couple of months."

My phone rang and I ran into the house to answer it. My timing always sucked when it came to this guy.

"My sister thinks she's going into early labor and Eric is out of town," I told him. "I should go get her, and you probably need to deal with whatever is on the other end of your pager."

"The tile should be good enough to set the toilet."

"Crap. I totally forgot. Yes. I have to have a toilet."

"Why don't you take care of your sister, that can't wait. I'll let myself out.

I was nervous about leaving him here and more nervous about leaving the alarm unset. "I don't know how long I'll be."

Carrying the dishes inside, he said, "If you loan me a key, I can set the dead bolt."

He freaked me out when he read my mind that way. I handed him my only spare key and our date ended as they usually did, abruptly.

As it turned out, it was a false alarm with Shannon but the doctor at the hospital told her she needed bed rest up until the baby was born. We sat in the emergency room while the doctor wrote up her release forms.

She was wringing her hands and frowning. "What am I going to do about the wedding?"

"Connor will understand," I said dabbing sweat from her brow.

"You can go in my place."

"I don't think so."

"Sure, you can. Mom can take in my dress for you."

"We need to talk to Connor and Bridgett first."

"Are you bringing Rick as your plus-one?"

"Oh, hell no."

"Do you have someone else?"

I thought about it. The Bobby fiasco came to mind. Asking Sawyer would send a weird message. Jason wouldn't go. Inviting Rick would make that whole mess blow up again. He'd called while I was on vacation, but I let the answering machine pick it up. Dave? He would probably go if he thought I'd put out afterwards.

"No. Just gonna be me."

CHAPTER 31

By the time I got home it was too late to call Sawyer. I couldn't decide if that was a good thing or not. Seeing Shannon and thinking about Connor getting married made me think about settling down. Sawyer was the closest thing I had to male companionship, but the whole beeper thing had me worried. He didn't look like someone who sold drugs but that isn't exactly the kind of thing you ask a guy. The words of a familiar song played in my head. *"It's a losing proposition, but one you can't refuse. It's the politics of contraband, it's the smuggler's blues."*

Julianne was waiting by the door when I got home at six in the morning. "Sawyer is an agreeable man. You would do well to summon him more often. He brings a vivacity to your being."

"He is nice."

"Why do you keep him at arm's length?"

I couldn't really explain. Was it because he was a lot like Dirk and a lot like my dad? I saw what my mother went through, and I lived it with Dirk. Both men were charming "lady's men" who had an untamed, exciting, yet alluring wild streak.

"I don't know," I lied. "Maybe he's just not the one."

"I have a friend who tried to steer me in another direction when I fell in love. He meant well, but the heart wants what the heart wants. I'll not pressure you further."

"Who is you friend?"

"My friend's face is clear to me. We played music together at a place uptown." Her eyes looked off in the distance as she remembered the night. "Billy was the door man. I asked him about the north wind." She paused. "It was a password, I'm certain. Another man who was new to me asked about the traffic on Colfax before opening the door. The place was hopping, though we hadn't set up the band."

"This was a place where you sang? Was it the Baxter?"

"No." she said slowly and then thought for several heartbeats. "I was feeling nervous and unsettled. I was speaking with…" she frowned. "There was to be a gathering at the river, a meeting. I feared for his life. It was those ruffians he knew." She stopped speaking and paced the room.

I wanted to pressure her on to tell me more, but I could tell she was struggling with the memory.

She sat on a five-gallon bucket of drywall mud. "I tried to keep him from going to the meeting, but he would have none of it" Her eyes filled with tears. "Rory was a gem of a man."

"Rory? Is that your boyfriend's name?"

She looked startled to see me there, almost as if she had forgotten where she was. "No. Rory was the one who gave me counsel. It was his sister, Josie with the lovely hair of red."

Names! I was so excited. She was starting to remember names. "Anything else you can recall from that night? Josie's last name?"

She looked sad and shook her head slowly. "I remember not."

I needed to get some sleep because I had to be at work at four. All the work, moving the tub, and tiling the floor, and then the hours at the hospital had me done in.

I laid down and got about six hours of sleep. What I didn't get was a bath. My tub and sink were still sitting in the master bedroom with the boxes of bath tiles and the vanity. I was tempted to call in sick so I could finish the bathroom.

I didn't.

It was a tough night. When I pulled up to the front door, there was an ambulance with lights flashing. That was never a good sign.

"What's going on?" I asked the doorman as I came in.

He set down the Rubik's Cube he'd been trying to solve for several days. "I guess one of the managers told a girl she was fired, and she went into epileptic shock."

"No way!"

"Way."

"Oh, he must feel terrible."

"I think she might be faking it."

"What do the paramedics think?"

"They'll take her to the hospital. Won't take the chance she isn't faking."

The rest of the night was better. The club was all abuzz with speculations about the incident. Sometimes I felt sorry for the managers. It seemed like a pretty thankless job. I knew I was being a pain in the ass, but I did ask for Thursday and Friday off again so I could at least get the new bathtub installed. Nick needed me on Saturday but that gave me a couple days. When I got to it, I had to do still more framing to set the tub because the room was a little wider than the length of the tub. As it turned out, that left a nice two-foot shelf at the rear of the bathtub to stack towels or nice decorator items. I drug the new tub from the bedroom, which was a fraction of the weight of the old tub, into the bathroom and set it in the framework. The drywall went up better than in most of the other rooms and by eight in the evening I was able to set the vanity and sink.

I was looking forward to moving my bed back upstairs. The parlor seemed a little claustrophobic, probably because of the door covering the only window in the room. I'd never covered the master bedroom windows with any more than aluminum foil.

The phone rang. It was my mother wondering if I was going to wear Shannon's dress. I hadn't called my brother and soon-to-be sister-in-law yet. I hated being in weddings.

By midnight on Friday, I had the tile on the shower walls and the taping done in the remaining walls. It was a miraculous change. I sat in the tub and imagined my first shower. I had no shower curtain, so it wasn't going to be tonight.

∞

Morning light crept in around the door nailed over the window, waking me. I had a lot to do before work on Saturday night. First stop, K-Mart for a shower curtain. I went to a wallpaper store and picked out some trim paper and found some for the master bedroom as well. A little paint and I'd have a real bathroom for the first time since moving to Denver. And a real shower, something I sorely needed at the moment since I'd been working two days straight.

After K-Mart, I swung by the hardware store to pick up a medicine cabinet and a large mirror. I also need a light fixture. The one I'd originally bought wasn't going to work. That's part of the problems with buying things on sale before you have a good working plan. I was trying to decide on a new light when Sawyer came over. "Bathroom light?"

"Yeah."

"How's your sister?"

"Good. False alarm, but she has to stay in bed. I'm stuck being a bridesmaid in her place."

Sawyer laughed. I'm sure it was because he couldn't imagine me in a gown. I had trouble picturing it myself. As it was, I was dressed in filthy cut-offs and a stained t-shirt with my hair in a scraggly knot on my head.

He sobered. "I couldn't get away the last two days. Would you like help setting the tub and sink?"

I beamed. "Done."

"Really? I thought you had to work."

"I skipped work."

"Good for you."

"I still have the lights to mount and the mirror to hang. I was hoping to get it done before work today at nine."

Sawyer looked over at a man in a dark suit. I'd seen the guy there before. That had to be the boss. "I can't get away today," he said. "I have to go to the Englewood store."

"I understand. Thanks for setting the toilet for me."

We both stood there without talking. After a minute, he reached into his pocket and drew out my key. "It's was no trouble."

I hesitated but held out my hand. He was giving my key back and I didn't know if I should be thankful or, insulted.

He took my hand and placed the key in it. "Anytime you need me. Call." He grinned. "Just not today. Okay?"

"Okay. Can I get some more pallets?"

"You bet."

∞

When I got home the answering machine was going crazy.

Mom: "I talked to Connor and Bridgett. They would love to have you fill in for Shannon. Call me." Click

Bridgett: "Hi Freja. This is Bridgett. Shannon can't make the wedding. Would you be a doll and fill in? Call me."

Shannon: "I'm home now. I talked to Bridgett. It's all set."

Mom: "I have Shannon's dress. You'll have to come by so I can make the alterations. Call me"

Connor: "Hey Freeman. Bridgett wants you to fill in for Shannon. I know it's not your thing, but she really needs you. Rehearsal dinner is next Thursday night."

Mom: "Shannon tells me you don't have a plus-one. I have a friend who has a son about your age. He's divorced. Call me."

Rick: "Hi. Haven't heard from you in a while. The offer to sell the place is still on the table. Call me."

I rewound the tape in the machine and called Bridgett first to tell her I would be honored to fill in. I told my brother I wouldn't let them down. I told my mother I wouldn't show up for the wedding if she tried to set me up, but I'd be by on Sunday to have her fit the dress. I couldn't bear to call Rick.

Monday morning, as I walked into the kitchen, I heard the sound of dripping water. After close inspection I found the shower was leaking into the parlor. "CRAP! I'm getting tired of this." I went upstairs and checked the connection. It was behind the wall. I must not have got a good seal in the plumbing. I studied at the wall in the second bedroom and shuttered.

"What are you brooding over so darkly?"

I jumped and let out a squeak. "You scared the crap out of me again."

"I believe you're over done."

I shook my head. "I believe you're right. It's the shower. There is a leak. That means cutting a hole in the wall."

"You make such a grievance of trifles. I've seen you do much more."

"Cutting a hole in a newly finished wall is not a trifle!" But I knew, compared to her problems, it really was a trifle. "I'm sorry. It isn't that big of a deal."

"You have such great heart and pluck."

I got out my hole saw and started in on the wall. The trick would be to cut enough drywall out between the studs to get at the plumbing. I would have to nail blocks to the studs to attach the new drywall when I was done.

Once I had a decent hole in the wall, I could see where the PVC pipe attached to the shower fixture. That was it, the leak. I went downstairs and shut off the water. Grabbing my plumbing box, I headed back upstairs and disconnected the shower fixture. I'd forgotten there would still be water in the pipe. Water sprayed in my face. "#@%*&#@!" I got the fixture screwed back in place with fresh plumbing tape.

Julianne quietly watched me wipe up the water on the floor. "You have the goods."

"The what?"

"I am enormously astounded. You might do anything if occasion warranted it."

"It was just a leaking pipe."

"I'm not so resourceful. It was difficult to weather the profitless intervals which punctuated my professional engagements."

I had to stop and digest her words. "What did you do between engagements?"

She sat on my one and only step stool. "I made up rooms at the hotel."

"The Baxter?"

The doorbell rang and Julianne evaporated. "It must be Sawyer. He promised to bring some pallets over today." I tossed the towel in the laundry basket and headed down the steps to open the door. He was already unloading the pallets, so I went to help him.

"Hi. Thanks for bringing these by."

A smile lit his face. "Working hard today?"

"Yes, there was a leak in the new shower."

There was a distinct twinkle in his eyes—cornflower blue with a misleading softness in them that charmed every woman he met. I felt a blush rise to my cheeks.

We carted the pallets around the house to the backyard and stacked them up against the house. He was really staring at me. I'm used to guys looking at me at work; mostly because I'm usually half naked. I smiled my best come hither smile, thinking about our last date. His eyes crinkled and his dimples deepened. He was definitely flirting with his eyes, and I found him hard to resist.

"Come in for a bit," I said, "Would you like a soda?"

"Sure," he said, and he followed me up the back steps into the kitchen. He was looking at me so intently I started to feel that warm tingle in my belly.

I grabbed a can from the fridge and handed it to him. He was staring into my eyes as I took my most provocative pose leaning against the old metal sink.

He sipped the cold drink; not taking his eyes off me. "You're really something," he said. His voice was husky and ultra-sexy. Either that, or my hormones were freaking out. I could have done him right then and there.

"I've almost finished the upstairs. Would you like to see it?"

He placed a hand on the sink beside me and leaned closer. "Tempting," he said, still looking into my eyes, "but I can't stay. I've got court this afternoon."

"You get a ticket or something?" I purred, praying it wasn't about drugs.

"No, renewing a license."

I took a chance. "I'm pure as the driven snow—but I've been known to drift. Are you sure you don't want to come upstairs for a few minutes and test my new shower?"

He looked as if he was contemplating my offer; a grin lighting his face. He ran his thumb across my lips and leaned forward. "When we go upstairs, I'm going to need more than a few minutes." He taped me on the nose with his finger. "I'll see you later." He downed the rest of the soda and slipped out the back door still smiling.

I stared after him. Julianne appeared by my side. "Wow," I said to her. "Sawyer's never come on to me like that before. Seems silly to flirt; knowing you can't stay. I don't know why he didn't act that way last week; when we had more time." I shook my head in frustration. "I don't get this guy at all. One minute he acts like he likes me and the next he's running away."

Julianne perched on the table. "He may be as unsure of your intentions as you are of his."

"I made my intentions quite clear today."

Brooding, I went upstairs to the bathroom to test the shower. As I passed the mirror, I was horrified by my reflection. The water that sprayed me in the face earlier had run my mascara. Sawyer wasn't flirting with me; he was probably wondering why I look like Alice Cooper. Oh, and I held nothing back. I am such an idiot. Note to self—Always. Always look in the mirror before you answer the damn door.

CHAPTER 32

On the way to Connor and Bridgett's wedding, I had to stop and write down a bit of graffiti on a building on Twentieth and Grant. *"Everyone wants to live at the expense of the state. They forget that the State lives at the expense of everyone."* I knew Aiden would like it, and I wasn't entirely sure he hadn't written it. As much as I didn't want to think about things like city council, my brothers were Libertarian activists and rarely did an evening with them go by without some reference to the overreaching government.

As I joined the wedding party in the prep room, Aiden was deep in conversation with Bridgett's brother about gun laws. "The Armed Career Criminal Act increases penalties for possession of a firearm for people who are not allowed to own a gun. What makes anyone think steeper penalties will be a deterrent? These guys already don't care if they are breaking the law."

"But they would have to spend more time in jail if they got caught," I said.

"Jails are just breeding grounds for better quality criminals. Three meals a day and a roof over their head while they hone their trade."

"I have faith that at least some of these guys value their freedom."

"Some do. I just think we should be repealing laws, not adding more. Harsher penalties never work. There is nothing harsher than death but there are still murders in states with the death penalty."

We lined up as the music cued the start of the service. My mind went back to Julianne and how she might have died. She apparently had a strong fear of the police which led me to believe her death had been violent. If it had been expected, surely, she would have gone to wherever it is souls go.

The service was glorious. I'm not usually one for big weddings but it was impressive. They were married at the Grant Humphreys Mansion which was built in 1902. The mansion's interior featured a grand staircase, ornately detailed fireplaces, elegantly appointed rooms and a classic ballroom. They were married on the south terrace with its fabulous views of the Front Range.

At the reception, Aden pulled me aside. "I just lost my business partner," he said. "What are you doing these days?"

"Seriously? You think Connor's going to quit the business?"

"Bridgett is loaded. Old Colorado silver money."

"I was wondering how they could afford this place." I watched the newlyweds dance. "Connor won't quit. He has too much dad in him. Pride will keep him showing up to work every day, and Bridgett's money might help you expand the business."

"That would be helpful."

"Here's a little something I saw on the way over here." I handed him the graffiti message. "There are actual other people who seem to agree with you."

Aiden laughed and punched me gently on the shoulder. "I knew I could count on you to cheer me up. You look great in that dress; too bad you didn't have a date."

I punched him back, a little harder than he punched me.

My mother came over to the table with a man who looked about twice my age and introduced him as the son of her friend. He was round faced and round bellied. Aiden punched me again.

"Ow." I rubbed my shoulder. The round guy looked confused and uncomfortable.

"It's nice to meet you," I said. "This is my brother Aiden. He likes to hit me when he can't remember how to talk."

The guy relaxed a little. "Nice to meet you. Your mother was telling me you were looking for a dance partner."

Now I wanted to punch my mother in the arm—but refrained. "Later?"

He nodded. "Sure, I'll come back."

After he walked away my mother frowned at me. "Couldn't you have been a little more inviting?"

"I don't feel like dancing right now."

"Sometimes we have to do things we don't want to do."

"I'm not looking for a dance partner, or a partner of any kind right now."

"He's a nice man. He has a good position at Sears as a corporate buyer."

"Mom."

Aiden slipped away from the table and found a pretty girl to dance with. "See there," she said. "Your brothers have no problem finding dates."

"She's our cousin. If it will make you feel better, I'll go dance."

"I don't want you to be lonely. You spend all your time and money on that old house your father dumped on you. You won't always be young and beautiful."

"Thanks for the reminder, mom."

"You know what I mean. I want to see you have some fun."

"Okay. I'll go dance."

I did go dance with the round guy and a half a dozen other men, both older and younger. I had a great time. I'd forgotten how much I liked dancing and by the time we put Connor and Bridgett in the limousine to the airport, I was exhausted but happy.

I worried that Aiden hadn't spoken with our parents about his situation. He would have to do it sometime but with all the commotion over Connor's wedding and Shannon's baby, this probably wasn't the best time.

∞

I drove to work with the car windows down. Autumn is a beautiful time of the year in Colorado, for at least a week or two. Although, sometimes an early snow kills the leaves before they have a chance to change color. It had been in the upper sixties all month with the exception of the eleventh and twelfth when the temperature plummeted to thirty degrees causing the leaves to change to bright yellows and oranges. As a native of the state I'm used to carrying several sweaters and jackets in my car, not to mention the shovel and boots in the trunk.

In between taking the doors off the windows and finishing the drywall and wiring on the first floor, I spent a lot of time looking through the obits for anything about Julianne and after several days, I concluded they may not have put her obituary in the paper at all. Sawyer was right, the light in the house made me feel much better. I went to Ace Hardware to have new glass cut for the front window. I walked around and analyzed the work I'd done. Julianne walked silently beside me. We stopped and stared out the new front picture window.

"It's lovely," she said. "I am enamored with your talents."

"I wish I would have practiced on the parlor first. I learned a lot about what not to do in here."

"An invitation to Sawyer is warranted. He has always held an interest in your work."

"He usually makes fun of me."

Once I had the molding replaced, I hung drapes in the dining and living rooms. I still needed to finish the texture and paint, but I didn't want the neighbors looking through the windows. There was also the possibility that a city inspector might happen by and see all the work I'd none without the benefit of a permit.

I was avoiding the hardware store because I was still embarrassed by my flirting. As it was, I had plenty to keep me busy because in late September, Eric and Shannon found the perfect house in Englewood. It was a 1970s, split-level brick house in a great neighborhood by the Cinderella City Mall. Not wanting Shannon to lift any boxes, everyone in the family helped them get moved in. She was big as a house by now and ready to be done with being pregnant. Watching her waddle around reinforced my fear of having children.

In between finishing the texture and painting on the upper floor and working at the club, I was helping Shannon and Eric decorate the baby's room. Everything was in yellow and lavender. Shannon was hoping for a girl. Every day, I found myself more excited by the thought of being an aunt. I stopped a K-Mart for new baby items on my way to Shannon's. It's amazing how many things babies need. I picked up a baby bathtub, a crib and a cute little dresser with daisies on the front.

∞

On October fifth, Shannon gave birth to twins, a boy and a girl. As a second baby shower gift, I bought them another crib. Mom was at their house every day with gifts and advice for raising the little ones. Shannon's children gave new life to both my parents. Dad was already picking out colleges. Aiden and Connor gave them a new Ford Bronco which I suspected Bridgett had paid for. The whole family was driving Shannon and Eric crazy for the first couple of weeks. By Halloween, they tired of family and family advice. I knew this but I couldn't help myself. I'd given them a week off and now I needed to see the babies again.

I stood on the doorstep; my arms loaded with gifts. Having my own children didn't seem as important as being the coolest aunt ever.

Eric answered the door looking beat. "Hi Freja," he said quietly.

"I can just leave these if you want,"

"No. Don't be silly. Come on in. Shannon is trying to take a nap."

"I won't wake her. I'm guessing that means Tony and Tonia are sleeping, too."

Eric nodded. "I would be as well, if I didn't need to get this laundry done."

"I'm off today and tomorrow. Let me do it."

He shook his head, no, but his eyes were saying yes.

"Really," I said. "It's the least I can do."

Eric nodded and sat down on the couch. Two minutes later he was snoring loudly.

I stuck a load of clothes in the washer and cleaned up the kitchen. My thoughts strayed to my own unfinished laundry, unfinished kitchen, and unfinished life. Was I missing out by not getting married? Not that I had someone to marry at the moment. As I dried dishes, I wondered, not for the first time, if I was staying in that run-down house to avoid growing up.

Three loads of laundry later, I slipped out the door and contemplated my next move. I drove aimlessly around town. I didn't feel like going home to my empty house. It was better, now that most of the drywall was up but it was still a wreck with unfinished walls between the dining room and the kitchen.

When I turned on the radio, The Boss was singing, '*You can't start a fire without a spark. This gun's for hire. Even if we're just dancing in the dark…*'.

CHAPTER 33

In late October the stock market had suffered the biggest hit in years. The Dow went down twenty-two percent in one day. I could feel it in my tips as the regular brokers stopped coming in for happy hour. We still had good evening crowds and the holidays brought out the best and the worst in people.

Halloween in any bar can be crazy. Bar people are kids who never grew up. But the strangest thing I can ever remember happening happened the week after Halloween. Two guys in their mid-thirties came in to have a drink. They sat at stage two and slammed a beer each. Although they were buzzed, they ordered a shot.

"You might want to slow down a bit," I said in my mother knows best voice.

"We're celebrating," said the more sober of the two.

"What's the occasion?"

He lifted his empty bottle. "To friends."

The other guy stood. "Scuzz me. I got to make my bladder gladder."

I pointed to the men's room at the top of the Breathalyzer ramp. "If you can't negotiate the ramp you can't have any more to drink."

I went to the bar to retrieve their Jack Daniels, but before I could set their shots on my tray, a police officer marched up to the stage. In a moment of panic, I thought I might get a ticket for over-serving.

Standing at the bar, I watched the show. The manager was standing near them as the police handcuffed the first of the two men and waited for the other one to come back from the restroom. A few minutes later, he was cuffed, and the police escorted the two men out.

I set the shots back on the bar. "I guess I won't be needing these. I just lost my customers."

Bobby set the drinks behind the bar. "Jack, that's an easy sell."

The manager came back inside a short while later.

"What happened?" I asked. "I had a couple drinks for them."

"I was making a sweep through the parking lot," he said, looking a little agitated, "and I saw this guy sleeping in the back of a car." He paused and ran his hand through his thinning hair. "I knocked on the window really hard, but he wouldn't wake up. I had to call the cops." The manager took a handkerchief out of his pocket and mopped his brow. "Apparently the guy was dead."

"For real? The guy in the car was dead?" I shivered. "Did those two guys kill him?"

"No, I don't think so. They said he was their friend. He died this morning so they thought they would bring him here."

I felt my knees weaken. "Why would they do that?"

"I guess they brought him to the club for one last hurrah. Obviously, they couldn't bring him in, so they left him propped up in the car."

"No way!" I said. I wasn't sure if that was the coolest thing two buddies could do or if it was the creepiest.

∞

I spent my Sunday at Shannon's place, but I suspect I was more in the way than of any real help. While much of the time I was holding the babies, I vacuumed and washed the dishes before Eric sent me home. "I love you, Fre, but your mom was here all day on Saturday, and Jacky Jo was here both Thursday and Friday. I just want to see my wife for a few hours."

Having been kicked out so they could rest, I went back to work on my house. Although I had rocked the walls in every room but the kitchen, I was still using extension cords on the main floor. I decided to leave enough Romex wire to reach any corner of the kitchen so when I finally did figure out where the breaker box would end up; I'd have enough wire to reach it. I connected the main floor outlets and lights into the existing box. It wasn't pretty: wire going in all directions, tied to the kitchen ceiling, running through holes in the walls. There was a real sense of accomplishment when I was able to turn the lights on for the first time.

The original molding was mostly stripped clean and ready to go back on the walls. Some of it needed to be altered because the thickness of the lathe and plaster wasn't always the same as the sheetrock. Over the next week, I got lots of practice shaving off the edges of the molding and having trimmed too much, inserting wood spacers.

"I feel a sudden madness has come over you." Julianne, in her elaborate dress, sat on a stool.

"I'm ready to be done with this. I hate sleeping in the dust. I want real furniture."

"It's catching, I expect."

"Catching?"

"This mood. You are all about the house in a frenzy and I feel overwrought."

"I'm sorry, I haven't been much company these days. I'm feeling like life is passing me by. My baby sister has children and I don't even have a steady boyfriend, let alone, a husband."

"You have your work and this house."

I dumped a dustpan full of drywall scraps into a five-gallon bucket and stared at it. I let out a heavy sigh. I was feeling lonely. Lately, I'd been contemplating what would happen if I called Dirk. When the guy was sober, he was wonderful. I knew he loved me with all my faults and that was a gift. I swept up another pile of crap. "One day you will leave me."

"I am only one amongst your many friends."

"I've never had a friend quite like you."

"Perhaps there is a remedy. You should send for Sawyer. He has been long in coming to the house. Is he on a new endeavor?"

I peeked over at my friend. "I don't know what I'm doing there."

"You can see he cares most assuredly. You ought to have choked him off months ago if you only mean to turn him down at the finish."

"I definitely like him, but his endeavors might be dangerous."

"You have treated him rather badly."

Had I? "I don't want to get hurt."

"There are some hurts worth baring, rather than lose the joy that goes in hand."

She was right, but it wasn't totally up to me. "I'll go by the store tomorrow."

I was running out of excuses to avoid seeing Sawyer. It had been three months. I was embarrassed because he gave back my key, and that I'd come on to him and been refused. I spent every free minute with Shannon's new family to avoid thinking about the emptiness in my life. I hated to admit it, but I missed his company.

At Julianne's urging, I took a chance and stopped by the store to order more drywall for the kitchen, hoping he would deliver it. I wanted Sawyer to see what I'd done upstairs. He was out of town, again. It figured, I was dressed for work and not covered in mud or paint. I skipped the drywall order. I could always order it next week.

∞

At work that night, one of our new regulars came in wearing a full-length black mink coat and his black cowboy hat. John was from Texas. He talked a lot about how important and well known he was in Texas. Entertainers didn't sit with him for long. That was a sure sign he was all hat, and no cattle. He wasn't much different from several others who frequented the place. Julianne would have called them drugstore cowboys. He talked a good game and had the manager convinced he should be a VIP. That meant he didn't have to pay the cover charge. The manager usually bought him a drink or two during the evening as well. It was the second week of November and although the weather had warmed back into the sixties; John still wore his mink coat everywhere. It was odd, but we get plenty of odd ducks in a place like this.

Because Wednesday night was slow, I asked if I could leave early. I wanted to spend the next day going through old news clippings at the library, hoping to find the name Julianne Florence Rosa Parker somewhere amid thousands of stories and obituaries.

As I was leaving, John was at the front door talking to the doorman, regaling him with exciting stories about Texas ranch life. I waited for the valet to escort me to my car. It didn't matter that I was parked twenty feet from the door; the valet always chaperoned the girls in case some strange guest was hanging out in the lot. I was standing at my door giving the valet a five for keeping me safe, when I saw John exit the club. Not ten feet away from me, he climbed on to a little green and pink Vespa and cranked it over. He must have lost his license due to a DUI or something. I choked back a laugh. Seeing him with his ten-gallon hat and mink coat pulling on to Colorado Boulevard on his Vespa was unexpected, to say the least.

I stopped at the Village Inn for a quick bite to eat. I didn't have anything in the house, and I didn't feel like stopping at Queen Supers on my way home. It was a great twenty-four-hour store because most of the men who shopped there were gay, meaning I rarely got hit on in the middle of the night. As usual, while I ate my dinner, I drew pictures of my kitchen, trying to decide how to finish it. Staring out the window, I saw John putt-putt by and laughed out loud. A few heads turned but I couldn't explain to them what I saw.

∞

Getting home about midnight and not ready to sleep, I sat at the kitchen table, playing around with my drawings. I re-measured the space between the back door and the west wall, hoping the numbers had changed and I could get all my kitchen on the west side of the room. If I put an island in the middle, I would just end up with two hallways instead of one. It made no sense to put any appliances in the little nook area so that corner would hold the washer and dryer. At least I had that much of the kitchen plan finalized.

As was my habit lately, I fell asleep surrounded by half-finished drawings and lists of things to research. The doorbell woke me, and I grumbled. My neck hurt from sleeping at the table. I'd drooled all over my latest kitchen drawing, leaving spots and wrinkles in the papers. It was a terrible plan anyway. Getting up from the table, I grabbed the plan, wadded it into a ball, and threw it in a corner with lots of other scrap wood and trash. Walking to the front door, I checked myself in the mirror over the fireplace. Last night's make-up was smeared around my eyes, there were lines on my face from the papers I'd slept on, and my clothes were wrinkled. Overall, better that I usually looked when Sawyer came over.

I opened the door with a yawn. "So, what brings you to my neighborhood?"

"I heard you stopped at the store."

"I shop there a lot."

"You didn't buy anything."

"Didn't find what I was looking for."

"What were you looking for?"

I couldn't say it out loud. I was feeling lonely and looking for him. "Uh…um…nothing."

He laughed that soft and warm way that meant he was happy.

"I'm glad I can make you laugh," I said.

He tucked my hair behind my ear. "So am I." He looked up the stairs at the loft with the new wood railing. It didn't quite match the stairway banister, but it was close. The room was taped but still needed paint.

"That was a great idea," he said. "The loft really opens the place up. Looks amazing."

He wandered into the living room and then the parlor. "Your taping skills are good."

"I've had more practice than I like."

"That light fixture is nice in here." He walked through to the dining room. "I see you found a good match."

"It took some time. I picked that up at the big box store."

He puffed his lower lip out in fun. "You've been cheating on me with the local chain store? I'm hurt."

"I don't go there often but sometimes they have some pretty good sales."

He followed me into the kitchen, and I nodded to a tea kettle. "Want some tea?"

"Sure. I only have a few minutes. I have to get back to the store."

"I looked at my watch. Noon. "Lunch break?"

"You might say that. Just getting back from the Englewood store. How was the wedding?"

"Gorgeous. Really." I gave him the highlights.

"Did your sister have the baby?"

Wow. So much had happened since I last saw him. Now I felt silly for avoiding him. He never cared enough to worry about how I was dressed or what I was doing. We could not see each other for weeks and pick up right where we left off. Friends are like that. I told him about the twins and my plans for Thanksgiving with the family. "Are you planning on going out of town again?" I asked.

He looked at me oddly. "No, at least not over Thanksgiving. The week after that I might be gone."

"Someone at the store said you were out of town. It's hard for me to keep up. You travel a lot. Are you a traveling salesman?"

A grin lit up his face and he downed the last of his tea. "No, it was other business. I've been trying to work some deals." He set the cup down and looked at his watch. "I have to go. I wish I could stay and help you paint." His smile told me he was being sarcastic. "I'll try to find more time in the future."

"Sure. I'll still be working on it."

When I closed the door behind him, Julianne said, "What did you say you called a good man? A stud? I do believe that man is a stud."

The words sounded funny coming from her and I burst out laughing. "So he is."

$$\infty$$

Shannon bounced back to her original Wonder Woman self and invited the entire family over for Thanksgiving again. I was astounded when she insisted on cooking for everyone when she had two babies only a month old. Eric was handy in the kitchen so Shannon would have help, but even with that, turkey with all the trimmings was a lot of work. Connor and his new wife would be flying to Maine, where they would spend the holiday with Bridget's grandparents. Mom and Dad were going to Las Vegas again, so it was only going to be Shannon's family of four and four guests. I picked up some fresh rolls from Queen Supers and Jackie Jo offered to make the Watergate salad. Aiden would probably bring more pies than we could eat, but you can never have too many pies.

As I slipped on my favorite turtleneck sweater, I told Julianne that I'd be home late. "We usually play cards or assemble puzzles after we eat."

"You have a tight relationship with your family. You are lucky."

"We get along. I'll admit, I'm a little jealous of Shannon. She's got two beautiful babies. Not that I want a baby right now but it's cool for her. She has a great husband, too."

"I remember a Thanksgiving dinner. I was with him."

"With who?" *Another clue?* I stopped short of slipping into my leather jacket.

She frowned in frustration. "I cannot utter his name."

I took a stab at it based on the look in her eyes. "The beautiful man from the park?

"Yes. It was him."

"And," I prompted.

"His parents had a lovely home. I should have imagined we were talking about music. We would not be sharing anything more intimate. Even I am not quite such an optimist as that. There was an unwonted touch of sharpness in his mother's voice."

"What did she say?"

"I can't recall the words." Julianne began pacing the floor. "She'd no right to do it. I needed to tell them something. I'd not been especially lucky." Lines wrinkled her forehead and she was wringing her hands. I had never seen her so upset.

She squeezed her eyes shut, trying to remember. "It was so important, my story. Alas, I never had the chance to speak it. His parents were frightfully upset with him for bringing me into their home."

She paused and her eyes widened in shock. "I wasn't one of them and they wouldn't stand for it." She sat down on the bed and started to cry. "I ran away. I was so ashamed, I ran away."

I didn't know how to comfort her. The boy she's mentioned was black and so was she. He was also a musician and she a singer so that couldn't be the cause. I didn't understand why his parents didn't think she was one of them. Her religion? Being an average white girl, I had no idea how other cultures interacted. I never understood bigotry and could rarely tell a Latino or an Italian from a Jewish person.

Whatever made her run that day was tearing her apart.

"What happened," I asked as gently as I could. "Why did you run?"

"They hated me and told their son to never be in my company. I was frightened and I knew they were not wrong in their hatred."

"No, Julianne, hatred is never right or deserved."

"You are a dear delight. I am blessed to be whom you give the privilege of friendship." She brushed the tears off her cheek with a graceful hand.

"If you don't want me to go, I'll stay here with you," I offered.

She studied me with big dark eyes. "I shan't ask that of you. This moment has proved so... inopportune. I've behaved abominably."

"Don't be silly. We have been trying for months to help you remember your past. I can't leave you like this. I'll call Shannon and tell her I'll be late."

"I shall be fine here with my memories."

Ignoring her, I went to the phone and Julianne relaxed slightly. When I finished the call, she appeared less stressed out but nowhere near happy.

I sat down next to her. "You remembered quite a bit this time. Let's try to learn who your mystery man is. What can you tell me about the house?"

"It was a grand home with a spruce tree to the left of the house. A large silver maple tree was spilling its last leaves on the front yard. The porch had a swing. There were four or five steps."

"That's good," I said. "What else do you remember?"

It was a brick house, dark brick, brown not red. There were lots of leaves in the yard and a red wagon."

I started to sketch a house with a porch. My drawing skills were limited, but I was able to determine that it was a two-story house with a porch across the entire front. It had a small window in the middle of the upper floor. "This is great. I can drive around the city and photograph houses. When we find the right one, we'll look up the owners. We can at least figure out a last name."

From my research on the Rossonian Hotel, I knew Denver was intolerant of interracial neighborhoods during the last century. During the twenties, Black people weren't allowed to live south of 20th Avenue. That would help me locate the house, but that still left a lot of streets to cover.

We changed the subject back to music and I played her favorite album. After sunset, Julianne was in better spirits. I headed for my sister's house to enjoy left-over turkey and pie. It was good to see my brothers and I thanked my lucky stars that I had a family to spend time with. Poor Julianne was caught in a strange world and couldn't even remember her family.

CHAPTER 34

Over the next couple of weeks, I snapped pictures of any house that came close to her description. The biggest challenge was the years of changes to the neighborhood. Once developed, I showed the pictures to Julianne. Every once in a while, a glimmer of recognition would light her eyes only to be gone a moment later. The neighborhood was filled with two-story houses with porches across the entire front. Some of the porches had been turned into additions to the house. The large maple may have been cut down sometime in the last sixty years and other trees might have been added.

Most of my time that month was spent at the library, driving around taking pictures, or at Shannon's house. If Sawyer stopped by my place I wouldn't have known. Part of me hoped he had, while the other part of me felt good not having that complication in my life right now.

I was still going to the shooting range about once a month. Dave flirted shamelessly. I know he would have jumped at the chance to jump my bones, but he respected my space. I think he understood my reasons for not accepting his generous offers and his flirtation made me feel pretty. Everyone wants to feel wanted, and Dave with all his playful flirting, never made me feel bad when I refused him. I suspected he got plenty of tail and I would have been just one more notch on his belt.

Coming home to a silent answering machine was a blessing. Mom had given up on introducing me to her friend's son and, thankfully, Rick had taken the hint and stopped trying to sell my house. I picked up the phone and called Aiden.

"Hey Bro. How's it hanging?"

"A little to the left tonight. What's up?"

"I was wondering if you might like me to help you talk to mom and dad."

"Why the rush?"

"Your friend Bill is very nice. I'm glad you brought him over to Shannon's for Thanksgiving."

The phone was silent for several heartbeats and I thought I'd upset him.

"Mom isn't ready," he said.

"Mom is incredibly strong. She just wants you to be happy. Besides, I want Bill to be with us for Christmas."

He drew in a breath. "I'll tell you what. If you bring a date for Christmas, I'll bring Bill."

"You know I don't have a boyfriend."

"Well, then you had better start working on it."

"Sheesh."

∞

December was kind of depressing. I dreamed of the day I could decorate my house in Victorian holiday charm. Right now, the kitchen was still a wreck. Although most of the wiring, plumbing, and sheetrock was completed I still had a lot to do before I would feel comfortable hosting a family gathering. I bought a Christmas tree that could set on my dresser and decorated it with tiny crystal ornaments. Julianne seemed agitated by the decorations but couldn't express why. She didn't remember anything specific about Christmas, but it upset her in some way. I wondered if she might have died during the holidays.

The upstairs was ready for paint. Taping plastic to the floor near the walls, I'd hoped to save myself some clean up. The good thing about this project was all the upstairs trim and walls were going to be the same color. I set a can of off-white paint on the plastic and went to find a straight screwdriver, a great tool for opening paint cans. Sometimes it can be used to convert common slotted screws into non-removable screws, butchering your palms in the process. It's like the Philips screwdriver which is good for stabbing the vacuum seals under lids or for opening old-style paper-and-tin oil cans, splashing oil on your shirt; but can also be used, as the name implies, to strip out Phillips screw heads.

Mixing a little drywall mud in with the paint gave it a little texture and helped cover some of my not so perfect seams. It took a couple days, but I managed to finish painting the entire upstairs.

Once my walls were shiny and new, I rented a floor sander. I would have done the floor first, but I generally track paint everywhere so I would need to sand it off. It was a good thing I practiced sanding on the upper rooms. Sanding with a five-hundred-pound belt sander proved to have a slight learning curve. Thankfully, the bed would cover most of the really deep gouges. I mixed the some of the sawdust with some wood glue, stain and varnish to make a paste to fill in the large cracks between the floorboards. Once the concoction dried, it looked pretty good. You could hardly tell where the floor had been patched.

As a Christmas present to myself, I bought furniture for the two bedrooms. Black lacquer for my room and white wicker for the second bedroom. I painted the walls in each of the bedrooms and hung new curtains. The upstairs was not only livable, but quite nice now. For the bathroom, I found a perfect pink and grey wallpaper boarder with a fabulous Art Deco shell pattern. It was a little feminine, but I am a girl after all.

My old furniture found its way to the alley to be snatched up by someone in need.

On my way to work I drove by the H B Woods. I didn't need anything just then, but I missed Sawyer. He wasn't there, again. As I drove to work, I wondered how many days he worked. It seemed to me he was gone more often than he was there. Was his other job paying the bills? If that was the case, was he just working at the store to pick up girls? The thought had my tail a bit twisted.

∞

My shift was over at two, so it was after four o'clock when I crawled into bed. The alarm went off. I hit the snooze button and pulled the pillow over my head. Sundays are tough. I work hard on Saturday night and it demands a little recovering to get back on the horse. By noon I was ready to tackle sanding the living room floor. The floor sander smoothed out the scratches, but the big gouges need more help. As I'd done upstairs, I saved some of the saw dust to make the repairs.

I like to wear my pants dragging on the floor. It's an old habit from the seventies. Unfortunately, the sander got a little to close and grabbed the hem of my jeans. The sander gobbled up my pant leg and attached itself to my leg. I quickly shut it off but still had trouble dislodging the material. Dragging the heavy sander with me, I found a pair of scissors on the kitchen table. Just as I was leaning over to cut myself free, I heard the doorbell. From my place in the kitchen I could see Sawyer through the window. I had a choice, I could ignore the bell and cut myself free or drag the sander with me to answer the door. I hadn't seen him since before Thanksgiving and I really didn't want him to leave, so the sander came with me to the door.

I unlocked the door. "Give me a minute. I'm caught in the sander."

He had the good sense not to laugh. He took the scissors and gingerly released me from bondage. Then, being the good sport he is he unclipped the sanding pad and removed the bottom five inches of my jeans. "I hope you can still wear those as cut-offs. They fit you nice."

"Thanks, I think."

He grinned. "You never cease to amaze me. The floor is looking good."

"I practiced upstairs. Do you want to see it?"

"Sure. If you don't mind, I need to pay the water bill, anyway."

I was so proud of my new bathroom; I would have invited the entire neighborhood to see it.

"You look pretty nice today," I said, leading him up the stairs. He was dressed in a light-blue polo shirt and dress slacks. "You have a date or something?"

"Or something. Wow, this looks great. When did you get the furniture?" He was standing in the doorway of the spare bedroom. I'd done the entire room in white lace and wicker.

"It was a Christmas present from me to me." I opened the bathroom door and did my best Vanna White.

"Great wallpaper. Your skills are improving; the tile is perfect." He turned and crossed the hall to the master bedroom. "Very nice. I recognize the light fixture. Spot-on match to the bedroom set."

"I only had it for about a year before I could put it up. I knew exactly what I wanted in here." Seeing him in my room had me conjuring up all kinds of erotic thoughts about what else I might want in this room. He looked totally sharp in his polo shirt and dress pants. I, on the other hand, was covered in pine dust from head to toe with one pant leg five inches shorter than the other.

I led Sawyer back down the stairs. I needed to get him away from my bed before I did something dumb and embarrassed myself again.

"You came by the store but didn't buy anything. Again." He was chuckling. "Don't tell me I'm the only one at the store who can sell supplies to you?"

"No." *Well maybe.* "I was thinking about ordering some drywall, but I still don't know what to do with the kitchen."

"It will come to you. The rest of the house is really coming along."

"Would you like a soda or some tea? Shot of whiskey? I also just got a fresh pizza."

"Sure," he said looking down at his watch. "I have about a half hour."

"Oh yeah, the something."

The corners of his mouth turned up. "Wait here. I need to run out to the truck. Be right back."

A few minutes later he opened the screen door holding a big red-metal box with a huge white bow on top. "Merry Christmas."

"Uh, thank you." I was stunned, and a little embarrassed. I hadn't bought him a gift. I was still confused about just what kind of relationship we had. "It's beautiful," I stammered.

Sawyer laughed. "Only you would call a toolbox beautiful."

We tracked dust down the hall into the kitchen.

"Do you have plans for the holidays?" he asked.

I set the toolbox on the kitchen table. Of course, I had to move a hammer, a saw, and some drawings to find room for it. "Same as last year," I said, putting the hammer and a crowbar into my new toolbox. "Christmas with the family. And you?" I pointed at the tea kettle and he nodded.

"I'm picking up Christine at the airport at six."

"Where was your sister? I asked, pouring each of us a cup of hot tea and setting the pizza on the corner of the table. "She go on vacation or something?"

"She goes to school back east." He absent-mindedly sipped his tea looking uneasy.

"Oh, I forgot. That explains how she can shop at Macy's. We only have The Denver, or May D&F around here."

He took a slice of pizza. "She's coming to Denver for Christmas this year. I hate it when she flies home."

That shocked me. "You don't like your sister?"

"Oh, I love my sister, I just hate it when she flies. I can't think straight until I know she's safe on the ground again."

"Oh. You don't like planes?" I helped myself to a piece of pizza.

"No." His answer was so curt I didn't press him for more details. I hoped I hadn't said something to hurt his feelings.

"Well then, how about those Broncos?"

"You follow football?"

"No, everyone is talking about how good they are this year."

"Yeah, they might go to the Superbowl."

"That would be good for business." I took a second slice.

"I need to go," he said rather abruptly.

"Ok." I said, setting my pizza back down, contemplating how our "dates" always seemed to end unexpectedly. I led him to the door, trying not to appear judgmental. "I hope everything is alright."

"Me too." I thought for a moment he was going to kiss me on the cheek again, but his mind was clearly on getting to the airport.

I closed the door and went back to the kitchen to throw away the box full of pizza bones. I never liked eating the crusts. If I were to design a pizza it wouldn't be served on bread and you would eat it with a fork.

Julianne stood beside me. "He was very upset tonight," she said softly. "He's frightened."

"I know. He was fine until the subject of his sister came up. I thought he was going to bite my head off."

It was late, and I didn't feel like working on the floors any longer. I played with my new toolbox for a while then went to bed. I couldn't sleep. I wanted to call Sawyer and see if his sister landed okay, but I didn't have his phone number.

CHAPTER 35

The following night at work, I was beating myself up over Sawyer when Pepper, aka Debbie on her voter registration, asked me if I was going anywhere for Christmas.

"No, I'll be spending it with my parents. I have three brothers and a sister here in Denver."

"I'm scheduled for Tuesday and Christmas Eve, but I want to go to New Hampshire. Can you cover for me? It'd be a colossal favor."

I set empty glasses on the bar. "Sure. We do the family thing on Christmas day and I could use a little extra money."

"Terrific. I owe you. I'll let Nick know."

"So, when are you leaving?"

"Monday, the twenty-first. I'll be back on the twenty-seventh."

"Do you think you could do New Year's Eve for me?" I asked.

"I'm probably going to be scheduled," she said. "I usually work on Thursday."

That had me feeling depressed. I didn't have plans, but I wanted to be able to do something if someone asked. "It's okay. You can pick up a day for me in January." I could have asked for New Year's night off, but I didn't have plans and I always tried to cover my shifts. When I lived in Vegas, I scheduled waitresses. I always appreciated the girls who covered their shifts instead of making me juggle all the other girls around. It was an unwritten rule among the staff.

Ginger, aka Carolyn on her social security card, traipsed into the waitress well. "Ted is over by the shoeshine booth. He asked me to get you. As long as you're going that way, do you want to deliver his Bacardi and Coke?"

"Sure. I didn't see him come in." I added his drink to my order. "Did he say what he wanted?"

Ginger shook her head. "Probably what they all want."

At the table, Ted asked me to sit down.

"I can't. They don't want us sitting on the job."

He shrugged. "I've got tickets to a party at the Adams Mark Hotel for New Year's Eve. I was hoping you could go with me."

"Really? What about your wife? Will she be joining us?"

"We're separated."

Crap, why couldn't someone nice ask me out? Ted was older and I wasn't convinced he was actually separated from his wife. He was still wearing his wedding band.

I glanced back at the bar. Bobby was a total moron with a dead-end job. Jason never asked me out again. I guess that wasn't the end of the world. Especially since he had kids and I didn't really want to raise someone else's kids. I wasn't so certain I wanted to raise my own kids. Rick was wealthy and nice looking. Unfortunately, his expensive gifts made me feel like a kept woman. I wasn't comfortable with that. I turned back to Ted. "I'm sure I have to work that night."

He looked a little sad. "When will you know?"

"Sunday at four."

"I'll call you."

"No, you should ask someone else. I didn't request it off and a lot of other girls did."

∞

The money I made the week before Christmas surprised me. It was nearly four times my average. That gave me money to buy extra presents for my family and still have money for my biggest house project: the kitchen. I wanted to buy something for Sawyer, but I didn't know what to get him. What he needed was a paint job and a back bumper for his truck. It was totally lame, but I bought him a leather holder for his pager.

I went by the store on Monday but the salesgirl told me he was out. "Family stuff. He'll be here tomorrow after three and then back on the twenty-sixth."

Of course, he would be spending time with his sister. Unfortunately, I would have to be at the club on Tuesday because I was working for Pepper. I handed the wrapped gift to her. "Could you see that he gets this tomorrow?"

She smiled knowingly. I realized he must have a dozen girls giving him presents.

On Tuesday, December twenty-third, I had a couple large office parties who were very generous and right before I got off work a squirrelly looking dude handed me seven hundred dollars for a four-dollar beer. That was the best night I'd ever had. I was tempted to ask the manager if I could stay a little later, but the club was nearly empty by midnight.

The next day Sugar, aka Corrine on her Blockbuster video rental card, told me the squirrelly guy had given her twelve hundred dollars. "You saw the case he had, didn't you?"

I nodded, stocking the napkin holder. "Yeah."

"Well, it was full of money, cash, thousands of dollars. You won't believe what happened after you left yesterday."

She called out her drink order to Bobby and turned back to me. "He was sitting in the shoeshine booth when a Denver swat team surrounded him. They came in from every door, loaded for bear."

"A swat team?"

"Yeah." She laughed. "The case was full of cash from a bank in Northglenn. Apparently, he robbed a bank and came straight to Shotgun Willies to spend it."

"What a moron. Did you have to give the money back?"

"Well," she rearranged the drinks on her tray, not meeting my eyes. "It wasn't like they had serial numbers. I gave the cops fifty dollars and some of the other girls gave some back."

"I should take mine to the police department. Crap. That sucks. I had plans for that money."

"They have insurance," Ginger said as she came into the well. "The cops don't know you have it. If the guy wanted to spread a little Christmas joy, why not keep it?"

"But it was stolen," I said. "It's against the law to keep stolen property."

"Whatever, Miss goody two-shoes," she said, rolling her eyes. "The news said he got away with over eight hundred thousand dollars. They aren't going to miss the couple hundred you got."

I carried my drinks to a table in the VIP area where a group of stockbrokers were having their Christmas party. Four entertainers were sitting with them. Snow ordered a shot of tequila.

"You know I can't bring you a shot," I said.

"Don't spaz out on her," Rain said, sucking down a Sex on the Beach. "You're such a dweeb."

"I'm not spazzing." I countered. "I'm just doing my job. Entertainers can't have shots."

Rain shook her head. "You're such a tight-ass. The other waitresses look the other way."

I knew that wasn't true. Most of the waitress staff was very careful about drink tickets. It wasn't worth losing your job to get some underage dancer a drink. Sunshine ordered a coke because she was only nineteen, and Windy asked for an Alabama Slammer.

Snow handed me her drink ticket. "Okay. I'll have a Long Island Iced Tea instead," she said, getting up from the table. "Excuse me while I go powder my nose." She nearly bumped my tray out of my hand as she rounded the table.

One of the guys who had been drinking Jack and Coke asked for a shot of tequila and a shot of rum. I wasn't going to argue with him but on the way to the bar I stopped to tell the manager that I suspected the rum would end up in Sunshine's coke and the tequila was probably meant for Snow. These were the times I felt like a glorified babysitter.

On my way home that night I stopped at the police station next to City Park. It was a small station with one lonely car in the parking lot. Inside, a single uniformed officer sat behind a desk.

"Hi," I said, approaching the counter. "I need to return some stolen money."

He cocked his head. "Come again?"

"There was a bank robbery yesterday. The guy came to Shotgun Willies and gave me some of the money."

"And you want to return it?" His thick brows lifted as his forehead furrowed.

"No. I really want to keep it, but it was stolen, and I don't want to get arrested for accepting stolen property."

Shaking his head, he said, "Give me a minute to call someone."

I took a seat on the little bench against the wall and waited as he dialed the phone. To the person on the phone, he explained why I was there. "Just a minute," he said, and he covered the mouthpiece. "How much money are we talking about?" he asked me.

"Six hundred dollars." After all, I did wait on the guy so some of it was a legitimate tip in my book. "It's different money because he gave it to me yesterday and what I'm giving you is from the tips I made today. I don't know if you have the serial numbers. I can go get the original money if you want me to."

He asked the person on the phone if they were tracking serial numbers. "Ok," he said. "I'll call a local car to come get it. Yeah, it's pretty strange, but it is Christmas Eve." He laughed at whatever the other person said in return. "Just like an angel."

He made another call and motioned for me to come back to the desk. "This is an evidence bag. I need to send the money to the robbery unit."

I filled out a form with my name, address, and how much money I was returning. Receiving the stack of bills from me, he sealed them in an envelope. I was feeling good and bad at the same time. I knew I was doing was right thing, but damn, it was hard to do. A few minutes later, two uniformed policemen came through the door.

"Is this the angel you were telling us about?" said an older cop with a coffee and donut paunch.

"She is."

The younger cop was gorgeous, tight body and dark wavy hair. "What's your name, angel?" he asked in a soft and sexy voice.

My tongue swelled making it hard to spit out my name. "Freja O'Connell."

"Really? Freja?"

"Yes. It's Swedish."

His eyes dilated and he smiled. "You're a pretty honest girl. Most people would have just kept the money."

Now I was feeling stupid. "Yeah, I know. They call me 'Miss goody two shoes' at work."

"And where's that?" he asked.

"Shotgun Willies. I'm a waitress there."

He grinned wider. "Fitting name, I suppose."

"Come on, Vic," the older cop said as he picked up the evidence bag. "I've got a ton of paperwork to fill out and you know how much I hate paperwork."

Vic looked me over with sultry, dark Latino eyes. "We'll escort you to your car if you're finished here."

Escort me to my car? Hell, I wanted him to escort me to my house, and to a few other locations. I glanced over at the man behind the desk to see if I was done. The sergeant nodded.

From inside my car, I watched the squad car pull out of the parking lot and head south on Colorado Boulevard. I was tempted to follow but I had family plans in the morning.

∞

When I told my family about the robbery and the money I returned, all three of my brothers totally gave me a ration of crap. My mother was proud of me. As for what I thought, the jury was still out.

After pie and ice cream Aiden cornered me out of earshot from the rest of the family. "No date again," he said.

I stuck my tongue out at him. "You didn't bring one either and, you've had four more years than me to find one."

He wrapped an arm around my shoulder. "Do you really think Mom is up for this?"

"I don't know if I'd do it now, not in front of the whole family. Mom's kind of private."

"Damn, I'd almost screwed up enough courage to tell them tonight."

"Pick a day that doesn't relate to anything else. No birthdays or anniversaries."

He cocked his head. "Why?"

"Depending on how they take it, they might not want a yearly reminder."

"Thank you, O wise one."

I kissed him on the cheek. "Anytime."

"I still think you were an idiot for returning all that cash."

"Maybe I was."

"No maybe about it."

∞

Nick gave me New Year's off because I worked both Christmas and Christmas Eve. I'd hoped Ted wouldn't ask around about the schedule. That being the only date offer I had, I decided to stay home and work on the house.

When I mentioned to Julianne that it was New Year's Eve, she wanted to know why I didn't go out with friends.

"I don't mean to razz you, but I am enormously astounded you are home." She followed me from the bedroom. "I should have imagined you would be getting dolled up and changing into your glad rags. A bearcat like you should be hoofing all night."

"It would have been nice to have some charming man take me out for a New Year's Eve party but the only offer I had was Ted." I carried papers and books back to the kitchen. "New Year's parties aren't all that great," I said.

"I have a friend who has the most wonderful masquerades. We were invited to play. The grand ballroom was draped in blue and silver." She stared off at something I couldn't see. "All the guests in costly evening gowns and swallowtail coats. I was most beside myself in awe. Josie was such a dear to invite me."

"Josie, she's the sister of Rory, right?"

She nodded. "We were engaged to entertain on that occasion. In Josie's home. I met a most peculiar girl that night. She removed her gloves before shaking my hand as the introductions were made. Most unconventional."

"Do you remember her name?"

"I do not. It was a gathering of artists. A man whom I did not know was reciting lines from a play and another was displaying oil paintings. She was thought-provoking as were most of the guests."

"How do you know Josie?"

She cocked her head to one side. "Her brother was a musician. A saxophone." Her eyes glazed over as they often did when she was reaching for distant memories. "It was not this night, but another, he encouraged me to seek the help of the police." She frowned. "I do not like speaking with bulls."

"I met a really cute cop the other night."

"I hope you are not in trouble. You don't need that kind of hooey."

I smiled to myself. Her oddball phases made me stop and think. "I didn't get in trouble. A guy came into the club and gave away a bunch of money he robbed from a bank. I gave it back the police; you know, stolen goods and all."

"That's just berries!"

I took that to mean I'd done the right thing in her eyes.

Her eyes clouded and she shook her head sadly. "So many people are dishonest unless they know someone is watching."

"There's always someone watching," I said

"There's no one watching you now." She followed me through the gauntlet of scrap lumber in the kitchen.

I turned to look at her. "You're someone."

"I can't leave the house. Who could I tell?" Her red lips settled into a frown.

"You won't always be stuck here." I had an inkling she was figuring things out.

"It is my nature to be curious. You never told me as much, but I perceive a long while has passed from the time when I came to this house."

"Did you remember something?" I sat down at the table and sifted through old drawings. "Did you come here during the day?"

She perched on a bucket of drywall mud because every other surface was covered with books and drawings. "The radio talks about things I've never heard before and the way you dress is very odd. The automobiles that pass the window are noisy with percussion and sleek in design."

This neighborhood loved their car stereos. Months passed before I had been able to sleep through the rapping and hip-hop music every car seemed to shriek as they drove up and down the street. "Yes. I'm not crazy about loud music either."

"You are not modest in your clothing choices."

"What? I'm modest."

"No, you are not. The shorts you wear show your legs in their entirety when most women would blush to show her knees." She got up, slipped past me, and pointed to the copy of House Beautiful. "Look the date on this magazine? Somehow, I've landed far in the future. I was born in 1907."

"You remember."

"Only that, nothing more. I don't understand how I arrived or why I'm trapped in this house. I've searched for a machine that might have conveyed me to this future world, however there is nothing here. There is a large metal construct in the basement that breathes fire, though I see no way to enter it."

"The furnace? You think the furnace is a time machine?" I bit back a smile.

"I am familiar with the concept. Mr. Wells explains much in his book."

"That's fiction."

She went back to the bucket. "What is real and what is fantasy? I do not belong here."

She was right. Is time-travel any crazier than being a walking and talking ghost? She could be still alive in her time and merely a pretty hologram in mine.

She let out a soft sigh. "If I could only find the right doorway out of here." Leaning back against the wall, a small part of her disappeared into the plaster, and I had an epiphany. "I got it! I know how to solve my problem with the kitchen. Thank you so much!"

Julianne seemed interested but not overly excited. "You have another plan now?"

"Yes. I'm going to put the back door right there where you are. By positioning the back door next to the basement door I'll have a full fourteen-foot by sixteen-foot rectangle to install the kitchen cabinets, appliances, and counters. I can brick up the lower part of the window and insert the sink in front of it." Newly energized, I skipped around the room, pointing out my plan. "I'll set the stove right there where the backdoor is now, and the refrigerator can go here. That will leave space for a three-foot counter between them." I was getting more excited by the minute. "I can have a Lazy Susan and a corner cabinet connecting the stove and the sink. It's perfect. And over here," I crossed over to the nook that held my currently unused stove and seldom used sink. "This will make a wonderful laundry. A short wall here will separate the two rooms without blocking the light from the window."

Julianne gazed at the drawings on the table. "You have quite the imagination. We did our laundry in the washhouse. What notions! I would have never thought to wash clothes in the kitchen."

"You had a wash house?"

She looked surprised. "Yes. My sister and I had to wash clothes every other morning. Mable! I remember her name. She is a few years younger than me."

"That's great. What can you tell me about her?"

"We lived in a very small house in the country and didn't go into town often. I remember horses; not many, about five or six. Mama worked in the garden and raised chickens. My father," she said quietly, looking uneasy. "My father is not negro."

That was a revelation. Julianne's skin wasn't particularly dark although she had a broad nose and full lips. Knowing her father was white was a big clue to who she was and why her boyfriend's parents had rejected her. Interracial marriage was probably illegal at the turn of the twentieth century. It would have been nearly impossible for her parents to find a place to live in Denver. Even here in the west where large numbers of black cowboys roamed the plains, they would have been shunned for marrying. "Do you remember your father's name?"

She shook her head and drifted out of the room. I'd learned that when she left the room there was no point in following. I don't know where she went, but I knew she was gone.

Excited by what I'd learned from Julianne and even more excited by the kitchen possibilities, I grabbed my tape measure and went to work. The library would have to wait until morning.

I drew the outlines of the room and, on paper, closed off the back door and put a new one in directly across from the dining room entry. It was such an obvious solution, I mentally kicked myself for not see it sooner.

CHAPTER 36

I woke to the sound of someone ringing the doorbell. I'd fallen asleep at the table and had a terrible crick in my neck. I rubbed the sleep from my eyes and stumbled to the door. As I passed the mirror over the fireplace, I noticed the tracks from my spiral notebook running across my forehead. On the radio, Hall & Oats were singing about private eyes watching you. I felt like crap, so I knew it had to be Sawyer. Using my left hand to cover the indentations on my face, I opened the door with the right.

"Seriously, Sawyer?" I said. "It's not even ten o'clock on New Year's Day."

He smiled; his dimples melting away my annoyance.

I tried to sound irritated. "You have impeccable timing."

"Is that so?"

"You know, I might have had a date last night." I turned around and headed to the kitchen where I could get a glass of water to help me wake up.

"I should have called," he said, "but it's fun to surprise you" He followed me into the kitchen. "I never know what I'll find you doing."

I stuck my tongue out at him, and he laughed.

"I have drywall in my truck. You mentioned needing more when I was here a few days ago. Would you like me to bring it in?"

"I need a minute or two. I just woke up."

He thumbed through the new drawing on the table. "This the latest kitchen plan?"

"Yeah. What do you think?"

"I think you're talking about cutting a hole through a brick wall."

"It's pretty soft brick."

He laughed. "Brick is still brick."

"I looked it up in this book." I slid a home remodeling book towards him. "See, I can cut out a small channel above the door. I'll cut it wider than the door and insert a steal header. Once that's in place, I can remove the bricks below."

He shook his head. "Brilliant."

"That doesn't get you off the hook for waking me up today."

"What if I stay and help you tear out the rest of the kitchen?"

"Maybe."

"I could give you tomorrow too."

"Why do you do this? Are you a masochist who likes to remodel houses?"

"I could ask you the same thing."

"Touché."

"I like spending time with you."

I blew out a sigh. "I could have guessed that might be true."

"That scare you?"

"Sometimes."

"Then we're even. Let's go get that sheetrock."

I was glad to change the subject. Sawyer did scare me. He reminded me of Dirk in too many ways and I couldn't bear to have my heart broken again. Sawyer didn't drink often that I knew of, but pretty girls followed him around like puppy dogs. I still hadn't figured out if he was into something nefarious. He never seemed to be at work and his pager went off on a regular basis.

As promised, Sawyer stayed and helped me finish tearing out the remaining walls and ceiling of the kitchen. By two in the afternoon, we were ready to haul away the stove and metal sink. His pager had chirped three times in the last hour. My Sony radio was turned up so we could hear it over the sound of falling plaster and the Saws All. Duran Duran belted '*…lost in the crowd, and I'm hungry like the wolf.*'

"All this work has made me ravenous," I said. "We can have a pizza here in twenty minutes."

"Sure." He didn't sound particularly excited.

"Would you rather have Chinese?"

"No. Pizza's great. How many do you eat in a year?"

"Too many."

I found the number on the box of yesterday's pizza and began to dial.

"I would have thought you would have the number memorized by now," he said, sitting down at the kitchen table.

"This is Blackjack Pizza. Sometimes I like to switch things up."

The pizza came and we settled on the couch in the living room to eat. It was cleaner than the kitchen and the dining room table was still wrapped in plastic. I briefly thought about eating upstairs where the interior was pretty much complete, but that would mean sitting on one of the two beds and I knew I couldn't trust myself with that kind of temptation. I set the sodas and pizza on the box that served as a coffee table in the living room and turned down the radio.

Sawyer popped the plastic lid off one of the sodas and took a long drink. "Nice digs," he said.

I'd cleaned it up a little since our last date, it was mostly covered in dust from tearing out the kitchen. "It works for now." I grabbed a slice of pizza. "My mom gave me this hideous furniture, but it's better than nothing."

"My mom left me lots things I didn't like so I gave most of it to my sister."

"Your mom left you?"

"My parents died."

"How awful." My parents might be a little odd, but I would be devastated to lose them. "How old were you when they died?"

"I was going to DU at the time; had to quit. Christine was still a freshman in high school. She took it pretty hard.

"Oh, that's harsh," I said sipping my Pepsi. "Like being a parent for a teenager when you weren't much more than a teenager yourself."

"We got along. We kind of needed each other."

"It's too bad you had to leave school. DU is an awesome college. You could have landed an excellent job if you'd had the chance to graduate."

He gave me a lopsided smile. "I'm not doing so bad."

I didn't want to say anything but, being a salesclerk at the local hardware store wasn't what I considered the greatest job. Was he talking about his sideline? "Why don't you go back to school now? With your sister off in college, you could go to night school."

"My college days are done. How about you? Why don't you go back to school?"

"I was a bad student."

"I can't believe that. You're brilliant." He snagged the last piece of pizza. "You managed to read enough books to remodel a house with no practical experience."

"It's not that I got bad grades. When I went to class, I got As. My problem is, I couldn't make it to class. I dropped out of high school three times. Then a couple years later I thought I wanted to try college. I got my GED and I made it seven months before dropping out of college. Like I said, I'm a bad student."

"But you're a heck of a drywaller."

I smiled at that. I was good at hanging sheetrock and my framing skills improved every day. Sitting beside him on the couch I studied Sawyer's face.

"What has you so fascinated?" he asked.

"I was wondering how you shave your dimples."

"I have this special razor that's round on the end."

I stared at him, thinking about it.

"And if you believe that," he said tucking a curl behind my ear. "I have some land in Florida I'd like to sell to you."

"Oh, cool," I said. "I need a place to put the bridge I bought last week."

Sawyer's pager went off again and he had to leave this time.

"I have to work tomorrow," I said. "Could you help me another day?"

"Just call."

After Sawyer left, Julianne appeared in the doorway. "He's a nice man. I'm glad to see him in better spirits."

"He is nice. I wish he had a better job."

"Is money important to you?"

I picked up the empty pizza box and soda cans. I didn't know the answer to that. Most days, having a man at all, wasn't important. "If I'm going to have a man, I don't want the kind who will cheat on me, or the kind who will sponge off me because he can't keep a job, or the kind who sees me as a pretty face. That's the kind of man who will trade you in for a new trophy wife when you turn fifty."

"As a man, he is not so much at the mercy of his temperament."

"You underestimate the temperament of a man."

I shut off the lights and turned the radio off as Dire Straits sang, *'…money for nothing and your chicks for free.'*

CHAPTER 37

I hated going back to work when I had so much to do at home. The kitchen was going to be costly. I would need thirty cabinets and all new appliances. The Stock Show was in town, so the money was good.

One of the bartenders bought a new truck a few days before and refused to let the valet park it. I guess he thought they would wreck it or something. It was extremely cold that night and the valet played a little joke. Every hour or so, they would pour a bucket of water over the truck. By two in the morning, the truck was incased in three inches of ice.

The guy was mad. He couldn't chip the ice off without damaging the paint. Unfortunately for him, the temperature stayed in the single digits for the next four days.

Practical jokes were mutual and a source of entertainment for the staff. It wasn't uncommon for a manager to staple a bartender's ones together while he was in the restroom or a bartender to pour coke on a waitress' tray if she wasn't paying attention. A manager once sent a barback out the backdoor knowing there was a bucket of water poised above the door. I was in on the joke when the waitress staff filled five hundred balloons and stuffed them in the office so the day manager had to pop a couple dozen before he could get into the room.

I was much more comfortable now. The money was good, but it was the staff I was getting to know and like. Occasionally Pepper and Cinnamon would join us for breakfast when Ginger or I worked until two.

Pepper was going to school to get her helicopter license. She wanted to fly Flight-for-Life. We were all surprised when she told us she was a trained Emergency Medical Technician.

"How did you end up an EMT," Ginger asked, "and why are you working at Shotguns?"

She played with her scrambled eggs for a bit before answering. "I make good money at the club. Why do you work there?"

Ginger laughed. "I like the smorgasbord of men." She tipped her spiced coffee to Pepper. "And the money is pretty good."

Cinnamon said, "I wouldn't work if I didn't have to. I'd rather be a housewife. I'm really good at that."

I suspected she would be a great wife. She would have the house spotless, the meals planned and prepared, the children decked out in matching clothes, and the laundry would never stack up. It made me wonder why her husband left her.

By Sunday, I was excited to get back to work on the kitchen. Once I knew the door could be moved a flood of ideas came to me. I went into basement and shut off the gas to the stove. I like a gas stove, but I wasn't sure of my skills. Running a new gas line to the other side of the basement was a bit iffy. If a water line leaks you get wet and a bit of a mess to clean up. If a gas line leaks; KABAM! The whole house goes up. Rather than get rid of it, I would use the existing gas line to hook up a gas dryer when the time came. For now, I capped the pipe. I shut off the water and detached the metal sink and cabinet. There was a hundred-year's-worth of grime behind it. The upper cabinet came off with the help of my saws-all and I dragged it out to the alley. There was a man going through the dumpster, looking for things to add to his shopping cart.

"Hey," I said. "Would you like to earn twenty dollars?"

He squinted at me suspiciously.

"I have a big stove I need to move, and it's too unwieldly for me. I have a dolly but it's still too much."

I hadn't seen his friend half a block down.

"Frank," he called. "Wanna make some cash? Lady has a stove to move."

The two men moved my stove to the alley in less than an hour. While they were at it, I had them haul off the old refrigerator. I was going to get one with a real freezer. I gave them each twenty dollars and a six-pack of Pepsi. I placed a FREE sign on the sink, stove, and refrigerator. All three were gone by the following morning.

The huge room was empty and ready to be remade. I wasted no time tearing out the last of the lathe and plaster in the small nook. Framing the walls took another day. I needed to use two by fours in order to hold the weight of the cabinets on the south and west walls. I wanted a heavy backdoor; something solid but something with a Victorian flair. The front door had a nine-pane window and I went looking for something similar for the backdoor.

Removing the kitchen window would take more than a day. The lower half needed brick installed to countertop height and a new custom window installed. The door was going to be a problem, too. I hadn't had anyone break a window since I took the doors off but leaving the back door wide open for two to four days wasn't smart. I called my brother.

"Come on. It will be like a camping trip. You can sleep on an air mattress and I'll buy beer."

"I don't know anything about brick," Aiden said.

"It's not hard at all. I'll show you. I just don't want to be here alone without a back door."

"You should sell the place."

I laughed at that. "No one is going to buy a house without a kitchen. I need to see this through. Will you help me out for a couple days?"

"Sure, as long as you have some cold beer."

I didn't tell him I didn't have a refrigerator anymore.

The call to Connor was about the same.

"I need to talk to Bridgett," he said.

"I'll call her. I'm sure she'll understand."

True to their word, my brothers spent the next two nights at the house. Aiden did a fantastic job on the window. It made me think I should have asked him to build the fireplace mantle. Cutting the door out was easier than installing the new one in. The brick almost melted under the saw. We used Connor's truck to pick up my new back door. It was beautiful four-panel solid-oak door with a nine-pane window, with double deadbolt locks, slightly more secure than the front door.

Kitchen cabinets were next on the list. Last November I had stumbled upon a discount warehouse that bought up used and discontinued building materials. They had odd sized, unfinished, oak doors for five dollars each. It would take some creativity to make the doors work in the space I had. I could pick up a new basement door while I was there because I didn't want to strip the paint off any of the doors my father had left in the basement.

Now that I had a working plan, I knew the breaker box would be staying where it was. Connor had experience with wiring having worked for an electrician for several years before going into business with Aiden. He helped me tie all my brand-new outlets and lights into the new box. I still need a licensed electrician to give it a final inspection, but that could wait until I needed the 220 for the stove. I finished the sheetrock in the kitchen and had my final measurements for the cabinets.

At the building warehouse, I purchased thirty-three solid oak cabinet doors. I even landed an entire matching lazy-Susan corner cabinet for twenty-five dollars. I could build the rest of the main cabinets from particle board and make the styles and rails from oak one by twos and one by threes. The whole room of cabinets was going to cost less than seven hundred dollars. The real challenge would be making the cabinets fit the doors I bought. I was less enthusiastic by the end of the January.

Julianne was away while my brothers were visiting. It was good to see her again.

"Well, what do you think?" I asked, pointing to the new door.

"I wasn't confident when you told me what you had planned. I had erred. It makes the room appear larger."

She glided into the empty space that would soon hold a bank of cabinets. Are you going to have a sink? I like having a sink in the house."

"Yes. Right there under the window so I can see the weeds in the backyard while I wash my dishes."

She cocked her head. "I don't recall having ever seen you wash dishes."

"I have been known to do it on occasion."

"We had a shared kitchen in the rooming house."

"You lived in a rooming house. When was that?"

"I was new to the city. I had ambitions to make a life on the stage."

Her nose crinkled and she frowned. "It isn't clear."

We went on to discuss music. It was a less distressing topic.

∞

The next morning, I got up and slipped into my favorite red turtleneck sweater and my best pair of jeans. I brushed on a touch of eyeshadow and mascara, tied my hair up in a banana comb and back brushed fluffy curls into it. I was tired of Sawyer catching me at my worst.

On my way to H B Woods I stopped for a burger and a Frosty. Although I would need the particle board sheets delivered, I could start making the stiles and rails for the cabinets right away. My list was long and expensive, but far less than I would have had to pay for factory-made kitchen cabinets.

At the store, I picked out several pieces of oak for the styles and rails, then scanned the store for Sawyer.

"Can I help you?" said a heavy man loading boxes of nails onto a metal shelf.

"I was looking for Sawyer."

He shook his head. He's in Kansas City this week. Can I help you?"

"Oh," I was deflated. "Well in that case, I need some quarter and some half inch particle board delivered to my house."

I gave him my order, picked up some deck screws and wood glue and checked out with one of the pretty cashiers. I'd been spoiled by the discount Sawyer gave me on things, but the price was still fair, all things considered.

∞

The particle board was delivered the next day and I went to work building cabinets. I only wasted three sheets before I figured out how to balance the sheets on a sawhorse raised to table saw height.

Julianne talked to me while I built the stiles and rails. I'd ask her questions and she'd answer until she couldn't remember any more details.

"In the rooming house, we worked together on Wednesday to clean the bedding." Julianne sat on a kitchen chair and watched me measure and cut the heavy sheets of pressed wood. "We set six dining chairs face to face with about three feet between each set of chairs. Not like this one," she indicated the chair she was sitting on. "They were wooden dining chairs. We then set three big washtubs on the chairs, one to be used for rinsing and two for scrubbing on the wash board. We would boil water on the stove and add a cup of Fels-Naphtha soap." She had a faraway look in her eye as she brought up the memory. "We shared the work. I often as not, I had to hang the bedding on the line. I was taller than many of the girls. The clothesline was strung from pipe to pipe because it was snowing that day."

I slid the next sheet of particle board onto the table saw. "I'm glad we have machines for that now."

"I would love to see one of your magic laundry devices."

"I'll get one when the kitchen is done."

"Oh, goody. I'm breathless with anticipation."

I stayed up all night working on my cabinets. The front door was locked, and the alarm was set. I played my music loud enough to hear over the table saw. If someone came to the door, I never heard it.

∞

It took most of February to finish the kitchen cabinets. After staining the cabinets, Aiden came over to help me set them and install the countertop. Since Connor was out of town, Aiden didn't feel like leaving the shop unattended, so I was left to hook up the new sink and lay the new vinyl flooring on Monday and Tuesday.

The local used appliance store delivered a shiny, white refrigerator, stove, washer, and gas dryer. As expected, Julianne insisted on seeing how each appliance functioned. While I was most impressed with the microwave. The appliance had been around since 1955, but very few homes could afford one. By 1975 the microwave was out-selling dishwashers. Julianne's favorite was the clothes washer. She liked the dryer but pointed out that the sun did most of the work in her experience. I was just glad I didn't have to schlep to the laundromat anymore.

My new kitchen was beautiful, and for the first time since moving into the house, I felt a real sense of pride. The house was starting to feel like a home. It wasn't finished by a long way, but having a working kitchen was major. I wanted to invite someone to dinner. I hadn't seen Sawyer in weeks and the all guys at work sucked. I called my little sister.

"We would love to come over," Shannon said, "but the Tonia has the sniffles. I don't think we should take her out."

"How about next week? I want to show off my new kitchen."

"Are you cooking?" There was genuine shock in her voice.

"I can make a few things."

"For sure, we'll come over in a couple of weeks."

That was better. It would give me time to buy some dishes.

CHAPTER 38

While painting the dining room, I played a movie soundtrack from the sixties. When Elvis crooned, *"Frankie and I were lovers. Lordy how we could love,"* Julianne burst into tears.

"Whoa, what's wrong?"

"I died!" she sobbed. "I died here in this house. In the front room."

I dropped my paint roller in the tray and followed her into the living room. "What happened? What do you remember?"

"It's all the fault of that wretched gangster. I'm with him. I hear a loud popping noise and my chest is burning. I can't breathe. I'm so woozy. Oh god it hurts!"

She gaped down at her fingers with alarm. "There's blood on my hands. Help me!"

She vanished.

"I'm sorry," I shouted to her, "Please come back." But she didn't come back. For days she was gone, and I wasn't sure she would ever return. Maybe all she needed to move on was to know she died. I was horrified to know she had died while standing in my living room. A loud pop may have been a gun. Blood on her hands could be her own or someone else's. The thought made me shudder.

Work was as insane as usual with the DJ jumping over entertainers on an Adult Size, Big Wheel Drift Tricycle. It sounds crazy, well yes, it was crazy. The DJ would start at the top of the wheelchair ramp by the restroom, pedal as fast as he could, hit another wooden ramp facing the other way. A prone entertainer would lie on the floor at the end of the second ramp. It made my heart stop every time he did it. I guess that wasn't any crazier than having all the male staff dress in summer dresses or Easter bunny costumes. A lot of the craziness wasn't something you would expect to see in a topless club.

I turned my back to the fire-tricycle spectacle and waited on Gene. He was sitting with four new girls. Apparently, his lust for Desire had waned. The Winter Olympics had recently concluded, and the group was talking about the Jamaican bobsled team. "Seriously," Lily said. "Where would they train? It's not like they got a lot of snow in Jamaica."

"I think they train on a water slide," Zinnia said.

Dahlia shook her head. "It wouldn't be the same. You need snow."

Gene held up his USA 1988 knit stocking cap he'd picked up while in Calgary for one of the downhill races. "Before I became a history teacher, I was training for the Olympics," he said. "That's what brought me to Denver. Colorado has some of the best skiing in the world."

Poppy studied the logo on the hat. "I didn't know Audi sponsored the Olympics."

"What?" Gene said.

"The rings. Everyone knows that's Audi's logo."

Gene chuckled. "Oh, Poppy."

I just shook my head as I sat her drink on the table. I wanted to ask Gene if he knew anything about Denver in the twenties. It wasn't until my second trip to the table when Lily and Poppy were called to stage, and Zinnia got up to hit the head, that I was able to distract him long enough.

I set his drink down. "Do you know anything about Denver gangs?"

"You mean like the Sons of Silence and the Hells Angels? I know there are several in Denver."

"No. Not motorcycle gangs. I'm looking for gangland shootings in the twenties?"

"Nothing comes to mind, but you might look up the name Smaldone. They own a North Denver restaurant called Gaetano's. Some people think the vestiges of the old mob family still run numbers and sell cocaine out of the place."

Dahlia looked up at me. "That was a long time ago. Why are you interested in gangs?"

"I'm doing research on an old house," I told her.

"They were Mafia," she said.

"Really? Do you know about them?"

Dahlia stretched out her long legs and smiled. "I married into the family."

"No way. They're still around?"

She shook her head. "Most of the family is gone. Some in prison, some just gone. My ex-husband used to brag about it. He told me Clyde and his younger brother Chauncey used to rule North Denver."

Is your ex still involved?" It was hard to picture this pretty girl mixed up with mobsters.

"I don't think so. His uncle still runs the restaurant, but he isn't participating in gang matters now. My ex used to talk about a police informant named Robin Roberts who was found shot to death in 1963. That was the year my ex was born. His uncles went to jail in 1983."

Gene nodded "It might have had something to do with a guy named La Guardia."

Dahlia shook her head. "They went to jail for loan-sharking and book-making. Skip La Guardia was killed in seventy-three and Ralph Pizzalato in seventy-four."

Fascinated, I sat down in the chair next to her. "You don't think his uncles had anything to do with those killings?"

She shrugged noncommittally. "Pizzalato was shot in his car in the parking lot of the Alpine Inn."

"The place right over here? The bar on Leetsdale?"

"I think so. Supposedly, Pauline Smaldone and her daughter barely escaped a house bomb the same year."

"I had no idea Denver had mafia gangs. You expect it in Vegas, but not here." I was thankful my father had cut way back on his gambling. Having been dragged out of bed in the middle of the night as a child made a lot more sense now. A shiver ran up my back. These were present day gangs or nearly so. I needed older information.

"I was hoping to learn something about Five Points in the 1920s or early 1930s."

She sipped her coke. "My ex used to talk about some guy named Joe Roma. I guess he was a mob boss who was murdered in 1933. He used to tell me his uncles, Checkers and Clyde killed Roma, but were never caught. He wanted me to think he was a tough guy. In reality, he was a bit of a mamma's boy."

From across the room I could see the manager giving me dirty looks for sitting down. I stood but before I left, I ask her if she knew more about Roma.

"Not really. You might look into the name Carlino. It's a name I've heard tossed around."

"Thank you so much."

I went back to the bar, bopping to ACDC's, *Dirty Deeds Done Dirt Cheap.*

∞

At the library the following day, I spent a lot of time looking for a shooting in Five Points. I was sure it was sometime between 1927 and 1933 but didn't have any luck. Without the year, it was nearly impossible to search all the records. It may have been a small paragraph somewhere since the people involved weren't famous.

I hoped Julianne would be able to tell me more about what

happened that day. I wasn't entirely sure she would come back, now that she knew she was a ghost. Several days had passed without seeing her. I worried and I missed her terribly.

Old newspapers at the library were filled with stories of gangland activity, a lot of it related to the KKK. It was surprising how many politicians of the twenties were connected to the group. Haddie had talked about it but it was unnerving to see it in print. They didn't even try to hide their connection.

Under the name Carlino, I found an article about a bootlegger's convention. Joe Roma set up a convention to stave off gang war between the Carlinos and other bootleggers in 1931. Evidently it didn't work, most of the more powerful gang leaders were dead within the next few years. With the repeal of prohibition, the gangsters had to change rackets. These people have no problem offering anything the governments wants to outlaw; from guns and drugs to gambling and prostitution. There's no market like the black market. The more the government outlawed, the more goods criminals were able to make bank on.

I was hoping the information about local gang activity might lead me to Julianne's killer, at least the situation that led to her death. There had been a few other deaths in addition to the ones Dahlia had mentioned but nothing about a woman who might have been a jazz singer at the Baxter Hotel.

I was deep in microfiche when Ted found me in the library. He knew my days off, and since I'm a regular at the library it wasn't hard for him to track me down.

"Hi pretty lady."

"Oh, hi Ted."

"Are you still looking for twenties information?"

"Yes." I start to pack up my notes. "Good seeing you."

"Is it? You know I got a divorce."

"Really? I'm sorry to hear that."

He shrugged. "What are you looking for? I'd like to help."

I didn't want to encourage him, but he seemed so sad I let him help me go through the microfiche.

"I'm looking for a shooting in Five Points sometime in the late twenties or early thirties."

"You have very strange hobbies."

∞

On Friday, about three-forty-five, Ginger, aka Carolyn on her electric bill, came racing in ten minutes before she needed to be on the floor. Late just meant not early in her case. She usually arrived thirty to forty minutes before her shift. She was on vacation last week, and I could tell she hadn't been to sleep. "Are you Okay?" I asked as we were putting on our uniforms.

"I just got back from Vegas."

"Did you have a good time? How was the flight?"

"I drove, and like, I just got here." She pulled her tray out of the locker. "I left Vegas this morning at five-thirty."

"That's a twelve-hour drive; even with the new seventy-five mile an hour speed limit. I've done it a few times, myself."

"Ten and a half hours. I drive fast."

"No way."

"I'm late today because I got a ticket in Utah." She closed her locker, and we headed up the stairs to the ballroom floor. "I was somewhere between Parowan and Beaver. The state trooper said he clocked me at one-twenty-five."

I stopped and stared at her. "I've driven that stretch. It's a wide-open stretch, but a hundred and twenty-five? What did you say to him?"

"He asked me if I knew how fast I was going, and I gave him my best dumb blond look and said, 'My speedometer only goes to ninety.'"

I understood, the speedometer on my Celica only went to ninety, as well. The National fifty-five mile an hour speed limit had just been raised to sixty-five that month in Utah. But to make it to Denver in less than eleven hours meant she had to average about seventy miles an hour and the stretch between Interstate Fifteen and the beginning of Interstate Seventy was narrow winding mountain roads not to mention the two-lane stretch of road through Glenwood Canyon.

She placed napkins on her tray and pulled out her twenty-dollar bank. "The trooper shook his head and told me if he wrote me up for anything more than twenty-four over the speed limit, he would have to take me to jail. He was just getting off a twelve-hour shift, so he wrote the ticket for eighty-nine."

"Wow, you were lucky."

"Lucky I didn't hit a deer at that speed."

Over the sound system Sammy Haggar was belting, *'I can't drive fifty-five.'*

∞

Two weeks later, while painting the living room, I saw Julianne on the stairs, again. She looked sad, almost angry.

"You were aware of my situation," she said, pulling on the sleeve of her dress.

"Yes." I set my brush down on the top of the paint can. "I didn't know how to tell you. I wasn't sure if you knew. There was so much you couldn't remember. I'm sorry."

"I perceived something was wrong. Time travel didn't make sense, but I utterly did not want to believe the alternative. Now that the knowledge of what has happened to me has crystallized into significance, I shan't ever be able to forget." She raced down the stairs and stood in the doorway to the living room.

I took a step back. "Maybe now we can find out why you're here."

"I came to tell him. I have to tell him about Opal."

"Opal?"

"Our daughter. He does not yet know he's a father." She turned and looked toward the front door as if she was expecting someone to be there.

"Who doesn't know?"

"Lincoln."

A distressed look settled in her eyes. "Oh, how could I have ever forgotten about my baby?" She vanished.

"Wait Julianne." I searched the hall and stairwell. "Lincoln lived here? And you came to tell him about his daughter?" I had so many questions. When did you come to tell him? Where was home? What is Lincoln's last name? I went for the one preoccupying her thoughts. "Where is Opal now?"

She reappeared in front of the fireplace. She looked weary. "I was going to tell him I was with child the day we had dinner with his parents. After his mother sent me away, I knew I couldn't tell him."

I tried not to frighten her with my questions. "Then what happened?"

"I went home to have the baby. I arrived here this day to make it right." Wringing her hands, she said, "Opal is only a few months old."

"Where is home?"

"I don't know." She moved about the room frantically. "My sweet lord! I don't know where my baby is." Her hands flew to her face and she began to cry. "How could I have forgotten that beautiful face? She is delightful."

"Is Opal her full name?"

"Opal May Parker. We never married. He doesn't know."

"I'll look for her. She might be nearby." It was going to be a challenge, finding a woman by her maiden name. If she married it would be next to impossible. I needed more information, but I was afraid of upsetting her. "Do you remember Lincoln's last name?"

Julianne stopped pacing and stared at me. Barely above a whisper, she asked, "How old will she be?" The passage of time was beginning to register.

I had to do some quick math in my head. "Fifty-something. When was she born?"

"March the twenty-second, 1930. It was snowing, the kind of late spring snow that is heavy with water. My mother delivered her with the help of my sister. As much as my heart ached to do so I dared not go to him. My mind was conflicted with my heart."

Julianne faded. I knew it would be a long time before she returned. Each memory seemed crueler than the previous one. I closed the lid on the paint can and washed out my roller. I had a name and a birth date to go on. Trying to find Lincoln would be like looking for John or Michael.

CHAPTER 39

EEEEEP *"What the hell is that?"* I sat up in bed and stared into the hallway. Across the hall, the motion detector for my alarm was flashing red. Still fuzzy from being woken from a deep sleep, I slipped into the hallway and look down the stairs toward the front door. The security panel was signaling a loss of power although my nightlight and clock radio still had power. Creeping back to my bedroom, I pulled out my rifle and checked to see if it was loaded. *"Not again, you f'n hoser. Let's see how you like a bit of lead in your tail."*

Back to the stairway, I glided down past the landing and checked the living room. Clear. My heart pounding in my chest, I crept down a couple more steps and leaned over the rail to look into the kitchen. Sure enough, a big man was standing right in front of my back door; dressed in black from head to toe.

I couldn't get my rifle over the banister to take the shot, so I sprinted down the last six stairs and drop a bullet in the chamber. Ka-Ching. A crashing noise came from the kitchen and the back screen-door was now swinging open. Angry, I fired at the door, knowing the guy was probably already over the fence. I took a deep breath and still shaking, I enter the kitchen, rifle at the ready in case there was more than one intruder. The room was empty. The basement door gaped wide and the kitchen window hung open.

I scanned the back door for a bullet hole. He'd pulled hard enough on the door handle to rip my brand-new molding off the wall. *"Damn. I just put that up."* The kitchen window was small, explaining why he broke the door jamb to get out. The dead bold held tight, the wall, on the other hand, gave away like butter. On the counter, sat my bottle of 1800 tequila. The dickhead had poured a drink for himself.

The alarm was still whining but the main security panel was in the basement. I don't like going into the basement on a good day, so I let it whine.

There's nothing like the sound of gunfire to get the neighbors to call the cops. Ten minutes later, four policemen were checking out my house. I told them what I saw and one of them graciously went into the basement to see if it was clear. He came back to report that the phone wires had been cut. Thankfully, that was what woke me.

By the front door, a good-looking cop reached for my SKS. As he stood there staring at me, a fraction of a smile played across his lips. He was obviously impressed, but I wasn't sure if it was regarding my semi-automatic rifle or the t-shirt that wasn't quite covering my neon pink panties.

"Is this yours?" he asked.

"Yes." I answered, pulling my t-shirt down.

"Where were you standing when you fired it?"

"About here," I know a bullet can go five hundred yards. If I pointed it down, I might have hit the furnace, and I just finished putting new sheetrock on the ceiling.

"Hey Joe," he said to one of the other cops, "let's see if we can figure out where that bullet went."

In the dining room Julianne was pacing nervously. "I saw him," she said. "If I could only leave this house, I could have followed him. I could tell you where he went."

I didn't answer. The guys searching my house would surely believe I was nuts.

I woke to the sound of my doorbell. I'd slept in the t-shirt, but I scrambled into my jeans. The good-looking cop from the previous night was standing on my porch looking at the dilapidated posts barely holding up the roof. His face was lean with a squarish jaw. Dark brown eyes and lashes. His coloring and heritage were Latino; his body build, Greek god.

"Hello," I said. "Can I help you?"

"I wanted to let you know we didn't find anything last night."

That was no surprise. They never found the kid who broke into my house the first time and they had his fishing license to go on. Apparently, he dropped the license when he was stuffing my costume jewelry into his pockets. "It's ok."

"If it's any consolation. You probably scared him pretty good."

"I hope so."

"How are you doing?"

"I'm pretty rattled. I'm going to by a handgun this time."

"Have you ever shot a handgun?"

"No, but until last night, I'd never shot an SKS at anything other than paper."

"You're the girl who dropped off the bank heist money on Christmas Eve, aren't you?"

I was surprised he remembered me. "I guess I was frightened last night. I didn't recognize you when you came in."

"I thought that was unusual of you. Not the part about not recognizing me, the part about the money."

"It was kind of silly of me to do that."

"I guess. No one would have been the wiser."

"Well, thanks for coming by." I was about to shut the door, but he stopped me.

"Can I take you to lunch?"

"I don't know. I just got up."

"How about breakfast then? I just got off work."

I glanced at my watch. "It's nine o'clock."

"I work the grave shift. Next month I'll be on the swing shift, four to midnight."

"That's what I work."

"About that breakfast, then?"

Feeling scared and vulnerable I gave in. It was comforting to have a cop on my doorstep. "Let me change clothes. Would you like to come in?" I opened the screen door for him.

"Sure," he said as he stepped past me, "My name is Vic. Victor Alverez."

He took me to a little place on Colfax and Josephine called Pete's Kitchen. The food was great; mostly what I would eat to cure a serious hangover, but it seemed to work well for rattled nerves. Two hours later we were still talking. I was captivated by his steamy good looks and dark eyes. He was built like a man who spends hours at the gym every day. His tight-fitting black t-shirt outlined his pecs and deltoids. When he leaned back to grab the ketchup off the table behind us, I could see a six-pack you could bounce quarters on. He told me his family was originally from Pueblo, and he had joined the police force when he was twenty-three. He had a serious girlfriend in college but nothing since then. If he told me more, I didn't remember at the time.

∞

Later, when I was home alone, I started freaking out. It was finally hitting me that a man had broken into my house and cut my security alarm before I woke up. I didn't know the creep's intentions, but I could guess, and that really frightened me.

Julianne came into the bedroom as I was getting ready for work. Last night was the first time in over two weeks she'd appeared to me. I had so many questions to ask her, but I certainly couldn't talk to her with a house full of cops.

She sat on the edge of the bed. "You would be the envy of many of my socialite friends who tied rags in wet hair each night."

"Huh?"

Your hair is lovely, and to curl it as you do each day without the need of sleeping on rags is a wonder to behold."

Not quite a wonder, but much better than sleeping on uncomfortable plastic rollers all night.

"That is to say, you would be quite the catch. Hither and thither men hurry about their business though any man would offer up his prospects in return for your engagement. You are not such a rag-a-muffin, you know."

I set the brush down and sighed. "I'm not looking for engagement." I was looking for answers.

"You are at odds once more."

"I had a tough night."

"That man who came in, he might have hurt you. He was a perfect beast of a man."

"I'm well aware of what he might have done."

"I wanted to go after him."

"I know."

"I cannot protect you and my poor little efforts at consolation are utterly trivial."

"Don't be so hard on yourself."

"You have the whole of your life to live and I would destress to see it cut short."

"You have bigger problems."

"I've not been especially lucky." She sighed loudly. "You never get your wishes until you've outgrown them."

Or you're dead, I thought morbidly. She was trapped in a half-life. Not here and not truly gone. It was very much like traveling into the future, seeing hot rollers for the first time, and hearing new productions of old music. I tried to see things from her point of view. Someone had killed her, or she had taken her own life. That was a heavy price to pay to see the future.

She had only wanted to tell her boyfriend about his daughter, but never got the chance. Imagine what it would be like to relive dying like I recall what I had for breakfast. How could she think my close call could compare?

"Can you remember anything more about that day?" I asked, hoping to forget my own problems.

"I was brought to understand Lincoln accepted a business engagement. It would convey him to Kansas City. For years he labored, unacknowledged, with increasing bitterness for he knew his own worth. His gifts were undeniable."

"His musical talent?"

"Yes. Lincoln was a master trumpet player. We shared a love of jazz and he brushed the bloom off the world for me. I wouldn't shackle him with an unwanted child. I had only wanted to explain why I went away. Much was owed to the destiny which had made our love a forbidden thing. His family wouldn't have me."

"They would if they had spent the time to know you."

"I would wish for you a happy life without fear of intolerance."

"Things are better now, but we still have a long way to go." I slipped into a clean shirt and jeans. "Why couldn't the cops see you that night?"

"I didn't want them to see me," she said.

"You can control who sees you?"

"In truth, I don't know. I like it that you can see me and talk with me. I like your friend Sawyer, too."

He's never seen you."

She smiled. "He's not ready."

∞

Work was a blur. I didn't want to tell anyone about my latest break-in. I felt silly after all the people who tried to talk me into selling the house and living someplace nicer. As much as I felt like moving, I had to finish the remodeling. No one would buy the house until I finished the front porch. The outside of the house still looked like a dump.

I asked to leave early because I hadn't had much sleep the night before. Nick said it was too busy. He probably thought I was tired from partying all night. As it turned out, he needed me until one.

I drove a new way home just in case some creeper was trying to follow me, so I drove up Clarkson Street from the north. There was a police car in front of the house and my first thought was that someone broke into my house again. Anger surged through me as I stomped past the car.

"Hi," Vic said, rolling down the window. "I thought you got off at midnight."

Relieved, I nearly laughed. "I had to work late. What are you doing here?"

He got out of the car. "Just want to make sure you were safe."

It was a nice feeling; being cared for like that.

"Thank you. Would you like to come in?"

He glanced over at his partner, and the partner shrugged.

"Sure. I can stay for a few minutes."

I made a pot of coffee for him, knowing he would be working until eight in the morning. I grabbed a beer for myself. I was still keyed up from work. It's hard to listen to pounding music for eight or nine hours and then go right to bed.

An hour later, his partner called to make sure he was coming back.

"Thanks for stopping by," I said. "That was nice of you."

He leaned over and kissed me softly on the lips. "It *was* nice."

I watched him slide into the front seat of the car and drive away. My mind went to that place I try to avoid; wondering what it would be like to be married to a cop. The little girl in me was feeling safe and warm just knowing he was watching my house.

I couldn't sleep so I got up, thinking I might take an allergy tablet. It usually made me sleepy but this night I worried about sleeping through my alarm and having some freak break into my house again. I stared out my east bedroom window and saw Vic's cruiser drive by. I rested better after that.

The doorbell rang, stirring me from a sound sleep. As I tramped down the stairs I was thinking about Vic, but it was Sawyer I saw through the window.

Opening the door, I tried to remember the last time we spoke. "I didn't order anything," I said, looking past him at the truck. It had a new back bumper and primer grey tailgate.

"I just thought I would see how you were doing. I haven't seen you since we tore out the kitchen."

"That was your fault. You're never at work anymore." I opened the door to let him in.

"I heard you ordered oak one by threes and some particleboard. Sorry, I was in Vegas."

"Yes, my kitchen cabinets. It was a whole lot cheaper to build them myself. Did you win?"

"Win what?"

"In Vegas."

He smiled. "Kind of. At least I didn't lose."

"Vegas can be fun for a while, but my money is safer here."

"I'll bet. What do you have left to do in the kitchen?"

"I just need to fix my new backdoor." The truth was I wanted his company. I hated being in the house alone. I led him to the new kitchen.

He took a step back. "Whoa! Your kitchen is stunning. Good job."

"My brothers helped."

He looked slightly crestfallen.

"Sorry, you were out of town for a month. Would you like some coffee? I bought a coffee maker."

"Only for two and a half weeks. I've been at the store every day since February twenty-fourth."

It was now the middle of March. "I guess I was busy." I held up a cup.

"Coffee would be nice."

"So how are you at fixing bullet holes?"

"What?"

"Yeah, some guy broke in and I took a shot at him."

"What?" he repeated and took me into his arms. "Why didn't you call me? You must have been scared silly." He touched his lips against my hair, and I could feel my knees threatening to buckle.

"Mostly, I was angry." I said, nearly pouting. "I ruined a perfectly beautiful door." Reluctantly, I pulled away and showed him the bullet hole, just above the door handle. "I wasn't scared until the next day. After I had time to think about it. The guy was in the house long enough to sneak into the basement and cut the phone line. The alarm woke me. It signals with a high pitch whine when it loses power." I turned to Sawyer and puffed out my lower lip. "He also had the nerve to drink my Cuervo 1800."

Sawyer wrapped his arms tighter around me this time. "I'm glad the alarm woke you. I hate to think what would have happened if he'd made it upstairs."

I shivered. "I can't think about anything else."

CHAPTER 40

He drank coffee while I filled him in on all the work my brothers and I had done in the kitchen. The gory details seemed to interest him, and I was damn proud of my cabinets.

I refilled his cup. "Measure twice-cut once. Or in my case, measure four or five times, cut, and then do it all again."

"Well, they look great."

"I couldn't have done it without their help. Aiden is far better than me when it comes to brick and mortar. I have to admit; I was a little nervous about hooking the new wires into breaker box. I like my hair straight. Connor helped me there."

Sawyer's electronic leash was going crazy. The pager was neatly tucked into the gift I'd given him, making me feel good. I had to admit, he couldn't be a very good drug dealer, or he'd own a better car.

"Do you need to answer that?"

He cringed. "Do you mind if I use your phone?"

"It's in the dining room."

He made a call to someone named Vinny. Something about a shipment out of Mexico being held up at the border. Crap. I just knew he was a drug dealer. He returned to the table after having Vinny contact some guy Hernandez.

"Everything okay?" I asked.

"Fine. Just a delay on an important product. I had most of it already sold and my customers won't be happy if they have to wait."

I topped of his cup once more. It was wonderful to have someone sitting in my new kitchen, drinking coffee. I didn't want our time to end, but I need to make a stop before work.

As he left, he turned to me and smiled. "Brilliant."

∞

On my way to work, I swung by Dave's store. The lot was full. I wouldn't have much time to chat with him. I was still debating asking him about his security service or buying another gun.

He smiled, when he saw me at the counter looking over scary looking handguns. "I see you're in a shopping mood."

"Yes, I might need something smaller than the SKS."

He must have sensed my apprehension. His smile faded and was replaced by a genuine look of concern.

"I had another break in. I was asleep at the time."

He placed his hand over mine and gave it a little squeeze. "There is nothing wrong with using a gun for self-defense."

"I wish I didn't feel like I needed one."

"Cops are great for showing up after the crime and writing reports. You need to survive long enough to call them."

I shrugged. He was right. "What would you recommend?"

"The Smith & Wesson Bodyguard is an excellent revolver for women. It's a fairly light handgun. Excellent quality. The synthetic grip makes it easy to hold and reduces recoil."

He pulled the gun out of the case and released the cylinder. "There is an ambidextrous cylinder release and it comes standard with an integrated Crimson Trace laser sight. This allows for easier aiming in reduced lighting." He pointed it at a wall target. Used properly, the laser sight can provide a psychological edge in a stressful situation. Imagine breaking into a house and seeing that little red light on your chest."

"That would scare the crap out of me."

"As it should."

"I fired my rifle the other night to let him know I was armed."

"That was sound thinking. Most thugs are easily frightened. He probably won't come back, but he isn't the only one out there."

That's what truly scared me. I would never know when another creep would try to break in or attack me on the way to my door. I never thought of myself as fragile, but this last incident had me totally freaked out.

I bought the Smith & Wesson.

∞

I still hadn't told anyone at work about my break-in. Most of the shoptalk was about Jimmy Swaggart these days. Cinnamon, aka Barbara to her ex-husband, was incensed that Swaggart came down so hard on Jim and Tammy Faye Bakker last year. "He completely destroyed Jim and Tammy's ministry."

I set my tray on the bar. "I didn't know you followed television evangelists."

"As a rule, I don't watch very much tv but it's all over the news."

"You would think the news would have something more important to cover."

"Like the Iran Contra debacle?" Pepper, aka Debbie on her plane ticket, said as she cleaned her ashtrays.

I hadn't been following either story. All the time we were working on the kitchen, Connor and Aiden were ranting about Reagan selling arms to Iran and funding the Contras. "We shouldn't get involved in other countries' wars." I must have heard that ten times a day. They swore those same weapons would be used against us one day.

Apparently, Pepper felt the same. "Reagan claims the arms sale was to secure the release of our hostages, but the first Reagan-sponsored arms sales took place in 1981 before any of the hostages had been kidnapped. The president is not above the law. Bush would be even worse than Reagan."

I made a mental note to introduce Pepper to Aiden. My brothers were registered Libertarians. They hated all government. They were all about responsibility and freedom of choice and that was something I could get behind.

∞

When I got home, Vic was waiting in his patrol car in front of my house. I invited him in for coffee again and took a cup out to his partner.

"Have you ever thought of selling this place?" He asked as he poured milk in his coffee.

"Every day."

"This isn't a good neighborhood for a single woman." He moved closer to me. "You need a big, strong man to watch over you." He leaned over and nuzzled my neck.

Vic was hot and it had been a long time. On the radio, Robert Palmer was singing *'addicted to love,'* and I was mulling over the idea of asking Vic to tuck me into bed. My moral compass is slightly bent. I jumped in with both feet, like I do with everything.

He didn't stay long after. He was still on duty. We met the following night after work and again the night after that. He was attentive and skilled. It didn't hurt that he was built like an athlete. Lying in his arms, I felt safe and warm.

Vic rolled over and lit a cigarette. "They're moving me to the swing shift next week."

"Four to midnight?"

"Yeah."

"Then we won't be having these late-night trysts?"

He nuzzled my breasts. "It means I don't have to leave you in the middle of the night."

If I were a cat, I would have purred. "Awesome."

"I'm a morning man."

"Morning man?"

He laughed "You'll see."

"I guess you'd better go. Your partner has been very patient."

Vic sat up and pulled his shirt on. The muscles of his back rippled making me want him to stay until morning.

"I have poker with the guys tomorrow night, but I'll see you on Monday." He stood and pulled up his pants. "I'll take you to breakfast about ten."

"That sounds wonderful."

∞

At the hardware store later that day, I ordered several four by eight sheets of oak plywood to make a window seat and bookshelves for the south wall in the parlor. When I asked if Sawyer was around, cashier pointed to the office. "He's in there."

The door was closed. I hoped he wasn't getting in trouble. I hadn't seen him since the day after the break-in when he helped me fix the bullet hole in the door. I paid for the order, asking to have it delivered on Sunday.

"Is Monday ok? Our delivery crew is off Sunday."

Sure, that's fine." I would go visit my sister and the babies. I hadn't seen them since Christmas.

∞

Tulips and daffodils were blooming in the park as I drove by. I stopped at American Furniture Warehouse to find living room furniture. The dining room was sporting the fabulous oak set my sister gave me, but I planned to get rid of the Formica table and chairs in the kitchen. I wanted something with a country feel, not something out of the 1950s. The parlor would have to wait until I finished the window seat. I was almost late for work that night, but I found what I wanted.

After work, I missed having Vic's patrol car waiting in front of the house. I drove around the block twice, making sure no one was hiding in the bushes. Once I was satisfied that I could make it to my door without drawing my gun, I parked the car and got out. The house was eerily quiet. I turned on every light in the place and cranked up the radio. Bon Jovi belted out, *'Livin' on a prayer.'* As I changed into cut-offs and a flannel shirt.

I opened a new five-gallon bucket of paint and started on the parlor. On the outside chance someone wanted to remove the bookcases, it would be nice if the walls behind them were painted. Not three rolls into the job, I turned to see Julianne perched on the bucket of paint.

"I feel like a bottle of champagne that's been uncorked for a week."

"That's odd. Why do you say that?"

Of course, I should be frightfully hurt if you were to finish your work here and move on."

"I'm not going anywhere."

"This new man in your life, he is not liking this house."

"Why do you say that?"

"His is wary. He does not rest here."

"That's because he has to go back to work."

"I do not like him. It's as if he is on the lam."

"I'm sure he doesn't want to get caught boinking me while he's on duty."

"He smokes."

"Yes. That's a bummer but he's a cop. He makes me feel safe."

The doorbell rang; startling me into kicking over the paint tray. Julianne evaporated. Since I was covered in paint, I was certain it was Sawyer. It was Vic.

"Hi, I wasn't expecting you tonight." I opened the door and he rolled in.

"We finished the game early, early in the morning." He leaned over and nuzzled me. I could smell beer on his breath. I looked at my watch. It was nearly five-thirty in the morning.

"Come in," I said.

"You look busy. You got time to tame the dragon?" He wrapped his arms around me and carried me up the stairs keeping me from tracking paint all through the house. The roller was going to dry out and the floor would have to be sanded, but at the moment I had more important things on my mind. In an instant his arms were around me, pressing me back, tenderly but determinedly, against the pillows.

∞

Sunlight was bleeding through the window when the doorbell rang once more. I stumbled out of bed and made my way down the stairs.

"Sawyer. Hi. I wasn't expecting delivery until Monday."

He grinned and his dimples deepened. "I never miss an opportunity to see you. Haven't you noticed?"

The fact was, I had noticed and now I was feeling uncomfortable. I could feel Vic standing behind me and the look on Sawyer's face told the story.

"This is my friend, Vic," I said, stepping aside so they could see each other. "Vic, this is Sawyer. He's delivering some oak plywood I ordered."

Vic gave a quick nod of the head and turned around. "Shouldn't come over so early on a Sunday morning. Some of us like to sleep in."

I grimaced. "Thanks Sawyer. I'll help you with this stuff."

"I guess I should have called."

"No need, you can come over anytime."

"I didn't know you had company."

I helped him unload the truck, putting the plywood in the parlor. It was the only room without furniture now. As much as I wanted to, asking Sawyer to stay for coffee would have been awkward in the extreme, so I just let him drive away.

CHAPTER 41

Over the next month, Vic asked me to go to his place almost every night, but I couldn't leave Julianne. Since finding out she was dead, she got upset when I left her alone very long. She was aware I had to work but hated me leaving her to go to Vic's place. Most nights he stayed in my house grudgingly.

He moved a few things into the house, mostly some clothes and his TV. Throughout May, I worked on the bookcases on my days off while Vic was at work. When he was home, he took up all my time. Between cooking, cleaning, and sex, I didn't have time for building projects. Evenings that I had previously spent working on the house were tied up with Magnum PI, Matlock, LA Law, and St. Elsewhere. When we weren't on the couch, we were in bed. Bed was preferable to the couch, but both had their appeal.

"Where are you going," Vic asked, as I grabbed my purse from the newel post by the front door.

"To the library."

"Why?"

"I'm doing research."

"What kind?"

"Geez, Research. You know, like on the house."

"Why?"

I rolled my eyes so hard; I gave myself a headache.

"I'll be back in a couple of hours."

I was starting to feel a little trapped. The only time I could meet with Julianne was while Vic was away. I still hadn't found her Lincoln. For all I knew, he could be dead, too. Lots of men die before they reach their eighties.

The library held nothing new for me. Without a last name, it was hopeless. I spent the next hour looking through old newspapers. The area had been through some tough years and didn't seem to be improving much. Photos in the current issue of the Rocky Mountain News showed a nineteen-year-old kid being carted away on a gurney after a shootout in front of Manual High School. He'd been hit in the neck by several scatter shots as school was letting out. The school was only a couple blocks from my house. I was thankful Vic was willing to stay with me at night.

I decided to go by the hardware store. The weather was warm, and I wanted to pour a new cement porch and set the new posts.

I didn't know what to say to Sawyer, but I felt like I owed him something.

Although Sawyer's half restored truck wasn't in the parking lot, I went inside anyway.

"Can I help you," a salesman asked as I roamed through the lumberyard.

"I'm looking for porch posts. Is Sawyer around?"

"He's out of town."

"Ah, yes."

"Said he would be gone for a week."

I was a little depressed as I trudged out of the store. I didn't know what I would have said to him, but it would have been nice to chat. I had gotten used to seeing him often and it had been over a month since he'd stopped by the last time, though I couldn't blame him. I missed my friend.

∞

That night at work, Ted asked to marry me.

"I have a boyfriend," I said.

"Is it serious?"

I didn't know if it was or not. Vic was living with me most days. "Yeah. We're living together."

"I don't see a ring on your hand."

I had never noticed how needy Ted was. Some of the guys who come to clubs like this have more self-esteem issues than the dancers. It's quite therapeutic in many ways.

"We haven't decided on that yet."

"Have you decided on the important things, like kids?"

Aries ordered a coke, Gemini asked for a Corona.

"Do you have a drink ticket?" I asked.

"Yeah," she pulled the little white slip out of her bag. Ted asked Aquarius if she wanted anything.

"No, I'm fine."

"Yes, you are," Ted said with a smile. All three girls giggled.

Libra sat down. "I got life insurance on my new watch," she said. "It's a Rolex."

Ted looked up at me then at Libra. "You don't buy life insurance on watches, only on people."

"Yes, you do. If they cost a lot of money."

Gemini agreed with Libra. "I bought life insurance for my dog because she's a purebred Akita."

"I have a purebred English Mastiff," said Aries.

Ted smiled, looking totally entertained "That's a lot of dog."

I shook my head and walked away.

∞

When I got home, I found a note from Vic, saying he was playing cards with friends. That was cool. I had work to do. My bookcases were installed and just needed some finishing touches. I was excited to fill them with my LPs and the assorted books I'd purchased to remodel the house. I had the entire Time-Life series of Home Improvement books in a box by the bed.

Julianne sat next to me as I finished staining my new bookcases. We had been talking about the virtues and vices of Vic again, a subject she brought up often.

"You bestow far too much importance on the outside of the cup."

"Well, no one likes drinking champagne out of a plastic cup. I simply apply the same principle to men."

"If you can be assured there is champagne in the glass." She got up and wandered around the room. "He is a knave and his manners are atrocious. He has taken it into his head to remove you from this house."

"It's the way he was raised, things are different now." I tried to explain the changes in men and women that had occurred over the last sixty years.

"Decent manners aren't external. Though visible from the outside, they come from a depth of understanding and respect. No amount of time can change a selfish man to an unselfish man."

"He works hard, and he makes me feel safe."

"By your own admissions, chaperones are out of date. You are qualified in ways I've never witnessed before our introduction."

"Well, sometimes I feel lonely."

"He has cut a niche of his own in your world. I like it not. I fear for the sale of your soul."

"Now you're just being dramatic."

"It's true, every word of it."

I knew she was right. Vic was corrupting my motivation; not only for the house but for the research I needed to complete. I had searched the birth records in the four counties closest to Denver without finding an Opal Parker born in 1930. Surely, her birth would have been recorded. She was probably born at home, wherever that was.

"Tell me more about Lincoln." I said, rubbing the stain in. "How was he different from Vic?"

"Link had crossed swords in many a wordy battle; quick as lightning. I loved to hear him speak of music." She flitted across the room as she spoke. "His understanding was immeasurable. Such tenderness, almost maternal in its selfless, protective quality, as is only found in a strong man—never in a weak one." A smile drifted to her eyes. "He had reached the mature age of three and twenty when we met. I was twenty."

I did a quick calculation on a cardboard box. If she was twenty-one or twenty-two when she had the baby and he was three years older… "He would be eighty something, now."

She grimaced. "His whole life vanished while I waited in vain."

"You were born in 1907." By my calculations. "If Lincoln was three years older, he would have been born in 1904. Do you remember his birthday; spring, fall?"

She shook her head. "My mind suffers holes. It is filled with fragments of memory which do not make sense to me."

I sealed the can of stain. "We will keep trying." The world had changed over the fifty-eight years she had been sleeping in the bowels of my house. Even if I could find Lincoln, what would I say? Would Julianne even recognize him?

Vic wandered in about six in the morning. I'd just crawled into bed and was dog-tired. He nuzzled me and worked his way down to my belly. Somehow, I found a pocket of reserve energy to tame the dragon before drifting off to sleep.

∞

Sundays were always a good day for house projects. Vic often slept late after a night of cards if he came over at all. Today Vic headed out to meet the guys for a softball game leaving me the entire day to work on my house.

I made a peanut butter sandwich for breakfast and headed out to examine the front step. My plan was to pour new concrete over the old concrete. If I threw a little rebar in there, it ought to hold up, and not break away from the original step. As far as the step had dropped, I was sure it would make a decent footing for the new porch.

First, I needed to raise the porch roof and support it so the damaged posts and railings could be removed. Using a twelve foot two by six stud, I wedged a notched end under the corner of the roof and pushed it back toward the house. With a second plank under the other corner I was able to move the roof another half inch closer to the house. I repeated the steps, going back and forth until I couldn't see light between the house and the roof.

By two in the afternoon, I had the old posts in the dumpster, and started building the frame for the cement. It was hot, and I was sweating in cut-offs and a bikini top. At least my tan was improving. Working in a dark bar gives one a true appreciation of sunlight.

Sitting up to wipe the sweat out of my eyes, I saw Sawyer's truck pull up to the curb. In addition to a new bumper on the truck, more primer was reapplied so most of the truck was gun metal grey.

I glanced down, happy to see I wasn't covered in cement, yet. Either his, or my timing was getting better. "Hi." I waved. Standing up to meet him, I tripped over a pile of lumber and hit my head on one of the roof supports. Rattled, I stumbled over to curb where he was unloading my new posts. "I wasn't expecting these today."

"Want me to return them?"

"Oh, no. I'm glad you brought them. I should be ready to set them up by Tuesday if I get the cement in today."

He eyeballed the timbers supporting the porch roof. "Anyone ever tell you, you're brilliant?"

I could feel my cheeks warm. I loved it when he noticed my ingenuity. "It took all morning."

"I'm sure. You have any help?"

"No. Are you offering?"

His cheeks dimpled. "Sure. I have some time today."

I helped him lay the last post down on the grass beside the porch. "Let me show you my plans for the second bathroom. The basement is a wreck still. I'm running new pipes for the second bath." I drew a kerchief out of my back pocket and wiped the sweat out of my eyes. "Working in the basement really makes a mess. I've had to clean the kitchen every day.

He grinned. "Most people clean their kitchens every day."

"Most people use their kitchens."

He laughed, and I stuck out my tongue at him making him laugh harder. I rolled my eyes.

"So, show me," he said, biting back another laugh.

We stepped over the frames for the new porch and through the front door. "The walls are painted, and I bought new things for the living room," I said.

Sawyer followed me through the house as I showed off my new furniture and draperies. The floors were shiny and looking so much better than when I moved in. I was peacock proud. You would have thought I was showing off a million-dollar mansion.

"Almost done, I see."

I led him through the kitchen to the basement. "Isn't this great? I'm getting better every day."

"Tell me something I don't know."

I reacted just like an entertainer when a guest told her she was fine. Biting back a giggle, I led him to the corner where the new water pipes were stubbed up to the floor of the back porch for the sink, bath, and toilet. I was delighted with my plumbing skills.

"Nice," he said, running his hand over the sewer pipe. "So, where's the door to your new bathroom?"

"I'm going to put a door in the west wall of the parlor. I already framed for it under the sheetrock. When I sealed off the backdoor, I knew the old porch would make a perfect bathroom, and every house should have at least two. I didn't know how long it would be before I could get it done so I rocked that wall."

"I was wondering why you held onto the old sink and tub."

"It's going to look awesome. Very turn-of-the-century."

He shook his head and beamed at me. "Brilliant."

A couple hours later, Sawyer and I put the finishing touches on the cement. My construction could have been better. I noticed a few places where the concrete was bulging, but thankfully the framing held, and I didn't have cement spewing over the lawn.

In the back yard, I cleaned the trowel in a bucket of water. "Would you like something to eat?" I asked. "We've been at this for hours."

Sawyer eyeballed the door; a wary look crossed his face. I turned to see Vic in the back doorway. The game must be over.

"Vic, you remember Sawyer, don't you?"

Vic glared down at him and belched. "Sure, the kid that works at the hardware store. Who could forget?"

"No thanks, Freja," Sawyer said. "I have dinner plans." He rinsed his tools in the bucket and helped me empty the dirty water near the alley.

"Thanks for your help today. I never would have finished this if you hadn't come along."

"I heard you were asking for me yesterday."

"Just wanted to say hi." I dried my hands on my shorts and walk past the side of the house to his truck with him.

"Hope everything is good with your sister and the kids," he said. He opened the door and slid in the driver's seat.

I leaned in the passenger window. "She's doing fine. Someday you'll have to meet her."

He gazed passed me. I turned to see Vic watching us.

"Thanks again," I called as he pulled away from the curb.

When I got back in the house, Vic was slamming pans in the kitchen. "Don't we have anything to eat in this house?"

I took the pan away from him. "I'll make some spaghetti, give me a few minutes."

"How long has that little turd been here?"

"What?"

"You heard me. How long has Sawyer been here?"

"He brought over the posts. Must have got here around one."

"I don't want him sniffing around here."

"Sawyer is just a friend."

"Bull. Men don't have women friends." As if to mark his territory, Vic opened the door and peed off the pallet deck.

"I hate it when you do that," I said. "The people in the apartments across the alley can see you."

"No one's paying attention."

"It's my yard, damn it, and I don't want you peeing on it." Sometimes you absolutely must recognize your inner bitch.

"Fine. I'm out of here."

"Great. Pee on your own yard."

Vic stomped down the hall and opened the front door before he realized the front porch was still three tons of wet cement. It's hard to look dignified when you have to retrace your steps. The windows rattled when Vic slammed the backdoor.

Totally pissed, I went up and turned on the faucet, stripping down for a hot shower. Julianne met me in the bathroom; taking a seat on the counter, looking as upset as I was feeling.

"Vic has become prejudiced against him. The man is about making people thoroughly uncomfortable until he gets his way, unless they happen to be stronger than him. Incidentally, a good many innocent folks who have nothing to do with the matter, get badly hurt in the fray."

I wiped away tears. "I can't blame him for being jealous."

"It is our very friendship he contests. You never play music for me anymore. Always the moving picture box is on."

"I know. I'm sorry."

CHAPTER 42

I was almost glad to pick up an extra shift on Tuesday. I was still feeling angry with Vic for pissing in the yard, but mostly I was angry with myself for dropping the ball when it came to Julianne. We used to spend hours together talking and listening to music. She needed my help, and with Lincoln in his eighties, we may not have much time left.

As I pulled up in front of the club, I laughed. Part of the neon sign was out, and the SHOTGUN WILLIES now read SHOTGUN LIES. I told Nick on the way to the dressing room. Apparently, it had been that way for a couple days. Neon was expensive and had to be custom made. Fortunately, it was just a transformer out and it was fixed the next day. That didn't stop the local newspaper from snapping a picture and publishing an article. Must have been a slow news day.

The usual subjects were there. We call them regulars because they come in so regularly. I was pretty much over Jason, so when he flagged me down, I smiled and brought him a drink.

"How have you been, lately?" He gave me a twenty and told me to keep the change.

"I've been good. Still working on the house."

He turned to the goth girl to his left. "Would you like something to drink?"

"Thank you. I'd like a Sex on the Beach, please." Montana appeared mean as hell but was one of the politest entertainers I've ever worked with. I collected her ticket and turned to Georgia.

"Corona," she said, handing me her ticket. Alabama was still nursing a rum and coke.

I started to turn away when Jason grabbed my hand. An unwanted flutter swept through me. "Will you bring a coke for Arizona? She'll be joining us when she gets off stage."

I swallowed back my insecurity. "Sure. I'll be right back."

As I threaded my way through the crowd to the bar, a bachelor party of eight guys had picked up stage two. They were carrying it in a circle, dancing to *Walk Like an Egyptian*. The girl on the stage was sitting down, as her head would have hit the chandelier if she were standing. It's all good fun until someone falls off the stage.

Bobby came scurrying back to the bar as I set down my tray. "Sorry," he said. "I had to hose down the porcelain."

"I didn't need to know that. Could I get a Corona, Sex on the Beach, Bacardi and coke, and a coke?"

"Not that it's any of my business, but you look like someone ran over your cat."

"Men are annoying."

Bobby set the drinks on the bar. "Does that include me?"

"Sometimes."

"I thought we had a pretty good thing."

"It was only like three dates." I turned and looked at Jason then back to Bobby. "I'm sorry. I didn't mean to be so flippant. You're a nice guy, just not what I'm looking for in a long-term relationship."

"You think Jason is?"

"What? No."

"I see you mooning over him."

"It's not like that."

"Whatever."

I dropped off the drinks and headed to Ted's table with the Bacardi and coke.

"Hi. I saw you come in." I set down the drink.

"Did you have any luck finding your friend's aunt?"

"No. I'll try again on my day off."

"I found something you might find interesting." From his mysterious briefcase, he pulled out a faded and yellow newspaper clipping. The date in the corner read June 22, 1929. The headline read, "Local Jazz Ensembles to Perform at Independence Day Rally." I sat in the chair next to Ted and read the copy. "City Park will feature local bands this Thursday along with top acts from Kansas City and Chicago. Thursday Night's line up will include Glenn Miller, Rossonian Hotel house band, Jewels of Jazz, and Benny Mark's Horn Boys. Trombonist Glenn Miller, singer and pianist Julianne Parker, saxophone and trumpet player Lincoln Smith, bass player Wilson Hemet, and drummer Benny Mark are local to Colorado."

"Wow! This is awesome," I said.

"Are you going to tell me what this is about?"

I leaned over and kissed him on the cheek. "No."

He smiled and shook his head.

Argentina and Ireland sat down, and Ted offered them a drink. By the time I got back from the bar, China and India had joined them. They were talking about the drought and stranded barges on the Mississippi.

"People are dying from the heat," China claimed.

"It's global warming," Ireland added.

Argentina sipped her drink. "More than forty-five percent of the country is suffering. This is the worst drought since the dust bowl." She turned to Ted. "Do you think we'll have another depression?"

Ted shrugged. "Can never tell. I'm stocking up on gold and silver at any rate."

The girls kept him preoccupied, so I couldn't ask him more about where he found the news clipping. The information lifted my spirits and the rest of the night was excellent. I couldn't wait to get home and tell Julianne what I knew. The only downside would be trying to tell her when Vic was out of the house. He had been mad at me on Sunday, but arrived at my house Monday night after work, all my sins forgiven.

Nick let me leave a little early but asked me to stop and see him after I changed clothes. I waited in the office for a good thirty minutes before going out to find him. He was escorting a guy in a wheelchair out the front door. Apparently, the guy had repeatedly crashed into the toilet in the men's room, smashing it to pieces.

"I could come back at a better time," I told him as he helped the guy into a cab.

"No, give me a minute." He paid the driver and told the idiot in the back seat to have a nice night. Smiling as if he was having the best night of his life, he said, "Did you think about my offer to become a manager?"

I had. I was torn. Watching him in action was impressive. I don't know that I would have been so nice to the guy. "How many days would I have to work?"

"All of them."

"No, seriously. You're here six days a week and usually for twelve hours or more."

He held my elbow and led me to the side of the building. "What can I say? I love what I do. I believe you do, too."

"I love the money."

"I see how you do the extra things like picking up napkins on the floor and straightening the tables. You're invested."

"I need two days off a week to work on my house."

"Granted. I've been paying attention. You're almost done."

"I still need to finish the fence and the second bath, oh, and I need new shingles on the roof."

"I can give you Tuesday and Wednesday off. I need a day manager. Ten to seven-thirty."

"That's a long day."

"You've been working four to two in the morning most days."

"True. But only four days a week. When would I start to train?"

"What are you doing now?"

I watched as Nick checked out the bartenders and closed up the club. Most of it was just common sense. After work, we went for breakfast and he filled me in on the philosophy of the business. Surprisingly, the entertainers were the focus of the entire business. Drinks and food took second place. "If the girls aren't making money," he said. "We'll have no girls. Without pretty girls, we have no business. That's all you need to know. Make the pretty girls happy."

∞

Wednesday morning, Vic sat around most of the day watching the Dodgers-Expos game. I sat on the couch beside him. "Nick asked me again last night if I wanted to be a manager."

Vic growled. "Why would you want to do that?"

"I can't waitress forever."

"You don't have to work there. Lots of other waitress jobs."

"I'd like a new challenge; something different."

"A new place would be different."

I got up and let him finish watching the baseball game he'd recorded. I wasn't sure if I wanted the job, but it was nice to be asked. In truth, I'd come to really like the people who worked there. They were open and honest, sometimes more graphic than I was accustomed, but it was always truthful. I went up to take a shower and get dressed for work. Vic came up a few minutes later. It didn't take him as long to dress because he didn't have to wear make-up.

I got my chance to share the news bubbling inside me when he left for work at three o'clock. I had about twenty minutes before I had to leave.

"Julianne," I called. "I have some terrific news for you."

She appeared almost instantly beside the bed.

I pulled the last of the hot rollers out of my hair and back brushed it into a halo of curls. "A friend found an article about a music festival in City Park. Does the name Jewel of Jazz mean anything to you?"

She looked thunderstruck. "Yes."

I sprayed a quarter can of Aqua Net on my hair to keep it in place. "Your name is unusual, so it has to be you. The paper said you would be performing with a saxophonist named Lincoln Smith. That's him, isn't it?"

"Jeepers creepers, how could I have forgotten?" Julianne nearly danced off the bed. "Of course, I remember that day. We played with several musicians. That was the day I met Glen. Jazz was all the rage. Link was living with Willie in a house on Franklin; one house down from 31st Street."

Now I felt like dancing. "I'll go there on Sunday. Maybe I can find him."

Julianne's dark lips puffed out. "He wouldn't still be living there after these many years. And to tell him of a child he never knew would be cruel beyond reason."

She was right. He wouldn't still be living with Willie and it wasn't likely Willie would still be there. I had moved more than ten times since leaving home.

"Can you remember anything more about him?"

His birthday is October the twenty-seventh. We met in City Park. I was showing my Mable the gardens."

"Who is Mable?"

"My sister. My sister's name is Mable. I left the baby with Mable," she moaned. "He doesn't know. He is the most wonderful man in the world, and he doesn't know about Opal."

Julianne vanished as she often did when something stressed her out. I didn't expect to see her anytime soon.

∞

Before work on Thursday, I went to the library. What were the odds I'd find a woman named Mable Parker, who was born sometime near the turn of the century? I hoped to find her in the National Archives. I didn't have time that day but planned a trip for Tuesday morning since the Archives would be closed on the Fourth of July.

When Ted came in, I brought him a drink and asked him about the archives.

"You can find information by county. I would start there."

"Thank you. I don't really have a county."

"Then you have a lot of searching ahead of you."

I turned to leave, and he grabbed my hand.

"Are you still with that guy?"

"Geez, Ted. Of course. You just asked me that a week ago."

He let go of my hand. "Still no ring. I'll keep checking."

I could never date Ted, let alone marry him. Not that he wasn't nice looking. He obviously took care of his health but like Rick, he wasn't my type. "It won't change anything. Vic and I are together."

"*Time is on my side.*"

I rolled my eyes. "Song lyrics? You've got to be kidding me."

"I know what I want, and I don't give up easily."

On that note, I walked away.

CHAPTER 43

Vic didn't come over Thursday night, so I was up early Friday morning. It was cloudy and cool. Colorado had bipolar weather. I slipped a light jacket over a t-shirt and jeans. By two in the afternoon, it could be ninety degrees or fifty. The drive to Lakewood was crappy. I'd forgotten it was the first of July and everybody and his brother would be leaving town for the mountains.

Once in the Archives building, I was able to relax and get to work. It took several hours to find a Mable Parker and Lincoln Smith. The problem was there was more than one of them. In fact, there were several. By guessing the birthdates on Lincoln, I was able to narrow it down to sixteen in the Denver area during the 1950s. Mable was a quite common name and the archives didn't often list middle or maiden names. I wrote down all the information and was just about to leave when Ted came in.

"I see you've been busy." He was looking at my capacious notes.

"I found a lot of information, but I don't know if it's right."

He sat down and pulled a piece of paper across the table. "I thought you were looking for a Julianne Parker. Who are Opal and Lincoln?" He studied my notes. "One day you're looking for gangs of the twenties and the next your looking for people in their eighties."

I swept the notes into my bag. "If you must know, I'm doing a history on my house. I believe a man named Lincoln Smith lived there with a woman named Julianne Parker."

"And this was in the twenties? People didn't just live together in those days."

"I know. I'm trying to figure out where they went."

"What does that have to do with your house?"

I stood up. "You sure ask a lot of questions."

He surprised me by laughing.

"You are quite the mystery. I can't wait to see what catches your interest next week."

I blew out a sigh and left him sitting there. I needed to get home and ready for work.

∞

On Saturday I stopped at the hardware store. I felt bad about the way Vic had treated Sawyer. I wanted to apologize, but in truth, I didn't know what to say. Sawyer and I didn't have *that* kind of relationship. Sure, I thought about it often enough, but we had never done more than harmless flirting. So why were my panties in a wad over this? I pulled into the parking lot and sat there like an idiot. Sawyer's Ford was parked by the door. It was freshly painted, looking super nice. I cringed as a couple guys loaded old pallets in the bed of the truck. They were going to scratch it to hell. He was probably delivering them to some girl who had the hots for him. The thought twisted my gut. I needed to figure out what I was doing. Vic was a stellar guy with a great career. He didn't drink too much and never mentioned other women. So I didn't like watching television as much as he did, but he was good to me.

I was about to pull away when a shadow crossed my dashboard. It was Sawyer. I hit the lever, and the window slid down. "Hi," I said sheepishly.

"Hi, yourself. Are you coming in, or just window shopping?"

I felt the heat rise to my cheeks. "Just stalking."

He laughed. "I hope it's me you're stalking."

"I wanted to say I was sorry for the way Vic treated you the other day."

"No need. Vic's a big boy. He can make his own apologies."

"He was rude. We got into a fight over it. Well, that and the fact he likes to pee on my yard."

Sawyer shook his head. "Marking his territory."

"I suppose. It's annoying, but it makes him happy."

"It's *your* happiness that matters to me."

"What does that mean?"

"Does he make *you* happy?"

"Yes, I feel safe with him."

Sawyer touched my nose with his forefinger. "Safe and happy are two different things."

Before I could say anything more, he turned away and strolled back to his truck. I thought about what he said as I drove home. Vic did make me happy, but I missed the easy way Sawyer and I could talk. Even now, his mere presence sent my blood racing with a speed that frightened me.

∞

Saturday night was as crazy as always. I called it amateur night because the average age of the clientele was about twenty-five, not much older than the entertainers. This was the kind of place that catered to bachelor parties, and these guys didn't have much experience with dancers. While some were in awe of the girls, others were just rude and most of them didn't have much money.

I made my way through the crowd and reached Dave's table. December joined him at his usual table by the DJ booth. "I'll have a white zin," she said.

Dave nodded; saying he would buy it for her. "You haven't been shooting lately."

"I've been busy with the house."

"I was afraid I'd chased you away."

He made me nervous but I'm a big girl. "Just busy."

He grabbed my hand. "I could try harder."

I gently disengaged my hand. "I have a boyfriend."

"All these girls have boyfriends. Never stops them from fooling around."

"I'm not that way."

"Too bad."

June and April sat down. They were continuing a discussion about the election coming up in November. June said, "I'm voting for Bush. His tax policies are better than Dukakis."

April ordered a Coors from me and then told June that Bush would be a terrible president.

"Well I'm going to vote for Bush and cancel your vote."

"You can't cancel my vote; you don't know where I vote."

January joined them. June asked her, "Who are you going to vote for President?"

"I don't know," she replied. "I'm from out of town."

Dave couldn't resist. "Don't you have presidential elections where you're from?"

"I don't think so."

I walked away as Guns N' Roses belted out, *'Sweet child of mine.'*

At the bar, Dan was talking to Nick. When Nick left, I asked, "What's all that about?"

Dan said he found a packet of coke on the floor. That wasn't unusual. I found lots of things on the floor. The club was extremely dark. One day a found a wadded up hundred-dollar bill. I'm sure it was from some guy was tossing money on the stage, but I always wondered if he had meant to throw a hundred.

By midnight my feet hurt, and I wanted to go home. I found Nick in the office with Dan. "Sorry," I said. "I didn't mean to interrupt."

"It's okay," Nick said inviting me to have a seat. "Dan was just going home."

It was highly unusual to have a bartender leave before the night was over.

"Is he okay?"

Nick shook his head. "He suffers from TSTL"

"What's that?"

"Too Stupid To Live. He just asked if he could have the coke back that he found. He needs some time off to think about it."

"Wow. So much for *Just Say No*. He probably should have thought of that before he turned it in."

Nick smiled. "Probably. I'm guessing you want to go home."

"It's okay. It's still pretty busy, and now you're short a bartender."

"Do you know how to make drinks?"

"Yes."

"Wicked. You now have the back bar."

At the end of the night, Nick asked me if I would help him close again. "Next week, how would you like to be responsible for the waitress schedule and the hiring?"

I had already been his go-to girl for training new waitresses. "Sure," I said.

"Your management training will start as soon as I have Mark up to speed." Mark was the newest manager they'd hired.

∞

Even having gotten home well after three in the morning, I got up early. I was eager to find Lincoln. I slipped out of bed and started dressing in the closet

Vic rolled over and lit a cigarette. "Where are you going?"

"I'm checking out a couple of leads in Aurora, Thornton, and Arvada."

He sat up and frowned at me. "Leads? What the hell?"

I pulled on my jeans. "I have some names of people who might know someone who lived here in the twenties."

"You're kidding? You plan to drive a hundred miles to see if someone knows someone who lived here sixty years ago? That's about the stupidest thing you've done, and believe me, there are some contestants."

"What's that supposed to mean?"

"Come back to bed. You don't need to know who lived here. What you should do is sell the place. Make it someone else's problem."

"I LIKE my house."

"Don't get upset. Your house is fine, but you have to admit; it still needs a second bathroom. That, alone will cost a small fortune, and I can't see you on the roof putting on new shingles."

"I can do it. Although, it would be nice to have some help."

"It's not my house. Just sell it." He got out of bed and wrapped his arms around me. "We should buy our own place. My apartment is too small, and this place gives me the willies."

"Are you asking me to marry you?"

"One step at a time, sweet cheeks. Let's find a house we can both be happy living in. Now, come back to bed, will you?"

I did, and we spent the entire day there.

Later that night while fixing a sandwich for Vic, Julianne appeared by the sink.

"You didn't try to find Lincoln today."

"I'm sorry. Vic kind of asked me to marry him and I would have been a butt to leave him after that."

"Victor doesn't like it here. He exudes the old-fashioned notions about a man being the master in his own house; whose forebearers from one generation to the next, have always been the masters of their women."

She faded away, and I felt like a butt anyway. I would have to find him tomorrow.

CHAPTER 44

The following morning, I got up early, trying not to wake Vic. I didn't want a repeat of Sunday. The sex was awesome, but I'd let Julianne down and she disliked Vic as it was. I dressed as quietly as possible; waiting to slip my shoes on until I was down the steps. In the kitchen, I started a pot of coffee and nibbled on a bagel, sans the cream cheese. Only because I didn't have any.

With the list of names from the archives, I started searching phone books. There were seven possible Lincoln Smiths living in the Denver area. Unfortunately, the phone book didn't give me their age. The closest was in Aurora.

I pushed away from my kitchen table and set my coffee cup in the sink. I could hear the shower running upstairs. Slipping my jacket off the back of the chair, I grabbed my bag and left through the backdoor. Less than a minute later, I swung the car into the street, waving at Vic who was standing at the door frowning.

My heart raced as I pulled up in front of the small brick house on Oneida Street. The neighborhood had seen better days, but the homes looked mostly well cared for. There was a mixture of large and small homes, manicured lawns and weeds. Being this close to the airport, many of the homes belonged to airline workers, pilots, and flight attendants.

In my head, I had a story worked out about being from the census bureau. It seemed reasonable that I would ask about their family and occupation. Dressed in a new Jaclyn Smith power suit with impressive shoulder pads, I took my note pad and slid out of the car.

The bell rang. I was about to leave when a tiny, very pale woman of about eighty opened the door. Note to self: old people don't move fast.

"May I help you?"

I swallowed my nervousness and asked if Lincoln Smith lived there.

"Yes. He would be my husband. What can I do for you?"

"Do you know if he ever played the trumpet in a jazz band?"

She cocked her head to the side and her watery eyes narrowed. "Who did you say you were with?"

"I didn't." I realized then my census story was the wrong tactic. "I'm doing genealogy research for a friend who said her grandfather, a Lincoln Smith, played in a jazz band in the twenties."

"I think you have the wrong man, but I'll ask him." She turned from the door leaving me standing there feeling like an idiot. A moment later a grey-haired, pale, and wrinkled man stood before me.

"Are you asking about my grandkids?"

"I have the wrong Lincoln. Sorry to have bothered you."

Fifteen minutes later, I was in Thornton, sitting in front of an apartment building. It was a secure building. I waited until someone came out and slipped inside. The place smelled of fried chicken and my stomach rumbled. My bagel had been eaten away by my anxiety. I was never good at cold calling.

I knocked on the door of apartment 301 and waited. An elderly black man opened the door. "Yes?"

"I'm trying to locate a jazz musician from the twenties. He was born about 1905. He played in a band called the Jewel of Jazz."

"Well, I wish I could say it was me; I could use the company."

"You never played in a jazz band?"

"Oh, yea. But it was called Big Six."

"Cool name."

"He smiled. "It was fun. I was a young man and the times were good."

"So, did you ever know a girl named Julianne Parker?"

"Sorry, I can't say that it rings a bell."

"Her boyfriend's name is Lincoln Smith."

"My son is Lincoln. My name's Henry."

"Thanks for your time." I turned and slinked away. I still had five more names on my list.

A quick stop at Wendy's and I was on the road again. The next address was in Arvada.

I pulled into the parking lot of Shady Rest Nursing Home. This was a complication I hadn't considered. He might be in a wheelchair or too feeble to go anywhere.

At the front desk, a young woman studied me warily. "Who are you?"

"My name is Freja O'Connell I'm doing genealogy research for a friend. She is trying to track down her father. His name was Lincoln Smith."

"I know Lincoln. He's been with us for a couple of years now."

"Do you think I could talk to him?"

"We don't usually let non-family members in."

"Could you ask him if he would see me?"

She stared at me for a while without answering.

"How about if you just ask him if he knew someone named Julianne Parker."

She nodded and motioned for another girl to occupy her place at the desk.

It seemed like an hour before she came back and said, "Follow me."

She led me to a recreation room where several old people were engaged in watching TV and playing cards.

"By the window," she said, pointing at a frail black man who was intently watching us approach.

I stuck out my hand. "I'm Freja. I have a couple of questions, if you don't mind."

He took my hand and turned it over in his. "Are you a detective?"

"No. I'm doing some research for a friend."

"What friend would this be?"

"I would rather not say until I know I have the right Lincoln Smith. Were you in a jazz band in the twenties?"

He nodded. "I was in a few. I moved around a lot."

"Could one of the bands be Jewel of Jazz or Benny Mark's Horn Boys?"

He laughed. "Benny Mark always was a sap. I'm fairly certain his band broke up over a dame."

"That wouldn't be a girl named Julianne Parker."

His demeanor soured. "No."

I showed him the newspaper clipping about the Festival in City Park. "Is this you?"

His eyes watered and he shrugged.

"I don't want to bring back bad memories. I have a friend who would like to meet you."

"Everyone I know is dead. One of the drawbacks of living too long."

"You don't have any family?"

"No. I had a brother, but he passed last year. What's goin' on? You sure you ain't a cop?"

"No, I promise." I sat in the chair next to him. "I live in an old house on Clarkson Street. I found this under the floorboards." I opened a drawstring bag and poured the contents into my hand, the old money, the ring and the bracelet. "Have you ever seen these before?"

Tears filled his coal dark eyes. He began to sob quietly. I pulled a tissue out of my purse and gave it to him.

After a moment he looked up. "It was my fault she died. I was just a kid trying to make good. Times were hard back then."

"Julianne?"

"Yes. She, and music, were the most beautiful things to enter my life. How do you know about her?"

I looked around the room at the other residents. "Can we go for a drive? I have something to tell you, but I don't want anyone to overhear."

He eyeballed me warily. "Child, are you pranking me? I don't know how you figured out these things belonged to me and my connection with Julianne, but you best be on the up and up."

"I promise. I'm on the level. I just don't want anyone to overhear us."

He nodded. As I helped him stand, he eyeballed me closely. "All these years, you were the first to find that ring."

"Undoubtedly."

We walked down the hall. The attending nurse came from behind the desk. "Where are you going?" she asked Lincoln.

"This little lady is taking me out for a beer and a pizza."

She looked surprised, and then dubious. "You have P.T. in an hour."

"I know. I'll be back." He smiled at the girls. "Unless she wants to keep me."

His sudden change of mood was disarming. He seemed like the kind of man who used humor to cover his feelings. Before we left, the attendant reminded me that Lincoln had a three o'clock appointment with his physical therapist.

He was frail but surprisingly limber. Celica's are rather close to the ground. I held the door open and he slid into the seat.

"Nice car. I had a Mustang back in sixty-three."

"I like it a lot." I fastened my seat belt and started the car. "Are you going to fasten your belt?"

"If you insist. I hate these things."

"I wouldn't want to have you killed in an accident."

"All got to go somehow."

"Hopefully, not on my watch."

"So, are you going to tell me why you came to see me?"

I turned off Vance Street on to 56th Avenue. "Julianne is haunting my house."

"Say what?"

"I know it sounds crazy, but she really is. I've been talking with her for two years. That's how long we've waited for her memory to clear up enough to find you."

He stared straight ahead. "You best take me home."

"Please. It's true. In the twenties you lived with a friend named Willie in a house on Franklin and 31st. I know your parents lived in a two-story, brick house with a porch across the entire front. It had a small window in the middle of the upper floor. And I know you played the trumpet and the trombone. Julianne was the lead singer in your band, and she died the day she came to see you."

His eyes slid to the left and he studied me. "You could have found that out other ways."

"She was wearing a red sequin dress with black tassels that day. She had a beaded bag and a gold cigarette case. Please believe me. She wants to see you."

I glanced over at Lincoln and he was shaking. "I don't understand why you're doing this to me."

He was pale and I thought he was going to have a heart attack. I pulled over on a side street. There was half finished coke in the cup holder from my stop at Wendy's. I offered him a drink. "I know how this sounds. You've got to believe me."

Swallowing the rest of the coke, he turned to look at me. "They never let me have coke. Not good for me."

I was relieved to see he had calmed down. "We won't tell them."

"Can I see the ring and bracelet again?"

I pulled them out of my bag and handed them to him. He turned the ring over in his hand. "This ring was for her. I was going to marry her if she'd have me." He studied the bracelet for a long time. "And this bracelet took her life."

"I'll let you keep all of it if you come with me."

"My Jules is a ghost haunting that house." He sounded as if he was beginning to understand.

"Yes. And she will never have any peace until she can see you again. I believe she needs you to cross over."

"I never want to go back to that house. It was the worst day of my life."

"Please. I know it's hard, but she needs you."

"I have an appointment in fifteen minutes."

"I can pick you up tomorrow. We need more time."

We made plans for me to pick him up at three o'clock the next day. He had a regular Cribbage game in the morning, and he was the reigning champion. "We play a penny a point and I've nearly doubled my Social Security check."

I dropped Lincoln off at the home feeling sad, certain Julianne would be leaving me soon. I pulled on to the Boulder turnpike, wondering what kind of love would keep a man single all his life and a woman from crossing to the next world. *Remember, after the fire, after all the rain. I will be the flame…'* blared from the radio as I merged with the Valley Highway and headed south.

CHAPTER 45

When I got home, I wanted to talk to Julianne, but Vic was sitting on the couch watching TV and drinking a beer. He looked at his watch. "Where have you been?"

"I was doing research on the house." I went upstairs to see if Julianne was around; not surprised that she wasn't. She rarely showed herself when Vic was in the house. I took out my notebook and made notes about Lincoln's address while the TV blared MacGyver.

"Julianne," I whispered. "I have news."

After an few minutes, I gave up and went down to the kitchen to find something to eat. Vic followed me and slid his arms around my waist.

"I don't understand why you spend so much time on this old house."

"It's interesting," I turned around to face him. He was sexy as hell. "Did you know the rose bush in my backyard is over a hundred-years old?"

"You sure spend a lot of days to learn this." He pulled away and grabbed another beer from the refrigerator. "Seems like a colossal waste of time. Are you going to make dinner?"

"I thought I'd order a pizza." I hadn't found anything good in the kitchen.

"Didn't we just have pizza last night?"

"Yes, so? I like pizza."

∞

Vic went to the shooting range before work on Tuesday. I didn't want to go with him because I wanted to speak with Julianne. I hadn't had a chance to tell her I'd found Lincoln.

The moment the door closed behind Vic; Julianne was standing by my right arm and I spilled my coffee on my shirt. "Crap, you scared me. I wish you wouldn't sneak up on me like that."

She looked hurt. "I do not sneak. I have no method of forewarning you."

"I'm sorry. You're right. I should be used to it by now." I watched Vic's Chevy Blazer pull away from the curb. "I spoke with Lincoln. He didn't believe me at first. Not that I blame him. It is a pretty wacked story." I went to the kitchen and poured more coffee into my mug. "I'm picking him up this afternoon."

Julianne looked pale, well paler than normal. "How is he?"

"Older." I wasn't sure how much of a shock it was going to be. Julianne was still in her early twenties and Lincoln had seen eighty years. "He has a great sense of humor." I pulled out a kitchen chair and sat down.

"Yes," she said. "He made me laugh. Amusement and laughter being quite desirable even at one and twenty."

"It's one of my main criteria for a man."

"Odd. Vic seems so stern. Much the primitive man – the man with the club."

"That's harsh; man with a club?"

"Sawyer is more to my liking. He's always supported your need to do things your own way."

"You can't choose whom you love. Even the nicest guys have flaws."

"It's a trifle early to be so definite. Vic has been one to cause a ridiculous storm in a teacup with his questions."

"You think Sawyer would make a better husband than Vic?"

"Oh yes, heaps."

"I don't know. There are a lot of things I don't know about Sawyer, like why he wears that pager."

"It's a silly notion, but mightn't you ask him?"

I was afraid of what I'd learn. I'd done my share of illegal drugs, but the notion of Sawyer mixed up with the kind of guys who escalate turf wars, and sell women to their friends, just made my stomach hurt. I couldn't help comparing my life to Julianne's. She was killed, probably shot, because she was running with the wrong crowd. Vic was a cop. Sawyer was… unknown.

"Vic would carry you along the road which leads to your own destruction. He thinks little of your accomplishments."

Julianne had a way of seeing things clearly. Even when Sawyer suggested another course of action, he never made me feel stupid.

I downed my coffee and went up to take a shower. Less than a minute into it, I heard the doorbell ring. Throwing a towel around me, I dripped over to the front window. Sawyer's newly painted truck was parked at the curb. "Damn. He has impeccable timing." I pulled on a pair of shorts and the bell rang a second time. "ONE MINUTE," I yelled, and jerked a t-shirt over my wet hair. I sprinted down the stairs pulling my shirt down as I opened the door. Sawyer smiled. Behind him I could see four by fours sticking out of the back of his truck. I twisted my hair into a knot and stuck a wooden pick through it.

"What's this?" I asked. I was sure I hadn't ordered anything.

"The other day you mentioned wanting to install a redwood privacy fence."

"Seriously?" I couldn't remember when I'd mentioned it although I'd been thinking about it for more than a year.

"Call it an early birthday present."

"Thank you. You shouldn't have."

"I wanted to."

"No, you really shouldn't have." Now I was feeling guilty. Vic was living with me most days, and I was getting expensive gifts from another man; a man I've had impure thoughts about.

I followed him to the truck. "This is totally awesome of you, but I wasn't ready to work on the fence today."

"I can get it started. I brought a posthole digger."

"I can't ask you to do that for me. Besides, I have to go pick up a friend this afternoon."

"I'll just stick these in the back yard." He dropped the tailgate. "And dig the holes."

I blew out a sigh. "Okay, I guess I have a couple hours. I can finish this when I get back."

We each grabbed an end of the stack of fence posts. "Your truck looks rad. Aren't you afraid of scratching your new paint job with these?"

"It's a work truck. If it gets scratched, I'll repaint it."

We measured and marked the location for the posts. Once the holes were dug, we mixed cement in a wheelbarrow to set the posts. I kept checking my watch because I didn't want to be late picking up Lincoln. As much as I wanted to, I couldn't explain my situation. Sawyer might think I'm a bit strange; but telling him I was meeting with an eighty-year old man and his dead girlfriend would convince him I was truly wacked.

By two o'clock, we had the posts set. I was washing out the wheelbarrow when Vic stepped out of the back door.

"What's goin' on?" he asked sternly.

"We just set the posts for the fence," I said, dumping the last of the muck out of the wheelbarrow.

He looked me over with a magnifying stare. "Fence, huh?"

Sawyer was packing up his tools and the auger. "I'll be back tomorrow with the rails and pickets."

"No. You won't. I'll pick them up for her."

"You have to work tomorrow," I said.

Vic gave me an icy glare. "Not until four, and it looks like you can get a lot done in a couple of hours."

I waved to Sawyer as he headed to his truck, never sure of what he was thinking. Following Vic into the house, I braced myself for his anger.

"You're working with Sawyer. Again," he said, without turning around.

"Don't start with me. Sawyer is just a friend."

He turned and looked me up and down. "I don't like what you're wearing."

"What's wrong with what I'm wearing?"

"For one, the shorts are too short, and for another, I can see right through your shirt."

I rolled my eyes and headed for the shower. On the way to the bathroom, I passed the mirror in the living room. CRAP. Vic was right on one count. I was in such a hurry to dress, when the doorbell rang, I wasn't wearing a bra. My white t-shirt was soaked with sweat and spray from the garden hose. I might as well have been naked.

"I need to take a shower."

"Looks like you already had one."

I rolled my eyes again but understood his anger. I also felt embarrassed that Sawyer had been working beside me all day, and I blithely went about with no clue how I looked. The message my attire must have sent would be all wrong. Was Julianne right? Was there a tramp lurking inside me?

"I'm late," I said. "And you should be leaving for work soon."

"I'll get ready at my place." He left without closing the front door.

"Fine," I said to his receding back. "I have to leave anyway."

Once I got upstairs to the bathroom, I could see that last night's make-up had left customary black rings around my eyes and my hair was sticking out every which way. I honestly looked like I'd been rode hard and put up wet. I found myself wondering if Vic had checked the bedroom before coming outside.

I finished my shower and jumped in the car. I was nervous about Julianne and Lincoln meeting after so long. Would he freak out? Would she freak out? Heading down 23rd Street, I turned on the radio and sang along with U2, *'I still haven't found what I'm looking for...'*

∞

At two-forty-five I parked my car in the Shady Rest nursing home parking lot. Lincoln's room was nicer than I'd thought it would be. A large TV and hi-fi cabinet filled one wall with two Lazy Boys facing it. The beds were small and neatly made with matching spreads. He shared the room with a man about his same age.

"Phil, this is my date, Freja. Don't wait up for me."

Phil laughed. "That girl either gonna keep you young or kill you. Can I have your old records?"

"Nope. I'll be back."

Lincoln held my hand as we walked to the door, partly to show off to his friends and partly to steady his gait. We waved at the residents standing by the rec-room door. The receptionist met us in the lobby.

"He can't be out after eight. And has to be in bed by ten."

"Don't you worry," he said with a wink. "I'll be in bed before ten."

I shook my head, thinking how much I would detest being told what time to come home. It didn't seem to bother Lincoln who merely grabbed her hand and kissed it.

"Don't worry about me. I'm in good hands."

Traffic in lower downtown was heavy and 23rd Street was moving like an inchworm; stop, go a few feet, and then stop again. When we reached Washington Street, Lincoln whistled under his breath. "That's new. Never was a Safeway store when I hung out in this hood"

"They've been building a lot of new stuff here."

"I wouldn't know the place; it looks so different now." He was shaking again; some of it from old age, but also a bit of anxiety, I suspected.

"RTD just purchased the railroad tracks that go out 13th Avenue. They say the light rail will stop just two blocks from here. The tracks are almost complete." I pulled up in front of the house.

"Just like them to plunk down railroad tracks in our back yard."

"It might help the neighborhood. You could work downtown and not need a car. Doesn't help me because I work on Colorado Boulevard."

I went around to his door and helped him out of the car. Getting in was one thing, getting out, quite another.

"This must be a new porch."

I hadn't had time to paint the new posts and rails. I unlocked the front door and led him into the living room. Julianne was sitting on a club chair in the corner by the fireplace as if it were the most natural thing in the world. Lincoln's knees folded. I held him up by the arm and led him to the couch.

She smiled demurely. "How have you been this long time I haven't set eyes on you?"

His voice cracked and was so quiet I could hardly hear the words. "Jules? Is it really you, love?"

"Yes, my darling. It would appear fate has given me one of her backhanders. You have changed."

"I've been forced to progress with the times." He shuttered.

"Can I get you a drink?" I offered.

Lincoln looked at me as if he's forgotten I was in the room, and he very well may have. It was a lot to take in.

"Do you have any whiskey?"

"Blended, bourbon, or Irish?"

He looked over at Julianne. "I like this girl." Looking slightly less stressed, he said, "Bourbon."

"Coming right up."

I hurried to the kitchen and poured each of us about three ounces. I didn't want to miss a word they said to each other, but I needed a stiff drink, too.

When I returned, Julianne was saying, "I've waited so long to see you. I have come on purpose to tell you something but first, I can't remember what happened that day. The day I died. I must know for it is driving me quite mad."

Pain settled in Lincoln's eyes and several heartbeats passed before he spoke. "You rang me up and said you needed to see me. There was something important you needed to tell me but not over the phone. I told you I was playing that night at the new lounge in the Baxter hotel. I guess it was the Rossonian then. I asked you to come with me and sing with the band. It had been so long."

"It was a year and three weeks," she said. "Since the day with your parents."

I pulled out my notes and looked at the calendar. That would have been the week before Christmas.

He sighed deeply "Yes, a very long year, but not as long as the years since that awful day."

"I'm sorry. It had proved a considerable strain. I meant it not to hurt you."

He shook his head. "I asked you to meet me at Walter Jackson's house." He looked around the room and frowned. "This house. You remember him? He was an old school chum."

"I remember. You needed to fetch something." She got up and moved toward him.

In his defense, his breath caught but he didn't flinch.

"Your voice that day is clear even now. You were excited like a puppy. I see you in my mind's eye."

Lincoln stared at Julianne who was now perched on the arm of the couch. "I asked you again, where you had been for the last year. You said you would explain when you got to the house. It was such a mystery. I was afraid it was something I'd done that drove you away."

"There are some things that can't be told over the wire. I struggled long with my secret." Julianne nodded slowly. "I wanted to tell you. I never got the chance. It pains me even now."

Lincoln shrugged, his dark eyes burning into her. "There was much I wanted to say to you, as well. I wanted you to marry me and move to Kansas City where we could start a new life." Lincoln's shoulders heaved, and he sobbed. "If I could only change one moment in time."

"Go on," Julianne said. "Tell me what came about that day. I must know the whole of it. Fragments of memory taunt me."

He wiped a tear from his cheek with the sleeve of his shirt. "Must have been about four in the afternoon when you arrived. I was nervous. I hadn't seen you in months. There was a Christmas tree there in the corner." He pointed to the corner of the room by the fireplace. "I knew how you loved the holidays, always buying little things for folks when you had no money. I had a ring for you and a beautiful plan. I set the room with spiced tea and a bouquet of carnations from the green house." He turned to the front door, remembering, a slow smile spread over his face. "I was giddy and anxious. So much so, I asked you to marry me the moment you came in the door spoiling all my fancy preparations." He looked down at his hands and the floor. "You were afraid of what my parents would say. You always did worry more about how other people felt. I told you I didn't care." He lifted his head, unsure, meeting her gaze. "I could see in your eyes the answer was yes. We came in here, in this room. I showed you the crystal bracelet that was supposed to be for my boss's gal. It was so pretty, I wanted you to wear it that night at the hotel gig." Lincoln sighed. "I was leaving the gang."

"Yes, the music prospect in Kansas. I was afraid I would lose you forever."

"I never stopped thinking about you." Lincoln sipped on his bourbon. "I was over my head with the bootlegging. I never should have gone for the quick buck." He shivered. "I lost everything."

"What happened next," I asked, enthralled with their story.

After several minutes and another long pull on the whiskey. I was afraid he couldn't remember. I was about to say something when he sighed deeply and looked through the new glass of my front window.

"Through the lace curtains," he said, "I saw The Italian's burgundy Ford pulled up to the curb. I knew they would be looking for the bracelet, so I stashed the ring and bracelet under the floorboards along with the money from the last job. I was in trouble. The boss wanted me to knock off this guy in the Highlands; a test of my loyalty. I didn't do it."

Lincoln's hands began to shake again although he kept talking. "Mario was The Italian's number one lieutenant. He kicked in the front door. '*You owe the boss big time, Piker,*' he yells loud enough for the neighbors to hear. He was always one for drama. The door was unlocked."

"*Lose the skirt,*' he says. '*We got business. Boss wants to know where's the scratch from the last gin run?*' Then he pulled out a gun and started toward me.

"Now, I was gettin' real hot under the collar, so I pulled out my gun. Don't tell me what to do or I'll plug you full of holes, I said to him. He was such an ass."

Lincoln stopped again and drew a deep breath. He looked at Julianne and his dark eyes filled with tears. "Jules, you stepped in front of me telling me to put the gun down when Mario fired. The bullet intended for me hit you in the back. I don't remember what I said to him then because all I could think about was, he shot my gal. I shot him three times in the chest."

Reliving the moment brought back all the original anger. His hands were clenched, and he got up and paced the room. "It was my fault. Always, it was my fault." He stared at the floor where I imagined Julianne laid, the life bleeding out of her.

Lincoln lowered his voice to barely more than a whisper. "My mind was blown. Jules was always a fast thinker. She could hardly speak but told me to give her my gun and tear her dress. '*I'll tell the bulls it was self-defense*', she said. '*A black man doesn't stand a chance when a white man dies.*'"

As he told his story I saw Julianne's image change. The once pretty dress was ripped on the side and a deep red soaked the bodice drowning the once shiny sequins in blood.

Lincoln began to cry, his breath ragged with sobs. *"You go',* she says to me. *'You can't be here when the police arrive. I'll be fine like china. Now go.'* I'll never forget those words. I'll be fine like china."

A floodgate of tears ran down his face as he looked at his lost love. "I'm so sorry. I was bull headed. I thought I could build a better life for us if I could only earn enough money to buy a house of our own. I had it all planned. I was such a fool, and it cost you your life."

He sat back down on the couch and placed his head in his hands. "I leaned over you where you laid on the floor and kissed you. I told you I loved you and that I would be back to make things right. You stopped breathing then.' He choked back a sob. "I knew then, the love of my life and my only reason for living was gone. I ran out the back door and jumped the fence."

He was shaking with grief and my heart hurt for him. Guilt is a heavy mantle to carry. I could see in Julianne's face that the memory of those last moments together enveloped her.

Touching her fingertips to her lips, she said, "There was only a moment for one last kiss." Tears rolled steadily down her cheeks. "I needed more time."

Lincoln bowed his head. "I was ashamed of my part in this. I holed up in Kansas City 'til I joined the army. After the war, I was on the lam, staying out west in Nevada. Only returning to Denver in the late fifties after my pappy died. The world had changed by then and most of the mobsters I ran with were in jail or dead. I never came back to this place."

Julianne moved to sit beside him. "I need to tell you now, where I was all those months."

He looked surprised when his hand passed through her cheek.

"Remember," she said quietly. "The day we attended Thanksgiving dinner with your parents?"

He nodded. "They were cruel, and you ran away."

"Your parents and mine had attended a funeral service a year ago, August, although, they knew me not then. My family sat next to your mother and father at Zion Baptist church that day.

Lincoln looked more confused by the minute. "Zion was our family church. Only five blocks from home."

Julianne blew out a heavy sigh. "I'd hoped you need never know, but the cat was out of the bag. I could see it in your mother's eyes. She would never have me."

"I don't understand," he said. "What did you see in my mother's eyes?"

"Link. Darling, my father is white. That is why we moved here from Alabama. We had hoped the west would be tolerant of our kind." She got up and paced the center of the floor. "That day, at dinner, I wanted to get their blessing on our marriage." She stopped and looked into his eyes. "You see; I was carrying your child."

His mouth dropped open. "What? You were pregnant?"

"Yes. Your mother made it clear I was unwelcome. I knew how they would feel if I told them I was with child. I went back to our farm in Salida." The corners of her mouth lifted slightly as happier memories came to her. "There were happy times, too. Mable and I used to make blackberry jam and sell it to the railroad workers. There is little to complicate the lives of a child."

She stopped and looked off in the distance. "Fate had changed everything for us."

"But, what about the baby?" he asked.

"That no other man had any claim upon me, I was forced to live there, with my family and bare the shame of raising a fatherless child."

Lincoln sipped his drink looking ashamed. "That must've been frightening."

"I had the baby in the spring. She's lovely. I see your eyes in hers."

Lincoln motioned for Juliann to sit down. "And the day you...?" He couldn't say the words.

"Opal was with Mable and Arthur when I came to Denver. She was always the best auntie. I couldn't know what you would say when I told you of her. Had I been certain, I surely would have shared my feelings with Mable as we were two pees in a pod, but I never told anyone your name in case you disowned us. My poor baby girl never knew either of her parents." Tears welled up in her dark eyes once more.

"I'm a very old man now. Too late to be a father, but I would like to see her, tell her who I am. Tell her who you were."

"She wouldn't still be living there after these many years"

"Would your sister know where to find Opal?"

Across the room, I sat in a club chair watching Julianne and Lincoln. "I think I can find her now." I said. "I found thirty-four different Opals in the census reports, but I had no way to know which Opal was your daughter."

I left them alone while I retrieved my research from my room. My stomach hurt. I ached for their lost love and their suffering. If Lincoln was her reason for being here, Julianne would be leaving me soon, and that also distressed me. I was a little surprised she didn't leave after telling Lincoln about the baby. I now hoped her leaving would be after meeting her daughter. Could that be the connection that was holding her to this world? What were the chances I could get Opal here, if I found her?

If Julianne was about twenty-three when she died; Mable would have been only eighteen. That was awfully young for raising a new baby. Born in 1930, Opal may have been married by the time of the 1950 census. I looked through my notes from the archives, checking the census again. Now that I had names and a location, it was so much easier. There were other interesting things in the census, but the clincher was an Art and Mable Henley who had three children named: Opal May, Robert Lee, and Marianne. In 1950 Art was still with railroad, and Mable was a teacher. That was forty years ago. I couldn't access anything newer unless I could prove a relationship. I could just see me trying to claim I was a long, lost grandchild.

When I returned to the living room, Lincoln and Julianne were in deep conversation. "Excuse me. I might be able to locate Opal, but I need to check the Salida phone records at the library. Will you be okay here?" I wouldn't normally leave a stranger in my house alone, but I couldn't bear to part them now that they had found each other once again. Besides, this guy was eighty-four years old and I didn't believe he would do anything to harm me with Julianne there.

"I'll be fine." Lincoln said. "Thank you for bringing me here."

I slipped out the door and raced to the library.

∞

In the Salida white pages, I found phone numbers for six different Henleys but no one by the name of Art. I switched gears and looked up old news clippings from Salida. The city was far larger and more industrial than I'd thought, a big train center. Most of the articles from the twenties were about trains, horses, and a prediction for an influx of automobiles with the new automobile road over Monarch Pass. Few roads went through the mountains then. I marveled that Julianne could have made the trip to Denver.

In 1931, I found a wedding announcement for Art and Mable but there was no mention of a child. They lived on a ranch north of Salida as of the 1950 census, but that was thirty-eight years ago. They may have retired to Florida by now. Unfortunately, I didn't have access to the more recent census reports. I didn't know if I should try to contact Mable. If I were Mable, I'd want to know about my sister.

Opal might have married at eighteen, that wasn't uncommon then. That would mean sometime between 1948 and 1958. I blew out a sigh. Hundreds of newspapers to search, one microfiche at a time.

I found the one I was looking for. Opal Henley of Salida married John Redhill in 1951. Bingo!

Opal was fifty-seven years old and John was sixty-one. From the phone book, I wrote down the number and the address. I had no idea what I would say to them. They were going to think I'd lost my mind.

∞

When I pulled up to the house, I saw Vic's patrol car parked in front of the house. This couldn't be good. I dashed into the house to find Lincoln held at gunpoint.

"Vic," I cried. "Put down the gun. Lincoln is a friend of mine." Poor Lincoln had been so frightened he'd wet the front of his pants.

Vic turned, angry, and gaped at me. "I found this guy sitting here talking to himself when I came in. What's he doing in here when you're not home?"

"Put down the gun, Vic." I stepped towards him and out of the corner of my eye I saw Lincoln panic.

I raised my hand, motioning Lincoln to calm down. "Vic! I had to run an errand and I asked Lincoln to wait here."

Vic harrumphed, but put his gun away. "You take too many chances. You leave your doors unlocked and you come and go at all hours of the night. You never listen to me. This isn't a safe neighborhood."

"I always listen, Vic. I just don't always agree," Crossing the room to face him, I said, "Look. I've got a policeman here with me at least five nights a week." I wrapped my arms around his waist. He was rigid, still upset from finding Lincoln in the house.

After a moment, he acquiesced and hugged me back. "Sorry, man," he said to Lincoln. "I didn't know who you were. Freja's had her share of trouble here."

Lincoln nodded. "I'd like to go now, if you wouldn't mind driving me home."

"Of course." I said. "I have Opal's number and address if you want it."

"Who's Opal?" Vic asked.

"She's Lincoln's daughter. They've been separated for nearly sixty years and I was helping him find her."

Vic's forehead furrowed. "You said you were researching information for a female friend."

I ushered Lincoln to the door. "I've been doing both."

"No offense, man," Vic said. "But Freja, why is his family so important to you?"

"Some things just are." I shut the door behind us, leaving Vic there to think what he might.

In the car, I handed the address to Lincoln. "How do you want to go from here?"

He studied the paper. "I don't know. She might hate me for abandoning her all those years ago."

"Then we need to make it right. Hate is a cancer, and if she's carrying that around it's only hurting her. Call me if you want to make the drive to Salida."

CHAPTER 46

When I got home, Vic was in the kitchen with the refrigerator door open. "Shouldn't you be at work?" I asked.

"I'm on break."

"Oh." I set a bucket of chicken on the table. "Hungry?"

"Yeah."

He pulled out a breast and gnawed on it. The silence between us gave me chills. I wanted to tell him what was going on but if Julianne didn't want to be seen, I'd just sound crazy.

"They're changing my hours again," he said between bites.

"Back to over nights?"

"No. Days."

"That's great. I'll be going to days too starting the first of August."

"Can you make good tips during the day?"

"I'm going to be managing."

His head shot up and he glared. "Are you crazy? You need to get a real job."

"It is a real job. I actually like working there." I was astonished by my own words. Somehow, I had gone from hating the place, but needing the money, to actually liking the job.

"I don't understand you." He got up and went to the living room. I could hear sounds of Andy Griffith, as Matlock, asking a suspect a pointed question. I went up to my room and put on my headphones. The Pet Shop Boys made me feel better, singing, *We've got no future. We've got no past. Here today built to last...'*

∞

It was eight in the morning on Wednesday. I was glad to be off work; Vic curled up next to me in bed. His new hours would start on Thursday, so today was made for sleeping in. His steady breathing was comforting.

From the bedside table, I grabbed the book Nick had given me, *Management by Guilt - and other uncensored tactics.* The first lines read: *'So, you want to be a manager. Are you crazy or what?'* I was definitely in the crazy column, but like everything else I've ever done; I jumped in with both feet.

Vic stirred about nine, and then stirred me for another half hour. He apparently forgave me for getting involved with Lincoln, but I wasn't going to push my luck by bringing it up. I made breakfast of left-over chicken and sat with him as he cleaned his gun. In the back of my mind, I was mentally scolding myself for not taking care of my own weapons. Certainly, as long as I had Vic, I would never need a gun.

"My Dad's coming up from Pueblo today," he said. "I thought we could go to lunch."

"Sure." I had been hoping to pick up the rails and pickets for the fence, but I didn't want to remind Vic of Sawyer. Especially not when he's proposing an introduction to his father.

"I told him you were a waitress at Denny's."

"Why would you do that?"

"He's pretty conservative, it's better if he meets you without any preconceived notions about what kind of girl you might be."

"And just what kind of girl do you think I am?"

"Not the kind of girl who works in a titty bar."

I was mollified by the idea he thought better of me than I thought of myself.

"I want to work on the porch today. It needs paint in case it rains. Do you think you could help me? Then I would have time to go to lunch."

"You can do it after lunch."

As it turned out, his father was very nice. He was a deacon in the church, so I understood Vic's hesitance to tell him about my job. We sat at Pete's Kitchen, Vic's favorite place, for about two hours. The subject of my job never came up and I was relieved not to have to lie.

We got back to my place about two-thirty. I spent the rest of the day painting the front porch while Vic watched a recording of the Cardinals-Dodger game on the VCR.

∞

Lincoln called the next day and wanted to meet Opal. I couldn't go until the following Sunday. Salida was a three-and-a-half-hour drive from Denver. If we left early enough, we could get up there and back in one day. The problem came from the rest home. He couldn't leave before eight in the morning and had to be back by six. That left us less than four hours in Salida to find Opal and convince her we weren't totally wacko.

I was antsy for the week to be over. At every opportunity I asked Julianne about her childhood. "I recall horses. Certainly, I rode for pleasure as well as travel. The red mare was a delight."

When Julianne reminisced like this, she often paced, and sometimes accidentally walked through a wall. It was totally unnerving. I met her in the dining room, where she continued with the story she had begun in the living room.

"There was a dreadful storm as you have never witnessed. My papa was drenched with its trapping of rain and snow as he bolted the front door. The electric burners quivered and went out. In the darkness my mama played the piano to keep the thunder at bay."

She sat down on a club chair and stared into the void. I was about to ask her how the storm ended when she giggled.

"We lighted candles. The wind thrummed against the windows and we feared they would be broken. Papa stoked the fire in the stove and began to sing with Mama. Mable was five years younger than I, and an accomplished seamstress."

She appeared to be holding something I couldn't see; turning it over and then holding it up. She began sewing the air.

"We are making a quilt for the baby," she explained, but she was talking to someone in the void. "The yellow fabric is utterly perfect." There was a joy in her voice I'd never heard before. "It will be darling."

Seconds later, she came back to me with disappointment etched on her pretty face.

"Are you okay?" I asked, sitting on the couch across from her.

"We were making a lovely yellow blanket. My time was near. We had been taught quilting by our great-grandmama before we left Alabama. I miss her."

∞

Vic was adjusting to his new earlier hours. He was often asleep by the time I got home. His days off were now Saturday and Sunday. This gave me Monday and Tuesday to work on the house without him getting in my way. That meant we only had Sunday off together and would have no days off together when I started full-time managing in two weeks. I was going to ruin this Sunday, too.

That morning, I told Vic I was going to help my little sister paint. Vic wasn't big on household maintenance, so he opted to stay home. Before leaving, I used the phone in the dining room. "Shannon, It's Fre. I told Vic I was going to be with you all day, Okay?"

"Sure. What's up?"

"I have to go out of town, and I don't want to explain."

"Are you alright?"

"I'm fine. I'm driving to Salida."

"Alone?"

"No, with a friend."

"I hope you know what you're doing."

"I do." I'll see you next week for Dad's birthday. Bye."

"Bye."

∞

I picked up Lincoln at eight. He was dressed in a snappy looking suit with a skinny tie. We stopped at Winchell's Donut House on our way out of town. My days usually started about ten; getting up at six was cramping my style. I needed caffeine and sugar. On the trip through the mountains, Lincoln shared stories about growing up in Denver at the turn of the century.

"I lost my mother to consumption. Lots of people had it."

"I'm sorry. Were you very young?"

"It was the year after Jules died." He sipped his coffee.

I was only twelve when the war started. I enrolled in an agricultural garden club to help free up young men for the war."

"From what you said, you were selling booze when you were in your twenties." I was curious to hear about prohibition since I made my living selling alcohol.

"The prohibition movement was big in those days. Scary stuff." He seemed to drift off and I thought he was asleep. I minute later he began as if trying to understand it for the first time.

"Crime and corruption was associated with large immigrant populations. In them days, the prohibitionists made up this thing called "nativism." They had the notion America was great because of its white ancestry. Odd they singled out Germans and Catholics as having a bad impact on Denver, but they did. Nativism picked on immigrants. These neighborhoods they was against, was usually in favor of abolishing prohibition. That added a more political angle to the fight."

I tried to imagine what Denver might have been like in the twenties. From the movies I'd seen, I thought most of the young people in those days were wild and free. I'd never given much thought to the politics of the day. The simple fact cars were limited, and rural people still used horses for travel would have made a difference. We went over Kenosha Pass and I tried to imagine how difficult it would have been for a young woman to travel to Denver in those days. Kenosha Pass was followed by Red Hill, and Trout Creek passes; all over nine thousand feet. "Have you ever been to Salida?"

"No. Never had a reason before now."

"Julianne said she never drove a car. How would she get back and forth to Denver?"

Lincoln looked over at me as if I was an interesting piece of artwork. "The train."

"Of course. Salida was a big train town." During the 1980s most train traffic was relegated to coal and lumber.

"During the twenties, there a trolley that ran down Colfax and Broadway, but the tracks have all been pulled up. Silly that they're putting 'em all back."

"I forgot. They had track on Broadway when I was a kid."

"Times change." He stared out the window. "The dust bowl came, and times got harder for people like me. One thing you can always count on, no matter how broke people are, they gonna drink and they gonna want music."

By the time we pulled into Salida, I knew most of his life story. He had worked for the CCC, the Civilian Conservation Corps. He had served a brief stint on the Denver Urban Renewal Authority and loved architecture.

I checked the address again and pulled into the drive of the thirty-acre horse farm outside Salida, off County Road 105 and Highway 50; same house Mable and Art had lived in during the 1950s.

"Do we have our story straight?" I asked, helping him out of the passenger seat.

"We spend a lot of time at the library."

"Yes, and I found you while doing research on the late jazz singer, Julianne Parker."

A big brown dog ran towards us, barking loudly. The tail was wagging, so I hoped it was just a greeting and not a warning. The screen door opened, and a wrinkled woman shouted to us, "He's friendly enough. Just wantin' to tell you to behave."

I smiled and introduced Lincoln as my partner. "We've been doing research on jazz singers. Lincoln is an old jazz musician. "Is Opal Redhill here?"

"Went to town. Be back," she turned her arm over and glanced at her watch. "Back in about twenty thirty minutes I'd say. Can I help you folks?"

"Are you related to her?"

"I'm her mother. What's this about?"

I held my excitement in check. This had to be Mable. "We were hoping you might remember a woman named Julianne Parker."

The woman blanched for a fraction of a moment. "She was my sister. Can't tell you much. She died when I was eighteen."

"Did she ever talk about her musician friends in Denver?"

Mable took a small paper fan out of her apron pocket and fanned the summer heat away. "She had a band. Cain't remember the name right off."

Lincoln listed slightly to the right.

"Good lord, where are my manners, would you folks like to come in and sit? My name's Mable."

"Thank you very much.' I said, helping Lincoln up the steps of the oversized porch. "We've been on the road since eight this morning."

She held the door open for us and it was cool inside. The farmhouse was neat and decorated in early 1950s eclectic. Mable led us to a Formica table in the kitchen and poured a glass of lemonade for each of us. "You want to tell me ag'in what's this got to do with Opal?

Lincoln took a long drink out of the glass and said, "I used to work with Julianne at the Baxter. We had a few other gigs, but mostly house band work. She was my gal."

Mable's shoulders slumped. She wasn't stupid. "You knew she had a daughter, and that's why you're here. You got a lot of nerve showing up sixty years late."

Lincoln shook his head. "Not quite. I only just learned of her a few days ago. Freja here," and he pointed to me. "She told me Jules had a baby."

I patted Lincoln on the wrist. "I was researching the family surrounding the death of Julianne Parker and discovered she had a daughter who never met her father. I got most of my information from the library and when I found Lincoln, I wanted to let him know. I guessed he was the father because he and Julianne had been an item for several years before she had the baby.

Mable's eyes flashed darkly. "She don't know about you, or her mother. I've been her mother all these years."

"Of course," he said. "I understand. I was mixed up with a bad crowd. Julianne was trying to protect her daughter by returning to Salida. She never told me."

The old woman eyeballed me warily. "How'd you find out? There ain't no birth certificate."

I was starting to panic; afraid Mable wouldn't let us meet Opal. "That isn't everything, Mable. I've been in touch with Julianne. That's how I learned about you, Opal, and Lincoln."

"That's a bunch of hooey if I'd ever heard some." She got up. I was sure she was about to kick us out.

"It's true," Lincoln said. "I didn't believe it myself at first. Mable, I've seen her."

Mable stopped and stared at the decaying old man. "Even if it was all true, it's too late."

"Please," said Lincoln. "I just want to tell her what happened."

"She got no cause to be hearing a different story after all these years. Art and me, we're her parents."

"If you could talk to Julianne just one more time," I asked. "Would you do it?"

Mable sat back down looking like she'd been punched in the gut. "I don't figure your angle in this."

"I bought this house in Five Points and found these things buried in the floorboards." I showed the items to Mable. "One day this beautiful girl in a red sequin dress shows up and starts singing. She couldn't remember much the first year. She told me you and she would make jelly for the railroad men. Said you had washhouse out behind the house. She hated doing laundry."

Mable took a drink of her lemonade; her hands were shaking.

I tried to remember everything Julianne had told me about her family. "Julianne told me about a baby blanket you and she made for Opal. A yellow quilt."

"How will I tell Opal," Mable began to cry. "I knew she'd been mixed up with bad folk, so I never told her who her mother was."

From behind Mable I heard a new voice. "You aren't my real mother?"

CHAPTER 47

Opal was dubious. Mable showed her the blanket. "No way on God's green earth they could'a known about this. You was just a baby, too young to remember your mama."

Opal sat staring at the blanket. It was several minutes before she peered up at Lincoln. "And you're my real father?" she said.

"I didn't know about you until just a while ago, honest. I would have come for you sure as you please."

Opal let out a heavy sigh and stood. "Where does that leave us now?"

I handed her a sheet of paper with my address. "Julianne would like to see you."

Opal rubbed her chin. "This is insane. I don't believe in ghosts. I'll have to think about it."

I understood her hesitation. It was a wild story. "It would be best if you came by in the morning or early afternoon. My boyfriend doesn't know about Julianne."

Mable's eyes narrowed. "Why doesn't he know?"

"He wouldn't understand, and Julianne doesn't like him."

Lincoln burst out laughing. "That's my Jules. A most opinionated woman, our boss used to say."

Lincoln napped on the long drive home. The ordeal had been exhausting for both of us, but I imagined more for him, having met his daughter for the first time. He'd never married, and never gotten over Julianne.

I dropped him off just before six. The receptionist was friendlier now but still admonished him for cutting it so close. Once he was seated for dinner, she came over to me. "I don't know who you are to Lincoln; but thank you. He seems ten years younger these days. It's good to see him smile."

"He's an awesome guy. Used to be a Jazz musician."

"I know. Before you started coming around, he was so quiet. It seemed like he was just waiting to die."

∞

When I got home, Vic's Chevy Blazer car was idling in front of the house. Parking in front of his car, I could see Vic get out. He was at my window before I could open my door. Hitting the lever, I slid the window down. "Hi, Babe."

"Where were you? And don't say you were with your sister."

"I went to Salida with Lincoln. He has family there."

"I don't believe you."

I opened the door into him. "I don't care if you believe it. That's where I was."

He followed me into the house. "You were with Sawyer."

"I wasn't. I just didn't tell you where I was going because you would have told me I was an idiot for driving him halfway across the state."

"Damn straight. Sometimes you can be a ditz."

"Oh really?"

I tried to push past him to go upstairs, but he grabbed my arm. "I'm not done with you."

Turning to face him, I planted my feet "Yes. You are."

He pressed me against the wall. Normally, I would have found his gorgeous body pressed against me like that very hot. Tonight, it was pissing me off. I tried to push him back; he was heavy in all his police gear. After a minute, I gave up. The moment I stopped pushing against him, he backed up.

"I'm sorry," he said sheepishly. "Sometimes you're too damned independent."

He leaned against the door frame; arms crossed. "Were you actually driving that old coot to Salida?"

"Yes. Lincoln lived here in the twenties. He had a daughter, who he didn't know about. I was helping him track her down."

"I don't understand why you would get mixed up in his drama, but I guess it's a nice thing for you to do."

At that moment, Vic looked like a puppy that had been kicked. I felt bad for having lied to him. I slid my arms around him and kissed him on the cheek. "I'm sorry I didn't tell you the truth. That was lame."

He pulled me tight and kissed me deep, his tongue tangling with mine. A moment later, he was naked beside me, all our angry words forgotten. At least for a while.

∞

At work the following Saturday, Ginger, aka Carolyn on her mailbox, announced she was moving to Las Vegas. I would miss her. When we talked about men, I could count on Ginger to have a fresh perspective. The girl was a free spirit.

I was telling her Vic and I were going to buy a house together. "He wants me to sell my house," I told her. "And get a place in a better neighborhood."

"Why would you do that? It's such a part of who you are."

"I would much rather he move in with, but he doesn't like my place."

"Men are tricky. If you don't ask something just the right way, you won't get the answer you want."

"I guess I need lessons."

Overhearing the conversation, Pepper, aka Debbie to her motorcycle posse, said "You can always trust a man to do what is in his own best interest. Politics change, but greed is forever. You just need to sell him what he wants most."

"I'm not sure what he wants."

"Pepper set her tray down and looked me in the eye. "Are you even sure you know what you want?"

"I think I know."

"Do you at least know what you *don't* want?"

I glanced across the crowded room. I liked my job and I liked my house. I also liked Vic, a lot. "I'm still working on the list."

Ginger smiled wide. "Aren't we all?" She downed a shot of Jameson, encouraging me to do the same.

I didn't usually drink at work, but this was a special occasion. Ginger had been visiting Las Vegas more often over the last few months, and it turns out, she was in love with a pit boss from the Sands. In the background we could hear Billy Idol singing, *'Nice day for a white wedding…'* We started with shots of Jameson and ended up sampling some odds and ends the liquor reps gave us. Nick had a basket full of disgusting liquor samples.

∞

Sunday morning, I learned there isn't enough aspirin in the world to make up for a truly bad decision.

I drug myself out of bed and stood under the shower. The water soothed the headache, but I still felt like I'd been hit by a train. Vic was mad at me for staying late and drinking with Ginger.

Over the sound of the water I could hear him. "Bad enough you drive after you've been drinking, but where the hell were you until four-thirty?"

He opened the bathroom door so he could see me through the shear shower curtain. "The bar closes at two," he said.

"We stopped at the Landmark and had breakfast."

He crossed his arms over his chest. "Why do I always feel like I come last in your life?"

"It was a going away party. I wasn't expecting it."

"Call me when you get it figured out. I'm going to my place 'til you do." He slammed the bathroom door and I cried. I'm such a mess when it comes to men.

After my shower and a cup of coffee or three, I decided to clean out the basement. My new paint sprayer would make quick work of the walls and ceiling. Even the floor was going to be white. I couldn't do anything with the crawl spaces, but painting would be a huge improvement.

I had three-dozen doors to get rid of before I could paint. The doors were stacked against the west wall, nearly stretching to the east wall. Leaning on the east wall were the doors I'd recently taken off the windows. One at a time, I started flipping the doors from the west to the east. I'm not really sure how it happened, but there was a major shift in the weight of the remaining doors. Like dominos, they seemed to flip by themselves trapping my arm between doors. Try as I might, I couldn't get my arm free. I kicked off my shoe, hoping to grab the doors leaning on me and push them back. I couldn't get a grasp on the last door and it was too heavy to lift more than three at a time. #$%&$#. How do I get in these predicaments?

Julianne usually followed me everywhere when I worked on the house. Today she had been telling me about a speakeasy downtown that didn't allow black performers. She fretted.

"How can I help you?"

I blew out a sigh and thought about it. "I'm not sure you can."

"I wish I could leave this place. I can't lift the doors. They are far too heavy."

"She had tried, but of course, she couldn't move anything in this world. That she was even visible was a miracle in its own right. I tried yelling, hoping a neighbor might hear me. I watched the light from the coal chute shifting as the day wore on. I grew tired of yelling and began to worry that I could be trapped for a long time.

Julianne winked out.

I heard the doorbell. YEA!!

I yelled, "Help! I'm trapped in the basement!" It seemed to take a long time before I saw Julianne leading Sawyer into the room. Tears of happiness streamed down my checks. I had been more frightened than I'd realized.

Sawyer immediately pulled the doors away, freeing me. I collapsed into his arms, still crying.

"Are you hurt?"

"My arm is asleep and I'm not sure it's ever going to wake up."

He massaged the arm until the tingling became painful.

"So," I said softly. "I see you've met my roommate."

He nodded. "I was about to leave when she appeared on the front porch. She told me you were trapped down here."

"She's never been outside before."

Sawyer looked across the room where Julianne stood smiling. "You know, I don't believe in ghosts."

"Neither do I, but here we are."

"She always been here?"

"Yeah. I couldn't see her at first. I think she has to trust you."

"Brilliant."

"Does that freak you out?"

"A little."

We stood there, looking like idiots for a while.

"Sorry I didn't make it back to finish the fence," he said.

"It's okay I understand."

"Sometimes my job gets in the way."

"That's what jobs are for. If we didn't have to work, we'd all get in trouble."

"Can I make it up to you by helping you haul out these doors?"

"Because saving my life wasn't enough?" I involuntarily shuttered.

He wrapped his arms around me. "I hate to think about it."

I pulled back slowly. I didn't want to but, Julianne was watching us, and it felt weird. "I'd love your help."

CHAPTER 48

Sawyer and I hauled away door after door. The dumpsters directly behind my house were overflowing, so we used the ones three doors down. As we carried doors, I told him everything I knew about Julianne. "I found her lost lover and her daughter. I don't know what's keeping her here."

"Do you think the ring or bracelet have something to do with it?"

"It does seem to have a connection. The first time I saw her was the day I found the ring. I was taking a bath and she scared the crap out of me."

"That's why you screamed when I knocked on the door."

I could feel the blush rising to my cheeks. I was barely covered with a hand towel the first time Sawyer had come to my rescue. I turned away and changed the subject. "I'm picking up Lincoln on Tuesday." I led Sawyer back to the house. "I'm really going to miss her if she goes, but this isn't the place she should spend eternity."

His pager was chirping every twenty minutes or so. Back in the house, I offered him a soda.

"Sorry, I'm going to have to leave you again."

"I understand. Got to make a living."

"Please ask for help. I worry about you."

"I got this. Besides, I have Julianne to help me."

I closed the door behind him, but through the curtain, I could see him shaking his head as he closed the front door. I didn't want to take advantage of Sawyer. He was so nice. I also had erotic notions when he was around too long and that conflicted with my self-preservation instincts.

Julianne looked pleased with herself. "I believe the introduction went well."

"He didn't go running for the hills."

"The man has character."

"Yes. I'm just not sure what kind. You loved Lincoln and it cost you your life."

She grimaced. "He was young and foolish."

"Not a lot different from Dirk or Sawyer."

She floated down the hall. "Fate has a way of getting in the way of our plans."

I went to work painting the basement. It was well after three in the morning before I cleaned out the sprayer. I was exhausted. I couldn't help wondering how the revelation of Julianne would affect my relationship with Sawyer. In one sense, it was very personal. Would he think less of me for not telling him sooner?

∞

Vic didn't come back Sunday or Monday night. It was just as well. I was going to pick up Lincoln today and I couldn't have him meeting with Julianne if Vic was in the house.

I rolled out of bed and turned on the shower. I was sore from the doors and the painting. Days like this, I missed the old claw-foot tub. I stepped in the shower and let the hot water ease my aches. The doorbell rang, and I genuinely didn't want to get out of the shower.

It rang the second time, and it crossed my mind it might be Mable and Opal. I hadn't heard anything all week, but I did tell them they could come by anytime on my days off.

I wrapped a towel around me and headed down the steps. I could see Sawyer through the window. He smiled when I opened the door. He had a three-day old beard. The scruffier he got, the sexier he was.

"Do you know how many times you've caught me in the shower?"

"Yep."

I rolled my eyes and asked him to come in. "I have to go pick up Lincoln in a few minutes."

"Vic never picked up the rails and pickets for the fence."

I looked out the door. "So, you brought them? Thank you. I almost forgot."

"I can carry them to the backyard."

"I'll help."

He ran a finger along my hairline, tucking a wet curl behind my ear. "You might want to put some clothes on."

A bolt of lightning shot through my belly. "I uh…uh…"

His cheeks dimpled ever so slightly, and he ran his thumb softly over my lips. "What would Vic say if he saw me here with you dressed in nothing but a towel?"

"Vic's a reasonable man. He'd understand."

Sawyer locked eyes with me. "Just so you know, for future reference, *I* wouldn't understand."

What was he saying? I had trouble thinking straight around Sawyer. One day we're buddies, talking about sheetrock and paint, the next moment my nether regions are all hot and bothered.

I stood there in a stupor, long enough for Sawyer to make a move. He leaned into me, pressing me against the wall. He kissed me lightly on the ear. His leg slid between mine and I could hear the roughness of passion in his voice. "You drive me crazy."

Without thinking, I let go of the towel, wrapped my hands around his face, and pulled his lips toward mine. His breath was ragged, his lips, almost touching mine. I had enough experience with men to understand the feral side of Sawyer's sexuality. I pressed my lips on his, and the phone rang. I tried to ignore it, but it kept ringing.

"I have to answer that."

Disengaging, I grabbed my towel before it could hit the floor. I now grasped why Sawyer wouldn't have understood if the tables had been turned. I certainly couldn't be trusted around an attractive man. I was shaking as I picked up the phone. "Hello?"

Sawyer motioned to me that he would unload the truck. I nodded.

On the phone a woman's voice said, "This is Mable, Opal and I would like to visit today."

"I'm going to get Lincoln now. I'll be home by eleven. Can you find the house?"

"Yes, we'll see you then."

I hung up and Sawyer was still staring at me. Julianne was beside him. "I should go," he said.

"I have a boyfriend."

"I know. I was out of line."

"I'll get dressed and help you unload."

He gave me a half smile and walked out the door.

"I'll be right back."

I watched through the glass. He had the overgrown schefflera plant Rick had given me in the back of the truck, covered by a protective sheet.

He set it on the floor in the corner of the room. "When I saw you had painted your living room, I thought you might like this back."

"Thank you. You didn't need to give it back. I meant for you to have it."

"I was just looking after it while it needed me. It doesn't need me anymore."

I ran up to get dressed but by the time I got back downstairs his truck was pulling away from the curb. I did have a boyfriend and, apparently, I needed a good scolding.

∞

An hour later I was back with Lincoln. He was in better spirits now. He seemed to have come to grips with what a gift he was given;

being able to see his love one more time. We should all have that kind of closure.

He sat on the couch telling Julianne how we found Opal and Mable. "They're on the way to see you," he said, toying with the small diamond ring and the crystal bracelet.

"I feel the pull to leave but wish to hold on."

"I hate to see you trapped here, but I don't want to give up a moment with you."

"Even eternity itself can't give us back the hours which have been flung away."

"I've never loved another."

"There remains always a secret and very tender corner of my heart for the man who, having loved me unavailingly, has still found no other to gain my place, even sixty years later."

He hung his head. "We can yearn to our hearts' content, but we are from different worlds now. I will soon join you in that other place."

"You have a daughter now," Julianne said softly.

Watching them made my heart ache for a love that could bridge the ages.

The doorbell rang, and I nearly jumped out of my chair.

Holding the door open to Opal and Mable, I said, "Come in. They're in the living room."

The two women rounded the corner and stood still. Julianne, in all her grace and beauty, was sitting on the arm of the couch. Mable was the first to react. Her hand flew to her mouth and she burst into tears. "I never would have believed it, but it's truly you. I helped you make that very dress."

Julianne stood and glided across the room to Mable. "Thank you for being the mother I could not be; for raising my baby."

Mable tried to touch her and was startled when her hand passed through air. "You always were so beautiful. Opal looked the spittin' image of you growing up. Mama and I never told anyone. When we heard you were dead, we just told everyone Opal was mine. I'd been married to Art for dern near a year by then. People always suspected when we married so young."

Julianne looked at Opal. "I'm sorry I wasn't there for you. You need never wonder if you were loved. I always loved you." She turned and regarded Lincoln. "I always loved you, too." She seemed pale and her voice was softer.

He wiped a tear off his cheek with the back of his hand. "You got into my system, Jules. I'm sorry for my part in this. I was running with the wrong crowd and didn't get out in time. I thought I could do one more job."

Lincoln held up the ring and bracelet. "I have no use for these things. Bringing me together with my family was worth more than I could ever repay."

"Give the ring to Opal," Julianne said. "I wish it could be more."

He handed the ring to Opal and gave the bracelet to me. I stared at it for a long time while Mable told Julianne about her marriage and their other children. Opal still stood by my side in silence, staring at the mother she had never known.

I slipped the bracelet on my wrist and Opal placed the ring on her finger. An electric chill ran through me and I could see it reflected in Opal's eyes. The life force that was holding Julianne here was vanishing.

Julianne drifted over to me as she began to fade. "Fre; such a lovely and suiting name for you. Thank you from the very bottom of my heart. If you sometimes feel sad and miss the old friendship—as I know you will—just remember, I'm only in the next room."

A moment later, my friend stepped painlessly across the borderline which divides this world we know, from that other world whose ways are hidden from our sight. My throat contracted and a burning mist of tears blurred my vision. I sobbed loudly. Opal put her arms around me, and although she never knew Julianne, she cried too.

Mundane though it may appear, the fact remains, the strain and anguish of parting, even from those we love best on earth, can be mitigated by such material things as food and drink. I pulled out a left-over pizza and warmed it in the microwave. We sat silently, each of us reflecting on his own part in Julianne's life, and now her passing.

CHAPTER 49

Vic came home that night to a somber house. He would never know my loss and I could never share it with him. Grabbing a beer from the refrigerator, he asked me again, "What has you in such a foul mood, today?"

"Nothing," I said, not looking up from my bowl of ice cream. Having a real kitchen had its benefits.

"You should sell this house. It feels like a tomb."

"I'm not done with it. At least let me finish the fence and the second bath. And the shingles."

He looked out the window at the back yard. "I see your boyfriend brought over the fence pickets."

"He's not my boyfriend, you are. And you never went to get them." I felt guilty. I could still feel Sawyer's kiss.

"I had to work," he said.

"I'm working five days a week now." I set my empty bowl in the sink. "Finishing these last projects will be hard without help."

Vic glared at me. "Don't invite handy man to do it."

"Will you help me?"

"Yes, if that's what it takes." He wrapped an arm around me, and at that moment, I believed he would.

There it was: my real dilemma. Vic always made me feel safe because he was a big strong man. It didn't hurt that he was also a cop.

He made me feel loved because he was jealous of Sawyer and my job. Although he was quick to anger, he was also quick to forgive.

Unfortunately, on his days off, he always had more important things to do than helping me with the house. I managed to get the fence finished by myself in one weekend. Once I learned how to use a nail as a spacer between the pickets, the project went fast. It really helped to have a power screwdriver.

I still wanted to do the shingles before the winter, but my new position was much more grueling than I thought it would be. I hired a roofing company to finish the job.

∞

Later that week, Cinnamon, aka Barbara to the PTA, surprised us all by announcing she and Ted would be getting married. It took me by surprise since he'd been hitting on me only a few weeks before. You could never tell about the guys that hung around the club. Some of them were looking for love and others just loved the looking.

Ted was sitting at his usual table. "Hi. Ted," I said handing a drink ticket to Amber and one to Jade. Now that I was a manager, I was handing out drink tickets instead of collecting them; radically better. "I hear you're getting married."

He gushed. "Yes. She is just the perfect girl for me. Barbara and I have a lot in common. She's the bomb."

I couldn't help smiling; he was so happy. "When's the big day?"

"We leave for Italy next week. She won't be back here."

"Good to know." Since I was doing the schedule for next week later that night. "I hope you will both be very happy."

"I never told anyone this, but my ex was very mean and such a slob. I was afraid to eat anything in the refrigerator most of the time. It drove me insane."

He wouldn't have that problem with Cinnamon. She was OCD about cleanliness. I realized then, Ted had always looked particularly sharp; always sat at the same table and always placed his briefcase in the same place. I found myself wondering if he'd been hitting on all the waitresses, hoping to snag one, or if he was just a lonely guy looking for someone to talk to and fell in love with the girl who was looking for a man.

Dan was back at the bar. Shotgun Willies never actually fires people, we just give them a month or two off. Dan would be teased about asking for the coke back for years. I stood by the end of the bar and watched him ring in a drink. "Do you need change or anything?" I asked. "I'm heading back to the office."

"I need to squeeze the lemon if you wouldn't mind watching the bar for a few."

"Sure. Don't squeeze it too long."

Pepper, aka Debbie to her city council, came to the bar and asked for two buds and a shot of Jack. She had been working more lately and I'd come to genuinely like her. She was a no bull-crap kind of girl, a lot like Ginger. "I see you bought a new Honda CRX," I said, opening the beers. "It's pretty sharp. Did you sell the Harley?"

"PIFFF. You don't sell a Harley once you have one. The car is just better in the rain." She flashed a striking smile at me and sauntered away. She'd changed her mind about becoming a Flight-for-Life pilot and spent two days a week giving tours of the front range. I discovered she'd been on her own since she was thirteen. She never had a steady boyfriend, but she and Dave were something she called "friends with benefits." I'd introduced her to Aiden at the company trip to Water World. They hit it off and were both activists in the Libertarian Party.

∞

I finished my shift at seven and was on my way home by eight. It was very warm even though the sun had set. The weather along the front range had begun to cool into the lower eighties, but the temperature drop was too late for some places. The dry summer led to fires in the mountains and the worst one was Yellowstone. I was angry with myself for not having made the time to visit the park. Now it would be a wreck if they opened it at all. Tuning the radio to the oldies station, I sang along with Mick Jagger, *Time is on my side,'* but I didn't believe it. I felt like time was slipping away.

I was washing the dishes when Vic came in. He was late. His shift ended at four and it was nearly nine o'clock. I never knew if he was going to come to my place or go home. He seemed more comfortable since Julianne left but he still wanted to be in his own place most of the time. I could understand. Though I felt my house was empty without her, I always slept better in my own bed.

"What's for dinner?" he asked.

"I'm making a tuna casserole."

"It's too hot to eat casserole. You have anything cold?"

"Let me stick it in the refrigerator. It will be cold soon enough."

"How about we go out tonight?"

"Seriously?"

"Sure. I was going to show you this later." He pulled out a real estate magazine. "But we can look at it over dinner. I need air conditioning."

"Let me get my shoes on." Air conditioning had been his big complaint throughout July and August. It was in the mid-seventies now, and I had the windows open, but it was still quite warm.

The White Spot café on Colfax is a twenty-four-hour diner that is a common hangout for the homeless. I was reminded of the Eagles song, *Sunset Grill*, as we watched the working girls walk by. Over dinner, he showed me an article about the re-gentrification of Five Points. It was forecast to be Denver's hottest market over the next ten years.

"You should sell the house now, while the market's good."

"I haven't finished the second bath."

"If you sell now, you can get your money back."

I wasn't sure if that's what I wanted; to get my money back. A part of me had hoped to make money. I had about $70,000 tied up in the house not counting my labor. With my new position using up all my free time, it would be a while before I could finish the second bath. Most people wanted two bathrooms. I blew out a sigh. "Fall isn't the best time to sell a house."

"Technically, it's still summer until mid-September."

"Where would I put all my furniture? Your apartment is too small."

"You can put it in storage until we can find a place."

There it was again. The offer to move in together. "I'll see. It would be nice to have an air conditioner."

CHAPTER 50

The next two weeks I spent every day off working on the second bathroom thinking about Vic's offer. Somehow the house didn't seem to hold the attraction it once had. The project was quite simple since I'd saved the old sink and claw-foot tub. I picked up a toilet at one of the big box hardware stores because I still felt ashamed of coming on to Sawyer while I was practically living with Vic.

Between work and home, I made the occasional trip to the grocery store. Vic was in the living room watching TV when I got home from Queen Supers. As seemed more common over the last month, we got into a fight. This time it wasn't Lincoln, or Sawyer, or pissing in the yard that had us snapping at each other. He was mad because I was working fifty to sixty hours a week. Apparently, he needed someone to be there when he came home from work every day. He expected me to wash his cloths and cook his meals; my leaving at nine in the morning and coming home at nine in the evening was not to his liking.

I was mad at him because he never supported my ambitions. He hated my house and hated my job. The strong hold of his arms that once felt safe, now, so often, felt like chains.

As I was putting groceries away, he asked why I was so late getting home.

"I stopped at the store."

"Not today, last night. You got home after ten."

Over the sounds of football, I said, "I had to work late. When I see something that needs to be done, I can't just walk away." I stacked canned goods in the cupboard.

"You always put something in front of me, either your house or your job."

Was that true? Did I always make him second? "I don't mean to do that I just want to make a good impression. I'm new at this job." I headed upstairs to gather a load of laundry.

"You should decide what's more important, me or your job."

The accusation was familiar. "That's not fair. I have to work."

"You don't have to work there."

"And you don't have to live here." The words were out before I could stop them.

"Fine," he said. "Go live with someone else, like Sawyer."

That was uncalled for. I hadn't seen Sawyer in over a month. "Maybe I will." I stomped over to the stairs and tossed his duffle bag over the rail; his laundry spilling out.

I watched Vic gather up the clothes in his bag, which was everything he had at my house other than his TV. Without a word, he carried it to his car. I few minutes later, he hauled out the TV and put it in the back of the Blazer.

Of course, Vic and I made up the next weekend. It wasn't in his nature to admit he was wrong, but I could deal. Over the next couple of weeks, I spent Monday nights at his place because I was off on Tuesday. Vic never brought back his duffle bag and I was okay with that. I asked him to meet my family at the twins first birthday party, but he had a hunting trip planned. My mother never mentioned the fact I was alone again, but it was a small relief.

∞

The club was feeling the downstream effects as recession took hold. The market had crashed hard the previous October, and Sugar had to pick up more days at the club. Brokers were struggling, so Jim restarted his law practice. They'd lived beyond their means during the boom, believing the money train would never end. My check wasn't as much as I had been making in tips as a waitress even after the initial crash, but after watching the clientele change from the regular stockbrokers and construction company owners to mostly lonely old men, I was thankful it was steady. One exception to the malaise was a guy who brought in sheets of one-dollar bills. I discovered you could buy sheets of uncut bills from the mint, but the entertainers still thought they must be counterfeit. I guess not everyone was hurting for money. It gave us hope and made for a fun day.

∞

Aiden finally took my parents out to lunch the first week of November and told them about Bill. My dad had a lot of questions about how long the two had been dating and my mom had questions about what kind of wedding they wanted. She was all about the theme wedding and Bill was just as excited. Mom wanted a beach luau theme, but Dad reminded her there were no beaches in Colorado. Bill and Mom settled on a Halloween party to be held next October.

"Why are you waiting so long?" I asked Aiden as he was helping me mow down the weeds in the back yard. The only reason he was there helping me was because it was his mower I was using.

"Bill wants to finish college and spend some time in Canada with his parents. He's hoping they will get used to the idea and come to the wedding."

"Where are you planning to have it?"

"Civic Center Park was our first choice but that's a little public. The State doesn't exactly let same sex couples marry. We're just going to have a big party at a hotel, probably the Adams Mark."

"Sounds like fun."

"I'm going to expect you to have a plus-one this time."

"Vic and I are talking about buying a house together."

"You two have been talking for months. When do you think you'll actually do it?"

"I don't know if I want to sell my house and I don't really want to rent it."

"With all the remodeling, you should make some good money."

"I used to think I wanted to live there but now I don't know. Seems silly to do all that work and never enjoy the finished product."

"So, don't sell it."

I couldn't explain it to Aiden. The house was so empty without Julianne. "It would make Vic happy."

Aiden thumped me on the nose. "Do what makes *you* happy."

CHAPTER 51

Vic couldn't make Thanksgiving with my family. I understood; he was awfully close to his father. Unfortunately, my mother didn't understand.

"I don't see why he couldn't come over for an hour or so."

"It's a long drive to Pueblo. And he had to work today."

My mother set the turkey on the table. "Boys come to dinner. He could come by after his shift. You said he gets off at four."

"He's working a double so a coworker could spend the day with his kids."

My mother inspected me as if she wasn't sure I was telling the truth. "Someday we'll meet him." I could tell by the look in her eyes, she didn't believe it.

"Aiden, Bill, Connor, come and eat. You can play with your Nintendo games after dinner." My brothers were hooked on Donkey Kong. Turning back to me, she said, "I just want you to be happy. If you're okay being alone, who am I to try to change you?"

I was comfortable in my relationship with Vic because we only spent a couple days a month together and my new job was exciting and challenging, much like the house had been. Vic still asked me to move my things into his apartment, but I wanted a place that was ours, not a drawer or two in his place. Not to mention when I was at his place, I felt compelled to do his weeks-worth of dishes and clean the bathroom. Most men don't realize when they stand in front of the toilet, not all of it hits the water, leaving a mist of piss on the walls and floor. I shouldn't have bothered.

∞

After Thanksgiving Dinner with my family, I stopped by his apartment with some tickets to a hockey game. I hoped to surprise him for his birthday, but it was me who got the jolt. He was in bed with another woman when I walked in.

My pride was hurt to the breaking point. Was my mother was right? Could I not catch and keep a man? I was so dumbfounded to see him lying there with her, I had no words. I was angry, of course, and the way he jumped up and started making excuses told me he had been as surprised as me. I turned and walked out, dropping my key in the fishbowl by the door.

By the time I got to work at seven that night, the weight of his betrayal began to seep in. I couldn't stay in the office and cry as I had wanted to do because I had a ballroom full of emotional entertainers and needy guests. When customers were rude or mean to the girls, I was their rock, but even the hardest rock will fracture under enough pressure.

Not having Julianne to share my feelings with made the house feel empty and cold. That night, I walked from room to room, talking to her, but knowing she could no longer hear me. Before going to bed, I emptied and washed his ashtray. The finality of this simple act brought on the torrent of tears I had been storing.

I was off the next day. I spent most of the morning in bed only to crawl into the old clawfoot bathtub I'd recently reinstalled. I could picture Julianne sitting on the edge of the tub telling me I was better off without him. In my mind, I knew it was true, but my heart pounded with its breaking. The next day I was more composed but not over the hurt. I had put myself out there, opened my house and my heart to him, only to be cheated in the end.

Throughout December I tried to forget the hurt. He called a few times, but I couldn't bear to speak to him. We had reached the end. He rarely stayed at the house that made him feel so uncomfortable, and I no longer needed a policeman to watch over me.

CHAPTER 52

My job had taken on more meaning over the next month because it was a way to ignore the hole in my heart. The weather was sucky and the appeal of living close to the club grew with every snowstorm. My big house was a constant reminder of yet another failed relationship and the loss of my closest friend. I was proud of the work I'd done, but it felt hollow on cold snowy nights. Even with the fireplace blazing, the warmth and soul of the house were gone.

At the end of January, I placed the house on the market, and it sold in less than two weeks. My dad told me I should have asked for more money, but I knew what was inside the walls and how much was done without permits. As it was, I cleared sixty-grand after paying off the mortgage and my credit cards, making a nice down payment on a new place.

One of the most annoying things about moving is having to change your phone number, and with it your business cards. My little black address book was filled with scratched out numbers and addresses. Learning a friend's new number took some Mnemonic game playing. Where I grew up, the exchange was 934 or 935 so remembering someone's phone number was a matter of learning the last five digits. The number I was giving up downtown was 7531, all prime numbers; while my new number was a war, 1812. It could have been worse.

I'd bought the furniture especially for the house, so I sold it as a package deal. Bringing it with me would have been like dragging old memories into a new life. The one thing I couldn't leave behind was the antique mirror I'd bought at the candy store. It was like a link in time to my friend. So much was wrapped up in Julianne. In my mind, I could still see her sitting in the living room, talking to Lincoln. I missed her terribly.

Leaving the furniture behind meant I didn't have anything in storage, much like the day I moved to Denver just over two and a half years ago. Not having furniture also meant I could fit into a small condo. In some ways I was starting all over, and in other ways I was leaps ahead, mostly because I had a bit of a bank roll now and just got another raise at work.

I bought a one-bedroom condo in Glendale so I could bury myself in my job as I had once done with my house. Ted and Cinnamon had moved on, but Gene, the history teacher, still came in a couple times a week. I went shooting with Dave on occasion, although I never took him up on his offers. He made it clear I would only be one girl in his harem. I wasn't cut out for that kind of relationship.

It surprised me that I didn't really miss Vic. His betrayal still hurt because you're never prepared for infidelity. It's hard to imagine someone you care about would rather be with another woman. Then I would remember the last time I saw Sawyer, and know it wasn't all Vic's fault we didn't work out.

Mostly I grieved for Julianne. I told myself she was in a better place, but I wasn't sure I believed that. It was heartbreaking to watch as fate tore her away from the love of her life so soon after finding him again. I hoped in that other world she would have no painful memories.

As for Lincoln, who had yearned for her through the years, only to have one fleeting moment to share seemed ungodly cruel. He told me once, her loss was a thing he would never get over no matter how many times he had to live through it. He was grateful for the chance to see her once more, but it was a bittersweet pain to lose her again. How many times does a love like that come into being?

The rest of February and March were unremarkable, and the only thing that stood out in my mind was the Exxon Valdez oil spill in Alaska. Like my heart, everything in the world seemed to be in chaos. In China, thousands of people were killed in Tiananmen Square. In June, the media and politicians were obsessed with the death of the Ayatollah Khomeini of Iran. People all over the world were protesting the Berlin Wall as Russia seemed to be falling apart. It was hard to know if the Cold War was ending or were we on the verge of another world war.

∞

Summer came and went. Big clunky cell phones were replaced by little flip phones and fax machines made the transference of written information instantaneous. The word on the street was how the world wide web was going to alter the human race more radically than the invention of movable type or the cotton-gin mill. I had a hard time believing in miracles of that magnitude. After all, we went to the moon and that was the end. I thought we would have colonies on Mars by the 1990s. The world was changing at increasing speed while I felt the space program and I were stranded in quicksand.

By the end of August, I was feeling better. I had fond memories of Julianne, but no longer grieved. I got over being betrayed by Vic in much the same way I got over being dumped after one night with Jason. I realized it was my pride that had been hurt, not my heart. I felt like a black veil had been lifted. I was learning to be a good manager and work was interesting again. Shotgun Willies was always unpredictable.

Like the evening I was doing the bar check-outs when April came into the office.

"I have a headache," she told me. "Do we have anything for it?"

"Check the first-aid box," I said, pointing to the metal box on the wall behind me.

"Thanks."

I could hear her rummaging around a bit. I turned to see her putting Aspercream on her forehead. I held back a laugh.

"I don't think that works that way," I said. "Here, take a couple of these." I handed her a couple Ibuprofen tablets.

Every day was a new, and interesting experience. Legwarmers and pumps were giving way to big sweaters and platform shoes bringing back images of the seventies. The waitress uniform changed but the entertainers still wore gowns or cocktail dresses. Fewer men wore suits, opting instead for blue-jeans and t-shirts.

Walking through the ballroom floor saying hello to the guests, regulars and new, I watched the bartenders jump up and dance on the bar when they heard '...*I study nuclear science, I love my classes, I got a crazy teacher, he wears dark glasses...*'

CHAPTER 53

At two-years old, Shannon's kids were growing up, no longer little babies, but people in their own right. Of course, Shannon threw a combination birthday party and end of summer backyard barbeque that would have made Amy Vanderbilt proud.

"I'm so excited about Bill and Aiden," Shannon said. "Look at what I made for them."

She pulled out a beautifully calligraphed marriage certificate.

"Bill is going to love that," I said. "He's still planning on going through with the vows. They have a friend who is willing to marry them."

Bridgett was helping herself to another hotdog. "They're very brave."

I preened. "Yes, they are. I hope one day marriages like theirs will be common."

Handing the condiments tray to Bridgett, Shannon said, "It really isn't anyone's business who we love." She scooped Jell-O salad into a cardboard bowl and handed it to Eric as he walked by. "Will you give this to Dad?"

"I hardily agree," I said. "And it isn't the function of the State to tell us who we can marry."

"Here, here," Aiden said. "This sounds like my kind of conversation. By the way. Mom is getting a real kick out of Pepper, I mean Debbie. Damn, I never know what to call her."

Shannon laughed. "That's Fre's first plus-one."

I stuck my tongue out at my sister. "She isn't my plus-one. Aiden invited her. They were working some political booth together last weekend."

Aiden nodded. "True enough. Freeman never has a plus-one."

"Did you get a costume yet?" Bridgett asked me.

"No. I need to do that tomorrow."

∞

The next morning, I was dreading the thought of buying a costume for the wedding/Halloween party. Instead of doing what I was supposed to do, I went for a drive. It was early afternoon and I had no place to be. I was off the next day and had no plans. I thought about taking a drive in the mountains, but I'd missed the turning of the Aspens.

Feeling melancholy, I drove by the old house. Pulling up across the street, I took stock of the changes. The new owners had installed a wrought iron fence in the front yard and the roses I'd planted had been cut back against the coming winter. I felt better knowing the place was being cared for. There were new shingles on the roof and the uneven flagstone had been replaced by a cement walk.

From there I just drove, listening to the radio. Garth Brooks sang, *'Looking back on the memory of the dance we shared...'* I pondered my lost loves and the good times we'd had. I hoped Julianne and Lincoln would be together one day but not too soon. Last year, I got a Christmas card from Mable and Opal, thanking me again for bringing them back together. Opal had her own daughter just out of college, and with Mable's prodding, they had named her Julia. The cash found under the floorboards went to help pay off her school loans. Opal now made regular visits to see her father and Julia was getting to know her grandfather.

I drove past H B Woods. Sawyer's bright red Ford truck was parked near the front of the store. On the radio Prince crooned, *'I guess I should've known, by the way you parked your car sideways, that it wouldn't last…'* I turned it up a little. My Toyota pulled into the lot and stopped in the space next to it. *Bad car.*

I sat there for a few minutes trying to think of something I needed to buy. My condo was small and not so old it needed any major remodeling. Deflated, I turned the key in the ignition. When I looked up, he was standing there, arms folded over his chest, casually leaning against his truck; six feet of perfectly toned muscle.

I shut the car off and got out. Mimicking his posture, I leaned against my car.

He smiled in that way that always melted my heart. "Well, hello there," he said.

"Hi."

"It's been awhile."

"Fifteen months," I said, biting on my lip.

"Can I buy you a beer?"

"Whiskey would be better."

He smiled and nodded toward the tavern across the parking lot.

"That works," I said, locking my car.

CHAPTER 54

It was dark inside and smelled of stale cigarettes and cheap perfume. My kind of place. We found a vinyl booth in the back. The place was almost empty. Bar crowds usually don't usually come out before seven. I slipped out of my jacket and sat down. Sawyer slid in across the table from me. There was no pretense or formality, as if we had seen each other every day for the past year.

"Jameson?" he asked.

I nodded. "No ice."

The bartender came over and Sawyer ordered a Bud for himself and a Jameson neat for me.

"So, fill me in," he said. "I've missed you."

"Julianne crossed over" I didn't tell him it was the day we kissed but it was on the tip of my tongue. "I miss her."

"I would have liked more time to know her."

"She always liked you. Hated Vic." I laughed. "He hated being in that house but never knew why. Julianne would always disappear when he was around."

"I drove by your house last spring but someone new lived there." He looked glum. "You never said good-bye."

"I sold it in January. The place wasn't the same without Julianne.

"And your friend, Vic?"

"It didn't work out."

Sawyer reached over and placed his hand on mine. "Can't say I'm sorry."

It was hard to look into those blue eyes that missed so little and understood so much. I was embarrassed by the break-up much like someone admitting to a divorce. This was another botched relationship. I looked away.

"Vic and I could never go anywhere because we were doing it for the wrong reasons. Vic wanted to get me out of Five Points, and I thought I need someone to watch over me. I thought I wanted to be with him forever but forever grew long and uncomfortable."

Sawyer listened without judgement. Part of me wondered if he was hurt by my ramblings about Vic. "I thought about moving back to Vegas," I said. "I was afraid I'd get into trouble. I'm bad around gambling. How about you? Are you a high-risk junky?"

"I don't gamble with what matters to me." He sipped his beer, watching me. "But there are very few things in this world, worth having, that don't require some risk."

"I'm kind of an adrenaline junky." I ran my fingers around the rim of my whiskey glass. "I miss working on the house."

"Were you missing the store, too?" He grinned and his dimples deepened.

"When I came here, today, I didn't know what to expect." I couldn't meet his eyes.

He leaned back against the seat. "It's been years since I expected anything. Now I only hope."

"What are you hoping for?"

A ringing came from his pocket. He pulled out a flip phone and answered. "Yo."

I couldn't hear the other side of the conversation.

"That shipment should have been in yesterday."

"Yeah."

"Okay."

"Tell Rocky he has to come up with another eight grand or I'm pulling out of the deal."

"Sure."

"You know where to reach me."

He put the phone away, and I just stared at his pocket.

"Just business," he said.

I nodded, feeling the old fear. Sawyer didn't look like a drug dealer, he looked like a beach bum with a two-day-old beard. Lincoln didn't look like a mobster, either.

He reached over and placed his hand back over mine. "Are you happy?"

"I guess I haven't felt joy in a while, but I'm not completely without hope. The job is going well."

He was staring at me, and I could feel my face warm. I'm not sure if it was from the whiskey or the scrutiny of his gaze.

Reaching over he traced a finger around my ear and down my neck, across my collarbone and caught the front of my shirt. He leaned toward me and whispered, "I could make you happy."

That got my attention. There was a place between my legs that hadn't been delighted in a long time. I stalled. I wanted him. Of that, I had no doubt. Every nerve in my body was vibrating at the mere touch of his hand. I asked myself if this was a test drive or a joyride. Was this the kind of car I wanted to buy or was it just a rental? I sipped the last of my whiskey to avoid answering him.

Sawyer sat quietly. He waved to the bartender, and the man refreshed our drinks.

I got up. "Excuse me. I need to shake the dew off the lily. I'll be right back." I needed a moment to think without Sawyer watching me. In the ladies' room, I stared at myself in the mirror. "What do you want, girl?" Sawyer had never failed me in big things or little. But I didn't know if he had a dozen girls on a string or if he took regular trips to Central America to pick up drugs. I splashed my face with water and studied the lines around my eyes. Fear gripped me. I had been hurt before. Vic was painful, but I realized I had never loved him. I was using him because I was afraid to be alone, and afraid of my feelings for Sawyer. Dirk had always been a knife in my belly and

Sawyer made that ache go away when I was with him. The similarities were frightening, and I couldn't survive another loss like that. I combed my hair out of my eyes and took a deep breath. If I didn't return soon, he would come looking for me.

I passed the front window on my way back to the booth. It had started to snow. Someone had put money in the juke box and Richard Marx sang, '...*Whatever you do, I will be right here waiting for you...*'

At the table, Sawyer had moved to the back of the booth. He patted the seat next to him and smiled; his dimples undoing my heart strings. I was feeling cozy, and it had been a long time since I'd been close enough to touch a man. I blew out a sigh and slid in next to him.

"I ordered some chicken wings while you were gone."

"Cool. I haven't eaten all day."

He slid a finger under my chin and turned my face toward his. "Fre, you know I love you. From the first time I caught you leering at my lumber."

He'd never said that to me before, but I knew it was true. The scary part of all this was I realized I genuinely loved him. It came to me in an unexpected flash. Why was I so frightened? I was a big girl. I had a good paying job if things didn't work out. Was I that afraid of getting hurt again?

He slid his arm around my shoulder and pulled me a little closer.

There I was, sitting next to him in a dark bar, contemplating of all the ways he could make me happy. I nibbled on a piece of chicken imagining how he would feel naked.

He grinned, sensing the change in me, and his fingers dipped into my shirt and rested there in the cleavage of my breasts, making me very happy right there at the table. Pulling his fingers out, he traced my jaw and pulled me closer. His lips brushed mine. "I want to marry you," he whispered. "I have for a very long time."

I couldn't think straight with his lips so close to mine. I pulled away and glared at him. "I won't quit my job."

"I never asked you to."

"I'll always want to remodel or remake something."

"As long as it isn't me."

"I expect you to pull your own weight."

He smiled in that mystifying way and said, "No problem there."

"You know I don't really want children."

"Fine by me."

"Okay then."

He cocked his head and furrowed his forehead. "Really—you're saying yes—you'll marry me?"

"Yes."

He kissed me gently, but I could sense he was holding back. I tried to pull him closer and extend the kiss, but he placed a finger on my lips and whispered. "I want to take you to my house."

"Okay."

We left the half-eaten wings on the table. Normally I would have boxed them up to eat later, but my mind was on the tight blue jeans Sawyer was wearing. He held my hand as he led me to his truck. I was nervous. It felt like a first date, and in many ways it was. I suddenly realized how little I knew about him. I'd convinced myself it was Sawyer who was running from me, but thinking back, I realized I'd always held him at arm's length.

I slid into the passenger seat. Sawyer pulled the seatbelt over my lap and buckled it. As he did so, his knuckles grazed my breast.

I sighed.

"Too tight?" he asked.

"No. It's fine." *Very fine.*

I watched him walk around the front of the truck and open the door. My heart was racing. I was going to his house. We had been friends for more than three years, but I'd never been to his house. I never thought much about where he lived or with whom.

As we pulled onto Holly, I had visions of a small house in Edgewater.

"I wasn't much of a friend. You always came to my house."

"You always came to my store." He grinned as he glanced at me.

"It's a good store. I don't think I could have done all that remodeling without you and the store."

When he turned south on Colorado Boulevard; I guessed Littleton. "Is your house far?"

"Are you in that much of a hurry? We could stop at a hotel."

"No, just curious. You've never mentioned where you live."

"You've never asked."

I felt like a butt.

When he drove into Cherry Hills, I thought, there was no way hardware store sales guy could live in this neighborhood. Drug dealers could. My heart sank. It was too late for me. I was committed. I loved him no matter what he did for a living. If my mom could deal with my dad and all his schemes, I could handle Sawyer. Could he be a more successful drug dealer than I had thought? The truck looked nice since it was painted, a little scratched from use, but nice.

I turned to him hopefully. "Do you trade room and board for carpentry skills or work as a handy man?"

He looked at me as if he hadn't heard me, then laughed. "I do a lot of the landscaping and the maintenance."

CHAPTER 55

Pulling up to a large grey stone mansion–this was not a house–it was a castle, he hit the garage door remote and the last of six doors rolled up. He angled the truck inside and closed the door. The first thing I noticed was a '67 Mercury Cougar in the next stall. It was emerald green with black interior, beautiful. The hood was up and there were pieces and parts laying on newspapers around the vehicle. Next to the Cougar was a Jeep, with red mud on the tires and a large cooler in the back. Next to the Jeep was a pop-up camper sporting the same mud.

The next two spaces were empty, and I assumed the owners weren't at home. That was good. It would have been awkward to have to explain why I was coming home with their maintenance man.

Unlocking the door, he led me into a mudroom. I saw his denim jacket casually draped over the bench. He helped me out of my coat and hung it up. From the mudroom we trekked into the kitchen where a few dishes sat in the sink. A newspaper was spread out on the counter.

He turned to me. "Do you like it?"

"Well, duh. It's about the biggest house I've ever been in."

He grinned. "Let me show you the rest of it."

Across from the kitchen counter, the family room had that comfortable, but not too neat feel to it. It was more of a library, in truth. Bookshelves flanking the fireplace were filled to overflowing with hard cover and paperback novels, mostly science fiction and alternate histories. The bottom shelf housed a rad supply of how-to manuals. I was jealous. A family portrait graced the space over the fireplace. Sawyer with his mother and father and whom I assumed was his little sister, Christine. I gawked around the room and I was certain. "How can you afford a place like this working at a hardware store? The taxes alone have to be several thousand dollars."

"I never said I worked there." He opened the refrigerator and took out two beers.

"Hello? You were there. And you rang up my stuff at the register, and you helped me load my car. Are you a drug dealer?"

He laughed wholeheartedly. "Is that what you think?"

"Um…uh…no." *Yes.*

He set the beer in front of me. "Funniest thing I've ever seen, those studs sticking out of the trunk of your little Celica."

"I don't understand. If you don't work there, what were you doing there?"

"I don't work there, I own it."

"The store?"

"Yes. It was the family business. My parents left everything to my sister and me after the plane crash. Christine and I tried to run the chain, but it was overwhelming, so we decided to sell all but five of the seventeen stores. Two years ago, I sold the Englewood store, one in Kansas, and one in Nevada. I'm trying to sell the last Kansas store now."

"All the times you were out of town, you were in Kansas?"

"Sometimes Vegas." He sipped his beer. "Five stores were too much for me, and Christine isn't interested in running a hardware store. I don't need the money, but I like the Holly store."

"The eighteen thousand someone needed to come up with?"

"For the store in Kansas."

"The H B in the store name. What's your dad's name?"

"Howard." He was grinning like a schoolboy. "Howard Bradford."

I took a healthy drink of beer to hide my embarrassment. "When you said you dropped out of school after your dad died, I had assumed you needed to go to work to take care of your family."

"I did. Christine was only fourteen."

"And the reason you don't like to fly…"

"Yes. You never expect to lose your parents. From the time you can remember, they are always there for you. It was a shock to both of us."

"I feel like an idiot. I definitely misjudged you." I took another swig of beer. "But in my defense, you dress like a construction worker and you drive that beat up truck. …Well, it looks pretty sharp now."

"I like to be comfortable. Refurbishing cars is a bit of a hobby." He moved toward me and took the beer out of my hand. "If you want me to wear suits, I have a dozen or so upstairs." His hot breath singed my cheek. "Would you like to see them?"

Heat from his body enveloped me as he wrapped his arms around my waist, and it wasn't his business suit I wanted to see just then. "Uh, I would like to see more of your house." I suddenly realized that I didn't know this guy at all, the sales rep, Lynette, all the meetings in the back office with the guys in suits.

"Sawyer. I don't know who you are."

"I'm the same guy who helped nail a door over your front window. The guy who helped you move a clawfoot tub down the stairs." He nuzzled my neck. "I'm the guy Julianne wanted you to be with. She told me not to give up on you." He pulled back and met my eyes. "It wasn't always easy."

"When did she…"

"The day I brought back your plant."

"Julianne always liked you. She left me that day."

He tilted my head back and gently brushed his lips against mine and whispered, "You still want to see the rest of the house?"

"Let's start with the master bedroom."

He picked me up and carried me through a spacious living room where a grand piano took up an alcove. The black and white furnishings were dramatic against the wall of windows overlooking the front-range. Bright blue sky colored the room.

The bedroom was simply decorated in china blue and chocolate brown. The bed appeared to have been made in a hurry; made but not overly neat, comfortable. Several pillows stacked in front of the headboard, looked like they'd been used for reading in bed.

He laid me down on the bed and kicked off his shoes; my pumps drop beside them. And then we made each other exquisitely happy.

EPILOGUE

In November of 1989 I sat curled up in his arms watching as the Berlin wall came tumbling down and for a moment in time, all the world seemed at peace. It was the end of life as I knew it; the end of the cold war that had us scurrying under our desks as children. Who would agent 007 battle, if not the Russians?

The 1990s brought us the world-wide-web and instantaneous communication around the world. I carried a cell phone like millions of other people.

It was a new beginning. I had my plus one. And let's face it, having lots of boyfriends just sucks.

About the Author

Michele Poague is a native of Denver, Colorado where she currently lives. A special events planner and political activist, she is also the author of the multi award winning trilogy *The Healing Crystal: Book One-Heir to Power; Book Two-Fall of Eden; Book Three-Ransom*, and *The Candy Store*. For more information regarding Ms. Poague or her published works, visit michelepoague.com.

∞

Cover Design, Interior Design, and Illustration
Michele Poague

Editing and Production
Bette Rose Ryan and Lois Deveneau